THE ORACLE
OF SPRING GARDEN ROAD

Norrin M. Ripsman

Cassowary Publications
Philadelphia

This is a work of fiction. Names, characters, places and incidents either are the product of the author's imagination or are used fictitiously. Any resemblance to actual persons, living or dead, events or locales is entirely coincidental.

Copyright 2024 by Norrin M. Ripsman
United States copyright registration
numbers TXu-2-415-694

All rights reserved. No part of this book may be reproduced or used in any manner without written permission of the copyright owner, except for the use of quotations in a book review.

First paperback edition June 2024

Book design by Judy Sery
Cover design by Snir Ayalof

ISBN 978-0-9601245-0-3 (paperback)
ISBN 978-0-9601245-1-0 (e-book)

To Nathalie,
with love

Chapter 1

Freedom. That's what it always felt like to him. Freedom. Freedom to do what he pleased, to follow his whims. Freedom to think his thoughts without submitting them for anyone's approval. Waking up each morning was like a divine gift to him, an opportunity to connect with the world on his own terms, beholden to nobody. He reported to no boss, had no rent or mortgage to pay, no car to maintain, no family to feed, no obligations. True, he had his habits, his routines, his rituals. He spent his weekday afternoons in his "office," two squares of pavement in front of a bank on Spring Garden Road. A man needed to eat, didn't he? And he grudgingly frequented a local shelter in cold weather to avoid freezing on the streets. Aside from those concessions to necessity, though, he marched to his own beat.

Rousseau declared, "Man is born free, but everywhere he is in chains." Observing all that slunk around him, he couldn't help but agree. Take the bank manager, for example, the one who sneered at him every time she passed by, who viewed him as somehow less than human, a blight on the maritime landscape. She was perpetually scampering to and fro in fear of missing an appointment, a deadline, a daycare pick-up. A permanent scowl plastered across her face in deference to her commitments, her responsibilities, the joyless requirements of her important life.

Or the kind teller, who often wished him a good afternoon and sometimes shyly, respectfully, dropped a coin into his battered hat with a benevolent, embracing smile. He often overheard her on her cell phone pleading with her elderly mother to be patient with her during the workday, not expect her to visit until the evening or arguing with her husband about car loans or the cost of orthodontics for their son.

Or the owner of the dress boutique across the way, who had inherited the successful shop from his parents, but had neither the talent nor the inclination to keep it afloat. He, too, was inseparable from his cell phone, as he pleaded with his impatient suppliers, his loan manager, his landlord, as he tried doggedly to stave off bankruptcy, all the while chain smoking, consuming a steady diet of antacid pills.

Even the prematurely greying pharmacist's assistant, whose Syrian wife kept pressing him to move heaven and earth to rescue her brother and his family from the anarchy of her war-torn homeland and whisk them into Canada. "What more can I do?" he would appeal to his cell phone in desperation as he ground his crumbling molars together. "I've filled out all the forms. I keep calling Immigration Canada. I've pestered our MP. I'm doing my best!" But it was never good enough for his disappointed wife.

Ah, cell phones, the ubiquitous bell shackling the human cat! He had never owned a cell phone, never would. These were the ultimate chains, he reasoned. With these diabolical devices, employers, spouses, parents, children, and various and sundry other unsavoury parties could monitor you wherever you went, ensure you enjoyed no peace, were always at their beck and call. They call or send text messages just to reign you in, to remind you that you are never beyond their reach, that you cannot escape their electronic noose. And no conversation is private with those infernal machines. The most intimate declaration of love, the most intrusive medical consultation, all now occur on a city bus, a crowded restaurant, or on the street in front of his office, for all to partake in.

But it was worse than that, he decided. People walked around all day with their eyes glued to a tyrannical screen the size of a playing card. Checking their stocks, their electronic mail, sports scores, even the weather, for God's sake! All this to avoid paying attention to the beauty all around them: the sun, the clouds, the harbour, the storefronts on Spring Garden, the people passing by, some kind-hearted, some sad, some self-absorbed, all unique. To avoid thinking about justice, love, truth. All the delicious and manifold mysteries of life.

And they were forever in a hurry. Rushing to work, rushing home, even rushing to the theater or a restaurant for entertainment. How entertaining could it possibly be if they had to manage the stress of traffic, parking, arriving late? They all wear watches, glance at them constantly, in exasperation, in fear. The point of watches had been to help them control time, but there was no doubt who the diabolical master really was.

None of that was for him. He had shattered his chains long ago. He was free. And for that, they pitied him. *They* pitied *him!* They called him unfortunate – *The poor unfortunate man!* – as if freedom were a curse, an affliction. They called him homeless. But he had a home. The city. All of it. It belonged to him more than to anyone else. *He* slept in its streets, wandered its parks endlessly, woke up with its sunrise, vanished in its fogs, was cleansed by its rains. While they confined themselves to the small, constraining boxes they called homes, fretted about repairing them, financing them, he strutted through the Public Gardens, the Citadel, the waterfront, the university, Point Pleasant Park, the city's blood coursing through his veins. Halifax was part of him, and he was indistinguishable from the city. The less charitable called him a bum. That he could accept, since he didn't perform any of the activities they would identify as useful and *did* inhabit the streets. Mostly, though, people called him Crazy Eddie, although he knew that moniker to be doubly inaccurate. Crazy because he lived outside and didn't care. Because he dispensed his views on life and philosophy freely to any who would listen. Because he was content living a life they couldn't fathom, enthralled by its beauty. Eddie because that was what he told them his name was, if they asked.

Who he was, how he had arrived to occupy that particular corner of the universe, was a longstanding local mystery, the subject of idle speculation and fanciful lore over a pint at the neighbourhood watering holes. Initially, they hadn't cared at all, hadn't noticed him. He had been just another invisible homeless man who drifted through with the wind. Most still ignored him, crossed to the other side of the street to avoid him, to pretend he didn't exist so their humdrum middle-class existences could continue untarnished by guilt. But due to his longevity, his obvious intelligence, his desperate though reluctant sociability, his flagrant assurance of his own superiority, many of the locals took notice, viewed him as a curiosity, almost a municipal landmark.

No-one could remember exactly when he had graced the city with his idiosyncratic presence. After nearly two decades it seemed there was something primordial about him. That like the trees, the hills, the harbour, he had always been there, that the city itself had been erected around Eddie and his two squares of sidewalk. Over a pint of beer in a dimly-lit pub on the waterfront, however, an old-timer with a head shaped like a coconut, a grisly beard and a moth-eaten royal blue sweater offered his wisdom on the matter to his younger companions.

"I heard that he was a young Navy man out of the base right here in town," he began, patting down the wispy gray coils of hair that framed his largely bald head. "He was a.... Aw whattaya call it? An ensign. Yeah, an ensign or sumptin. Well, he was engaged to his high school sweetheart – absolutely ga-ga over her. Loved her to pieces. But, ya see, he was sent on maneuvers in Europe or somewhere, maybe the Skagerrak, I dunno, for a long deployment. Well, our boy he wrote to his girl every single day and mailed the letters whenever he was on shore leave and was itchin' to return so that they could marry. Finally, after a few months, he sailed back home and showed up at her place to surprise her. He didn't call or nothing, you understand. Just marched right in, as pretty as the newborn snow, all gussied up in his Navy duds to lay claim to what was his. And, of course, he didn't find her alone. But you already *guessed* that, din't ya? But it was who she was with that was the kicker." He paused for effect. "Aye, it was his own father, yes it was! Can you imagine our boy's shock? After that, he lost it. He couldn't go back to her or go back home. He just plain *lost* it. You know what I mean? Took up his residence on Spring Garden that very afternoon."

His comrades were impressed, but the bartender, who had been eavesdropping on the old man's story from behind the large mahogany bar with brass rails, chimed in, "Aw, Hank. We been over this too many times before. He's too smart for the Navy. Book smart, I mean. Wicked smart."

"Shuddup, man!" the oldtimer retorted, raising his voice, his speech slurred by alcohol. "Navy guys can be smart, too."

"Yeah, but not like *him*. Philosophy and all," the bartender, a man in his late forties with a round head, graying hair and his own large bald patch, rejoined, an empty porter glass in his hand, ready to be filled at the tap. "He's a university boy or I'm the premier of Nova Scotia. From somewhere out west, no doubt. Probably a lawyer or somethin'. Who knows what brought him here?"

One of the servers piped up from a table nearby where she, too, had been following the conversation. "I dunno," she said. "I mean, I heard he's an American from the South. A member of the Klan. They say he killed a man and escaped across the border, but can't use no money or credit cards because they'd catch him. So he lives on the street. But every morning at dawn, he puts his white hood over his head in the park and does some Klan rituals."

"Aw, that's a bunch of hogwash, Charlene!" Hank exclaimed.

"No really! My sister saw it with her own eyes," Charlene insisted. "I mean, she went for a run along the Northwest Arm before work and saw him covered in his shawl, muttering some kinda chant. She was horrified to think there's some evil Klansman right here in Halifax!"

"Those are just a bunch of tall tales," the bartender chided. "You can believe 'em if you want, but they're just people talking. I even heard someone say he escaped from the looney bin in Burnside. But they'd have got him back by now, wouldn't they? It's not like he's hiding very well."

"Does it really matter?" one of Hank's younger friends, a chubby man in his thirties with oversized jowls, asked. "He's just some hobo."

"You know, I asked him once myself," the bartender confided, ignoring the younger man's question. "'Eddie,' I sez, 'where you from? Why do you stay here?' He just stared through me with the strangest expression you'd ever seen and sputtered out some claptrap about Rousseau and the Danube River."

The revellers laughed uproariously. "He's clearly out of his gourd," one declared, as she swirled her lager round in her glass and took a large draught.

But the man they called Crazy Eddie cared little what others said about him and paid it no heed. He had rejected their mediocrity, their pettiness, their ignorance, years ago. He couldn't expect them to understand his choices, what motivated him. As long as he had the glorious maritime sky, the salt air, the sublime trees and, of course, the harbour, he could dispense with them.

His was a very cerebral existence. Having renounced most of the social interaction attendant in human affairs, the empty small talk, the petty competition, he devoted his hours to cogitation, contemplation, reminiscences. At his trial, Socrates argued that the unexamined life is not worth living. Well, unlike most people, Crazy Eddie led an examined life.

In warmer months, he liked to sleep in Point Pleasant Park. A sprawling woodland at the southern tip of the city, cocooned on three sides by Halifax Harbour and the Northwest Arm, the park was Crazy Eddie's forested oasis. He would trek there in the early evening along South Park Street to enjoy its canopy of trees, to delight in its views of the churning grey water. Before ten o'clock, the park's official closing time, he would seclude himself in his "bedroom," a wooded area off the path overlooking the Northwest Arm, where he secreted his few treasured possessions that would have been of little interest to anyone who happened upon them: a ratty old blanket, a frayed sweater, a soiled, torn pair of sweatpants that was several sizes too large, a depleted bar of soap and other such sundry items. Lying in hiding on a clear night, with the sound of the water lapping the bank, the sea air, the perfume of the trees, the tableau of the sky with its magical stars above, Eddie was as close to heaven as man could ever be.

When the weather grew colder, he retreated inland, sheltering himself from the merciless, damp nautical winds behind a downtown building, often nestled between a dumpster and a brick wall. It meant separation from his beloved park, his home and lifeblood, but it still afforded him his independence, which he valued above rubies. The heavy Nova Scotia snow was daunting, often coating him in his blanket like a frosty alabaster cocoon. But the bitter winter rains, from which neither blankets nor extra layers of clothing, nor even the jagged bit of canvas that he purloined from the dumpster behind a hardware store could shield him, were far more formidable foes, that sometimes shook his faith in his abilities. In the worst of the winter, he had no choice but to surrender and sleep in a homeless shelter to avoid freezing to death. These were the hardest weeks for him to endure, this dependence on others.

Was he ever lonely in this solitary existence to which he had consigned himself? At times. Everyone craves at least a modicum of human contact. But, in truth, Eddie had often experienced loneliness more profoundly when surrounded by others, especially those that seemed at ease with each other, who fit in. Eddie had never truly fit in.

He viewed the universe so differently from them. Their raison d'être was to rise in the pecking order. To accumulate more wealth and status. Life was a never-ending quest for more, more, more. There was never a point at which they would survey all they had, their position in society, and say, "I have achieved my goal. I am satisfied." Instead, they slept fitfully throughout their anguished nights, scheming to procure even more, to cheat others of theirs, terrified about losing what they already had. He needed nothing, desired nothing more than to live freely on God's bountiful earth.

And their obsession with posing, with marketing! To him, everyone seemed so preoccupied with advertising themselves. With their clothes, their expressions, their attitudes. Like the unshaven, broad-shouldered, overweight man sporting a Harley Davidson cap and a shirt declaring "Beer made this body." As if slovenliness was an achievement to celebrate. Or the high school students with sweatshirts advertising universities which they did not attend, might never have the credentials to attend: University of Toronto, UBC, Harvard, Princeton, Oxford. Like somehow wearing the shirt made them part of the club! He simply couldn't fathom what the other ubiquitous symbols meant: the alligator, the man on horseback, the large beaver. Vanity of vanities!

Sometimes there was a mismatch between the bearer and the image. Like the nervous young woman with deep set, anxious eyes, attired in a garish mauve tee shirt bearing the caption "Party Animal" in bulging, electric white and red runes. As if it were more an aspiration to escape the chilling uncertainty that clouded her days and haunted her nights. But by far the most common image cultivated by the mass of humanity that passed before him each day was that of respectability: men in off-the-rack suits, women in pantsuits or skirt-and-jacket ensembles, the army of the responsible, the professional, the dreary, the dying-while-living. Thank God he no longer belonged to that sorry ilk.

He amused himself with what his clothing, his appearance, advertised about him. He was by no means dirty, but his unkempt salt-and-pepper beard, his shaggy, tangled mass of greying hair, which was progressively losing the war, surrendering more territory to baldness each month, his baggy khaki sweatshirt with its Swiss cheese holes, his mud-stained blue jeans and canvas military boots that long ago were beige, gave off the distinct air of neglect. Of a lack of concern for how others viewed him. And the cold, hard, unwelcoming aspect of his steel blue eyes, the tough, leathery, wind-worn patches of skin that were visible through his hair, deterred most from getting too close.

If they had gotten beyond his unwelcoming exterior, however, they might have noticed the ridges that had of late crept into his wind-worn brow. A growing worry, sometimes bordering on panic, that it would soon come to an end. Come crashing down around him like a chain of dominoes. Because, for the first time in his two decades of freedom he began to fear for the future. To fret like the rest of humanity.

Workdays in his office earned him a modicum of cash in the form of coins tossed into his cap by passersby, out of kindness or, just as frequently, amusement, in payment for the wisdom he dispensed. Having developed notoriety as the Oracle of Spring Garden Road, many got a charge out of soliciting his opinions on any manner of topics.

Crazy Eddie, is it right for the government to increase taxes?

Listen, Eddie, is rock and roll or classical music better for the brain?

Should morality take precedence over freedom?

Eddie, isn't there something wrong with using taxpayer money to fund abortions?

Which is better, Crazy Eddie, freedom or equality?

While all the questions were fascinating to him and of immense importance, he resented the questioners' derision, understanding that they cared little for his answers, save to laugh at his pomposity, at the beggar who saw himself as a sage. Yet he never failed to engage. After enjoying their sport, they usually recompensed him with their alms, which enabled him to supplement what he could scrounge from dumpsters or receive from foodbanks.

On this particular early autumn afternoon, with the sun a shiny brass penny high in the sky and a scattering of leaves blowing through the street on the back of a still-warm breeze, a young man in tweed pants and a brown leather jacket approached Eddie with a twinkle in his eye. "Hey, Crazy Eddie! Who do you think is gonna win the next provincial election?" he asked in a mocking tone.

"Politics is nothing but tribalism," Eddie replied dismissively. "You choose a team: the Conservative blue team, the Liberal red team or the NDP orange team. Then you try to crush the other teams. You lie when you need because it's more important to win than to be honest. And what's it all about? Controlling other people. Compelling *them* to follow *your* ideals. I have *no* interest in that."

"Well, what do you think about the silliness down in the US?" the troublemaker followed up.

"You see," Eddie explained, "that's the problem with democracy. The key to democratic rule is the principle of one person-one vote. Everyone's vote counts equally, and the masses determine who rules. But the masses are ignorant...."

"Ho!" the man laughed.

"Let me finish! They can't bother to evaluate the candidates' platforms carefully. They don't understand the complexity of the issues. Instead, they'll vote for someone they recognize from television, or someone who says what they want to hear, even if that candidate has no real grasp of the issues that matter to them, even if they suspect that's he's lying to them. Forget rule by the masses. We'd be better off with Plato's philosopher king," Eddie concluded.

"Oh, and who should rule us? You?" the young man taunted, fingering the zipper of his expensive jacket.

"Far from it. As I said, I have no interest in politics. As far as I'm concerned, let the small minds rule the day, as long as I remain king of *this* spot," the man they called Crazy Eddie retorted sarcastically, gesturing toward his concrete realm.

"Well, you've got all the answers. Don't you Eddie? We're so lucky we have *you* to set us straight," he mocked, tossing a loonie into Eddie's cap, and moseyed down the street, secure in the knowledge of his inalienable superiority.

It wasn't only clowns and posers who consulted the Oracle. Sometimes it was people in need of his unique talents. Later that afternoon, he amazed onlookers with his response to a diffident university student. The young man watched him hesitantly from a distance in the late afternoon sun for a while, his hands thrust into the pockets of his faded jeans, before screwing up the courage to talk to the bushy-haired nomad. "Uh, excuse me, Mr. Eddie, sir," he said with a weak, cracking voice. "I was hoping you could help me."

"And how could I do that?" Crazy Eddie barked.

"Well, I... I have a philosophy midterm and I was hoping you could explain something to me," explained the student. "I'd be willing to pay you five dollars if you could."

Five dollars was a princely sum to one such as Eddie. "Why don't you hire a *real* tutor?" Eddie challenged him. "Why come to a bum like me?"

"I... I don't have much money. I've borrowed a lot to go to school and can't afford a tutor," the young man replied, his face reddening. "They said you know these things."

"Well, what do you want to know?" Eddie asked impatiently.

"It's about Hume and the problem of induction. Can you help me with that?"

"Sure," Eddie said. "Sure. You know what induction is, right?"

"Not exactly. I mean, it's just reasoning, isn't it?" the student replied.

"It's a special kind of reasoning. It's basically generalization. If you see multiple instances of a phenomenon, you may use induction to conclude that these examples represent a category of events which share similar properties," Crazy Eddie explained.

"You've lost me," the young man complained.

"Well," Eddie continued patiently, waiting for the number one bus to discharge its passengers and proceed across the street so as not to drown out his lesson, "if you see five animals that you're told are dogs and observe that all of them have four legs and a tail, and you don't see any counterexamples, you may use induction to generalize that all dogs have four legs and a tail. You follow?"

The student nodded his head. Eddie continued, "Or alternatively, you can induce that because the sun rose in the morning every day in the past, it will do so again tomorrow morning. In *An Essay Concerning Human Understanding*, Hume takes issue with the logic of induction. He concludes that there's no basis for being certain that the next instance of a phenomenon will conform to the previous pattern. In other words, just because the sun rose every morning in the past doesn't mean it will in the future.

"But that's ludicrous!" the student exclaimed. "Of course it will."

Eddie sighed. "We can't know that. Maybe it rose in the past because of a specific set of circumstances that won't be replicated again in the future. Or maybe it's just dumb luck that it rose every time in the past — like a coin coming up heads a hundred times in a row," Eddie persisted, becoming ever more animated.

"But why would that be?" the young man insisted.

"Well, let's assume a different situation. You live next to a small house, owned by an old man. Every night just after dark, the old man lights a candle in the living room window. Okay?"

"Uh-huh."

"Well, now let's assume one day the old man sells the house and moves away. Will there be a candle in the window tonight?" Eddie queried.

"No," the student answered.

"Because the circumstances have changed. It's the same with the sun. Perhaps the circumstances have changed, even if we're not aware of them. So it's logically problematic to generalize through induction," Eddie explained, as the sun ducked behind a cloud, darkening the street temporarily, as if to emphasize Eddie's point.

"So Hume says we shouldn't use induction?" the student inquired, removing his cheap, plastic-framed sunglasses.

"Not quite. He says it's flawed. So, as philosophers, we should be aware of the limits of induction. Nonetheless, since we need to live practically as human beings, he says that of course we should use the lessons we've learned from experience. We just shouldn't expect them to be infallible," Eddie concluded. "Got it?"

"Yes. I think so," the student said gratefully. "I wish my professor were as clear. Thank you!" He reached into his back pocket for his wallet.

"Put your money away!" Eddie shouted. "I don't *need* your money!"

"Huh? I promised to pay you five dollars for your help," the student protested, donning his sunglasses once again as the sun re-emerged.

"Don't insult me! I know you were just asking questions to ridicule me, like everyone else does. I don't need to be humiliated. Just leave me alone."

The student looked flustered, almost to the point of tears. Again he reached into his pocket and again Eddie screamed at him. "Don't mock me! Just leave me alone. Go!"

Embarrassed, the young man complied, shaking his head in confusion. A couple of men who had been following the discussion were amused. "That Crazy Eddie, he's a genuine loony. S'got a real mean streak in him. Just flies off the handle like nobody's business, he does," one of them commented.

"Sure does!" his companion agreed. "What an asshole!"

But the teller, who had left the bank for the day on time to overhear the exchange, knew better. Later in the week, when Eddie strayed from his office for a few minutes, she discretely deposited a five-dollar bill from her own wallet into his cap.

Under the circumstances, it wouldn't be surprising to learn that the man they called Crazy Eddie had contempt for everyone he encountered, everyone under the sun. There is, of course, an exception to every rule. An older woman he knew only as Jane was the sole person Crazy Eddie respected, genuinely valued. In her early sixties, Jane had retired early when her older husband did, moving downtown to enjoy their golden years to the fullest.

Quick-witted, well-read, contemplative, the man they called Eddie saw in her an intellectual equal, something he rarely encountered on the street. Jane had taken an instant interest in him the first time she had heard him lecturing to a family of tourists several years ago. She would stop by, often with food or a cup of coffee, just to talk to him, as a human being, a companion, not to humour him or mock him. She seemed genuinely concerned about his well-being as she visited his office to chat almost daily while she ran errands around town. Acerbic Eddie actually looked forward to these social calls, had begun to view her as a companion, even a sort of friend, something he had not possessed in over twenty years.

"Good afternoon, Eddie," she said as the sun neared the end of its lazy journey to the West that day. "You must be enjoying this absolutely perfect day."

"Yes," he assented. "I'll take 'em as long as I can get 'em. How are you today, Jane?"

"I baked some cookies this morning. Would you like some?" she asked as she proffered a brown paper lunch bag smeared with translucent grease stains to him. Witnessing his discomfort, she added, "Vegetarian, of course. I wouldn't offer them to you if they weren't."

"Thank you," he grunted as he grabbed the bag. "Say, Jane. What do you think of the uproar over that Cornwallis statue?" Jane was the only person Eddie would actually ask questions of, whose opinion mattered to him.

"I don't know.... I understand what they're objecting to," she reflected. "In many ways, he was an unsavoury character. But he *was* the city's founder. To pull down the statue would seem wrong somehow. Like it would erase history. Why? What do *you* think?"

"I'm not fully sure," he confessed. "I see your point, but I also wonder whether the Miq'maq are objecting precisely because it erases *their* history. It's not a simple issue, but it strikes me that it's appropriate for the city to be having the conversation, regardless of what they decide. Human beings usually don't care what evils they do to others. To discuss it, to agonize over it... that may just be progress."

"I suppose.... But I fear the consequences if we can just purge people from history. It's very Orwellian. But listen..... I wanted to talk to you about something else. I don't want to intrude, but I'm a little worried about you. The winter's coming and they say it's going to be a bad one. Is there anything I can do for you to help you out, Eddie?" Jane inquired, perhaps sensing the turmoil that had been growing within his troubled breast of late.

Her sincerity, her genuine compassion, moved him. Instead of answering, he gazed forlornly past her, as if half remembering a deeply-buried secret of bygone times, when dinosaurs roamed a pristine and unblemished Earth, and disclosed, lowering his voice almost to a whisper, like he was divulging a secret too personal, too precious to share with the winds, "My name is Gabriel...."

Chapter 2

Maybe it was because of the traumatic circumstances of his birth, the precarious nature of his first few weeks of life, that Gabriel Morris Klein had a mortal fear of the dark as a child. At least that's what his father thought.

Gabriel made his grand entry into the world prematurely, on a kitchen table in the Outremont district of Montreal during what was dubbed "The Storm of the Century," on March 4, 1971. His parents, Esther and Isaac Klein, Hungarian Jewish emigres who resided in Toronto, had travelled to Montreal by Voyageur bus to attend the wedding of Esther's cousin, Albert. Since money was perpetually tight for the Kleins, Albert's parents had billeted them with nearby friends rather than sending them to a hotel. The morning of the wedding, Esther suffered her first contractions. Since this was her first baby, however, she had no inkling that she was about to deliver, especially with her due date still three weeks away. In the meantime, the city – which had already been inundated with above average snowfall for the winter – was blasted with gale-force winds and a whopping forty-seven centimeters of snow on that single day, paralyzing the roads, the transportation system. By the time the Kleins understood that Esther was on the verge of giving birth, driving her to a hospital was simply out of the question. Their hosts desperately banged on neighbouring doors in search of a doctor, but found only Hélène, a nursing student, who under the circumstances was unceremoniously thrust into the role of midwife.

The scene in the kitchen of the upper duplex apartment was chaotic. Isaac and his hosts frantically scampered hither and thither in search of blankets, towels, hot water and other utensils deemed necessary by acne-ridden Hélène, whose connect-the-dots face had assumed a sickly, panicked aspect. In the absence of anaesthetic or pain medicine, they plied Esther, who was lying astride the table alternately weeping and shrieking, with Tylenol. When the too small, wrinkled, red baby boy made his unceremonious arrival, a shiver ran down Hélène's spine. She crossed herself, whispering bleakly to the duplex's owner, out of earshot of the boy's mother, "This one won't survive, I'm afraid." But the scrawny infant with its plaintive cry had an iron determination far greater than that of Napoleon's Grand Army. After inexpertly snipping the umbilical cord and slapping him to make certain he was breathing, Hélène gingerly swaddled him in towels and, rather than handing him to his mother, placed him near a metal desk lamp in an effort to keep him warm.

Fearing that the premature baby would die without an incubator, "Nurse" Hélène urged Isaac to contact the police and request assistance getting him to a hospital. The best they could do in the winter pandemonium outside, though, was to dispatch an officer on skidoo. Within an hour of his troubled birth, therefore, the baby and his beleaguered mother were bundled up and strapped onto a snowmobile, battling the snow, the bitter winds, to arrive at the Royal Victoria Hospital, where he remained in an incubator for three weeks before he was deemed viable enough to be discharged.

And so it was that Gabriel spent the first month of his life in Montreal and had his *brit milah*, the Jewish ritual circumcision that normally occurs on the eighth day of a boy's life, when he was four weeks old.

Despite his inauspicious beginning, Gabriel grasped life with both hands and thrived. As an infant suckling from his mother's breast, he was always ravenously hungry, could never get enough. In that very same manner, throughout his childhood, his brain thirsted for knowledge, for greater challenges. He learned to speak early, at only ten months, exclaiming with delight on his first birthday, "Ooh! kandools and ice kweem!" He delighted his parents with his spongelike memory, which allowed him to complete the poems and songs they taught him as a toddler. So insatiable was the boy's quest for knowledge that his mother started teaching him to read prior to his third birthday. While she ran errands in the car, he would practice by reading street names – Wil-son, Bat-hurst – and business names – Shell, Fi-na, Mac's Milk. By the time he entered Kindergarten at five years of age, he was reading at a middle school level, in particular devouring the Hardy Boys detective books and the Encyclopedia Brown mysteries.

His early life passed agreeably enough in his family's Bathurst Heights upper triplex apartment. His parents, after having difficulty conceiving children, were over the moon with their gift from Heaven and lavished all their love and attention on him. Although they both worked full time, plump, auburn-haired Esther staggered her hours so she could pick her blue-eyed boy up from daycare, and later school, until he was old enough to make his own way home. She would then spoil him with cupcakes, mandlebrot cookies, or his favourite, her homemade chocolate kokosh, before bringing him along as she did her shopping. When they returned, they'd play games together until dinnertime.

His father would return from a long day of work mentally and physically exhausted, but never too drained for a story, to hear about what his "little mensch" learned in school or to read the paper on the living room sofa with Gabriel poised on his lap, happily chirping away. "Oy, what a day I had!" he'd invariably declare upon crossing the threshold of their dwelling, to be met with the exuberant padding of Gabriel's small feel before the boy catapulted himself into his father's arms, erupting, "Daddy's home!" Then, to Gabriel's delight, Isaac would chase him all around the apartment while Esther laughed, despite her injunction not to get the boy too excited before supper. Sometimes he'd bring his son a small gift that he'd picked up on the way home: a candy bar, a book or even some raspberries, which the boy practically inhaled after first wearing them as helmets on each of his chubby fingers. From then until he tucked Gabriel into bed for the evening, father and son were inseparable. Occasionally, when Esther finished cleaning up from dinner, she would find them in the living room, both fast asleep, Gabriel lying across his father's chest, one hand around his beloved stuffed cocker spaniel, which for reasons he could never explain he named Beemie, the other straddling his father's neck. When this happened, she would watch them for a while with a tearful smile before carrying Gabriel off to his room.

Over time, his intelligence and advanced knowledge presented his parents and his school, Summit Heights Elementary, with a problem when the dark-haired, fair-complexioned, pudgy boy with intense, blue-grey eyes entered Grade 1. Aside from the social skills children were expected to acquire, the core of the curriculum revolved around elementary reading and basic arithmetic, both of which Gabriel had already mastered under his mother's tutelage. So he found himself completely unchallenged, even bored. His teacher, meanwhile, was frustrated with him deriding all the math problems as "too cinchy" and the books as "baby books" in front of his classmates.

Initially, the principal tried to solve the problem by sending Gabriel out with some of the slower children to help teach them the concepts they were unable to grasp in class. This was convenient for the teacher, as it disposed of two groups of problem children: those who were unable to follow her lesson plan and Gabriel, who demanded much more than she could offer. The Kleins, however, were horrified that their little mensch wasn't actually learning anything in school. So eventually the principal agreed to skip Gabriel into Grade 2. In truth, he believed that Gabriel was advanced enough intellectually to jump right into Grade 3, but he and the Kleins feared that placing him so far beyond his age-level might disadvantage him socially.

The Kleins marvelled at all the questions their young prodigy would ask as he tried to make sense of a complicated world. One evening, while his father was putting him to sleep on the wooden bed he had built for his son, Gabriel quizzed him about his accent.

"Why do you and Mama talk funny," the boy asked without malice, propping himself up on his pillow with his elbow, his beloved Beemie grasped firmly in the other arm, and studying his father's square face, the scar above his left eye from an accident with a shovel when he was a child.

"We have accents," Isaac told him patiently, "because we were born in Hungary."

"Oh," he said, not quite comprehending. "Do all people in Hungry have accents?"

His father smiled indulgently, revealing his crooked teeth, the large triangular gap between his upper incisors. "Well, when they speak English they do. You see, we didn't speak English when we were young. Only Hungarian and Yiddish. We learned English much later."

The boy sucked in his lower lip as he turned this over in his mind. "So why'd you want to come here if you didn't know English?"

"That's a fair question. You see, Jews had a hard time in Hungary during the war. Many Hungarians hated Jews and treated them badly. They were friends of the Nazis, from Germany – very bad people who wanted to kill all us Jews. When the Nazis attacked Hungary in 1944, they made the Hungarian government send its Jews to Poland and Germany to be killed. That was just fine by many Hungarians. My aunt and uncle – may they rest in peace – were murdered in the Auschwitz concentration camp," Isaac said, stony-faced. This was too complicated, too upsetting for a young boy, he feared, but believing Gabriel deserved an honest answer he continued. "So, we Jews wanted to get away from such a terrible place, where people could treat us so badly. But after the war, Hungary was occupied by the Soviet Union, and we couldn't get away. After the revolution in 1956, though, many Jews escaped Hungary. That's when my family and Mama's family both got out and came here. So, we didn't choose to come to Canada. But we're thankful that Canada took us."

That was a lot for young Gabriel to process. At first, he said nothing while the wheels in his mind kept spinning. But when his father said "goodnight" and kissed him on the forehead, the questions came fast and furious. "Why did they all hate Jews? What did the Jews do to them? And, if the Hungry people were friends of the Notsees, why did they attack Hungry? Was it bad for the Jews when the Sovit Union took over? And__"

Proudly rustling his son's hair with his thick, hairy fingers, his father exclaimed in mock exasperation, "Enough questions already!!! It's time to go to bed. We'll talk about this another time."

Isaac kissed his son, moved toward the door and was about to extinguish the overhead light.

"Wait, Daddy!" Gabriel almost shouted. "Can you turn on the nightlight?"

"Sure," his father said, as he bent to flick the small switch.

"And... can you check under the bed? And in the closet?"

"Aw, what for? You're a big boy. You're not still afraid of the dark... of monsters, are you?" Isaac asked with a grin.

"Well, a little...." Gabriel admitted. "And also...."

"Also what?" Isaac asked, raising his left hand, palm outward, fingers spread, to punctuate his question. The hand cast a faint shadow on the door in the dingy yellow light from the overhead fixture, with its square frosted shade, held in place by a round, black plastic nut.

"Make sure the bogeyman's not hiding anywhere," Gabriel blurted out breathlessly.

"The bogeyman? I never heard of such a thing," his father puzzled, bringing his hand to his face to scratch his cheek.

"Jack says he's a nasty man that sneaks into your room when you're sleeping," Gabriel recounted breathlessly. "He says it's got claws and horns and stuff," he shivered as he related this, "and can see you even if you can't see him!"

"Well, he's not here," Isaac assured him, after making a show of inspecting the room. "Goodnight, little mensch!"

"Goodnight, Daddy!" Gabriel replied, visibly relieved.

The Klein's cluttered kitchen was a macabre study in beige linoleum. The counters, one for meat to the left of the sink, a separate one for dairy in accordance with kosher dietary laws to its right, were both shielded against foreign invasion by a light shade of the rubbery resin. Above them, the plywood cabinets housing both sets of dishes, meat and dairy, were themselves coated in a lighter, ivory linoleum laminate. The table, also covered with the material, was a darker, greener beige, almost olive in hue. Even the floor consisted of burlap coloured linoleum sheets with a rust-coloured floral design, giving the room a drab, institutional feel. All these elements were tied together by the peeling, dispirited sable wallpaper. It was a cacophony of beige. Yet, despite its unsightly dreariness, the kitchen was Esther's empire. As an immigrant woman for whom poverty and traditional social norms had precluded a higher education, an opportunity for a satisfying career, she always felt a degree of empowerment as the Cleopatra of her kitchen, an authority she exercised with an iron fist. And for Gabriel, with its magical aromas of Chicken Paprikash or his mother's mandlebrot cookies, the pencil-marked door frame where Esther proudly recorded his growth over the years, the small rectangular table where they bonded as a family, the drab kitchen was his little corner of Heaven.

A few weeks later, over dinner at the kitchen table, lost in that nauseating sea of beige, Gabriel puzzled over his father's occupation, his mother presiding, deriving *naches* – which in Yiddish implies a combination of pride and satisfaction – from her ascendancy.

"What do you do when I'm in school, Daddy?" he asked thoughtfully, twirling a tuft of his soft, chestnut hair around his index finger.

"Whaddaya think, little mensch? He works!" was his mother's reply.

"Yeah, but what do you *do* at work?" Gabriel persisted, as only a child could, rocking back and forth on the wooden kitchen chair, whose legs were slightly uneven.

"I work at an office," his father said.

"A *big* office. Downtown," his mother added, standing to refill a jug of water from the sink. "Now stop playing with the chair. You're gonna break it. And eat your potatoes," she commanded lovingly. "They're getting cold!"

Gabriel angled his fork like a shovel and scooped some mashed potatoes into his mouth while he imagined the office his father must work in, a big brass nameplate on the door, like on television.

"Do you have a desk?"

"What's an office without a desk?" His father often responded to a question with another question.

"And a secretary?"

"Of course I got a secretary," he assured his son with a perfunctory nod of his square cranium. With his square head and square face, he was built like a large cube with sandy, thinning hair.

Gabriel smiled. His father must be rather important, he surmised. The phone rang. Esther, who was always the first to answer the lime green telephone affixed to the kitchen wall near the door to the equally drab hall — heaven help Isaac or Gabriel if they usurped her right — pounced on it and lifted the receiver to her ear, while Isaac followed her with his dark brown eyes.

"Hello? Yes? Who is this please?" Esther queried, her narrow, still pretty face a contorted mask of concentration.

"But what do you do in the office?" it occurred to Gabriel to ask.

"What do I do?" his father repeated distractedly, still watching his wife, wondering who would be calling at dinner time. "I manage accounts. It's really not a big deal."

But to Gabriel, it was everything. He knew what his father did. He was no longer a little kid, oblivious to the world. He was almost seven and, he felt, could relate to his father almost as a big person would. As if to underscore this thought, he asked, "Can I go to your office with you? To see it?"

"Duck cleaning?" Esther asked incredulously into the telephone, her melodic voice rising. As she got flustered, her accent grew more pronounced, her command of English grammar slipped. "What for we should need *that*?" Isaac, now riveted by the phone conversation, ignored Gabriel's question. "We don't *have* any ducks!"

"Daddy?" Gabriel persisted.

"No, we don't have that too. No air conditioner, no ducks. We don't need *duck* cleaning!" Esther blurted in exasperation, her face reddening. "Goodbye," she said, replacing the receiver. "What a crazy call. He only wants we should clean our ducks!"

"It must be a joke," Isaac opined. "You know... whatta they call 'em? A crank call."

"So *can* I, Daddy?" Gabriel inquired again, his small frame rocking with impatience.

"Can you what, little mensch?" Isaac asked, still puzzling about the call.

"Can I see your office?"

His father hesitated for a moment. "They don't like children in the office. But when you're older I'll take you. Now be quiet and eat, will you? I want to get outside already and see if we can finish that snowman before bedtime!" His father tousled his hair lovingly.

Although Gabriel adored his parents, his strongest bond was with his maternal grandfather, his Zaidie. After school or on the weekend, Zaidie, who lived in an apartment two blocks away, was overjoyed to spend time with his only grandchild, teaching him to play Chess, reading classic books to him, or instilling in him a love for classical music. It had been Zaidie who had introduced the boy to the wondrous magic of *The Count of Monte Cristo, Treasure Island, Robinson Crusoe*, the 1812 Overture, Beethoven's Fifth Symphony. Although he suffered from an arthritic ankle which made him limp and support himself with a walking stick, he would often take Gabriel on long walks, during which they would discuss the old country, history, philosophy, Jewish tradition, the various and sundry jobs his grandfather had been compelled by necessity to work at after immigrating to Canada with little money. For Gabriel, this kind, sweet, bald old man with thin ribbons of cottony hair above his ears, whose love for him knew no bounds, was a fountain of information, an endless encyclopedia. A single walk with his Zaidie nurtured his fertile brain infinitely more than an entire year of school could.

On one such walk, after attending synagogue with his grandfather on a December Saturday morning, Gabriel sought more information than his father had provided about their lives in Hungary.

"Were you in Hungry during the war, Zaidie?" he inquired, as they headed southbound on Bathurst Street, past the 7-11 store. The traffic was heavy for a Saturday, and the stench of automobile exhaust spoiled the crisp winter air.

"Yes, I was," his grandfather admitted, grimacing as he shifted his weight onto his sore ankle. He spoke slowly, ponderously, with a pronounced Hungarian lilt. It was a point of pride for him that, though he immigrated to Canada as an adult and had a heavy accent, his English was almost flawless.

"Was it hard?"

"At first, no. The Hungarian government passed anti-Semitic laws, but it didn't really affect me. I was trained as a lawyer in Budapest and, although they restricted the number of Jews any firm could hire, I was lucky to be the only Jew in my firm. So I was able to keep my job." He paused at an intersection to check if was safe to proceed. "Eventually, though, they began to draft Jews into the Munkaszolgálat, a forced labour battalion. These unfortunate Jews were treated miserably, often beaten and abused. They were forced to do terribly dangerous work on the Russian front, including clearing minefields without proper equipment. Many of these Jews died or were horribly maimed. So when they called me up, I ran away."

"Ran away?" The boy's eyes widened. He had to steady himself to keep from falling, as his plastic boots slipped on a patch of ice.

"Careful, Gabriel!" his Zaidie warned, anchoring the boy with his gnarled hands. "Yes. I went to the farm of a friend of the family's, a Gentile, not far from Budapest, near the Duna... the Danube River. When the Nazis decided to deport all the Hungarian Jews to the death camps – it was terrible, you know – it became too risky for my friend to keep me. German and Hungarian soldiers were searching the countryside for escaped Jews. If they found me, not only would I have been killed, but my friend would have been punished, too. So I left and hid by the river. I stayed in hiding for many months, until the war ended. I was the only member of my family to survive," his grandfather recollected wistfully, his grey eyes narrowing with sorrow. He walked slowly, gingerly now to avoid slipping and putting undue pressure on his swollen joint.

Gabriel was bewildered. "But... where did you sleep? And what did you eat?"

"I dug myself a hole in the soft mud of the riverbank, behind some low bushes, and hid inside. I slept in that cold, dark hole. Because it was easier to move around unseen at night, I slept during the daytime and gathered food at night and in the early morning. My friend promised to hide some food for me in a rain barrel near the cowshed every day. So mostly I crawled back to his farm each night and ate that — a bit of bread, some cheese. He knew I ate only kosher food, so he never left me any meat. But I also hunted around for wild berries, plants and roots that I could eat. Whatever I could find."

Gabriel was awestruck with admiration. He painted a romantic picture in his head of his grandfather, Errol Flynn-like, eluding the entire Hungarian Army, stealing food from right under their noses. But he was still troubled.

"Zaidie," he asked hesitantly, sucking in his lower lip thoughtfully.

"Yes, my angel,"

"Why did Hungry hate the Jews? And why did the Germans hate us?" It was the same question he had asked his father. One that had been vexing him for some time.

His grandfather smiled sadly. "I wish I knew. Because we're different. Because our religion is different."

"That's a pretty dumb reason to hate someone!" he exclaimed, with the innocence of a child. They came to an intersection and stopped, while a steady stream of cars filtered by.

"Yes, it is," his grandfather agreed heartily, nodding his thanks to a driver that waved them across. "Promise me that you'll never hate someone just because he's different or believes something different, okay Gabriel?"

"Of course, Zaidie," Gabriel promised solemnly, as they reached the stairs to Gabriel's home.

Oh, the memories of his youth! His mother's high-pitched, indulgent laugh, which promised safety, comfort. The smell of freshly-baked kokosh. The whistle of cold winter air blowing through his poorly-insulated window, making him shiver with delight under his blankets at night. The telltale clap of his Zaidie's walking stick on the stairs, which announced a surprise visit even before the old man reached the door. Gabriel's breathless anticipation of Chanukah and its glorious candles. His grandmother's metal-framed magnifying glass, which she used to read magazines and novels. The filaments of the metallic space heater that glowed bright orange on a cold January night, mesmerising the boy. His father's resonant, confident voice chanting the blessings before dinner on the Sabbath. The sounds of traffic outside their apartment on Bathurst Street – the metallic screech of a bus braking to pick up passengers, the whoosh of a car speeding through a puddle in the rain, the powerful whir of a truck engine idling at the traffic light – the elongated reflections of headlights on the ceiling. The detergent smell of a freshly-mopped floor in his school. The deep peal of the *shofar*, the ram's horn, on Rosh Hashanah. And always on the stairwell, the sour, pervasive odour of cabbage, a relic from their neighbour's meal from the previous night, or perhaps the night before that.

One decision his parents made once Gabriel entered Grade 4 had a profound influence on the boy's mind, the way he viewed the world. To supplement his studies with religious and cultural instruction that would help him understand what it meant to be Jewish, they enrolled Gabriel in a religious night school with classes every Tuesday evening. At first, he resented what his nine-year-old brain viewed as a pointless waste of time. When all his friends were playing street hockey after school, he would ride a crowded, overheated bus up Bathurst Street to a brown, two-storey brick school north of Finch Avenue. There he would join a group of unfamiliar ill-behaved children, who also resented their parents for spoiling their evenings, to be lectured by rabbis with old world accents even stronger than his parents'.

Over time, however, he grew enthralled with all he learned. He especially loved the bible stories about Abraham, Noah and Moses. God told Abraham "Go forth from your land and your father's home and travel to the land that I will show you!" *Imagine that*, he thought, *God actually spoke to Abraham! How wonderful! But how? Probably through nature, Gabriel decided, through the trees, the wind, the water. Maybe He speaks to us all that way, but we've forgotten to listen.* And what a man was Abraham! God spoke truth to him and he obeyed, despite the immense sacrifices that entailed. Abraham abandoned his father's house, his wealth, his comfort, because his father's ways were wrong, immoral, an abomination in God's eyes. He persisted in following God's path, even though he was the only one who heard God's call, who understood its importance. Even though he was ridiculed by others. Was there ever a more heroic, just figure, a better role model for a young boy?

Or Noah, who heeded God's call to build an ark to rescue life on earth from the flood. Noah, who was "perfect in his generation." Although his generation was corrupt, had abandoned the ways of God, Noah didn't succumb to their peer pressure. He endured the scorn of his neighbours with equanimity while he built an ark and gathered two of every species in accordance with God's wishes.

Grandest of all, in young Gabriel's mind, was Moses. Moses grew up in Pharaoh's house, raised in opulence and splendour. Nonetheless, when he witnessed an Egyptian whipping a Jew merely because he was a slave, that stirred Moses' conscience. He renounced everything to pursue the course of justice. He would rather live as a humble shepherd in Midian than be worshipped as prince of Egypt and be a party to corruption, slavery, injustice. God chose this soft-spoken, lisping, humble Moses to be the harbinger of his deliverance and valued him above all men, to the point that he even revealed his sacred countenance to Moses and no-one else. Yet Moses' love of justice was so great that he was audacious enough to argue with God himself on behalf of the Jewish people, which only made God love him more. There was a man to admire!

How these stories influenced Gabriel, shaped his young mind! He learned to value truth and righteousness above all. He learned that it was wrong to compromise on matters of principle. Would Moses compromise with injustice? Would Abraham make his peace with idolatry? Although it was for only a single evening each week, the years Gabriel spent in Jewish school instilled a moral compass in him that would always point straight north and a respect for God that would remain with him always.

On a blustery autumn night, with the wind rattling the aluminum window frames, Isaac was unable to sleep and trudged into the kitchen for some warm milk. As he passed Gabriel's room, he was startled to see light streaming out from under Gabriel's door. He pushed it open to discover Gabriel wide awake, clutching his blankets tightly with white knuckles as he sat upright, his knees tucked under his chin.

"Gabriel! What's going on? It's after midnight!" Isaac exclaimed. "Why is your light still on?"

"Sorry, Daddy. The nightlight stopped working and I got scared," Gabriel said through heavy intakes of breath. He rubbed his eyes with his right hand, still clasping his blankets with the left one.

Isaac bent down over the nightlight and confirmed that the blackened bulb had indeed burned out. "I'm gonna have to get a new bulb. But what are you so scared about, little mensch? Mommy and I are in the next room," he said tenderly.

Gabriel furrowed his lips and looked away. After a delay, he said, "I'm just scared."

"Of what? There's nothing here that can hurt you," Isaac said. But Gabriel held his tongue. "Still of that Bogeyman?" Turning beet red, the boy nodded slowly.

"There's no such thing as a Bogeyman," Isaac asserted, trying to conceal his indulgent smile.

"Yes, there is! Jack says he's always looking for sleeping children to kidnap," Gabriel insisted, as he nervously ran his tongue along his loose upper incisor.

"You're almost ten years old! You can't still be afraid of that nonsense.... Listen, I've asked around. The Bogeyman is just like the *Mumus* our parents told us about in Hungary. Mommy and I never wanted to raise you with that silliness. But it's just something parents' sometimes say to their kids to make them behave. 'If you don't go to sleep, *Mumus*'ll get you.' It's not real," Isaac explained, ruffling his son's hair good-naturedly.

"Are you sure?" Gabriel asked doubtfully.

"I promise you, Gabriel. Don't you trust me? I'm your father and I love you more than the whole world. I wouldn't lie to you. There is no Bogeyman," his father said.

Gabriel sucked anxiously on his lower lip. After a long silence, he relaxed, his fingers unclasping, the knot in his shoulders loosening, and said, "Okay. I believe you Daddy."

"Now you can't sleep with the light on. Do you want me to leave your closet light on instead?" Isaac offered.

"No," Gabriel replied, without hesitation. "If there's no Bogeyman, I guess I can sleep without a night light."

Isaac nodded approvingly and tucked his son into bed. As he retreated to the hallway, Gabriel jumped out from under his covers without warning and ran to give him a bear hug, encircling his father's paunchy stomach with his small, rubbery arms and squeezing tightly. Then he returned to bed and fell asleep quickly in the dark.

By all accounts, Gabriel appeared to be a special child, gifted academically and possessing a maturity, a wisdom that belied his age. At Parent-Teacher night in Grade 4, his homeroom teacher, Mrs. Stewart, couldn't rave enough about his progress.

"Mr. and Mrs. Klein," she said, as they shuffled into her cluttered classroom awkwardly, twisting themselves uncomfortably into desks made for children. "You must be very proud of your son."

"Oh, yes," Esther admitted, brushing back an escaped lock of her auburn hair that obscured her opal blue eye. "But how is he doing in school?"

"How is he *doing*?" Mrs. Stewart repeated with enthusiasm, adjusting the arms of her round purple spectacles. "Gabriel's a wonderful student! He's excelling in every subject. He reads well above a fourth-grade level. He's serious, well-behaved, mature, sensitive.... Everything he puts his mind to he succeeds in. And not just his academic pursuits. He's one of the youngest members of the school's Chess club and, by all accounts, he's quickly rising up the ranks. The music teacher says he's got the makings of a gifted musician. He's truly a model student."

Isaac beamed. "But how is he doing socially?" he asked, as his eyes swept the Australia display on the far wall, complete with a map, photographs of kangaroos and koalas, indigenous artifacts, and other items of geographical interest. "He doesn't seem to have many friends."

"Well, that's true.... He's not one of the more popular students. He tends to read a lot at recess and sometimes seems to prefer to be by himself. But he *does* have friends. He seems to be very close to Jack Silverman," the teacher replied thoughtfully.

"I know him. He's been to our house once or twice," Esther volunteered. "What about the Lubov boy?" The Lubovs were a Jewish family that had emigrated from Hungary at the same time as the Kleins. The Kleins had helped them when they arrived in Toronto after living in Halifax for a few years, had even let them share their cramped apartment for a month until they found jobs and an apartment.

"Leibl? No, I don't think I've seen them together much. As I say, Gabriel isn't a social butterfly," the teacher reported.

"But he's not being picked on or anything, is he?" Esther inquired anxiously.

"No! Nothing like that that I'm aware of. He's just not the most social child. I don't think there's anything to worry about," Mrs. Stewart assured her.

"Thank you, Mrs. Stewart," Isaac said, as he extracted himself from the low desk and stood to leave, stretching to relieve a leg cramp.

"What I'm trying to say is," Mrs. Stewart continued, pushing her glasses further up the bridge of her nose, "your son is a special child. He's not like the other children. I think he's got a great future ahead of him. You've got to nurture that."

The Klein's exchanged proud, surprised looks. They had always thought Gabriel was bright, and like most immigrants dearly wished to see their son achieve academic success to enable him to climb the socioeconomic ladder. But they were still astonished to hear his teacher gush about him so. "We will," they assured her.

***

In light of Mrs. Stewart's advice, the Kleins decided to re-evaluate their priorities. As relatively recent immigrants who arrived from the old country with little but the clothing on their backs and, at least initially, a poor command of English and French, life in Canada was a constant struggle for them. Although they both worked full time, money was perpetually in short supply. They concluded, however, that it would be criminal to shortchange their beloved son by denying him the opportunities that he needed to unleash his boundless potential. *Nothing*, they agreed, was too good for their Gabriel.

Their first decision was to cancel their annual family vacation. Every summer, the Klein's had rented a cottage on Lake Simcoe for two weeks to escape the muggy city and fill their lungs with unspoiled country air. It was a restorative vacation that they all relished, as a rest from the rigours of work and a chance to bond together as a family. Isaac particularly loved fishing with Gabriel and cooking their catch on an outdoor bonfire. But that was the only real luxury that they could eliminate from their budget without causing undue hardship. Besides, Isaac reasoned, they could probably find affordable activities around town to replace the cottage.

In addition, Esther suggested that she could earn a bit of extra money by working as a part-time seamstress, altering clothing for people in the neighbourhood. During the week, she had full-time employment in Mount Sinai Hospital's kosher kitchen. But she believed that she could find time for alterations on some evenings and Sundays, if it would help Gabriel.

With the extra money they secured in this manner, they bought Gabriel a used violin and hired a music teacher to instruct him once a week. Gabriel was overjoyed, as he adored music and had always dreamed of an instrument of his own. In addition, since Gabriel didn't appear to be challenged academically at school, they hired a tutor once a week to teach him more advanced mathematics and science.

It amounted to a considerable sacrifice for the Kleins, but they were more than happy to do their parts to give their gifted son a leg up in life. And far from begrudging what they lost, they never once made him feel like he was in any way a burden on them, a yoke around their necks.

To compensate for their more austere lifestyle, the Kleins sought low-cost activities that the whole family could participate in. On Sundays in the summer, they would drive into the countryside and enjoy long hikes into the woods. They frequented free concerts around the city and Shakespeare-in-the-Park at High Park. And, at the end of the summer, they would splurge on a Sunday excursion to the Canadian National Exhibition on the waterfront.

The first year, despite these activities, Gabriel seemed dispirited by the cancellation of their summer cottage trip, so Esther, always a fountain of ideas, suggested that they paint his room. Gabriel had frequently complained about the drabness of the pasteboard white walls in his bedroom. "It's so-o-o-o boring!!" he would say. His friends had more vibrant colours on their walls, which they had been allowed to choose themselves. But his parents had been loath to hire a painter – "We're not Rockefellers," his mother had said – and, at any rate, weren't certain whether their lease allowed them to do so. So Gabriel had grumbled, but grudgingly accepted their verdict. Now, in the interest of cheering him up, Esther secured permission from the landlord, declaring that they would make it a fun family project during their vacation time.

The idea was a tremendous success. They bought the paint, a few brushes, two rollers, and other accessories at Canadian Tire. With the freedom to choose the colour, within reason, Gabriel opted for a bright lime green to which his dubious parents reluctantly consented. For three days, they donned old clothing and, with a battery-powered transistor radio playing in the background, sometimes music, sometimes radio plays, they slathered on coats of primer, then the green paint.

At one point, Gabriel dipped his brush into the paint can and turned to face the wall he was working on, only to smear paint accidentally all over his father's polo shirt. He inhaled deeply, fearing he had done an irreparable wrong. Isaac glanced at his stained shirt in surprise, let out a joyous shout of "You miserable cretin!" and proceeded to chase Gabriel around the drop cloth with his roller, occasionally scoring a hit and splattering paint on the boy's t-shirt, jeans, and arm. Seeing this, Esther joined in the mirth, defending her son by forming a united front with him against Isaac. It was light-hearted, raucous family fun. In the end, all three were stippled in paint from head to foot.

When the job was completed, Gabriel surveyed his room with satisfaction, declaring, "Now my room is the nicest in the whole apartment. We should paint the rest of the rooms, too."

"Oy! Take it easy, Michelangelo!" Esther exhorted him. "Let's enjoy this beautiful new room for now and maybe next summer we should do more."

"But that was so much fun," Gabriel insisted. "Hey, Dad, maybe we could paint your office, too!"

"My office?" Isaac echoed. "I don't think they need *us* to paint my office."

"Aw!" Gabriel whined. "Hey, what colour *is* your office anyway?"

"What colour is it?" Isaac asked, wiping paint smears from his cheek with a cotton handkerchief. "It's an office. Does it need to have colours?"

Not to be deterred, Gabriel persisted, "Well, what colour are the walls painted?"

"Like any other office," Esther piped up. "It's white. Or half-white."

Gabriel found that disappointing. But still, it *was* an office. He couldn't expect it to be purple. "Does it have a big window?" he asked hopefully.

"A big window? I don't know if it's big, but there's a window," Isaac replied. "Now stop asking questions and let's clean up this mess! Then I'll race you to 7-Eleven to get popsicles."

"You're on!!" Gabriel screamed in delight.

It had been a glorious family activity and Gabriel was thrilled with the improvement to his room. Looking back on it many years later, Gabriel viewed that as the high-water mark for the family, the time when they were happiest together, perhaps the last time that they truly acted as a carefree, harmonious family unit.

Another innovative family activity that summer had a profound impact on Isaac. Walking home from the bus stop one afternoon, his attention was drawn to an unsightly patch of weeds abutting the triplex's side wall, adjacent to the driveway. He shook his square head in disgust. How it cheapened the appearance of their already shabby abode! An idea struck him, however.

That evening, he telephoned the landlord and requested permission to use that patch of earth as a family garden. Although he had only been a young boy at the time, he harboured fond memories of the sprawling, verdant garden behind his parents' apartment building in Budapest. In his mind's eye, he envisioned this scrawny patch being similarly transformed. Bemused, the landlord agreed to investigate. The following day, like a benevolent genie, he granted Isaac his wish, provided that the garden didn't interfere with the driveway. The family now had jurisdiction over a misshapen spot of bad soil, approximately a metre wide and three-quarters of a metre deep, with poor access to sunlight, overgrown with chickweed, plantain weed and dandelions. This became the Klein family garden.

Over the next week, the Kleins toiled under Isaac's tutelage to root out all the weeds by hand. Next Isaac drove Gabriel to a hardware store to purchase potting soil. They then dug out the entire patch, replacing the hard clay with more fecund soil. When all that hard labour was finished, they debated what to plant. Isaac was eager to grow vegetables, particularly tomatoes, cucumbers and peppers. Like the impractical young child he was, Gabriel was partial to watermelons. Given the diminutive size of the plot, however, Esther strongly advocated cultivating herbs, which didn't require as much space. Eventually, they reached a consensus, whereby most of the patch was devoted to basil, oregano and parsley, but a corner was reserved for one tomato plant and one jalapeno pepper plant. To indulge Gabriel, they allowed him to plant a watermelon seed in a jar that they placed just next to the garden.

Over the next few weeks, the plants sprouted, flowers appeared, tiny fruit emerged. But by then, beyond the excitement of using some basil and oregano leaves for Esther's cooking, mother and son had lost interest in the garden. In contrast, Isaac was smitten. After work each day, he would pull out encroaching weeds, lovingly sprinkle water from a yellow plastic pitcher, and pinch off the flowers at the tip of the herb shoots to keep them growing steadily. It brought him such joy, such inner peace, to tend the garden. By the following year, they stopped referring to it as the Klein family garden, designating it, instead, 'Daddy's garden'.

Life has a way of unravelling sometimes. All can be proceeding smoothly, predictably, pleasantly, in a comfortable soporific rhythm. But then the powers that be unexpectedly place a small pebble, insignificant really, on the track, directly in the train's path. In many instances, the danger is averted; either by luck or deft skill, the engineer can steer through it, keeping the engine on track, a few sparks the only consequence.

Occasionally, it has disastrous effects, causing the locomotive to derail in a fiery explosion. More frequently, however, its impact is less immediate, less dramatic, although no less pernicious in the long run, leading the train to deviate, to shift tracks, to disrupt the natural flow.

When he was ten years old and just starting grade five, Gabriel's grandfather suffered a series of strokes rendering him incapacitated in the hospital. His months-long illness affected Gabriel considerably. Most immediately, it had the practical effect of thrusting Gabriel into the role of essential worker at home. With his parents at work all day and his mother visiting her father in the hospital after work, much of the cooking and cleaning devolved to Gabriel after he finished school, or else it simply wouldn't get done. With the help of his mother's cook books and some coaching from Esther on Sundays, he learned how to fry an egg, make an omelette, brown ground beef to make a meat-based pasta sauce. His mother also introduced him to the washer and drier so that he could manage the family's laundry in her absence. So the young boy matured by leaps and bounds in these months, accumulating responsibilities and life experience that would serve him valuably in the future.

At the same time, his grandfather's illness took the wind out of Gabriel sails. Zaidie was his idol. The man the Nazis couldn't crush. The giant who brought his family back from the brink of extinction, moving to Canada to begin anew. The moral force of Gabriel's life. How could he get sick and look so frail? Was he going to die? Gabriel couldn't bear the thought.

Gabriel telephoned his grandfather in the hospital almost daily to update him on the day's developments at school, his progress learning to play Chess, the gossip from the synagogue, to play some music on his violin. Every Sunday afternoon, he would visit his grandfather in his room at Branson Hospital near Bathurst and Finch. Taking a seat next to the bed, with the metal guardrails that lowered and raised enticingly, in the large four-patient room divided by curtains, he implored his grandfather to recover, willed him to rise out of the bed and walk with him as he did before, but to little avail. While his visits always put some colour into Zaidie's gaunt, wizened face, a weak smile to his grey lips, it was clear that his grandfather's health was deteriorating rapidly.

Matters came to a head when his grandfather had a massive bleed one night and lost consciousness. For a period of days, Zaidie fell into the coma from which he would never emerge. On Saturday after synagogue, where Gabriel recited a special prayer for his grandfather's health during the *Torah* reading, he and his father rode the Bathurst bus up to Branson to join his mother's vigil at her comatose father's bedside. This in itself indicated to Gabriel the seriousness of his Zaidie's condition; ordinarily, the Kleins avoided riding in cars or buses on the Sabbath out of respect for its holiness. In the elevator, on the way up to the Intensive Care Unit, Isaac prepared Gabriel for the change in his grandfather.

"He's not like he was last week, Gabriel," Isaac began gently.

Gabriel nodded. "Is he going.... Is he going to die?" he asked, biting his upper lip to prevent himself from crying.

"You're a big boy. I think I can be straight with you," his father responded resting his hand gently, lovingly, on Gabriel's shoulder. "It doesn't look good. The doctors don't think he has very long."

Gabriel repressed a sob in an effort to justify his father's faith in him. To show that he really *was* mature enough to handle this. All he could think, though, was *how can Zaidie, who beat the Nazis and lived all by himself on the riverbed, die?* But then he remembered that Moses, who extracted the Jews from Egypt and performed many miracles, whom God loved above all others, also died. So did Abraham. So maybe Zaidie had to die, as well.

In the room, Gabriel sat forlornly in the tan vinyl armchair adjacent to the hospital bed, staring at the tubes protruding from his grandfather which dripped at regular intervals, inhaling the medicinal, institutional scent of the room, while his mother stroked her father's limp hand sadly, whimpering softly. After a few minutes, Gabriel stood up and placed himself at the head of the bed. "Zaidie, you'll be proud of me," he announced as enthusiastically as possible under the circumstances. "I got the highest mark in the class on my History test. It was on Mesopotamia."

His mother turned to him sadly. "Oh, little mensch! There's no point in talking to him. He can't answer you. He's in a coma."

Gabriel smiled wanly. "It's just like talking to God, Mom. He hears you, but he doesn't answer. It's still worth doing." With that, he proceeded to tell his Zaidie about the name Mesopotamia, which meant 'between the rivers,' its geographical location in contemporary Syria, Iraq and Turkey, the striking features of its pottery and culture. Esther watched in wonder through the watery screen of her tears.

When he left the room later that afternoon, he gave his unconscious grandfather a kiss on the forehead and promised to return the next Sunday with details about his preparations for the school science fair later that term, for which he and his friend Jack planned to conduct an experiment on magnetism. It was a promise he never had the opportunity to keep, as his grandfather gave up his struggle the following night.

Although Zaidie's passing had not come as a surprise to Gabriel, it had a dreadful effect on the boy. His bitterness that the one person he loved the most, who had loved him with the fire of a thousand suns, could die was inexpressible. In the weeks after his grandfather's passing, Gabriel's usually cheerful disposition grew sullen. He became prone to angry outbursts.

On the morning of Zaidie's funeral, Gabriel exploded at his mother over the clothing she had asked him to wear. He insisted on a brightly-coloured tie, which his grandfather had given him as a gift. His mother judged it to be inappropriately festive.

"Gabriel," his mother said softly, the dark grey bags under her eyes glistening in the early morning light, "a darker tie would be better."

"No, it wouldn't!" he responded harshly, defiantly. "Zaidie gave it to me and I'm gonna wear it!"

"It's a lovely tie, little mensch, but it's not right for a funeral."

"I don't *care* what you say! I'm wearing *this* tie," Gabriel screamed, angry tears welling up in his eyes. "And don't call me 'little mensch' anymore. I'm *sick* of it!" He shook a tightly clenched fist at his mother.

"Listen, Gabriel. I know you're hurt. So am I. He was my Daddy, and I'm just torn like a paper right now. But we have to mourn him the proper way," Esther reasoned.

"You didn't love him the way *I* did! Nobody did!" Gabriel wailed, his rage bubbling over like hot lava. In the end, his mother gave in, shocked by her son's outburst, but preferring not to upset him more than he already was.

During the seven-day *shiva* – the traditional Jewish mourning ritual in which friends and family visit the bereaved in their home to offer them comfort and reminisce about the deceased – Gabriel largely hid in his room, avoiding what he viewed as a hollow pantomime of sympathy from people who didn't really care about his Zaidie. When Jack came to offer his own condolences, Gabriel emerged, only to leave the *shiva* house and talk outside with his friend.

Above all, Gabriel began to obsess over a watercolour his mother had painted of a bend in the Danube River, which hung proudly in the living room, over the sturdy wood-framed sofa, whose functional but not terribly comfortable cushions she kept imprisoned in a red and yellow floral cloth to prevent fading. With the irrationality of youth, he fancied that this rural scene depicted the actual spot where Zaidie had hidden during the war, that the bushes on the far side of the canvas were the very bushes that had shielded Zaidie from the Nazis. The painting became his relic, the physical manifestation for Gabriel of his grandfather's strength of spirit, his indomitable character, his righteousness. Sometimes, when his parents returned home after a long day of work, they would find their son perched on a cloth-backed wooden chair opposite the sofa, lost in thought, his lower lip tense inside his mouth, devouring the painting with his eyes.

Ever afterwards, when trying to come to grips with all that was to occur, Esther would return to this moment as the font of all their troubles. "It's my father," she would say with a sad tilt of the head. "He was never the same again after my father passed."

Isaac disagreed. "That's ridiculous, Esther!" he would shout. "People die! You can't break to pieces just because an old man dies!"

But Esther would just sigh mournfully and repeat, "He never got over my father's death."

Several weeks after the funeral, Gabriel's homeroom teacher, Mrs. Riveira, brought Gabriel's class downtown for a visit to the Art Gallery of Ontario. The weather that May morning was gray and rainy as Gabriel boarded the chartered TTC bus. His friend Jack urged him to sit with him on a two-seater bench so they could talk about their science fair project, but Gabriel preferred to sit by himself on a single window seat in the middle of the bus. Overcast days put him in a contemplative mood and he was eager to revel in the ethereal quality their silver, uncertain light lent to the somber sky, the newly-budding trees, the fresh grass. As they approached the museum, however, he was shaken from his reverie upon hearing one of the class bullies, Victor Runyon, yelling his name.

"Hey, Klein!" the hefty boy in a grey and white striped polo shirt called. His tone was menacing.

"Uh, yeah?" Gabriel replied distractedly, still gazing off into the distance.

"I thought your dad worked in an *office*," Victor bellowed, pointing out the window on the other side of the bus.

"He does. What's your damage?" he said, trying to tread the fine line between pushover and provocateur.

"Well then why is he dressed as a *garbage* man and picking up *garbage* on the street?" the bully taunted, a spider about to dine on a freshly captive fly.

To Gabriel's great annoyance, Leibl Lubov echoed the bully's charge. So much for gratitude. "Hey, that *is* Gabriel's father! He's a garbage man!" Lubov shouted with malicious glee.

Gabriel jumped over to the other side of the bus, peered out the window and, at first, couldn't see what his classmates were talking about. On closer inspection, though, he saw a garbage man of about his father's height and build emptying a grooved metal can into a truck outside a brown-brick residence on Spadina Ave. *What a coincidence*, he thought. *That can't be him.* As the bus came closer, though, he clearly saw his father's unmistakeable square face, the shovel scar above his left eyebrow, his father's squat, muscular body clad in a navy city sanitation uniform.

"Klein's old man's a garbage man! Klein's old man's a garbage man!" Victor began singing joyfully. Lubov and other classmates, smelling blood in the water, joined in.

Gabriel saw red. Although he was not a fighter, he lunged, a wounded tiger, at his nemesis, burying him in punches to the chest, the stomach, the face, scratching wildly. Victor was a much larger, heavier boy, but he hadn't expected this furious assault and was consequently powerless to ward it off. By the time he overcame his surprise and fought back, landing a powerful punch or two of his own, Mrs. Riveira arrived to break up the fight and sentence both boys to detentions. She was stunned that Gabriel, of all her students, would be party to a fight.

Gabriel couldn't contain his fury. All day at the museum, he said little and didn't pay much attention to the art, either to appreciate it or to ridicule it with his classmates. All he could think about was his father on the street in that uniform.

That afternoon, after serving his one-hour detention, he returned home and squatted on the wooden bench just inside their apartment, waiting furiously for his father to return. His mother urged to him to have a snack before dinner, but he refused, unable even to look at her in his seething rage. When Isaac finally walked in the door, Gabriel pounced on him immediately, not leaving time for him to remove his hat and shoes.

"How was *work* today, Daddy? Did you have fun at the *office*?" he sneered.

"Don't talk to your father with that voice! What's the matter with you?" his mother scolded.

"Well? How was the *office* today?" Gabriel persisted, glaring directly, angrily, defiantly, into his father's eyes.

"How was work? It was a busy day. Lots of files to follow up on. Really busy," his father sighed, a little nonplussed by the unfamiliar, menacing note in his son's voice, the hostility in his eyes.

Gabriel snorted in disgust. "I was downtown today with my class on a school trip. The school rented a TTC bus and drove us to the art gallery. On the way, you'll never guess what I saw...." he sneered. His parents exchanged frightened glances. "That's right, Daddy. I saw you at your *office*. Wearing your work clothes. Picking up *trash cans*!"

"Oy!" his father grimaced, wounded deeply by his discovery. His mother gasped and began to weep. But ten-year-old Gabriel, with uncompromising righteousness and justice on his side, was unmoved.

"You *lied* to me!" he wailed. "How could you?" *Abraham wouldn't have lied*, he reasoned with his precocious, but still childlike, brain. *Moses would have told the truth, regardless of the consequences. Zaidie would have been true to him. How could his father have lied like that?*

"Your father didn't *lie*," his mother equivocated. "He just didn't want you to know what you didn't need to know."

"Yes. He *did*. He *lied*! He *lied*! He told me something that wasn't true. That's *wrong*!" Gabriel yelled at the top of his lungs, hot, angry tears burning his cheeks.

"Look, I'm sorry. I didn't tell you... because I knew you'd be *ashamed*," Isaac, despondent and red-faced, admitted. "I wanted to save you from that."

"I'm not ashamed!" Gabriel yelled defiantly, hatred brimming in his ice-blue eyes. "Do you think it matters to me what you do? But you *lied* to me!!! You didn't *love* me enough to tell me the truth! I'll *never* forgive you for that!"

To his parents' bewilderment, Gabriel was true to his ten-year-old word. Recalling this incident years later, he would never see his parents' point of view, never empathise with their shame, their desire to spare him embarrassment, never pardon them on account of their boundless love for him. Instead, he would remember this as his first unforgiveable betrayal. Though he was still very young, from that day forward his relationship with his parents altered forever. Although, like the dusk it brightened and darkened at times, gone was the powerful, unconditional brimming love that he had felt for them. It was replaced by a more pragmatic, transactional ethos, devoid – from his part anyway – of any real warmth.

Chapter 3

Winters were very hard for Gabriel and becoming tougher. Living outdoors in good weather, enjoying God's resplendent nature, the trees, the water, the fresh maritime air, that was easy. In winter, however, the bitter winds, the relentless snow, the teeth-chattering cold, all conspired to push him indoors, into the shelter that he dreaded, that crushed his spirit. As always, he tried to delay the move as long as possible. In late fall, when he could bear the frigid gusts off the water no longer, he made his annual move inland, to the dumpster, but found it harder to endure than ever before. He slept little and woke up with every part of his body stiff, on fire. It was difficult for him to walk after sleeping on the hard, cratered asphalt. When the temperature plunged below the freezing point and the snow painted the city cottony white, he was almost grateful to retreat to the misery of the shelter.

As damnably cold as winter was, in the past Gabriel had always found a bright side to it. The harshness of winter made him cherish the remaining seasons of the year that much more. The resplendent springs, when nature stirred from its somnolence, tantalized with its bright pastel palette, its honey-infused perfumes, and reminded him of the majesty of creation. The warm, tranquil summers, when the sun beat down through branches upholstered in thick, luscious, verdant leaves, warming the very interior of the soul. The glorious crisp autumns, when the dazzling symphonies of yellows, reds, oranges and browns give solace even as winter prepares its malicious return. No-one appreciates summer, truly *lusts* for it, Gabriel was convinced, who hasn't endured a Canadian winter.

This particular year, after the trees of Point Pleasant Park had reluctantly surrendered their leaves in preparation for winter's onslaught, Gabriel found himself prone between a dumpster and the back wall of a commercial building fronting onto Spring Garden Road, attempting to shield himself from a biting rain. It was early in the evening, and he had a long, numbing night ahead of him, as he tried unsuccessfully to fend off the deluge with a bit of canvas, one side of which he affixed with duct tape to the outer edge of the dumpster, the other to a groove in the red brick wall.

More so than usual at this time of year, he felt fatigued, listless, worn out. A faded watercolour that had lost its sheen. After twenty years of this lifestyle, time had started catching up to him, as it must to all. Through the glare of a nearby streetlamp, the light escaping a window on the building on the far side of the alley, he stared at his tired, cracked, shaky, weather-beaten hands in disbelief. They were the same hands as yesterday, weren't they? He recalled the strong, supple, confident hands of his youth. Time and the ravages of outdoor living in a harsh climate had sucked the lustre out of them, sapped their vitality. How did they get so old? When had their skin lost its vibrancy, its suppleness, its shape? They resembled his grandfather's rheumatic hands more than anything he could connect to his own body.

It wasn't just his hands, though. Lately, his left ankle had started swelling up. It was harder to put weight on it, to walk on it when it flared up. Occasionally, especially when he camped on the pavement next to the dumpster, he would suffer back or neck spasms. And he caught colds, fevers, more frequently, found it harder to recover from them. Clearly the old machine was not what it used to be. And, if he were honest with himself, he would have to admit that at times he was losing the joy of it all. How would he manage as he aged?

The Oracle of Spring Garden Road

***

By late November, there could be no more pretence of invincibility, no more delay. The shelter was Gabriel's only recourse for the long, harsh winter. Once again, he needed to steel himself for the assault on his dignity, his independence. As he did every year, he grudgingly packed up his bedroom, his life, into his trusty duffle bag, bid a painful farewell to the park and began the disheartening hour-long walk to the shelter.

The first night was always the hardest. The dormitory hall was an unholy cacophony of irritating sounds. The man in the cot to his left snored loudly and irregularly all night. Had it been an even, regular snore, Gabriel might have been able to adjust to it, in effect to filter it out in his mind. Its unpredictability, however, its unevenness, at some moments the sonorous blast of a trumpet, at others the sedate purring of a kitten, made it all the more jarring. Elsewhere in the room, a man called out pathetically in his sleep, "I'm sorry, Bertha!" perhaps to a wife or a daughter he had wronged during his misbegotten journey through life. Another man, exactly which Gabriel couldn't ascertain in the dark, wheezed audibly and coughed throughout the night, no doubt suffering from Emphysema owing to an adulthood of smoking. From other corners of the room came sobs, the metallic shrieks of the cot springs as sleepers shifted positions, the staccato, flatulent eruptions from those who had difficulty digesting their meal, and the occasional profanity-laced tirade from dormers unable to rest on account of all the foregoing. And through it all, the incessant ticking of the round, white institutional clock, that cruel metronome heralding the passing of each second of lost sleep. If Hell had a soundtrack, Gabriel decided, this would be it. And yet what alternative did any of them have? Winter in Atlantic Canada was not made for sleeping outdoors.

Of course, it wasn't all bad. The shelter gave him regular meals and snacks, a shower with clean towels, laundry facilities. A barber occasionally visited to provide discounted grooming for the temporary residents. Most of all, it provided the necessary respite from the relentless Halifax winter, without which he couldn't survive. All that, though, came at a high cost for Gabriel's soul: the dependence on others, communal living, being caged indoors, no longer being in control of his own destiny.

Lying in bed that first night of the season, oppressed by the others, by their proximity, unable to sleep, he recalled his first brush with the shelter, with its associated foodbank, twenty years earlier. It had been his first winter on the street, before he had overcome the dysfunctional addiction to luxury that modern life inspires. Even before he had laid claim to his bedroom in the park. Only two weeks on the street in the late autumn sent him scurrying for the institutional protection of the shelter. How shocked he was by the cacophonous, malodorous dormitory, his misbegotten comrades! And how the nasty volunteer at the foodbank almost sent him scampering back to the horror he had escaped!

He had arrived at the foodbank absolutely famished, not having eaten for two days. He had not yet figured out how to earn money in his office and his small initial stake of cash had exhausted itself rather quickly. In desperation, he placed himself at the back of the disorderly queue to enter the church which housed the soup kitchen. Each of the unfortunate souls ahead of him grabbed a bowl and, when their turn arrived, presented it to the volunteer manning the pots to receive either the soup or stew on offer that evening. As Gabriel reached the head of the queue, he was horrified to discover that the soup was a seafood soup with shrimps and the stew was a meat stew, neither of which he could eat as a traditional Jew who adhered to kosher dietary laws.

The woman barked at him, "Soup or stew?" In his misery, his confusion, he asked under his breath whether they had any vegetarian food, but she couldn't hear him. Irritably, she ladled a portion of stew into his bowl. This drew him out. He thrust the bowl back at her, saying, "I can't eat this. Do you have anything without meat or fish?"

She adjusted her plastic hairnet officiously to convey authority. "This isn't a restaurant, you know," she snapped. What she said next, however, stung him. "Beggars can't be choosers!"

His torment was complete. The smell of food surrounded him, thrilled his starving senses, yet he couldn't eat a bite. The volunteer who should have welcomed him taunted him, and the man in the queue behind him shoved him aside, impatient with the delay. In humiliation, in disgust, Gabriel flung his bowl onto the counter and slunk toward the door. At the end of his rope, he was prepared to admit defeat, to tuck his tail between his legs and return home, whatever it cost his soul. There was only so much a man could bear. As he approached the door, however, he found it barred by a burly man, a full head taller than Gabriel, with a green Saskatchewan Roughriders t-shirt, broad shoulders and a kind heart.

"You haven't eaten anything, sir. Can I get you something?" the man asked with courtesy and respect.

"I can't...." Gabriel mumbled in desperation.

"You can't eat what we have? Is there something else I can get you?" he insisted gently.

"I.... Do you have anything vegetarian?" Gabriel asked weakly, not wishing to explain the reasons for his dietary restrictions.

"You don't eat meat?" Gabriel shook his head. "What about fish?" A second shake of Gabriel's head. "Oh," said the man, discouraged. "We don't have many options aside from the soup and the stew.... But I think I could scrounge up some bread and butter. Would that be alright?"

With tears in his raw, hollow, malnourished eyes, Gabriel nearly kissed the man. He practically inhaled two slices of buttered white bread, prompting the man to fetch a few more slices. "You haven't eaten much lately, have you, sir?" the man asked. Gabriel shook his head mournfully. "Then take it easy. Eat slowly. You wouldn't want to get sick. I'll make sure there's enough bread here for you."

For the next several days, the burly man took Gabriel under his wing as his personal charge, ensuring that there was enough vegetarian food for him to eat. His actions made all the difference for Gabriel at his lowest ebb. How different it was today, Gabriel reflected. Now, when Gabriel makes his winter appearance at the foodbank, he's always greeted with a "Good to see you, Eddie! The vegetarian options are on the left side of the table."

But how time passes, Gabriel lamented, still awake on his cot. Twenty years! Where did they all go? Somehow or other, each day, each wayward hour, added up, like the microscopic grains of sand in a giant hourglass, to an unfathomable sum. Especially now, as he aged, time raced by with abandon. Each week disappeared more rapidly than the previous one, each year seemed shorter than those which preceded it. He was almost unable to enjoy the miracles of nature he was privileged to witness, when all he could focus on was how many more springs, how may more autumns, he would be able to experience in good health. Perhaps that's the true curse of aging, he thought. This anticipation of decline, rather than the decline itself. How happy one would be if he could simply live in the moment, with no thought of the future!

On a blustery day in January, Gabriel escaped the shelter for the day, as was his wont, and plotted a course for the office, eager for a bit of relief. Every time he exited the shelter and gratefully rejoined the world, it never failed to amuse him that the first sight to greet his eyes was the casino. It underscored the folly of mankind. They deprive themselves of their daylight all week in pursuit of the almighty dollar, but then gamble it all back in the darkness, betting it on red, the pull of a handle, the turn of a card. Why sacrifice so much for the legal tender if they don't value it anyway? And, if they have money to burn, why pass by a shelter crammed with people whose lives could really be helped with a little cash, to fork it all over to the wealthy syndicate that runs the casino? These were exactly the kind of misplaced priorities that made him pity people. What a sorry race they were!

He navigated the icy streets slowly, carefully, anxious to avoid a fall. His toes were numb. Each nefarious blast of damp wind from the harbour chilled him to the bone. Eventually, he installed himself in his regular spot outside the bank on Spring Garden, shivering in the purple foam-filled jacket he had purchased from the thrift shop. The filling was uneven, having bled out from a jagged, pea-sized hole near the bottom, but the price had been right, and it did provide more protection than the threadbare flak jacket he wore in the warmer weather. After enduring the elements for only forty-five minutes, however, a strong gust of biting wind sent him scurrying for the protection of the library.

This was his usual pattern. To mitigate his trauma during the endless, excruciating months of winter, he resolved to break free from his prison as much as possible during the daylight hours, regardless of how treacherous the weather was. He continued to clock in at his office during weekdays to restore a sense of normalcy and purpose to his life. One advantage to working during the winter was that people are more generous to the homeless during extreme weather. Gabriel found that, even if he kept shorter hours, he could earn twice or thrice what he did on a summer day, enabling him to spend more on warm clothing and hot food.

When he could withstand the cold no more, he would take extended breaks in the Central Library, just down the block. The new building was particularly hospitable, with its wide, neon orange and lime green faux-leather chairs in the building's atrium. Often, he would fetch a tome from the shelves – a treatise on philosophy or a classic novel – and curl up on the green chair to read it in the warmth. In this manner, he completed Tolstoy's *War and Peace* in daily instalments during the first winter after the building's construction. Occasionally, after miserably sleepless nights at the shelter, he would fall asleep, book in hand, and dream for hours of a better world.

When the library was closed, he would warm up in the indoor shopping centre further up the street. This was a more complex operation, as the mall security viewed him as a blight, a deterrent to the desirable shoppers, and objected to his loitering. So, he reserved the mall for shorter visits. But, when he was flush with cash from sitting out in his frigid office, he often spent some of his haul on food and a hot drink at Tim Horton's, where he could linger to escape the wind. So, although he took fewer meandering walks in the winter, he still refused to confine himself to the horror of the shelter for the duration.

On this particular day, he selected a copy of Edmund Burke's *Reflections on the Revolution in France*, and plopped down into one of the orange chairs, finding his preferred green one occupied by an older woman in a mauve kerchief engrossed in a volume on horticulture. Having slept little the night before, he immediately drifted off for over an hour. Before waking fully, he inhabited that delightful, languorous half world between sleep and consciousness. In that cottony, soporific state, he overheard a library patron complain, "Look at that useless man taking up space over there. Like this is his own private manor!" Still drowsy and peaceful, Gabriel merely registered the insult, but took no offense. Slowly, he opened his eyes, gathered his belongings and returned to his office, leaving the book on his seat.

After another miserable hour at the office in temperatures too cold to enjoy, he bought a cup of hot coffee and called it quits for the day. *It's no use*, he conceded to himself. *I simply can't manage in the winter anymore. It's too cold and I'm getting too old. But what choice do I have? What am I to do?* As he trudged along Brunswick Street, slowly picking his way on the slushy pavement from his office to the foodbank on the other side of the Citadel, exercised by his predicament, his shoes – the beige, low-cut canvas boots he had purchased long ago from the military surplus store, whose treads were now entirely worn – encountered a patch of black ice. In an instant, he was completely upended, crashing into the cold, hard pavement with the full force of gravity, a few coins spilling out of his pocket on impact. Beyond the initial shock and embarrassment, he realized that he had hit his right hip and wrist hard in the fall. Struggling to recoup his money and right himself, he assessed the damage. No, he didn't believe anything was broken. That was fortunate. But he'd have himself some nasty bruises.

Wiping the sludge off his jacket, his faded trousers, he reflected on the catastrophe that might have been, but for the grace of God. Still in his mid-to-late-forties, he was by no means old, but a blow like that could have broken his hip. Worse, had he not shielded his face with his arm, he could have smacked his head against the pavement, causing a concussion or worse. Either injury would have been disastrous, would have spelled the end of his independence. He shuddered thinking about it, as he continued on his route, limping slowly, painfully, back to the foodbank.

***

After dinner, Gabriel selected a book from the shelter's makeshift library to take his mind off the throbbing pain in his hip, the dull ache in his wrist, his swollen ankle. The only offerings were beneath him: pulp romance novels, detective stories, thrillers. *All in such poor taste,* Gabriel lamented. *Why did they automatically assume that homeless people either had low tastes or were sub-morons who could not process literature more complex than your average high school dropout?* Reluctantly, he selected a detective novel and picked his way through the anodyne work for about half an hour before throwing it down in frustration and turning in early. Thus began another interminable, nerve-wracking, chaotic communal night, where sleep was all but impossible. Sartre had observed wryly that Hell was other people. *He must have spent time in this shelter*, Gabriel chuckled.

All Gabriel had to distract himself from the unpleasantness were his memories. So, like his neighbours no doubt, he plumbed the depths of his mind night after night, reliving past humiliations, recalling loved ones long forgotten. In the midst of his reverie, he heard the library patron's insult echoing off the walls of his mind:

Look at that useless man taking up space over there.

Now he took umbrage. "Nobody's useless!" he muttered aloud, as a memory from long ago floated through his head. When he was in night school as a child, two boys in the class had gotten into a heated dispute over a hockey card. In exasperation, one boy taunted the other, calling him a useless piece of trash. Their teacher, a young rabbi with a curly brown beard and psoriasis on his arms, separated the two boys and objected to this epithet.

"No-one is useless," the rabbi insisted, placing his Hebrew bible on his desk. "Everyone and everything has a *tafkid*, an appointed purpose that God created them to perform. We don't know what that purpose is. We may never know. But you can be sure that He put us all on this Earth for a reason."

The rabbi had captured Gabriel's imagination. Without raising his hand, as he was required to do, he blurted out, "What kinds of purposes do people have?"

Appreciating his interest and enthusiasm, something rare among the night school students, the rabbi ignored Gabriel's protocol violation. "Well.... It could be anything. It could be to perform a good deed. To help someone out in a difficult time. Or it could be to help the Jewish people or to invent something crucial for mankind. For Moses, it was to lead the Jewish people out of slavery in Egypt. But it wasn't to lead them into the promised land. That was Joshua's mission. Thomas Edison's purpose was to create light for mankind. Alexander Graham Bell's was to help mankind communicate. We're told that spiders were created to save King David."

"Spiders! Yuck! How did spiders save King David?" a tall girl with blonde pigtails secured by shiny red elastics asked with a shudder, leaving no doubt that she thought the universe would be more perfect if the Divine had decided not to grace us with that particular creation.

"Well," the rabbi said, scratching the flaky crust on his wrist, "before he was king, when David was trying to escape from King Saul, who wanted to kill him to prevent him from ascending to the throne of Israel instead of Saul's son, David hid in a cave. As Saul's guards approached the cave, a spider emerged and spun a web across its entrance. When Saul's men reached the cave, they saw the spider web and assumed that David could not have hidden inside without breaking the web, so they moved on to search elsewhere. Saving the future king of Israel and the ancestor of the Messiah was the crucial *tafkid* of the spider."

It was often hard for the rabbi to command the children's attention, as many of them resisted the idea of night school with every fibre of their being, having spent a long, draining day in public school before arriving. Consequently, the proceedings usually devolved into a chaotic mess of paper airplanes, spitballs blown through the empty clear-plastic casings of Bic ballpoint pens, and loudly-sung pop song lyrics accompanied by drumming on the desks and unholy gyrations, which the rabbi – Gabriel couldn't remember his name – was reluctant to clamp down on too aggressively, lest the children bear a grudge against Judaism forever on his account. The idea of the *tafkid*, however, had clearly resonated with the students, as evidenced by the comparative silence in the room, the dreamy expressions on their faces as they contemplated their own purposes in life, the wondrous contributions they were destined to make. Encouraged by this rare moment of genuine enthusiasm, the rabbi adjusted his stiff, metal chair and plodded on. "It doesn't have to be on such a grand scale, though. For most people, their important purpose is to do a single act of great importance, perhaps helping someone out in a time of distress or something like that, which though small is immensely important."

"Let me tell you a story," the rabbi continued. "Once, in a small village in Lithuania, there was a rich man whose wife had died during childbirth. He raised his only child, a boy he named Noam, with the help of a maid, sparing no expense on his cherished son. Unfortunately, the child was a bad seed. In his youth, he was undisciplined, cruel to other children and prone to violent outbursts. As he grew, his character showed no mark of improvement, but the evil he committed was exponentially worse. He stabbed a horse repeatedly just to watch it suffer and die." The pigtailed girl gasped. "He drank, gambled, cheated and behaved improperly to women. His father died heartsick that he had raised such a monster."

"Having inherited his father's dry goods business, Noam treated his workers miserably, occasionally firing poor employees just to make them suffer. He fired one very poor man who had worked in the company faithfully for many years and had no other means of supporting himself. The man pleaded with him, begging him to allow him to keep his job because he would starve otherwise and wouldn't be able to take care of his children. But Noam just laughed derisively, telling him that the business wasn't a charity organization and that the man shouldn't have had children if he couldn't afford to feed them."

"Wow," said one of the children, "what an asshole!"

"Watch your language, Mordie!" the rabbi admonished him with a sour face. "Anyway, one day, the maid who had raised him became very ill and was about to die. She was bedridden in the hospital in the nearest city, since the village didn't have its own hospital. Without any family of her own, she was all alone and terribly frightened. For some reason, when word got to Noam that she was dying, he was moved to pity. Perhaps she had been the only person to reach him when he was young. Perhaps she was the only mother figure he had ever known. Who knows? But he immediately picked himself up and travelled to the city to visit her, staying at her bedside the whole time, feeding her, reading to her, just holding her hand. It was like he was a completely different person. The effect on that poor old maid was remarkable. Instead of dying in fear, in abject misery, she felt comforted, loved even. That had been Noam's *tafkid*. He eased an old woman's suffering when she died."

"So, did he become a good person afterwards?" a freckled girl in the front row with shoulder-length black hair and a mouth full of braces asked optimistically.

The rabbi hesitated, stroking his beard with the tips of his fingers. "I don't think so, Becky. Sadly, I think he just went back to his regular ways. But at least he had fulfilled his appointed purpose."

Gabriel began sucking in his lower lip. "Does that mean that he didn't get punished for all the evil he did, just because he fulfilled God's mission for him?" he asked indignantly.

Once again the rabbi paused, staring down at his scratched, laminated desk for inspiration before answering. "That's not for me to say, Gabriel," he confessed. "It's God's job to judge people, not mine. But I would expect that he got punished for his wickedness. Nonetheless, I'm sure he also got credit for his great act of kindness with his dying maid, which might have lessened his punishment somewhat."

At the time, Gabriel had been beguiled by the story and the concept of a *tafkid*. Now, many years later, surrounded by the lost, the forgotten, the forsaken of Halifax, Gabriel laughed sadly, sardonically, to himself. *And what is my sacred purpose,* he wondered. *Surely, I've done nothing meaningful, nothing worthwhile thus far in my life. And that's not likely to change in my line of work. Perhaps I am truly the world's only useless person. Have I really wasted my life?* Agitated, he left his bed to get a breath of frigid nighttime air just outside the shelter, as he continued to mull over his future and the increasing challenge winters posed for him.

By the time he limped back and installed himself once again on the metal-springed cot that was his lot for the winter, it had all become clear to him. At long last, he had reached a decision. Sadly, he couldn't continue as he was indefinitely. His body couldn't hold out forever. After twenty years, he needed to make a change. And it would have to be soon. But how? And what would he do then? He would require a plan. But it had to be on his own terms. He couldn't completely surrender his glorious freedom, the beauty of his lifestyle, and throw himself at the mercy of the shelters, the foodbanks, the halfway houses, the government agencies, the rabbis and priests competing to outdo each other with their institutional kindness. With the smiles they store on the shelf for the front page of the annual report. No. That was not for him. He'd have to do it as he had done everything else in his life. On his own terms. *I'll figure it out,* he vowed. *I always do.* In the meantime, he'd need to save some money, he decided. Because whatever he was going to do in this crazy world of men, it would require money.

Chapter 4

"Need any help, Rabbi?"

Thirteen-year-old Gabriel was bundled up in his navy-blue parka on an icy December afternoon in the synagogue parking lot. He noticed the rabbi, Rabbi Plotkin, struggling to lift a heavy box out his trunk. In preparation for his bar mitzvah, the ritual celebration of a Jewish young man's coming of age, the previous March, Gabriel had participated in Rabbi Plotkin's weekly bar mitzvah class every Sunday morning to learn more about Judaism and what is required of a Jewish man. As usual, he was a model pupil and formed a strong bond with the rabbi, who also taught Gabriel to chant the Torah portion for the week of his celebration. Gabriel revered the rabbi for his soft-spoken self-assurance, his bedrock moral principles, his unpretentious kindness. In Gabriel's eyes, here was a truly holy man, doing God's work with little fanfare and little earthly reward. As a result, after the bar mitzvah, when other boys stopped attending synagogue even on Saturdays and resumed their normal Sunday morning recreations, Gabriel began to attend the rabbi's weekly Torah *shiur* (lecture) for adults. That was what brought him to the synagogue that Sunday.

"Yes please, Gabriel! I need to bring in this box of *siddurim* from the bookbinder, but it's really heavy," he said, referring to prayer books by their Hebrew name. The rabbi's ordinarily pale complexion was flushed crimson with the strain and the cold. "Would you mind carrying it in with me?"

"My pleasure," Gabriel replied with feeling. He supported one side of the box with both his hands and helped the rabbi raise it out of the rabbi's age-worn Pontiac, while Rabbi Plotkin freed one of his ungloved, chapped hands to close the trunk.

"I would have brought it in earlier, but unfortunately I had a funeral to attend to. Mr. Kuperman's mother just passed away, may her soul find peace in the afterlife."

"Oh, I'm sorry to hear that," Gabriel said politely, trying to assume an appropriately sombre expression. Together they lugged their cumbersome burden to the front steps of the building, where they stopped to catch their breath. Rabbi Plotkin, a short, overweight, grey-bearded man in his early sixties was huffing as he leaned on the bannister. Gabriel, still a chubby boy, breathed normally, but his eyes were fixed out into the distance, while he distractedly sucked in his lower lip.

"I know that look," the rabbi said playfully. "The wheels of your famous brain are turning."

"Huh? ... Oh, no. I was just thinking. You must really know people better than anyone else," the boy reflected.

"What do you mean?"

"It's just that... you see their true selves. When they aren't posing or trying to make a certain impression. You see everybody at their best. In pure happiness. At weddings, births, brit milahs, bar mitzvahs. They're too genuinely happy to try to put on a show or hide their true reactions. And you see them at their absolute worst. At funerals. Even *before* funerals, when they're still in shock. When they can't hide their sadness, their pain. You must really understand people better than anybody," he explained.

The rabbi stared at Gabriel in amazement, with something akin to fatherly pride. "Gabriel, you never cease to impress me. Yes, you're absolutely right. Rabbis do see a side of people that others don't."

"You're lucky," Gabriel commented, as they heaved the box up the stairs and into the synagogue. Mrs. Weiss, the cantor's wife who worked as the synagogue's secretary, held the door open for them.

"Thank you, Mrs. Weiss," Gabriel said brightly.

"My pleasure, Gabriel. It's so nice of you to help the rabbi out like that. Don't forget to stop by the office for something from the candy dish when you're finished." Mrs. Weiss was popular with all the boys in the synagogue, not simply because she was young and very pretty and was, therefore, every young boy's fantasy, but because she was kind and dispensed candy and chocolate freely. Gabriel was happy to take advantage of every opportunity to visit her.

"Sure thing," Gabriel assured her. "Thanks!"

They deposited the box of prayer books in the main sanctuary. Rabbi Plotkin rubbed his frozen hands together rapidly to warm them up, then turned to the door to ascend the flight of stairs to the library for his shiur.

Gabriel sidled up to the rabbi on the stairs. "What have you learned?" he asked.

"I beg your pardon," the rabbi said, perplexed.

"I mean about people. As a rabbi."

The rabbi was taken aback by the question. After a momentary hesitation, he recovered, replying, "The centrality of God to our lives. He comforts the bereaved, even in the depths of their sorrow. Yet happiness without God, celebrations without the proper perspective, without humility, are empty endeavours."

Gabriel swallowed his lower lip once again while he pondered the rabbi's answer. Rabbi Plotkin, studying his face, admiring the boy's precocious wisdom, was struck by an idea.

"You know, Gabriel, I think you're ready to give a presentation at one of our classes," he said.

Gabriel was astonished. "Me? But I'm just a kid. You always ask the adults to do that. I can't talk to the adults," he objected.

"Nonsense! You're every bit as intelligent as the adults in the class. Maybe more.... I'll give you a good topic to work with. Let's see.... How about the Ten Commandments? We read that in February. That'll give you a couple of months to prepare. You can ask me for help if you need it."

Gabriel mulled the idea over. "I guess I could try," he said at last, as they proceeded to the library for the class.

When Gabriel took his seat, he heard some of the adults in the class snickering about the rabbi's weight, commenting about how he had become fatter over Hannukah. "The Plotkin thickens," whispered Mr. Dimberg, a mustachioed man with an odious grin. The man sitting between him and Gabriel responded, "How many latkes did the rabbi eat over Hannukah?" Not hearing an answer from his friend, he supplied one himself. "Alotkin!" he said in a low voice. Both men giggled. Gabriel simmered inside, wondering why they bothered to attend the class if they had no respect for the rabbi. He eagerly wanted to tell them off, to defend the rabbi he respected so, but to his shame, he shied away from it.

He was still seething after the lecture, cursing himself for his cowardice. But, after visiting the office and raiding Mrs. Weiss' well-stocked candy dish, he let the matter drop and returned home.

At school, Gabriel was in grade nine, the final year of junior high, and had finally discovered the appeal of the fairer sex. Since grade one, he had viewed girls as rather a nuisance. They didn't enjoy the games he played. They had high-pitched, whiny voices and were always giggling. They wasted their time singing silly rhymes while skipping rope. *Miss Mary Mack, Mack, Mack, All dressed in black, black, black, With silver buttons, buttons, buttons, All down her back, back, back.* How babyish! Everything about them was annoying. Yet somehow, suddenly, now he began to notice them. Their hair. Their eyes. The same voices that had irked him were suddenly so charming. So beguiling. Although he was still a serious student, sometimes it was even a struggle to concentrate in class because of them.

And there was one particular girl who had captured Gabriel's heart without half trying. Lisa Ross. A pretty, dark-haired girl of average height with soft brown eyes and adorable dimples, she was all he could think about sometimes. He would lie awake in bed long after turning in for the night, mooning over her in the dark, imagining that she were harassed by Victor Runyon and the bullies of the class and that he intervened heroically to save her, earning her gratitude and affection.

After school one January day, he strolled to Earl Bales Park with his friend Jack to go sledding. On the way, he asked Jack with forced nonchalance, "So, what do you think of girls?"

"Girls?" Jack asked cagily, like he had never heard the term before, as his cheeks took on a crimson hue.

"You know. Do you like 'em?"

"Well, they're okay, I guess," Jack conceded after a short pause, trying eagerly to sound indifferent although he shivered slightly, his chest constricted.

"Yeah. I think so, too," Gabriel admitted, amazed that he had actually declared that out loud.

They continued their northward march on Bathurst Street, revelling in the intimacy of their discussion, the simultaneous relief and thrill of disclosing to another human being their innermost preoccupation. For some time, they said nothing as they tramped along the slushy sidewalk, Jack's navy-blue sheet plastic toboggan rolled up and slung over his shoulder, their school knapsacks adhering to their backs like misshapen tortoise shells. A fire engine sped by southbound, its siren blaring, capturing their attention for the moment.

"Is there anyone that you have your eye on?" Gabriel asked shyly when the noise subsided. "You know, someone really special?"

"Nah, not really. I kinda like them all," Jack said with a broad grin, displaying his perfectly-aligned teeth.

"Yeah. I know what you mean."

"What about you?" Jack asked with growing interest.

They reached the southern edge of the park and began to trudge through the thick snow. Gabriel started to answer, but the wind picked up, blowing loose snow in their raw faces. For protection, Gabriel wrapped his felt scarf loosely over his mouth and nose, stifling further conversation for the moment. The boys ventured through the layered snowdrifts, sometimes, to their excitement, plunging waist-deep, as they threaded their way through the immense park's ravines to a hill on the far side that was ideal for sledding.

When the wind abated, Jack said impatiently, "I didn't hear what you said. Is there someone you like?"

By this point, Gabriel had begun to lose his nerve. "I don't know. Let's just sled," he urged his friend.

"Hey! That's not cool! *I* told *you*!" Jack whined, his caramel eyes narrowing beneath his granite tuque.

"No, you *didn't*," Gabriel retorted. "You just said you like them all." He stooped and packed some snow into a small, fluffy snowball, which he tossed lightly, just missing his friend's face as it fell harmlessly onto the slope.

"But that's the truth!" Jack protested. "One day I thought I really liked Sandy Hoskins. But then the next day I was sitting next to Ellie Krakover and thought *she* was really cute. And when I went skating last Saturday night, Tracy and Heather were there and I had fun skating with them. I think I just like *girls*. Not any one in particular. They're all cool."

"Well, for me...." Gabriel began, but then interrupted himself. "Listen, you've got to swear yourself to secrecy. Okay?" Jack nodded eagerly. "No, I mean it. You've got to swear that you'll never tell *any*body, or I'm not going to say anything."

"Hey! We've been best friends for years. I won't rat you out," Jack said solemnly, gazing up at his taller friend.

"Promise?"

"Yeah, I promise," Jack replied, by this point desperate to know his friend's secret. "I'd pinky swear, but I don't want to take my mittens off."

"Well, there *is* someone I like...." Gabriel's voice trailed off.

"Who *is* she?" Jack pressed with growing impatience.

"Lisa Ross." Gabriel's face flushed as red as the fleshy inside of a watermelon. It made him feel good to speak her name, as if it imbued a fanciful hallucination with substance.

"Wow! She's cute," Jack said, his sparkling eyes widening. "Does she know?"

"No! We've barely said two words to each other. I don't even know if she knows I'm alive," Gabriel lamented.

"Still," Jack said with admiration, "Lisa Ross...."

"Well," Gabriel said sternly, at once relieved to have unburdened his soul and fearful that he had revealed too much, "if you tell *any*one I'll kill you." With that he grabbed his friend's sled and sailed down the hill at full speed.

Gabriel's love of music also continued to grow. At first, like most children, he developed a fondness for pop music, which was easy to digest. He had liked the Commodores, Michael Jackson, Wham. But he quickly began to eschew the simpler music, gravitating instead toward more sophisticated rock music, which he haughtily described to his friends as "better-written" and "more complex." At this stage, he listened to David Bowie, Yes, Genesis.

In his heart of hearts, however, his true love was the classical music that his Zaidie had introduced him to. As he explained to his violin teacher, a woman in her late-fifties named Lyudmilla, who dressed in garish outfits yet inexplicably paired them with black, horn-rimmed glasses, rock music was okay to talk to your friends about, to dance to, to listen to while doing homework. But when he heard Mendelsohn's violin concerto, or Beethoven's, it was "like listening to the voice of Heaven itself." It filled him with wonder, moved him. Sometimes it even made him weep, which made him self-conscious, so he preferred to listen alone.

With Lyudmilla's help, he had also progressed by leaps and bounds as a violinist. He was developing a rich, full sound and excelling at the vibrato and other key skills, such as the shift to fifth position. Yet his love of music, his quest for perfection, began to frustrate him and impede his progress. Although he played extremely well for a thirteen-year-old, he never found it sounded quite right.

After one music school performance of Monti's Czardas, with which Lyudmilla was particularly pleased, Gabriel complained to her, "I don't think I'm cut out to be a violinist."

"Whatever could you possibly mean, silly child?" Lyudmilla asked in horror, placing her hands on the hips of her orange and mauve midi dress in disgust, her elbows out, a ferocious beast set to devour her prey.

"I'm just not good enough," he stated flatly, dejectedly.

"Nonsense!" the teacher snapped, adjusting her horn-rimmed spectacles. "You made only one small technical mistake and you recovered well. You're doing fine for someone your age. You shouldn't expect to be Jascha Heifetz already!"

But Gabriel only sighed a deep and bitter sigh, one that would befit an old, wizened man far better than a thirteen-year-old boy. "It doesn't sound like it's *supposed* to," he said. "It's not perfect. There's no point in playing if it's not going to sound like it should."

Lyudmilla grabbed him by his shoulders and turned his face toward hers. "Gabriel, I like your attitude. It's important to keep trying to be perfect." Then she said something that stuck with him for the rest of his life. "But remember. Don't ever expect *perfection*. Perfection isn't possible when human beings are involved."

He reflected on that as he returned his violin to its case.

Ah, the splendid confusion of Gabriel's coming of age in the mid-1980s: his bar mitzvah, marking his transition from boyhood to manhood, although the metamorphosis was far from complete; the Sports Illustrated Swimsuit issue he hid between his mattress and box spring, especially the cover portrait of Paulina Porizkova with the V-cut magenta suit that revealed the sides of her perfect breasts and the translucent ivory bathing suit that showed a discerning thirteen-year-old the salient points of Cheryl Tiegs' magnificent body; exploring his own equipment in the presence of the aforementioned literary periodical, hoping that his perceptive, even hawklike, mother wouldn't notice the telltale stains on his sheets; the 1984 Olympics that didn't give him the opportunity to see the Hungarian team or any other country from the East bloc; the curve of Lisa Ross' neck as she bent over her notebook in English class; the posing; the urgent need to take a position on Trudeau's resignation, on his successors, Turner then Mulroney, without any clear idea of what they stood for, in order to differentiate himself from his father; the embarrassing croaking of his voice, which made him reluctant to sing and self-conscious when he spoke; the terrifying moments when he outwardly raged because his journey to adulthood, to independence, was taking too long, yet inwardly feared that life was moving far too quickly.

At home, relations between Gabriel and his parents had grown more tense, more militarized. As Gabriel became a pillar of synagogue life and embraced the religious precepts, he found his parents' conduct disappointing. For one thing, he felt his parents were lax with the kosher dietary laws. While they only brought kosher meat and fish into their apartment, they had no qualms about eating non-kosher food, excluding pork which they refused to touch under any circumstances, at restaurants or friends' houses. They argued that this was the way their families had been raised in Hungary and they had no interest in changing their practice. For his part, Gabriel believed fervently that God had not intended the rules of *kashrut* to be applied only at home, or when convenient. Religion, in his view, was not something to pull out of a drawer when it suited you; it was a matter of righteous principle.

A second flashpoint concerned daily prayers. For his bar mitzvah, his parents had furnished him with the accoutrements of Jewish manhood: his *tallit* – a ritual, four-cornered prayer shawl with fringes at each corner – and his *tefillin*, wood and leather phylacteries for his head and left arm, each housing sacred parchments. On the Sabbath and holidays, Jewish men were required to wear their *tallit* for morning prayers; on all other mornings, they adorned themselves with both the *tallit* and the *tefillin*. Since his bar mitzvah celebration, with the rabbi's encouragement, Gabriel made a point of praying each morning, making the appropriate blessing on each of these sacred articles. When possible, he did so in the synagogue, with the mandated prayer quorum of ten men, the *minyan*. On other days, when the requirements of school precluded that, he would don his *tallit* and *tefillin* at home before eating breakfast. He enjoyed his prayers, which bestowed upon him a sense of inner peace, of being in God's presence. In contrast, Isaac attended services in the synagogue on Saturdays and holidays, but did not pray during the week.

Over breakfast one morning before school, Gabriel took his father to task.

"Dad, did you *daven* today?" he asked, using the Yiddish word for "pray".

"What difference does it make?" Isaac responded evasively, as he doused his bowl of Corn Flakes liberally with milk. He scowled, observing that the bowl had a slight crack near the edge. Another dish that would need replacement.

"That's *not* an answer!" Gabriel snapped, his jaw clenching in disgust. "Did you *daven* today?"

"Why do you ask a question when you already know the answer?" As usual, to Gabriel's frustration, Isaac responded to his question with another evasive question.

Esther jumped in to defend her husband. "What is this, an interrogation? Your father escaped Communism so that he wouldn't have to submit to questioning by the KGB over breakfast."

"Very funny," Gabriel said sarcastically. Then, turning back to his father, he charged, "You didn't *daven*, did you? You never do!"

"No, I don't. Okay? Zaidie never did. Neither of your Zaidies. It wasn't how we were raised," Isaac replied, the veins in his right temple twitching in exasperation.

"How can you call yourself a Jew if you don't even *daven*?" Gabriel asked with contempt.

Isaac coloured. He slammed his spoon down into his bowl, splashing milk all over the table. "How *dare* you say that?" he raged, clenching both of his hairy fists. "We kept the tradition in the old country, despite pogroms, the war, Communism. Risking our lives! Now that you've got such an easy life you accuse us of not being Jewish enough?"

"Fine," Gabriel yelled back. "So now that it's easy to be Jewish, in a country that allows us to, why don't you *daven*? Why don't you keep kosher?"

"What are you talking about?" his mother intervened sanctimoniously, as she wiped the errant milk with a rag. Her hair had begun to grey in places, but her face was still vibrant.

"I keep a strictly kosher home. I only buy meat from the kosher butcher. You *know* that!"

"But you went out last Sunday and had cheeseburgers from McDonald's! *That's* not kosher!"

"Ah, Gabriel, that's the way we were raised. All the Jews back home kept kosher at home, but were more flexible outside," Esther explained, hoping to reduce the intensity of the dispute, which had shattered the order, the tranquility of her kitchen.

"Why do you need to be *flexible*?" Gabriel challenged, anger flashing in his steel blue eyes. "There are so many kosher restaurants and stores near here, right on Bathurst. What's wrong with Marky's? If you want fast food, why not Maven's? Why do you have to eat at McDonald's?"

"You don't appreciate all the sacrifices we made for you," Isaac shouted, ignoring his question. "We've done *everything* to give you a good life. To give you all the opportunities. A decent home. Violin lessons. A nice bar mitzvah. And all you can do is *criticize* us!"

"Oh, here we go again with the guilt. Listen, do you even believe in God, Dad?"

"Do I believe in God? I'm late for work and he asks if I believe in God. What kind of a question is that?" Isaac complained, the wind whistling through the triangular gap between his upper incisors. "Let's just say that I believe in him, but that God and I have an uneasy peace."

"If you believed in God, you'd keep kosher and *daven*," Gabriel reasoned. "It's as simple as that." It occurred to Gabriel in a flash of insight that family was an artificial construct. You choose your friends, but no-one gets to choose their parents, their siblings. If he were not related to his parents, he decided, he would have nothing to do with them. They would be like all the students at his school that he passed by in the halls without ever meaningfully interacting with them. Yet the bond of blood forced him to butt heads with these stubborn, selfish people each and every day.

"No, it's not so simple, Einstein. Religion isn't so absolute. It's very personal. Some people feel that it's not enough to *daven* every morning like you do. They do it every afternoon and evening, too. Some say the butchers we go to aren't kosher enough. Everyone has to make their personal choice of what they believe and what they're comfortable with. We're okay with you making *your* choices, even if they're different from *ours*. Even if you're stricter. But you need to respect *our* choices, too," Isaac said, as he stood up to leave.

But Gabriel refused to let his father get the last word. "Being Jewish isn't a cafeteria where you can pick and choose what you want. 'I'd like a little bit of *kashrut*, but not too much, please.' 'I want to *daven*, but only on Saturdays.' It's not about what *you* want, but about what God wants! Honestly, why do you even *own tefillin* if you never use them?" With that he grabbed the brown paper bag containing the lunch his mother made for him and stormed off to school in disgust.

All that morning at school Gabriel simmered. The nerve of his parents! What hypocrites they were! He was so upset and distracted that he couldn't concentrate on his classes. When Mr. Farrar, the History teacher, called on him to share his opinion of the importance the Riel Rebellion, Gabriel had not been paying attention and was uncharacteristically flustered and inarticulate.

At recess, Jack took his friend aside in the windy school yard. "You alright, Gabriel?"

"Ah, I'm just sick of my parents. That's all," Gabriel answered, pulling his navy tuque down over his ears.

"I hear you, man. Sometimes my folks can be tough to take, too. What'd they do this time?"

Gabriel hesitated. Jack was also Jewish, but his family was completely secular. He wouldn't understand the subtleties of keeping kosher and prayer. "They're just a bunch of hypocrites," he complained vaguely.

"Is there anything I can do to help you out? Do you wanna come over to my house after school for supper? That would keep you away from them a bit longer," Jack offered.

"Uh... will you have something I can eat?" Gabriel asked hopefully.

"Sure. In the worst case, even if we're having something you can't, I'll ask my Mom to make some eggs or some spaghetti with canned sauce for you."

"Thanks, Jack. You're the *greatest*," Gabriel said warmly.

"Hey, it's nothing. I'm glad to help out. *You've* really helped me lately. With Victor Runyon. If it weren't for you, he'd have everyone calling me Jackass," Jack said, lowering his face.

"Aw, that's nothing. You shouldn't show him that it bugs you, though. It only makes him do it more."

"Still," Jack insisted, "I'm glad to help *you* out for a change."

The bell rang and Gabriel returned to the classroom in a better frame of mind, grateful for his friend's sympathy.

Little in life can rival the good-natured chaos that prevails in a synagogue in the immediate aftermath of Saturday morning services. The order, decorum and sanctity of the prayer service melt away, and the sanctuary tilts more toward rowdy auditorium than house of worship. As the congregants remove and fold their *tallit* they greet each other jovially and discuss all manner of sundry items, from community matters, such as the cantor's miraculous voice, poor Mrs. Lupowicz's heart attack and the rabbi's thought-provoking sermon, to topics of more general interest, like the weather forecast, the upcoming provincial election and the Leafs' porous defence in the previous night's game. They call to friends across the room, hoping to reconnect after a stressful work week. Many jostle to ask the rabbi for his guidance, to query him on the finer points of his speech or merely to wish him a good Shabbat. Others rush to the banquet hall, avoiding the children playing raucously in the aisles, to partake in *kiddush*, a small celebratory gathering with food and drinks provided by the synagogue, while latecomers make a vain attempt to block out the tumult as they finish their morning prayers.

In this after-service pandemonium on the Saturday immediately preceding Gabriel's early February lecture, Rabbi Plotkin sought out Gabriel's father, finding him in one of the back rows near the exit, still folding his *tallit*.

"Good Shabbat, Isaac. How have you been?" the rabbi asked. A group of children in the aisle were tossing candies in the air to see who could throw the highest without hitting the ceiling.

"Rabbi, good Shabbat! That was an excellent *drasha* you gave this morning," Isaac responded. "I hope our new premier will be as wise a leader as you say Moses was."

A man in the next row, overhearing, harrumphed, "Hah! Miller's no Bill Davis. Grossman would have been a better choice."

"Well," the rabbi smiled sheepishly at the man, "I try to stay away from politics and stick to what I know: *Torah*." Turning back to Isaac, he said, "I've been meaning to talk to you for a while."

One of the children hurled the candy with too much force. It ricocheted off the ceiling, grazing the rabbi's beard before landing on the bench. Her friends laughed at her loudly, derisively. With an impish grin, Rabbi Plotkin grabbed it before the children could, unwrapped it and popped it into his mouth. "You know the rules, Sarah," the rabbi said mischievously. "If it hits me, I get to eat it!" The children groaned and pulled out another candy to continue the game.

"What can I do for you, Rabbi?" Isaac asked, smiling at Rabbi Plotkin's antics.

"Me? Nothing. I just wanted to thank you for sending Gabriel to my *shiur* on Sundays. He's such a wonderful boy."

Isaac's expression clouded. "I didn't send him. He goes where he wants to go."

"But you should be very proud of him. He's a *brilliant* boy! He may be the brightest young student I've ever had," the rabbi gushed. A woman who had recently recovered from surgery approached to thank the rabbi for his assistance during her illness. Rabbi Plotkin welcomed her back and wished her good health while the children cheered a candy that missed the ceiling by only millimetres.

"Thank you," Isaac bellowed above the din once the woman moved on. "But actually, Rabbi, could we talk somewhere quieter, more private? I'd like to ask for your help with something."

"Of course. Please come with me," Rabbi Plotkin said, as he threaded his way through the mass of bodies, conducting Isaac into the hallway, down a corridor and into his office. Once inside, he turned the tables on Isaac. "So, what can *I* do for *you*, my old friend?"

"Well, it's just.... I was hoping...." Isaac began, but petered out, uncertain of what to say.

"Yes?"

"Well, Esther and I have been having problems with Gabriel. Since he respects you, I was hoping you might... you know, talk to him," Isaac said uncomfortably.

"What's the problem?" the rabbi asked.

"He.... He doesn't respect us."

"*Gabriel?* I'm shocked. He seems like such a wonderful, well-behaved boy. Can I ask – you don't need to answer, if you'd prefer not to – *why* you think he's acting like that?" Rabbi

Plotkin inquired as tactfully as he could, his pudgy hand gliding thoughtfully through his wiry beard.

Isaac looked away from the rabbi. "Why he acts like that? Well, I think he's... he's embarrassed by us, embarrassed that we're immigrants... about what we do for a living. Maybe also because we're not as religious as he is."

"You know, Isaac, children sometimes go through a phase where they're embarrassed by their parents, where they give them a hard time," the rabbi said gingerly, still reluctant to believe that his prodigy, his model student, could behave so disrespectfully to his parents. "Perhaps he'll grow out of it soon."

"You think he'll grow out of it?" Isaac asked rhetorically, still averting the rabbi's glance in shame. "*I* don't. He's been cold to us for a long time. It breaks our hearts."

"I see.... I can't tell you how sorry I am to hear this. And of course, if I can help, I'd be happy to talk to him," Rabbi Plotkin assured him, his plump face registering grave disappointment.

"Thank you, Rabbi. I really appreciate it."

Their conversation concluded, the two men wandered into the social hall for the tail end of the *kiddush*, wishing the synagogue president, Mr. Haberman, and Mrs. Weiss, whom they passed in the corridor outside the office, a good Shabbat.

The next morning, Gabriel was a bundle of nerves as he entered the synagogue. Although he believed that he had prepared an excellent discourse on the Ten Commandments and had practiced delivering it to the mirror in his bedroom multiple times, presenting it to the rabbi and a group of educated, opinionated adults was another matter altogether. He wasn't even fourteen, after all. Sure, he had given a short speech at his bar mitzvah. But that was to a partisan audience which would indulge him, ignore his mistakes, forgive triviality and triteness.

This was the rabbi's *shiur* and he, an adolescent, was expected to teach well-educated adults something meaningful and novel about a topic they had doubtless learned much about over their entire lives.

He sat anxiously in the musty library on the edge of the front row of metal-framed chairs with black vinyl seats, absently scratching at the vinyl with the fingernails of his left hand. The rabbi stood with his back to the ark containing the Torah scrolls that were used when the library hosted auxiliary or overflow prayer services, facing the class, waiting for everyone to arrive and take their places. The lighting in the room was dim, several of the spotlight bulbs having burnt out, and as it was cloudy outside the window along the length of the side wall did not compensate much. To Gabriel, it lent a sombre, foreboding aspect to the class.

At last, at the appointed time, the rabbi cleared his throat audibly to signal the start of the *shiur*. "Ladies and gentlemen," Rabbi Plotkin announced with great fanfare, "we're in for a special treat today. Gabriel Klein will be leading today's discussion. Gabriel is only the smartest boy that I have ever had the pleasure of teaching. So I have every reason to expect that this will be worth listening to, worth giving your undivided attention to. Gabriel, the floor's all yours."

Gabriel stood up, surveyed his audience nervously and inhaled deeply, the musty odour of old books filling his nostrils. After thanking the rabbi, he began to address the crowd in his own unique voice, the voice of a precocious teenaged boy who desperately wanted to sound like a man, who wished to be taken seriously by adults, but had only the vocabulary of the playground to draw upon. He salted his prepared comments, which he scripted and wrote out by hand in large print on several loose-leaf, lined pages, with complex, adult words. Yet the phraseology was that of a teen. To his humiliation, his changing, croaking voice made his in-between status all the more salient to the class.

He began with a series of questions. Why was the first commandment not an actual commandment, but a statement: *I am the Lord, your God, who has taken you out of Egypt?* And were the second and third commandments, not to make or bow down to graven images and not to speak God's name in vain, really the most critical commandments to start with? Why not talk about theft, murder and adultery first? And why did God begin with five commandments between man and God, balanced by five social commandments, between human beings?

He started with trepidation, hesitatingly, trying to rein in his shaking hands, the quaver in his voice. He winced at each slight misstep, each mispronounced Hebrew word, bitterly resenting the indulgent, patronizing smirks on some of the adult faces in the class. As he proceeded, however, he gained confidence, drew strength from the unfeigned admiration and approval in Rabbi Plotkin's shining eyes. He explained what he described as the sheer genius of the Ten Commandments. How it all flows from the essential first non-commandment. How the point of the commandments was to regulate social life, to prevent strife and abuse. But God could not begin with that, or people would have resisted, would have questioned these rules. *Why* shouldn't they murder? *Why* shouldn't they commit adultery? *Why* shouldn't they steal? The purpose of the first five commandments, Gabriel explained, was to lay the foundation upon which the all-important social commandments would stand. Why should we behave decently toward one another? Because *I am the Lord, your God, who has taken you out of Egypt* and therefore you owe Me your allegiance. That had to be the first principle, or the rest of the edifice would collapse.

But the Commandments were forward-looking, too, Gabriel continued. How could God ensure that their respect for Him would not erode, that future generations, who had not witnessed God's miracles in Egypt, at the Red Sea, who had not been present at Mount Sinai, would still treat each other with respect? The second, third and fourth commandment were designed to maintain respect for God by proscribing other idols and acts cheapening God's name, by requiring Sabbath observance to acknowledge God's dominion. Finally, the fifth commandment, the requirement to honour one's parents – the key mechanism of intergenerational transfer of knowledge and ritual – was there to ensure that respect for God was passed from generation to generation. Only after laying this essential foundation was it possible to present the real aim of the *Torah*: the social commandments. Don't murder. Don't commit adultery. Don't steal. Don't bear false witness. Don't covet. In short, treat one another with respect and dignity.

"Therefore," Gabriel concluded, staring icily at Mr. Dimberg, "if you *daven* every day, observe the Sabbath, study the *Torah* and perform all the commandments between man and God faithfully, it's worthless in God's eyes if you are also belittling your friends and making fun of your teachers behind their backs."

In the question period following his presentation, a few members of the audience raised their hands, mainly to congratulate Gabriel and then ask some relatively trivial, benign questions. Having already completed the presentation, Gabriel was no longer nervous and was able to provide satisfactory answers before turning the podium back to Rabbi Plotkin to wrap up for the day.

As Gabriel returned to his seat, he received a standing ovation from the class. Even Mr. Dimberg stood clapping graciously. Gabriel was buffeted by conflicting emotions. On one hand, he was terribly proud to have led the class and met with their approval. At the same time, he felt humiliated, patronized, because the class never clapped for adults who presented and because the questions they had asked were not as aggressive as they normally would have been. Clearly, they were pulling their punches and protecting him. Still, he told himself, he had held his own and presented an excellent *shiur*.

After the class, the rabbi took Gabriel aside, remaining in the library after the rest of the class cleared out. "What an excellent *dvar Torah*!" he praised. "I *knew* you'd be able to do it. It doesn't matter that you're so much younger than the rest of the class. You have so much more to say than many of them."

"Thank you, Rabbi. Coming from *you*, that means a lot to me," Gabriel responded truthfully, beaming with pride.

"And thank *you* for sticking up for me there. You're a good boy."

"What do you mean?" Gabriel asked, shifting uncomfortably on his feet.

"Oh, I know some of them make fun of me. 'The Plotkin thickens....'" Rabbi Plotkin said with a self-deprecating smile. "I *am* kind of fat and dumpy looking."

Gabriel blanched. "You *knew*...?" he uttered in amazement.

"Oh, I'm more aware of what goes on here than people think. But you shouldn't judge people based on one character flaw. If you did, we'd all be doomed. Barney Dimberg is actually a really wonderful person. Do you know that he volunteers in a downtown foodbank every Sunday afternoon, caring for those who are less fortunate? When the synagogue's basement flooded last year, he came in and led a crew of volunteers waist-deep in foul water to clean it out and make it usable again. So I think we can look the other way if he pokes a little fun at a rabbi who enjoys his desserts more than he should. Don't you?" the rabbi asked playfully.

Gabriel sucked in his lower lip while considering the rabbi's point of view. "No, I don't think I agree," Gabriel eventually chimed in. "You don't ignore every mean thing a person does, every dishonest or cruel act, just because they also do some good. People have to take responsibility for their behaviour."

"Well then why did God give us Yom Kippur, Gabriel? He knows we're not perfect. He *created* us that way. But He gave us a day to atone for our sins, to try to right our ships and improve our behaviour. And if He can forgive us for a few mistakes, for the weaknesses of character we all have, shouldn't *we* be more forgiving, too?" It was a theme the rabbi returned to often in his Saturday sermons, and especially during the High Holidays.

"Well, I don't know. I suppose so...." Gabriel mumbled, not entirely convinced.

"And while we're on the subject, Gabriel, I was hoping you wouldn't get upset with me if I mentioned the fifth commandment, which you discussed briefly in your *dvar Torah*," the rabbi ventured gingerly.

Gabriel turned beet red, missing a breath, but said nothing.

Rabbi Plotkin continued, "The Torah says we have to honour our parents, even if we're angry at them, even if we're embarrassed by them." He paused and waited for Gabriel to respond, to engage him somehow, but the boy stood almost immobile, stone-faced, tensing every muscle to avoid betraying emotion. "Your parents are good people, Gabriel. They love you a lot and would sacrifice everything for your happiness. Try to overlook their faults and recognize the good in them."

Gabriel just stood there, his hands clenched into fists, buried inside the front pockets of his brown corduroy pants. The rabbi prodded gently, "Can you try, Gabriel?"

"It's a lot harder than you think," he choked, fighting to keep under control, to avoid screaming at the rabbi.

"It always is," Rabbi Plotkin agreed genially. "Do you want to talk about it? I can keep a secret."

"No," Gabriel stated flatly.

"That's fine. I don't want to pry. But will you at least think about it? As a favour to *me*?"

The loud, analog clock on the library wall audibly ticked off seventeen seconds before Gabriel's reply. "Okay," the boy relented, still not looking directly at his mentor. "I'll *think* about it. But just for *you*, Rabbi."

"Thank you," the rabbi said graciously, with a sombre nod. "That's all that I ask."

Gabriel stormed off annoyed, mortified, not even taking the time to visit Mrs. Weiss in the office to procure his weekly candy from her jar and chat with her a bit.

After school the next afternoon, a glorious winter afternoon with bright sunshine glistening on the pristine white snow that had fallen the prior evening, Gabriel was still brooding about his conversation with the rabbi when he headed with Jack to Earl Bales Park to hang out. He was annoyed that the rabbi dared to mix into his personal life. Worse, his parents must have gone behind his back to badmouth him to the rabbi. That really infuriated him. But then a part of him simultaneously wondered whether the rabbi might have a point.

Jack found his friend to be poor company that day, especially since he was bursting to tell Gabriel about an exciting development. "Hey! Earth to Gabriel. Come in, Gabriel! You seem like you're on another *planet* today," he teased.

"Huh? Oh, sorry. I guess I've got some stuff on my mind," Gabriel replied, absentmindedly digging into to the snow with the heel of his boot.

"Well, you won't *believe* what I have to tell you," Jack announced, stooping to gather some powdery snow into his gloves.

"What?" Gabriel asked with a distracted smile.

"Guess!" his friend said, as he showered Gabriel with loose snow.

"I don't know. Tell me," Gabriel commanded, wiping the powder off his face without further comment.

"Aw, you're no fun, today," Jack complained. "Just take a guess."

"Uh, Mr. Irwin was arrested for child abuse?" Gabriel suggested playfully. Mr. Irwin, their science teacher, liked to discipline rowdy students by throwing chalk at them. He was hated by the entire class, except Gabriel, who thought he was an excellent teacher.

"That would be sweet, but no," his friend replied, sitting down on a mound of snow. "Take another guess."

"Don't be a prick! Just tell me! I'm in no mood for games."

"Gee, you're a real spoil sport.... Okay, it's about Lisa Ross," Jack said.

That got Gabriel's attention. The unexpected mention of her name made his pulse race, made him forget about his parents momentarily. "Yeah? What about her?" he asked with interest.

"She likes you," Jack told his friend.

"What? Really?" Gabriel pumped his fist in exaltation. But then he furrowed his brow and inquired, "Wait. How do you know?"

"Well, she came up to me after drama club and asked, 'You're friends with Gabriel Klein, aren't you?' So I said 'yes.'"

"*She* came to *you*? And asked about *me*? Hoo hoo!" Gabriel rejoiced.

"Yeah, and she said, 'He's really smart, isn't he? He seems to know *everything*.'" Gabriel flushed proudly in the dazzling winter sunlight, a peacock on parade. Jack continued, "So I asked her why she was asking me about you. Did she like you? She blushed from her head to her toes and said 'no.' But I could tell she really did. So I helped you out."

Gabriel grew suspicious and asked, "What do you mean?"

"I told her it was okay. That you liked her, too. She seemed really happy to hear it__"

"You *what*? How *dare* you?" Gabriel exploded.

"Hey! Don't get angry! I was only trying to help. And it worked," Jack declared triumphantly.

"What kind of *friend* are you? What kind of *person*? You *promised* me that you wouldn't tell anybody. You *betrayed* me!" Gabriel raged.

Jack was stunned. "Look, I'm sorry, Gabriel. I was only trying to help you," he pleaded.

"I don't even want to *talk* to you, Jack. You're no friend of *mine*."

"Aw, come on, Gabriel. We've been friends *forever*. You know I wouldn't do anything to hurt you," Jack protested.

"Just shut up, *Jackass*!" Gabriel barked. As he said that, he rushed at Jack and pushed him hard, with both palms extended. Jack fell back under the pressure of the unexpected blow, landing in the snow while Gabriel stormed away.

Gabriel's head was clouded as he returned home, passing his father's beloved snow-covered garden near the entrance to the triplex. Once inside, he climbed the stairs to his parents' apartment on the top floor in utter turmoil. His closest friend had betrayed him. His parents were interfering with his relationship with Rabbi Plotkin, the person Gabriel admired and respected most now that his Zaidie had passed on. To top it off, he had given the rabbi his word that he would think seriously about making peace with his parents. He couldn't lie to the rabbi, betray him as Gabriel himself had just been betrayed.

Could he ever forgive his parents, he wondered as he unlocked the door with the brass key on the beaded silver chain around his neck and entered the apartment. Forgive.... What for? He kicked off his boots and tossed his coat on the hook.

Not for anything in particular. Sure, they had lied to him about so many things over the years. About his father's job. About how they had escaped Hungary. Gabriel heard them talking to his grandmother one night about how much they had needed to bribe the border guard to get into Austria. They had never told him that they had done anything illegal! They constantly embarrassed him, by bragging about how gifted he was to anyone who would listen. By claiming to be observant Jews, but then eating non-kosher food just because they preferred it.

But was the rabbi right? God commanded us to honor our parents, whether we respected them or not. He also taught forgiveness. Should he forgive his parents and overlook their many faults? *Could* he forgive them?

Crossing into the living room, his attention was drawn, as it often was, to his mother's watercolour of the Danube. Immediately, his thoughts drifted to his grandfather. Heroic, righteous Zaidie, who hid in the mud on the banks of that river to escape the Nazis. In the bright strokes of the painting, he saw the stark contrast between his Zaidie's integrity and his parents' hypocrisy. How could he forgive them?

But didn't forgiveness require repentance, a genuine effort to apologize and become a better person? *That* was the purpose of Yom Kippur. Not simply forgiveness, but repentance. Yes, he decided. That's what he would tell the rabbi if he brought the matter up again. He was prepared to forgive his parents for Rabbi Plotkin's sake, but only if they reached out to him and engaged in true repentance by correcting their behaviour.

To Gabriel's relief, however, Rabbi Plotkin did not bring the issue up again over the next two weekends. In part that was attributable to Gabriel himself, who studiously avoided direct contact with his mentor. After services on the Saturdays, instead of hanging around the auditorium afterwards for the *kiddush*, Gabriel quickly reshelved his *siddur* and walked home. After the Sunday Torah *shiur*, he waved perfunctorily to Rabbi Plotkin and rushed out with the other students. For his part, the rabbi had witnessed Gabriel's consternation and decided not to ride him too hard. Gabriel was a good boy, he judged. In time he would bring the matter up again, once the boy had time to mull it over, and Gabriel would do the right thing.

On the second Sunday, a cheerful sunny day in late February, the kind of winter day that restores one's belief in the coming of spring, Gabriel rushed out of the *shiur* so quickly that he forgot his knapsack under the metal frame chair with the black vinyl-covered seatback and cushion – the kind of chair one only finds in synagogue libraries, that must have been made for that purpose and that purpose alone. Only later in the afternoon, when he sat down at his bedroom desk to complete his science homework for the following day did he realize his oversight. He rushed back to the synagogue immediately, hoping the building was still unlocked.

When he arrived, the parking lot was almost empty and the building was dark, except for a solitary, orphaned light in the office. Mrs. Weiss must still be in, he thought. He would visit her after retrieving his bag. As he was ascending the steps to the library, though, he heard a single shrill, piercing scream, followed by more screams. He stood petrified, his feet rooted on two different stairs, uncertain of what to do. After what seemed like an eternity but couldn't have been more than five or ten seconds, Gabriel inched slowly down the stairs and tiptoed toward the office and the commotion. As he approached the room, holding his breath, fighting to control the involuntary tremors of fear in his legs, he could distinguish Mrs. Weiss' voice, no longer screaming, saying something that sounded like, "You're a naughty man!" Confused, afraid, but eager to come to her assistance if she needed it, to play the hero, Gabriel thrust open the office door and asked nervously, "Is everything alright Mrs...."

Nothing could have prepared the almost fourteen-year-old boy for the scene that met his eyes. Mrs. Weiss – the pure and modest young cantor's wife, who was kind to everyone and unimpeachable in conduct – was reclining on her back on the carpet behind her desk like Titian's Venus, naked at least from the waist up, while the bare-chested middle-aged synagogue president, Mr. Haberman, stroked her breasts luxuriously. Gabriel assumed that they were both completely naked, but couldn't be sure, as their lower halves were obscured by the desk, the very one that housed the candy jar he had partaken of so often. Their faces turned to him in surprise as he entered, Mrs. Weiss' blanching, while Mr. Haberman's reddened, so that remembering it afterwards they reminded him of the foreground and background of the Canadian flag.

In shock, Mrs. Weiss asked stupidly, "What are you doing here, Gabriel?" while Mr. Haberman ducked behind the desk to grab his clothing and cover up. Gabriel was left gawking at Mrs. Weiss in utter confusion. He had never before seen a woman's breasts and would never again lay eyes on as perfect a pair. But he recoiled in horror, in shame, in disgust, and burst out of the office.

As he exited the building and reached the parking lot, he stopped to gather his thoughts, to stop his head from spinning, as the president, now fully dressed, caught up to him. "Listen, son...." Mr. Haberman began, laying his firm hand on Gabriel's shoulder.

"I'm not your son," Gabriel cut in angrily, wrenching himself away from the president's grasp.

"Look, it's not what you think," Mr. Haberman attempted to mollify him, flashing a car salesman's smile.

"I may just be a kid, but I'm not stupid," Gabriel retorted, glaring.

The tall, lanky president inhaled deeply. "Okay. I understand you're upset. But you wouldn't want to hurt Mrs. Weiss' reputation, her *marriage*, by saying anything, would you?" He reached into the back pocket of his Harry Rosen trousers for his wallet and began to extract some bills. "I'm sure we can find a way to make this right."

Gabriel was horrified. "I don't want any of your stinking money. You're *disgusting*!" With that, he began to run toward home.

"Gabriel, wait!" Mr. Haberman called after him, but he just kept running until it was clear that his pursuer had abandoned the chase.

Instead of sprinting home, he headed straight for the rabbi's apartment on Bathurst Street. He realized that he couldn't discuss what he saw with his parents. Rabbi Plotkin was the only person he trusted enough, respected enough, to unburden himself to. Besides, the rabbi would know what to do. If there was anyone who could stand up to Mr. Haberman, it was Rabbi Plotkin.

Completely out of breath from running almost the entire four-block distance, he pressed the buzzer for apartment 201 on the large board in the entrance area of the rabbi's building. A short time later, Mrs. Plotkin's distorted voice squawked over the intercom. "Yes?" she queried.

"Uh," Gabriel said, disappointed that the rabbi himself didn't respond, "this is Gabriel Klein. From the synagogue. I need to speak to Rabbi Plotkin."

"Oh, he's busy now. Can I have him call you?" the tinny voice asked.

Gabriel was flustered. He couldn't wait. "It's really urgent!"

"Let me check with him," the rabbi's wife said.

The next raspy, distorted voice to speak over the intercom was the rabbi's. "Come on up, Gabriel," he said, as the electronic lock buzzed to admit him.

Once upstairs in the Plotkins' dreary apartment, the rabbi ushered him into the living room and directed him to a worn wooden sofa with rose-coloured upholstery, while the rabbi installed himself in a matching armchair. Mrs. Plotkin offered Gabriel some chocolate babka, which he declined, but she brought it out anyway, together with a glass of milk, before withdrawing to the bedroom.

The sense of smell is often the most indelible. Particular odours, fragrances, remain with us long after all other recollections have faded away. When Gabriel recalled this meeting afterwards – and he thought about it, brooded about it often – he associated it with the sickly-sweet scent of cream soda. Whether someone had been drinking that beverage, perhaps even spilled it on the sofa or elsewhere in the room, or whether something else merely mimicked the aroma, he couldn't say, but when he entered, the entire apartment smelled like cream soda.

Greatly agitated, Gabriel had immense difficulty recounting the jarring events that brought him there that afternoon. Though fiercely intelligent, his early adolescent brain lacked the vocabulary to explain exactly what he saw. Moreover, in his confusion and mortification, he was too embarrassed to relate the tawdry details. But the rabbi patiently attempted to put him at ease and slowly pieced together what had distressed him so.

The rabbi's oval, rubbery face assumed an ashen complexion and his eyes closed, as if he bore the brunt of his student's pain, as if it wounded his very soul. "That's a terrible thing to have to witness, Gabriel. I'm so sorry to hear it," he said genuinely. "Are you alright?"

Gabriel considered this. He felt as if he were in a daze, in an unreal world, where dreams and nightmares merge with reality, where kind, married secretaries fall prey to lecherous, predatory synagogue presidents, where best friends betrayed one's deepest, darkest secrets, where rabbis inhabited dingy but dignified apartments that smelled like cream soda. Only Rabbi Plotkin could put this right, he reasoned. Rabbi Plotkin: God's messenger, His fiery right hand, with the wisdom of Solomon. "No, I'm not," he answered at last. "I'm really... angry. How *dare* he?"

"No question. It was wrong of them," the rabbi pronounced, rubbing his cheek, his scraggly beard, with his pudgy hand.

Gabriel nodded fervently, adding, "You need to throw them out of the synagogue!"

"Ah, Gabriel.... I can't kick someone out of the synagogue each time they sin. If I did, we'd have nobody left in *shul*," Rabbi Plotkin said with a wry smile, using the Yiddish word for synagogue.

"Rabbi!" Gabriel uttered in shock. "It's not a joke. It's *adultery*!" The telephone rang, attracting the rabbi's attention, but Mrs. Plotkin answered it in the other room.

"Yes, of course. I didn't mean to be flippant," the rabbi said gently. "But we have to allow people the space to make their own choices, even if they're the wrong ones...."

Gabriel's jaw dropped. "They broke one of God's most sacred commandments. In the synagogue office! You can't just let that go! And what about poor Mrs. Haberman? And Cantor Weiss?"

"Ah, Gabriel," the rabbi said with obvious discomfort, "in principle you're right. But it's not that simple...."

Gabriel looked incredulous. "I don't understand, Rabbi. What's so complicated? He violated one of the Ten Commandments. How can you just ignore that?"

"Listen. I can guide the community, but I can't be God's policeman. Besides, there are also some practical considerations. Mr. Haberman is not only the *shul* president; he's the chair of the board and one of the biggest donors. I can't just throw him out of *shul*. I might even lose my job if I tried."

"You might lose your...." Gabriel couldn't believe that Rabbi Plotkin, the one man he admired and trusted, could sell out God's commandments for money. Crestfallen, bewildered, he stood up to leave, shaking in anger and confusion, accidentally toppling the plate of babka onto the carpet. Without stopping to tidy the mess he made or even apologizing, Gabriel staggered toward the door, tears streaming down his cheeks.

"Gabriel!" the rabbi called after him, but he ran out without heeding. As he stumbled down the staircase to the lobby, it suddenly occurred to Gabriel, with the force of an explosion, that Rabbi Plotkin had not been surprised by his revelation. That he already knew about Mr. Haberman and Mrs. Weiss. He *knew*.

When he left the rabbi's apartment building, he wandered aimlessly, his brain in an angry fog, eventually finding himself in Earl Bales Park. He clambered down into the ravines he used to tramp with Jack, still in utter bewilderment. He had been forsaken by his only remaining friend, abandoned by his last ally. "I am alone," he uttered aloud mournfully to the leafless trees, gathering his coat about him tightly although it was rather warm for a February afternoon. Then, remembering his Zaidie, he began to steel himself for the solitude that would be his lot from then on.

For the rest of his Grade 9 year, Gabriel was rather isolated. He remained in a state of belligerence with his parents, rendering his home life unpleasant. But they worked during the day, and he avoided them at night by studying in his room or taking walks in the park. Weekends were more problematic. He withdrew from the rabbi's Sunday lecture and tried, when possible, to avoid attending the synagogue on Saturdays. When his father insisted on dragging him, he sat in back, ducked out during the rabbi's speech, departed immediately after the service. Consequently, for all intent and purposes the rabbi ceased to be a personage in his life.

At school, his rift with Jack was never repaired and the two kept away from each other. While Jack continued to be a target for bullying by Victor Runyon and others, Gabriel never joined in. But he also refrained from intervening on Jack's behalf, instead remaining aloof.

Gabriel initially replaced Jack's friendship with Lisa Ross. He would walk Lisa home after school, even going so far as to carry her school bag and hold her hand. How creamy and soft it was, despite the frosty March weather! Their relationship fizzled out quickly, however, as beyond their physical attraction, they had few interests in common and little to talk to each other about. By mid-April, their puppy love had run its course and they each had their attention diverted in other directions: Lisa by a high school boy, Gabriel by his studies.

During the final two months of junior high, Gabriel largely kept to himself, focusing on his schoolwork, his violin, reading books. To his surprise, he adapted to his isolation, his loneliness, quite easily. It didn't really bother him. In his mind, there was something heroic about it. Like his grandfather, he didn't need others.

When the school year ended, and with it his junior high career, Gabriel was honoured as one of the top students in his class at the graduation exercises. Isaac and Sarah attended the ceremony, although their pride was tempered by their growing rift with their son. Not having any real friends in his class, Gabriel opted not to attend the graduation party afterwards, instead preferring to return home and read.

Over the summer, Gabriel secured employment as a busboy in a local restaurant to earn some money and remove himself from home. He selected as many evening and weekend hours as possible to minimize his exposure to his parents. During weekdays, when his parents were at work, he would often take walks through the ravines of the park, discovering a love for nature that he had never before nurtured. The only uncomfortable time was when his parents were on vacation, when his father toiled happily in his postage stamp plot of a garden. Then, he and his parents clashed, occasionally escalating to shouting matches. Overall, however, his last summer before high school passed agreeably enough.

At High Holiday time in September, Gabriel felt compelled to attend synagogue to pray and hear the *shofar*, the ram's horn blown to stir the community to repent. It was difficult, painful even, for him to look upon the rabbi and Mr. Haberman sitting in their gilded chairs like the biblical cherubs on either side of the ark. Had they truly repented of their sins, Gabriel wondered. Or, more likely, had they brushed them under the carpet so as not to interfere with their very obtrusive, very public, piety.

Gabriel reached his breaking point on Yom Kippur, the Day of Atonement. The climax of the Yom Kippur morning prayers was the *Avodah*, the recitation of a series of poems detailing the biblical Temple service that Aaron, the High Priest, performed in the desert on Yom Kippur to atone for the Jewish people's sins. They describe how he ventured with trepidation into the Holy of Holies and slaughtered a bull and a goat as sin offerings, the former for him and his household, the latter for the people, sprinkling their blood in an exacting ritual before the Ark of the Covenant. Even the slightest misstep could have incurred God's wrath and resulted in Aaron's death. When he exited the Holy of Holies safely at the end of the Service, therefore, the rest of the priests and the entire nation rejoiced, secure in the knowledge that they had been forgiven for their iniquities.

At this point in the modern Jewish prayer service, the congregation sings a stirring song of exaltation to celebrate the emergence of the High Priest all those centuries ago. The song – *Mar'eh Cohen*, "The Priest's Countenance" – is a poetic depiction of Aaron's splendour at the zenith of his glory. The Cantor would sign each verse: Like the image of a rainbow in the midst of the cloud, such was the priest's countenance. *Like a rose in the midst of a glorious garden, such was the priest's countenance.* Then the congregation would take up the refrain, *How truly magnificent was the High Priest's countenance when he emerged from the Holy of Holies in peace, without injury!* This was always the highlight of Yom Kippur for Gabriel, the moment he yearned for above all. For the whole synagogue, which had been fasting by this point for over eighteen hours, to rise as one and sing, often dancing around the aisles, ignoring their hunger, their thirst, their fatigue, their weakness, just to rejoice in God's sparing of Aaron. In Gabriel's young mind, it was as close to God as modern man could ever get.

As he stood this year watching the congregants rejoicing, listening to Cantor Weiss' heavenly voice, his eyes were arrested by Rabbi Plotkin standing on the dais with a rapturous, beatific glow, to all appearances the very image of piety, of Godliness, of the High Priest himself. Gabriel was suddenly filled with revulsion, with contempt. Instead of the usual emotional high, he felt dejected, betrayed, empty. This grew to the feverish pitch of fury, blurring his vision. He wanted to shout, *You fraud! How dare you? How can you defile God's sanctuary in this, the holiest of moments?* But who would listen to him? Would anyone care? No, he realized with sudden clarity, they would rally around the rabbi, even if they snickered behind his back afterwards. All they wanted was the public *appearance* of holiness at the appropriate times, in front of the appropriate people. They would beat their chests in the synagogue to expiate their sins on Yom Kippur, but would then return to their sordid little lives unaltered by God's grace. They didn't care a whit for God's will or His glory. It was all a sham.

Ashamed – of his corrupt rabbi, of the mealy-mouthed congregants, of himself for being taken in by their charade – Gabriel pushed his way brusquely to the aisle and marched in disgust to the synagogue exit, never to return again.

Over the ensuing weeks, his parents, who simply could not understand Gabriel's sudden change of heart, tried to persuade him to attend Saturday morning services, but he would not budge. The following year on Yom Kippur, his mother implored him, "Gabriel, it's the holiest day of the year! You *have* to go to synagogue." But he just rolled his eyes and responded defiantly, "I'll *daven* at home." Eventually, they reluctantly reconciled themselves to the fact that, as they understood it, their son had turned his back on Judaism.

But his parents' assessment missed the mark. Certainly, Gabriel's decision to leave the synagogue amounted to a rejection of organized Judaism, of organized religion in general. But it was not a repudiation of God Himself, or even Judaism. Far from it. He left because these people — the so-called standard-bearers of God — had forsaken His principles. He thought of Lyudmilla. *It's people that ruin religion, that spoil God's perfection.* In truth, Gabriel left organized religion *because* of God, *for* God. He continued to pray every morning with his *tallit* and *tefillin*. He kept kosher for the rest of his life and observed the Sabbath and holidays to the best of his abilities. But he never prayed in a synagogue again.

Chapter 5

The sun rose over the treetops of Point Pleasant Park, casting the maritime world in its ethereal glow. As the first rays peeked through the evergreen needles above him, Gabriel opened his eyes to greet the new May morning. Having survived another harrowing winter in the shelter, spring had finally vanquished his old foe and at long last Gabriel was back where he belonged. He blinked and surveyed his kingdom: the rippling waters of the Northwest Arm spread out in front him, with the Royal Nova Scotia Yacht Club flanking the other side, the trees and bushes lining the bank he occupied, the gulls circling above his head, the sparrows and goldfinches singing joyfully in the verdant branches, the fluffy clouds gathering in an effort to extinguish the nascent sun. This was the beauty of creation.

The splendour of it all was achingly beautiful. We're a funny species, Gabriel reflected as he luxuriated on the patch of earth that served as his bed. Ants don't cry. Neither do bats or pythons. Other mammals may howl about something lacking in the present: the pain of a wound, insufficient food. What is it about human beings that makes them weep at the zenith of beauty, that makes them uniquely aware of its ephemerality? Instead of revelling in the majesty of a spring day, delighting in its delicate blossoms, its ambrosial fragrances, we're stabbed to the heart by the knowledge of its inevitable decay, that we can't have it forever.

He reached under the torn sweatshirt that functioned as his pillow and retrieved from a faded plastic grocery bag a grubby, soiled, fringed shawl which had once been white, with faint black stripes of varying thickness spanning the section near its edges. With great reverence, he draped this sacred relic, his *tallit*, around his shoulders, placed a small, black, satin kippah on his head, and recited a blessing. Then, like he did every morning, he greeted the new day with prayer, his back to the water, facing east. Without a *siddur*, he began with the prayers that he knew by heart, the Shema – *Hear, oh Israel, the Lord is our God, the Lord is one* – several of the blessings, a few other scattered and sundry verses. Over the many years, he had forgotten much. These preliminaries completed, he addressed God more colloquially, with a heartfelt apostrophe. "Good morning, God! It's me. Gabriel. I want to thank you for the beauty. For the trees. For the beautiful music of your wonderful world. Please sustain it and teach people to appreciate it and to treat each other honestly and kindly." His prayer service over, he carefully folded his *tallit*, placed it back under the sweatshirt.

He remembered how he had appropriated it many years ago. One Saturday morning, he entered the synagogue on Oxford Street after services had begun, eager not to be seen. Given his shabby appearance and dress, the odour of the streets that permeated his clothing, he was bound to raise eyebrows. So he waited until they began to chant the weekly portion of the Torah scrolls, when he might escape notice. Then he crept inside in trepidation.

Although he had never stepped inside that synagogue before, it was wonderfully, tantalizingly, agonizingly familiar to him. The large entrance hall with plaques commemorating the donors who had built it; the sweet, musty smell of old books; the bookcases lining the walls on either side of the entrance to the sanctuary, crammed with prayer books and Hebrew bibles; the sing-song incantation of the Torah portion escaping from behind the closed doors of the sanctuary. It had a hypnotic effect on Gabriel, casting him back to his youth in Toronto. He peered through the patterned window on the wooden door, emblazoned with a large, angular, black wrought iron *menorah*, the sacred candelabra. Through it, he caught a glimpse of the rabbi reading the Torah in front of the ark, clothed in a curtain of red velvet, flanked by a six-headed candelabra on one side, a wooden appliance displaying the current page number on the other. To his disappointment, the synagogue was nearly empty. Unlike the packed sanctuaries he remembered from his youth in Toronto, there were no more than thirty people scattered around the large hall. *A synagogue shouldn't be empty*, he thought judgementally. *It's not right.*

His heart stopped. He heard a light footstep behind him.

"Excuse me, sir." He spun around to see a short-haired, middle-aged lady in a fancy silver-sky blue belted dress and a matching sky-blue tam studded with artificial jewels addressing him. She studied his face, his hair, his clothing, a tinge of sadness in her oval eyes. "I'm so sorry, but we don't keep any money on Saturdays because it's our Sabbath. But if you come back tomorrow, the rabbi would be happy to help you out," she said kindly.

He was frozen on his feet, bewildered. He found himself unable to speak.

"If you'd like, I can get you some food, though," she assured him with a warm smile.

He nodded his head. She excused herself and descended the stairs to the small downstairs auditorium where they ate their *kiddush* after the service. While she was downstairs, he quickly scouted the entrance hall and spotted a rack with prayer shawls for the congregation. Before she returned with food, he grabbed one, together with a black satin *kippah*, shoved them under his shirt and rushed out the front door, in mortal terror of being caught.

Did he have any qualms about stealing from a synagogue? Most definitely not. The way he viewed it, the synagogue furnished these shawls to enable people to pray and connect to God. That was exactly what he intended to do with the one he pilfered. In fact, he needed it more urgently than the other congregants, who all had the money to buy their own. So it wasn't really theft; it was an act of faith. He was only sorry he wasn't able to procure a prayer book or a pair of phylacteries, although he wouldn't realistically be able to preserve them, given his lifestyle. Since then, he donned these prizes every morning to commune with God.

 His prayers completed, Gabriel grabbed a surprisingly fresh bar of cheap soap and clambered down to the water. Scouting around quickly to make certain he was alone in his early morning routine, he removed his clothing, soaped up, and plunged into the edge of the water to wash himself. This was a daily luxury he could afford in the warmer weather that he had to dispense with during the long, cold months that Atlantic Canada provided with too beneficent a liberality. Emerging from his bath, he quickly towelled himself off with the sweatshirt that served as his pillow and dressed, spreading the damp sweatshirt out on a branch to dry.
 Once dressed again with the same clothing in which he had slept, he cached the soap and the ragged clothes and rags that functioned as bedding for him, retrieving instead a battered, bent toothbrush with dishevelled bristles and an empty old plastic Coca Cola bottle which he took with him on a short walk to the park's public restroom. After dunking the toothbrush under the tap, he swished it around his mouth, without toothpaste, and spat out. Then he filled up his bottle with cold water, drank it in one gulp, refilled it and secured it with the cap.
 He studied himself in the restroom's mirror. How grey his hair had become, how craggy his skin! He searched for a trace of the boy he used to be so many lifetimes ago. As a young man, he had seen a travelling exhibit of Magritte's paintings. One painting in particular, a canvas depicting an artist beholding an

egg but sketching a bird in flight, had captured his imagination. The idea was that entities were always in flux. The egg had no meaning if separated from the bird it was to become, just as the bird could never be distinct from the egg from whence it emerged. He wondered if he still bore the markings of the young Gabriel, whether this future could have been predicted for the young, promising boy. He sighed as he dried his face with a paper towel from the rusted dispenser. After returning to his "bedroom" to store his toothbrush and donning the threadbare, grey tweed peaked cap that he used to solicit handouts, he was now ready to begin his day.

    He commenced with a leisurely reconnaissance of the southern tip of the park, around the Northwest Arm Battery and Point Pleasant Battery to take in the beauty of the ocean, a privilege he never tired of, despite the pollution, the encroachment of industry. *Why did man always have to mess with perfection?* he lamented. He then enjoyed a luxurious walk through the wooded park toward the exit. It still wasn't the same as it was before Hurricane Juan, but at least it had recovered considerably, he observed with satisfaction. Like a snowflake, his path was anything but direct. He lovingly inspected his favourite trees, imitated bird calls, stopped to watch a rabbit scurrying into the brush, admired the Monet painting that was the sky, with its patches of brilliant azure blue rapidly being encroached upon, crowded out, by billowing cumulus clouds. *That's what people miss in life*, he thought, with a self-satisfied grin. *They're so eager to get somewhere that they ignore the magnificence of the journey.*

    Upon emerging from the park at the Young Avenue entrance, Gabriel continued straight to Spring Garden Road, neither quickening nor slackening his deliberate pace, despite his slight but noticeable limp. On the way, he took stock of his cash resources. He had a little over six dollars in his pocket. The rest – his savings – was buried in his bedroom, where it would be safe. It was far riskier to carry too much money on his person. With six dollars he could buy himself a bagel at Tim Horton's for an opulent brunch and still have some money left for dinner. Or he could conserve funds by picking up something to eat at the supermarket near the train station. Yes, that made more sense. He needed to save as much as possible of his daily earnings if he was going to make a change, whatever that may be.

A young woman wearing an expensive white polo shirt above a pristine white miniskirt and carrying a tennis racket scrutinized him in disgust as he passed her near the tennis courts on Young Avenue. He was used to that. Clearly, he did not fit her elitist, self-glorifying notions about which human beings were valuable and which were not. But she was no-one to him, so Gabriel just ignored her and turned right onto Inglis at the next intersection.

After reaching Barrington, the notion came to him that it would be more practical to scour the dumpster behind Tim Horton's, rather than squander money unnecessarily at the supermarket. While some of the establishment's patrons avoided him, avoided making eye contact, and others pitied him, Gabriel rummaged through the large green metal bin behind the restaurant, searching for scraps of food. He extracted a doughnut whose glazing someone had chewed off, and a quarter of a bagel smeared with cheese spread. That would feed him adequately at no cost. He could have also salvaged part of a meat wrap, but for religious reasons he eschewed meat and fish that conflicted with kosher dietary regulations.

What a waste, he reflected. *Throwing out perfectly good food. While some people starve, others dispose of food just because they can.* He gobbled the remains of the doughnut and sauntered off to his office, saving the bagel scraps for lunch. *A few more dollars for the kitty.* Now if only he could figure out what to do with the money he was saving. He still needed a plan. Oh well, there was still time.

The Oracle of Spring Garden Road

***

As Aristotle observed, man is by nature a social animal. The most reclusive human will still crave communion with others, although he may prefer to keep the circle of intimates small, perhaps restricted to only one other. Even one such as Gabriel, who intentionally withdrew from society, who spurned it in anger, in disgust, cannot survive long without human contact. Isolation works on the human brain, wears it down, causing drastic behavioural changes. In Gabriel's case it had two significant effects on him. It brought him to fill in for social intercourse with his own mind. He relived, almost obsessed over, past events and discussions or imagined new dialogues with people he knew years before. In this manner, he paradoxically retreated into his own mind precisely because of a yearning for human contact.

The second effect isolation, and the derision of the good people of Halifax, wrought for him was to alter his personality. Gabriel had possessed a gregarious, if shy and reclusive, nature. Although he never had many close friends, except perhaps in the final years of high school, it wasn't because he was in any way disagreeable or unpleasant. His years on the street as an outcast, however, had transformed him into a caustic, acerbic soul, with a sharp tongue and short on pleasantries. Even his manner of speaking, his voice, had altered, becoming more of a snarl than the rather pleasing, conversational voice that the fairer sex had found beguiling when he was a student.

To his credit, Gabriel recognized these dangers early, understood that he desperately needed to routinize contact with others, or he would go mad. For this reason, he resolved to hold court in his office daily and converse with passersby, even those that ridiculed him, to prevent himself from tumbling into an abyss. And he latched onto the kinder souls he met – Jane, the teller – in the hope of retaining some connection to the human race, despite his desire to maintain a prudent distance from it. Over time, he even began to derive some pleasure from his hours in the office, especially on sublime spring days like this, when the world was joyfully emerging from its extended brumal hibernation.

He sat on the pavement of his office, his back against the brown bricks of the bank, the graffiti-laden metal depository slot, enjoying the bustle of the business day. Outside the pharmacy across the street, the pharmacist's assistant was pleading loudly with his wife over his cell phone, clawing at his greying hair in frustration with his free hand. A university student in her bright yellow Dalhousie sweatshirt lazily perused the window of a craft store on the other corner. The number 10 bus was just pumping its brakes to stop in front of the office, ready to disgorge more pedestrians onto an already lively street. Somewhere further down, toward the park, the door opened at one of the bars and some brassy strains of jazz music drifted down the street. All the while, the clouds billowed overhead to sanctify the maritime main street scene. Gabriel soaked it up, revelling in the weather, the atmosphere.

Just then, through the small cut-out window in the narrow wall separating his little enclave from the rest of the bank's façade, from its entrance, he spotted Jane crossing Dresden Row toward him. Her appearance was uncharacteristically severe, not simply because her silver, matronly hair was pinned up in a bun, or because of her harsh, black rectangular bifocals. There was something in her expression, in the sallowness of her cheeks, in her eyes, cast down, searching the ground as she walked. To his surprise, she walked right past without even noticing him.

"Jane? Won't you stop and say hello?" he called after her, somewhat offended.

"Huh?" she murmured, turning around. "Oh, Gabriel. It's you. I'm so sorry. I didn't mean to ignore you."

"What's going on?" he asked. He wanted to sound more sympathetic, but he had gotten out of the habit of caring for other people. "And please don't call me that when people are around. They know me as Eddie...."

"Oh," she said, "Sorry.... My husband is sick. Very sick, I'm afraid. I'm just out to pick up a prescription for him."

Rather than showing her any sympathy, Gabriel merely flashed her a queer look. "Which pharmacy?" he asked gruffly. "You've passed both of them already."

Jane spun around in confusion. "So I have," she admitted. "I should have stopped at Lawton's. I guess I'm not myself today. Thanks for paying attention."

Gabriel nodded as she prepared to retrace her steps. He eagerly wanted to say something reassuring to her. "It's in God's hands. I'll pray for him," he offered.

"Thank you. If only I believed in God, I might find that comforting," she said. "But I appreciate the sentiment."

Her response disappointed Gabriel. He snorted as she retraced her steps to the pharmacy, deciding that he would need to follow that up with her when she had more time.

After spending the day at the office, Gabriel decided to take a walk further afield, to the Citadel, the Commons and beyond. Not merely for the pleasure of wandering, aimlessly, through the city whose heart was synchronized with his own. He had ulterior motives.

A homeless person, one who withdraws from civilization to rebuke society, reject its corruption, does not covet. Their palatial homes, their luxurious automobiles, hold no attraction for him. He spurns the delights of their table and their finery, their fancy vestments, as vanity. Such was Gabriel's attitude toward material possessions. There was one luxury, however, one item that Gabriel yearned for from the depths of his soul.

Not far from the Commons, Gabriel had espied a storefront luthier that sold handcrafted violins. Now and then over the past several months, he had lingered outside the shop window admiring these fine instruments, drinking them in with his eyes, imagining how they would feel in his hands, what wonderful sounds he could coax out of them. It was almost too much for him to bear. On this late afternoon, he could contain himself no longer. Despite his shabby appearance, he entered the elegant shop and sidled up to a display case, admiring the violin it held.

A salesman in a grey suit and brightly-coloured paisley tie looked him over in disgust. "Can I help you?" he asked condescendingly.

Gabriel resented the salesman's attitude, but the allure of the instrument, its pleasing wood grains, the symmetrical serpentine f-holes, its slender neck, stayed his anger. "Can I try this violin?" he asked breathlessly.

"Are you interested in buying it?" the salesman inquired contemptuously. "We only allow *customers* to play our instruments."

As Gabriel stared at the salesman with suppressed rage, the owner of the establishment approached. He had observed Gabriel pining away at the instruments through the window over the previous months and was moved by his obsession. "Do you know how to play, sir?" the owner asked Gabriel, waving away the salesman's astonished objections.

"I did," Gabriel responded simply.

"Well then, give it a whirl," the proprietor suggested with a magnanimous smile.

Gabriel nodded his gratitude, wiped his hands with a tissue from a box on the counter, and lifted the cherished instrument. He fondled the fine-grained wood, as the owner handed him a bow to use. Gabriel took a deep breath and suppressed a tear. It had been so long since he had held a violin, had felt its satisfying weight in his hands. He began warming up with scales before playing the Czardas that he had excelled at as a teenager under Lyudmilla's tutelage. The violin was a wonderful instrument, easy to play, with a clear tone. He, however, was out of practice. Though he had played the piece endlessly in his mind over his two decades in exile, his hands – bigger, stiffer, clumsier – could not keep pace. To his dismay, he made several mistakes, and his sound was only a pale reflection of his past glory. Although the proprietor was impressed by his performance, which he had not expected from a homeless person, Gabriel himself was despondent. He quickly replaced the instrument on its stand on the display case and returned the bow to the owner before bounding toward the door like a jackrabbit.

"You're welcome to come back any time you'd like, sir, and play some more," the owner assured him, as the salesman looked on in disbelief.

"Th... thank you," Gabriel stuttered awkwardly, then rushed out of the store ashamed.

Gabriel began his long walk home in the doldrums, dispirited by his disappointing performance. After several blocks, however, his mood picked up. The evening was cold and damp. Typical maritime fare. A heavy fog slowly rolled in from the Atlantic. Gabriel smiled. Although a Halifax fog was biting – the kind of dampness that chills one's soul – Gabriel adored the fog above all else. One could really lose oneself in it, as it blotted out the entire world. He wandered off through the side streets on the way to his bedroom, hearing the mournful dirge of the foghorn, which stirred him as no other sound could. The fog closed in, shutting him off from the world. The lights of the city, the cars, the buildings, the people all tumbled into its mystical vortex, vanishing before his eyes. *Was that building ever there? Is there a city called Halifax? Was it all a dream?* He felt like an angel in Heaven, with the earthly plane dissolving and only cloud, water,

God's glory itself remaining. He was joyously, miraculously whisked away from the pettiness of man, his treachery, his selfishness, to an ethereal plane of pure spirit.

Yet in the midst of his rapture, an incongruous memory took hold of him. Many years ago, too many to count, he had been hungry at the end of a long, blustery day. But he wanted more than simply the bread, cheese and vegetables he usually ate. After years on a restricted diet, he craved meat. But where could he find kosher meat? He remembered once seeing a man with a *kippah* emerging from a supermarket on Quinpool Road. So he counted the change in his hat, almost eight dollars, and trekked from his office to the supermarket in the hope of finding kosher food.

As it turned out, he was in luck. The grocery store did maintain a small kosher section, including some breads, frozen meats, a dairy/deli refrigerator. Unfortunately, the delicatessen meat was pricey. And, far from his usual haunts, Gabriel looked out of place, was an unwelcome intrusion, with his soiled clothing and unkempt hair. Tainted by the foul odour of the streets. He stood awkwardly at the deli fridge, fumbling nervously with a small package of sliced smoked turkey breast whose price was beyond his meager means.

At that moment, he noticed a man with a black hat and a dark beard staring at him. The man seemed lost in indecision. What should he do about this homeless man in supermarket? Perceiving that Gabriel was aware of his attention, the man approached him and asked politely, "Excuse me, sir. Do you mind if I ask you, are you Jewish?"

Although the man was younger, taller, thinner than Rabbi Plotkin, something in his demeanour reminded Gabriel of his former rabbi. For reasons he still could not understand today, Gabriel panicked. He averted the man's gaze, simply muttering, "No," before tossing the turkey package back in the fridge haphazardly and hustling out of the store. To his embarrassment, as he reached the pavement in front of the supermarket, he was shivering, shaking uncontrollably. That night he dined on whatever scraps of food he was able to find in local dumpsters, renouncing the idea of procuring kosher meat.

As curious as that episode was, he might have been able to put it out of his mind completely, if it hadn't been for what transpired the following afternoon. He was in his office talking to the kindly bank teller, who had just finished her lunch and offered him a square of brownie that she had prepared for herself, but then decided that she'd be better off without. Out of the corner of his eye, he spied the bearded man he'd encountered in the supermarket strolling down Spring Garden Road toward him. *What was he doing here?* Gabriel thought, seized by an unexplainable terror. *Was he following me?*

Gabriel quickly, awkwardly grabbed the teller's brownie and hurried away in the opposite direction, leaving his hat with the alms inside unprotected on the sidewalk. He ducked down the next side street and turned in to the alley behind the pharmacy, huffing mightily. There he sat for what seemed an eternity, still breathing heavily, berating himself for his cowardice, waiting for the man to return to his own part of the world.

Eventually, after he decided that enough time had elapsed, Gabriel slunk back around the corner. After a quick reconnaissance of the street, he determined that the offending man was nowhere in sight. That's when the first thought about his hat and the coins inside hit him like a concussion grenade. How could he be so careless? He raced back to his spot in front of the bank, relieved to find the battered hat still sitting faithfully on the pavement, like a mangy old mutt. Peering inside to verify that no money had been pilfered, Gabriel was taken aback. His hat was now home to two packages of the kosher turkey he had examined the day before, held together by a thin, crimson elastic band. Upon further examination, he found that tucked in between the brace was a crisp ten-dollar bill.

Thinking back on that incident, Gabriel now remembered that he had been unsettled, even enraged, by the man. Who did he think he was, barging in on Gabriel's private space? Did he think that Gabriel *needed* his charity? But why should he dwell on this now? Why was he ruining the splendid seclusion of a Halifax fog? Maybe it had been a mistake to visit the luthier today, to play the violin. If you indulge in luxuries, you're bound to become soft, he told himself. He tried to banish the incident from his mind.

It was a challenge to navigate back to his bedroom in the relentless fog. He knew the streets and paths well. But even so, the dank, viscous vapours disoriented one's senses. Had he already passed Ogilvie Street? Shouldn't the Cable Road path to the NorthWest Arm begin about here? Was this the copse of red spruce trees that he cut through to his bedroom in the underbrush? The throbbing pain in his foot, exacerbated by the dampness, the chill, made every step an agony. It took him quite a while and he stumbled several times, once nearly tumbling down the stubbly bank into the water. He managed to grab on to the trunk of a small tree and drag himself up, but his arms ached and his left ankle, which was perpetually flaring up nowadays, was on fire. Eventually, he felt his way and settled back into his cold, damp hideout, *his* Danube riverbed, nursing his wounds.

That night, with the foghorn crying out, he slept fitfully, feverishly, interrupted by vivid and haunting dreams. In one, he was patrolling Spring Garden Road near the Public Garden when he saw his father, dressed in his work uniform, loading discarded items onto the back of a compactor truck. Instinctively, Gabriel turned away, but as he did so, he noticed that his father was clearing away a perfectly good danish. He called out in anger, "Stop! Don't throw out that danish. *I'll* eat it!" But his father looked at him, an expression of disappointment, disgust, loathing on his face, and said, "I don't understand you, Gabriel. There's no danish here." Confused, Gabriel glanced down at his father's hands and, to his alarm, noticed that, after all, he had been mistaken. It wasn't a danish Isaac was tossing into the jaws of the compactor. It was a baby. "No!" Gabriel screamed in horror, but it was too late. The infant had disappeared into the bowels of the truck. Gabriel woke up screaming, salty tears streaming down his cheeks.

He peered around to take his bearings. The fog was still heavy, blotting out the stars, so he could not estimate the time of night. He was alone in a cocoon of damp, murky darkness and, rather than the giddiness, the elation, he normally experienced on a foggy night, he was overcome by an all-consuming dread. How did such a magical May day turn so wrong? It was foolhardy, he knew now, to think he could just pick up a violin and play after all these years. Some things are better consigned to the past, that long-forsaken country of our youth, whose hold on us grows stronger the farther we run from it. But there was more to it than that, he knew. He was just unable to put his finger on it now.

Unable to sleep, with untold hours left until dawn brushed away the darkness and the dread, he turned his attention back to his predicament. He could not spend another winter on the streets or in the shelter. That was clear to him now. He needed a plan to transition back, only on *his* terms. But how? That was the issue. Over the past months, he had spent many a night obsessing over this vexing problem, elements of the solution in sight, but the modalities elusive. On this night, however, with the Heavens blotted out of the sky, the comforting wail of the foghorn, it all became clear to him. He would solicit help from the one person he could trust, from whom it would not be a betrayal to enlist aid. From Jane. She would help him get a job – any job, as a dockworker, a janitor, a streetsweeper, it didn't matter. Maybe, he thought, maybe he could even see if the music store needed help. The amount of money he would earn was largely irrelevant. He already lived more frugally than anyone could imagine possible. All he would need was enough to rent the smallest, cheapest studio apartment to shelter him from the cold. Yes, that wouldn't be too much of a sell-out, he reasoned.

To do this, however, he would need to demonstrate to her, to them, that he was responsible, presentable, not a liability. That would take money. For a haircut, for clothing, shoes. The surplus store, the thrift stores wouldn't do. He estimated that three hundred dollars should do. A princely sum for him. But as he plotted it out, he decided it could be manageable. On any given workday, he could pull in between five to ten dollars. Often more. And with the help of dumpsters and, if necessary, the foodbank, he could reduce his daily expenses to near zero. With about five months until winter, that left about one hundred and fifty days, of which more than a hundred were workdays. He could even work on Sundays is necessary, although never on Saturdays. He already had over thirty dollars put away since the winter. If he could save almost three dollars each day, he'd be ready to implement the plan by the time the upcoming winter reared its frightful head.

Yes, Gabriel thought with satisfaction, as he finally drifted back to sleep. I now have a plan....

Chapter 6

As he entered high school, Gabriel was cast adrift. All the stabilizing influences in his life had fallen away like so many leaves in an autumn rain. He no longer respected his parents, whom he judged as weak and unprincipled. He had consigned the synagogue and its rabbi to the forgotten past. Even his school was new, as he moved to the William Lyon Mackenzie Collegiate Institute for high school, leaving behind many of his classmates and acquaintances – he couldn't quite call them friends – who chose different schools, closer to their old junior high. Jack Silverman enrolled in Willowdale High School, as did Lisa Ross. Victor Runyon had been held back to repeat Grade 8. Leibl Lubov, whose father had struck it rich in the dry cleaning business, had moved to Rosedale and registered at the exclusive Upper Canada College. For Gabriel, everything was new, different, strange.

In this turbulent new environment, Gabriel underwent a profound and disappointing metamorphosis. Now in an unfamiliar school, further away from his home, the precocious, overachieving boy with a fiery will to succeed had lost his drive, his sense of purpose. Having learned that he could earn good enough grades just by coasting, he was no longer motivated to work hard at school. He would rarely complete his homework, studied only superficially for his exams, put minimal effort into his papers and projects, which he often submitted unstapled and crumpled, having been crushed in his knapsack. The teachers at Mackenzie, knowing nothing about Gabriel's sparkling academic past, concluded that he was a slacker, a below-average student not worth their investment of time.

Instead, Gabriel grew more interested in the social pleasures of high school. Music, parties, girls, alcohol, drugs. The award-winning, socially awkward student now cut classes, chased skirts, attended parties. A pudgy boy no more, having sprouted tall and lean with a square jaw and piercing steel grey eyes, yet still with that lack of self-assurance around the fairer sex which made him even more adorable to some. He still had no close friends, but he had fallen in with a bad crowd, a group of miscreants in Grade 11 who called themselves "The Stoners," who swore, smuggled booze into school, and introduced Gabriel to beer, marijuana, hash. To his parents' alarm, he was rarely at home, staying out most nights and weekends, getting stoned at parties, at friends' houses, or just in a secluded park near school.

He was a raging river, a frantic waterfall, plummeting at breakneck speed, not to the ocean nor to the sea, but to the depths of an infernal abyss. Perhaps, had he still respected Rabbi Plotkin, the rabbi could have rescued him from his descent, his slide toward oblivion. But when he thought of the rabbi at all nowadays, it was with bitter contempt. For Gabriel, Rabbi Plotkin was the symbol of weakness, of betrayal, of hypocrisy, of all that was wrong with adults. He wasn't quite the prototypical rebel without a cause, because he wasn't exactly rebelling. One needs a sense of purpose to rebel, and he had none. Instead, Gabriel's descent was more of an abdication, a recognition, he would have said, that in a world where people were morally bankrupt and corrupt – *Perfection isn't possible when human beings are involved* – there was no point in trying.

And what of God? Had Gabriel abandoned Him, too? Not at all. He continued to pray every morning with his *tallit* and *tefillin*, and remained steadfast in his observation of the Sabbath and kosher dietary laws, at least to his standards. He troubled himself little, if at all, about whether his rejection of his parents, his drinking, the drugs, were an affront to God. If anything, he viewed his behaviour as a righteous castigation of the ungodliness all around him. Like Noah, who had to construct his ark under the gaze of an indifferent world which cared little for His word, Gabriel saw himself as alone in his devotion to God's truth amongst a sea of unworthy humans. It wasn't his rock-solid faith in God that was shaken; it was his rather tenuous faith in man that had crashed to the ground, engulfed by the simmering flames of his disillusionment.

Not surprisingly, his parents tried their best to rein him in. They constantly pleaded with him, harangued him, yelled at him, ordered him not to throw it all away on cheap thrills. But they had no way to reach him. They lacked the language, the tools, to break through his truculence.

They received his final report card of the first semester of Grade 10 in utter shock. "Gabriel!" his mother cried uncomprehendingly. "D in math? C- in Biology? C+ in English? D in History? How can this be? What have you been doing with yourself?"

"Lay off, Mom!" he snapped. "I passed the semester. So what's the big deal?"

"How can you talk to your mother that way? Have you no respect?" Isaac exploded.

"The goal in life isn't to squeak by," Esther persisted, absently playing with the emerging crow's foot over her eye. "Your father and I didn't worked so hard all our lives – worked our fingers to the bone – just for you to squeak by. Or not to. You owe it to us to put in your whole effort."

"Why is it always about *you*? It's *my* life! Let me do what *I* want!" Gabriel protested.

"You stupid, ungrateful child!" Isaac shouted, the jagged blue veins in his temple pulsating with rage. "Just because it's your life doesn't give you the right to throw it away. You think it's a big joke, but what you do now matters. If you mess up now, it will affect whether you go to university, what kind of a job you get, what kind of a house you're able to live in...."

"Geez!" Gabriel exclaimed. "You think you know everything. Just leave me alone, will you?" With that, he ran off in a huff, leaving his frustrated parents choking on their impotent rage. It was a scene that repeated itself too often in their apartment.

"You got any dough, Klein?" Devin, the unofficial leader of The Stoners, asked him. The sun had just started to set, and the group had gathered at their unofficial hangout, Wilmington Park, between the recreation building and the ice rink. They had been sharing joints and tossing stones onto the tennis courts when Devin and a tall, close-cropped blonde girl they called Suzy Q decided they need alcohol.

"No, I'm completely busted," Gabriel replied.

Devin looked at him rather menacingly. "You always use our stuff, but you never pay for any yourself. How about you steal us some booze?"

Despite the calming effect of the marijuana, Gabriel was ill at ease. He badly wanted to pull his weight with the group, but he wasn't willing to defy God's solemn commandment for anybody. "I don't steal," he said evenly, as his eyes were drawn involuntarily to a synagogue across the street that he had noticed earlier, on his way to the park. The sign proclaimed it to be *Beth Jacob V'anshei Drildz*, the house of Jacob and the men of Drildz. What a strange name! At the time, Gabriel wondered what Drildz could possibly mean. Now the synagogue's conspicuousness gave him the eerie sensation that God was testing him.

"You afraid of getting caught?" Devin challenged him.

"No. I just don't steal."

Devin remained silent, contemplating this response with narrowed eyes, an ominous scowl, so Suzy Q piped up, "Well, can you break the window so we can get in, Boy Scout?" The others laughed at the fitting moniker she had invented for him.

Gabriel sucked in his lower lip. "Yeah, I can do that," he replied slowly.

"Okay, we wait until the supermarket closes and then we go," Devin commanded.

Over an hour later, it was pitch dark when the supermarket lights switched off and the last cars vacated the parking lot. The group stealthily slunk across to the plaza under a starless sky, anxiously checking for any prying eyes.

"Stay away from the bank!" a tall, broad-shouldered boy Gabriel knew only as Tank, whispered urgently. "I think there's a camera in there."

Carefully, with a quick glance toward Sunnybrook to make certain that no-one had remained in the supermarket after closing time, they converged slowly toward the LCBO liquor store. Scrutinizing the storefront, Devin concluded the cavernous window, rather than the narrow glass door, offered the best prospect for access.

"Okay. Do your thing, Boy Scout!" Suzy Q commanded.

His stomach in his mouth, Gabriel removed his faded jean jacket and wrapped it around his left arm from the knuckle to the elbow. Inhaling deeply, he averted his eyes and hit the window with great force. The window splintered with glass tinkling and scattering as the shrill whine of the alarm pierced the air. A cheer went up, as someone in the group marvelled, "He did it!"

With the burglar alarm ringing, Devin took charge, barking orders to the group, no longer concerned about keeping quiet. "Get in quickly and grab something! We don't have much time before the heat gets here," he said. "Let's meet back at the rink in five minutes."

Gabriel escaped back to the park immediately, hiding next to the ice rink while his companions grabbed a couple of bottles and met him there before the police arrived.

"Nice job, Boy Scout. Want some?" Devin asked, thrusting a bottle of Canadian Club whiskey in his face.

"No thanks, man," Gabriel replied, as they heard the peal of approaching police cruisers.

"Why not?" Devin queried, his face a contorted mask of surprise and puzzlement.

"I don't drink stolen booze," he stated matter-of-factly.

Devin scratched his cheek quizzically. "But you're okay breaking the store window?"

"Yeah. I don't mind sticking it to the man. But I won't steal."

"You're a funny one, Boy Scout. But you're alright in my books," Devin mused. "Now let's get outta here."

The area was soon bathed in pulsating crimson as the police entered the plaza's parking lot. Devin and Tank quickly cached their haul and crept to the southern edge of the park, away from the plaza. Suzy Q took Gabriel by the hand and led him across the baseball diamond to the eastern edge of the park. As they were crossing Elder Street to escape to the side streets beyond, a police cruiser barred their way, and an officer ordered them to freeze.

Boy, did he get an earful from his parents in the backseat of his father's banged-up old Buick as they liberated him from the police station at three o'clock in the morning! "What the Hell do you think you're doing?" his father raged at him through the rear-view mirror. His mother, sobbing pitifully, lamented, "My own son, handcuffed and fingerprinted like a common criminal!"

Fortunately, after hours of questioning and, even more jarring, the endless hours waiting all alone in the interrogation room, wondering what would happen next, expecting the worst, he had at last been released with a stern warning. They had accused him of robbing the store, to which he steadfastly maintained his innocence, which was technically true. Since his comrades had backed him up, and no-one had mentioned that it was he who had broken the window, the police elected not to press charges against him. But that didn't comfort his parents much.

They continued to heap warning after warning upon him, hoping to reach him. "My God, Gabriel! Now you're robbing liquor stores? What's wrong with you? Do you want to flush your life down the toilet?" his father yelled. His mother resorted to guilt, "Don't you even care what you're doing to us?"

"Aw, leave me alone! I didn't steal anything," he asserted defiantly.

"Even if you didn't, you're guilty by association! You shouldn't hang around with hoodlums!" Isaac thundered. "At any rate, I hope you've learned your lesson here. You can't be proud of yourself, almost going to jail like that."

Far from scaring him straight, though, Gabriel was completely unaffected by the ordeal with the police, or his parents' rant. He felt strangely exhilarated, heroic even, as if he had finally done something worthwhile in his life. How thrilling it had been! How his stomach had lurched into his mouth as he ran to the park while the alarm shrieked and the police arrived! Had he ever felt so alive? And the gang hadn't sold him out to the police. Who said there was no honour among thieves? His adventure confirmed him in the dubious path upon which he had embarked, the lively, exciting friends he had chosen to hang out with.

His bravura at the liquor store clinched his reputation with the gang. Not only had he proven his mettle by breaking the window, but he had also been a good soldier, hadn't ratted his colleagues out to the police. Paradoxically, they embraced him all the more because of his perverse principles, which allowed him to break in but not enjoy the stolen fruits of his labour. Boy Scout was alright with the rest of the Stoners. He was rewarded with a central place in the gang, which was unusual for someone a year behind most of the group.

As it turned out, the police had released all the Stoners, with the exception of Devin, due to a lack of evidence. Devin, however, had been doubly damned with fragments of glass in one of his shoes and fingerprints left on one of the bottles of spirits the police had recovered from their search of the park. Since he already had a criminal record, he was charged with break and entry and theft under $5,000. He did not return to school thereafter, creating a leadership void in the gang that, in short order, Suzy Q filled. That boded well for Gabriel, whom she now held in special esteem.

For the rest of the rest of academic year and into the summer, Gabriel spent an increasing amount of time with the Stoners, most evenings and weekends, during the afternoons at times when he cut classes, sometimes late at night, drinking, experimenting with different kinds of drugs, listening to psychedelic music. All the while, his grades continued to plummet and his struggle with his parents escalated.

One late summer day, while his parents were working, Gabriel spent the afternoon in Tank's backyard, getting high on marijuana. When he returned home, still in the throes of a euphoric high, inspiration struck him and he pulled out his violin. Convinced that he could actually see the music, he suddenly understood where he had fallen short before, how he could transform his sound. He played without inhibition, filtering out the distractions, pure music flowing from his limbs through the instrument, creating a brilliant sound unlike any that he had ever heard before, unlike even the greatest violinists had ever been able to achieve. Gabriel was exultant, believing he had finally attained the perfection he had striven for since he first picked up the instrument. It was music as God had intended it. In awe, he fetched his cassette recorder and performed the piece once again, with the same intensity, the same genius, to capture the perfection forever.

By the next morning, he had forgotten all about it. But as he was dressing, he noticed the tape on his desk and the memory came flooding back. With a tremor in his breath, he inserted the cassette into the recorder and pressed play, eager to witness the sublime beauty he had wrought. To his dismay, his outright horror, it was absolutely terrible. He had missed several notes. The tempo was off. The sound was awful. This was God's music? The faintest blossom of a doubt sprouted in his mind: *What am I doing to myself?* With a shudder, he brushed it aside, quickly erasing the cassette and shoving it into his desk drawer, as if by burying it as far as possible from the light he could hide his shame from the world.

On a drizzly night in early November, while his parents attended a Parent-Teacher Night at Mackenzie with his Grade 11 teachers, Gabriel and the Stoners assembled in Wilmington Park for an impromptu party. Someone brought a battery-operated boom box. Others furnished two cases of beer, a few bottles of whiskey, bags of chips and other snacks. Suzy Q supplied the narcotics and other drugs. Gabriel helped himself to a few generous swigs of whiskey and joined a group dancing on the tennis courts. The boombox was blaring Billy Idol's "Dancing with Myself," and Gabriel began to shake his limbs furiously to match the song's frenetic beat.

"Hey, Boy Scout! Time to try something new. I think you're ready for acid," Suzy Q announced, beckoning him to the skating rink, where she was distributing drugs to the group.

"Acid?" Gabriel asked dumbly, as he stumbled over to her, already feeling the effects of the alcohol.

Someone asked, "Are you sure the boy scout should take acid? He's had a lot to drink."

"He'll be fine," Suzy Q assured him. She licked her right forefinger, lifted it to Gabriel's mouth and parted his lips. With her left hand, she placed a small yellow tab under his tongue. "Just let it melt, Boy Scout," she advised him gently, as she let her hand slide casually across his cheek, the length of his neck, and then down his shirt stopping just below his belt. Already buzzed, Gabriel was unsure of how to respond.

Zero, a Stoner in Grade 12, grew impatient. "Hey! If you want to fuck him, then fuck him. But give *us* some of that shit, first!" he whined.

"Chill out! You'll get your turn," Suzy Q assured him.

"At what?" Zero asked lasciviously, making lurid gestures.

"If you behave, maybe both," she teased, with a promiscuous wink.

Once the tab dissolved, Gabriel propped his long, lanky body up on the wooden ledge surrounding the skating rink and sat watching Suzy Q distribute acid to the rest of the group while he waited for the drug to declare itself. Suzy Q made Gabriel uneasy. She had taken a shine to him since the liquor store heist the previous year. But to him, she was an enigma. Like both poles of a magnet, simultaneously attracting and repelling him. Her close-cropped, boyish hair, the unsightly nose ring, the tattoo on her right bicep of a rose penetrating a skull, all that was off-putting. Perhaps it was even designed to repulse. Yet she had a powerful charismatic mystique about her, an innate sensuality, that beguiled him. He couldn't make his mind up about her. She was perfectly unsettling.

At first, the LSD had no discernable effect on him. He remained on the ledge for a while, merely observing, recording the group dynamics, as the rain picked up its tempo. Over time, however, he became acutely aware of sounds and shapes that he had never paid attention to before. The sound of yellow. The shape of time. The weightlessness of his soul. A euphoria unlike any he had ever known washed over him like a tidal wave. He felt all powerful. Glorious. Invincible.

He stood up and strained his eyes to see, really *see*, the rain, which lashed at them with shards of purple glass, pulsating with energy drawn from some unseen power source. Each beat of his heart bathed the rain in a new and ever-changing panoply of shades.

Purple-gold. Purple-grey. Purple-green. Raging purple. Regal purple.

"I am Caesar!" he shouted triumphantly with all his might.

"Hail Caesar!" someone beside him answered.

"Hail Caesar!" Gabriel screamed again.

"Hail Caesar!" more voices joined in, in ecstasy.

"I am Caesar!"

"Hail Caesar!"

They lunged at their foes across the shimmering battlefield, pikes in hand, thrusting, shrieking, taunting, the neon grass beneath their feet metamorphosing, now coarse sand, now flaming coals, now blazing diamonds. Skewering their enemies, punishing them for their betrayal, righteously hacking their faithless limbs from their lifeless bodies.

"Death to the barbarians!" he screamed.

"Death! Death!" came the answering war cry.

As one, united, they overcame the small pockets of resistance that remained on the battlefield, saving the kingdom from the enemy. Their foes vanquished, they charged on screaming, revelling, thrusting to capture the splendiferous spoils of war.

Still the rain raked the world, like multi-coloured machine-gun fire, proclaiming their victory to all. Blue-grey, blue-magenta, blue-purple. Always purple. Royal purple.

"I am Caesar!"

"Hail Caesar!"

"Hail Caesar!"

"Hail Caesar!"

"AAAAAAAAHHHHHHH!!!!!" Gabriel screamed, a primal, elemental scream from the core of his being, pounding his chest with both fists, announcing his triumph, his majesty, his glory, his unlimited power.

In the midst of a deep, treacly sleep, a loud gurgling filled his ears. Amused, he languorously lifted an eyelid and was assaulted by bright light, by rust-coloured fabric. He slowly raised his hand to his eye to block the glare and waited for his eyes to adjust. *What? Where am I?* His head was still floating, but his first reconnaissance suggested that he was on a sofa. He pushed his arms down to lift himself up, but they brushed against soft skin. He focused his eyes with effort and discovered that there was a slumbering girl underneath him. With a jolt, he sat upright, making an effort not to disturb her. *Is that Suzy Q? No, she has curly purple hair and silver earrings depicting a snake wrapped around a cross. She's also quite short. Who is she?* The next instant, a tremor of panic shook him: both he and the girl were completely naked.

His brain was working slowly, its gears still impeded by the cobwebs of the previous night's revelry. *Did I have sex with her? How could that be? My first time was supposed to be special. What have I done?* He scrutinized her once again, hoping to remember who she was. His eyes fell upon a tattoo on her stomach of a fiery pitchfork, leaving no doubt about whose handiwork was at play. This was only the second time he had ever seen a naked woman in real life, and it was as shocking and disturbing as the first, perhaps more so.

He gently pushed himself off of the dormant girl and stood up, teetering unsteadily before finding his balance. Trying to clear the fog in his brain, he concentrated on the room around him. A large glass pane with colourful fish: neon blue, magenta, crimson, mauve, bright lights. *Still the effects of the drugs? No. An aquarium. So that's why I hear gurgling. It's the oxygen pump.* The room was carpeted and had small rectangular windows at the very top of the wall on one side. *A basement? I don't remember coming here. Where are my clothes?* He peered around the room but saw neither his nor the girl's clothing.

A bewildered rat in an unfamiliar maze, he stumbled out of the room into a dark narrow hallway, at the end of which was a staircase, four steps up, a small landing, and six more steps in the reverse direction, which brought him to a large hallway with hardwood floors. It was a large mansion, unlike any Gabriel had ever been in, even larger than Jack Silverman's house. He wandered into the kitchen at the far end in search of his clothing.

"For God's sake, put some clothes on!" He swiveled his head sharply to discover a strange middle-aged woman in a white bathrobe with curlers in her hair, whom he hadn't noticed upon entering. She was sitting at the table nursing a cup of coffee, an open newspaper in front of her, an exasperated look on her long, angular face.

"I... I don't know where they are...." he muttered in embarrassment, as he covered himself with his hands. Never in his life had he been so mortified.

With a harrumph, she stood and walked to the counter, where she extracted from a drawer a red and white cotton apron emblazoned with the maple leaf. "Cover yourself with this for now," she ordered, tossing it to him. Instinctively, he caught it with both hands, blushing purple when he realized that, in doing so, he had exposed himself to her for a second time.

"Relax," she said, a trace of a smile forming on her mauve lips, before rapidly disappearing, to be replaced by her scowl. "I've seen worse." He quickly fumbled with the apron, tying it awkwardly across his back. It hung down to his knees, covering the front adequately, but leaving his back open. Still, it was an improvement, for which he was grateful.

"Where... where am I?" he asked, bewildered and ashamed.

"Joey must have brought you here."

He considered this for a moment, then asked, "Who's Joey?"

"Oh, Joey often brings stoners here with her," the woman replied with obvious distaste.

"Can you help me find them," he asked pathetically. "I should get to school soon...."

"*School*? It's already three o'clock!"

A quick glance at the LED clock on the oven confirmed what she had said. Ten after three. Had he slept so long?

They split up and each checked different rooms on the main floor, each spacious and opulently furnished. Gabriel explored the stately living room and a smaller room that connected to it that appeared to be a library, both in vain, when he heard the woman calling him from the dining room.

"Are those your clothes on the trampoline?" she asked with contempt when he arrived.

"I guess they must be," he reasoned. "Thank you, Mrs....?"

"Ms." She corrected curtly. "Now get going. Just leave the apron on the trampoline when you're dressed. Turn right out the door, then right at the end of the block. Follow Maxwell all the way to Wilmington and you should find your way from there."

She ushered him through glazed French doors on the back wall of the dining room that opened onto an enormous backyard with its own oval-shaped swimming pool. Having lived his whole life in a cramped two-bedroom triplex apartment, Gabriel was amazed. It seemed palatial. Yet he was repulsed by it. *Who needs all this? A person isn't a better human being just because he has a lot of money or lives in a big house.* Not far from the pool was a trampoline with clothes and shoes scattered around and about, sopping wet and reeking of vomit. With a heavy heart, he separated his apparel from the girl's and dressed self-consciously, hoping that none of the neighbours was watching.

He followed the woman's directions to Wilmington Avenue and then, without any conscious plan, trudged toward his school, passing by the strangely-named synagogue once again. Shivering in his damp, fetid clothing, Gabriel berated himself for his behaviour, his choices. *What have I done? I don't even know that girl. Was it worth it? What am I even trying to prove by getting stoned like that?*

As he approached Mackenzie, Suzy Q, who had just left the school for the day, called to him from the other side of the street. "Hey, Boy Scout!" she hollered. "You were *awesome* last night, loverboy!" *What did she mean by that? Did I...? How many women did I...? Oh God, please help me!*

As she walked away in the other direction, she giggled, pirouetted gaily and yelled, "Hail Caesar!" His mortification was complete. He had sunk so low, had reached rock bottom.

When he returned home, both his parents were lying in ambush for him. Neither had slept much the night before and both had taken sick days from work to track Gabriel down. They were extremely agitated.

"Where the Hell *were* you all night?" his father screamed. "You may not care, but we were *worried* about you!" Isaac's face appeared haggard and drawn.

"Get off my case!" Gabriel covered his guilt, his shame, with belligerence.

"Isaac, wait! He looks awful. *Smells* awful," his mother protested. "Are you okay, Gabriel? You need to eat something? Your father's right, we were worried sick about you. But you shower and eat first. Then you explain yourself."

It occurred to Gabriel that he hadn't eaten a bite since the previous evening. He was ravenous. He grunted his assent to his mother's plan and jumped into the shower. Once he had washed off the trappings of the previous night's failure and put fresh clothing on, he sat down to a bowl of pea soup and a plate of goulash. Then he steeled himself for his parents' onslaught.

"The principal said you hang around with the druggies," Isaac raged. "Is that where you were last night?" It was more an accusation than a question.

Gabriel glared at his father. "I was with friends," he spat out.

"What kind of friends keep you out all night? We were so worried we called the police," Esther bawled. "Why didn't you call us to tell where you were?"

"I should have," Gabriel conceded. "I'm sorry."

"Were you taking drugs? Or drinking? Is that why you came in smelling like a toilet?" Isaac piled on.

"It's none of your business!"

"None of my business? You're only sixteen years old! It's illegal for you to drink and drugs are illegal at any age. We're your parents and if you break the law, *we're* responsible," Isaac reasoned.

Feeling cornered, Gabriel said nothing. His mother continued. "And what's with you at school? Your teachers say you're failing Math and getting D's in History and French. How can *you* be failing Math? You're always the top of your class. Why are you doing this to yourself?"

"It doesn't matter. I'll pass the year," he retorted.

"Why should you just *pass*? With a mind like yours, you should be winning prizes. Why aren't you trying anymore?" Esther asked plaintively, the worry lines burrowing into her large forehead.

"Aw, just leave me alone! I said I was sorry. I won't stay out all night again."

"Not good enough!" his father screamed. "From now on you can't be out of the house after 8PM unless you clear it with us first. And if we even get a hint of drugs or alcohol.... Well, then you'll be *really* sorry!"

Gabriel stormed off to his room and slammed the door.

Later, when his wife had retired for the night, Isaac entered Gabriel's room uninvited.

"I know you don't like me, don't respect me," he said quietly as his son stared at him stonefaced. "But I'm your *father* and I have to put my foot down for your own good."

"Why can't you just leave me alone?" Gabriel wailed.

"Do you know why? Because I'm your father and, though you spit on me, I *care* about you. You've got to make something of yourself. Don't throw away all that talent! Do you want to be like *me* in life? A *garbage man*?" Isaac challenged him.

Gabriel glared at his father with unbridled hatred in his steel-blue irises. "No, Dad. I don't want to be like *you*, at all."

His words hurt Isaac more than Gabriel could know. But his father merely replied, "Well then *do* something about it! Take *responsibility* for your life."

"Aw, Dad," Gabriel responded. "Don't freak out. Universities only care about your marks in Grades 12 and 13. What I'm doing now doesn't really matter."

"That's where you're *wrong*! You're on the wrong track. Your teachers think you're a screw-up. You're wasting your God-given talent. You always talk about God this and God that, like you're some kind of Goddamn prophet or saint. But you're throwing away everything God gave you! Does God want you to dull your brain with drugs like some kind of criminal?"

That got Gabriel's attention. Although he hated giving his father the last word, he sucked in his lower lip and said nothing.

"Now listen to me. You got two years left of high school. I can't afford to pay for university. So, if you want to go – and you damn well *should* want to go — you need to get a full scholarship. So turn yourself around. And *now*!"

Gabriel took his father's advice and his humiliating escapade the previous night to heart. While he retained his grievances against his father, he evinced a grudging respect for Isaac for the manner of his entreaty, for putting his son's well-being ahead of his own dignity. In Gabriel's eyes, it bordered on the heroic. Who knew that his father had that in him? And, Gabriel realized to his surprise, a college education was truly very important to him. The very next morning, Gabriel began his long climb back from the abyss.

He resolved not to take drugs ever again, to drink only in moderation. He committed himself to resurrecting his academic standing. Since he had fallen behind in most of his classes, he stayed up late for the next ten days reviewing his textbooks from grades 10 and 11 to catch up. Finally, recognizing that the Stoners had been a terrible influence on him, had brought him in contact with the criminal element and threatened to undermine the moral fibre that defined him, he decided to sever his ties with them, at least informally, by avoiding them and their hangout.

After school two weeks later, Gabriel found the Stoners lying in wait for him near the bus stop on Wilson Heights. They looked distinctly unhappy.

"Where ya been, Boy Scout?" Tank demanded with a menacing sneer.

"We missed you," Suzy Q added, a note of melancholy in her accusing tone.

Gabriel squirmed. He had been avoiding them because he didn't quite know how to explain to them that he was going straight. They had been good to him, in their own way, and now he was rejecting them. Betraying them. "I've been busy. I have a lot of schoolwork," he said as brightly as possible, but there was a nervous flutter to his voice.

"*Schoolwork?*" Suzy Q repeated derisively. "You've never cared much about *that* before."

"That's true," he admitted. "But my folks are on my case. They'll kill me if I fail out of school."

"Well, come out with us tonight," she said. "We've got some more acid."

"Thanks, but I really can't." After a short pause, he added, "I can't drink or take drugs anymore."

Someone said, "He thinks he's too good for us," with a fake British accent.

Tank shouted, "No-one quits the Stoners!"

Just then, someone grabbed his arms from behind and pinned them behind his back. "Hey!" Gabriel shouted, struggling to break free as Tank punched him repeatedly, mercilessly, in the stomach.

After a few vicious blows, Suzy Q said, "Hey, don't go too hard on him, guys." Tank hit him twice more, then threw him to the ground, where he lay writhing in pain, breathing laboriously. "You guys go to the park. I'll catch up with you soon."

She kneeled on the sidewalk beside him in her faded black denims and stroked his cheek gently. "Sorry about that," she said simply. "Couldn't give you special treatment." She suddenly leaned toward him and kissed him full on the mouth, pressing her hand tenderly against his groin. "I'm gonna miss you, Boy Scout. You have an *awesome* dick," she whispered gently in his ear, before sighing, clambering to her feet and walking away.

In terrible pain, battling to catch his breath, Gabriel called out weakly after her, "Suzy, did we...?" The cloudy sky above him was swirling.

She spun around in surprise, her mouth curling in anger, pain bleeding from her eyes. "You mean you don't *remember?*" she sputtered.

"I... I was really high. I don't remember much." He muttered apologetically.

"Well, it didn't mean much to me *either*, you fucking *yid*!" she snarled. He could see her struggling against her tears as she charged at him and kicked him savagely in his stomach with the metal tip of her Kodiak work boot.

As she stormed away in anger, in humiliation, he kept repeating weakly, pathetically, "I'm sorry.... I'm really sorry...."

At the end of Math class the following week, Gabriel's teacher distributed the most recent exam he had graded. Instead of returning Gabriel's, he withheld it, saying, "Klein, please see me after class."

When all the students had cleared out, a time-consuming process involving bag retrieval, opening and closing desktops, conversations about the upcoming basketball tournament and a few bars of Kim Mitchell's *Patio Lanterns*, Gabriel approached his teacher's desk. "Yes, Mr. Graham?" he asked nervously. "You wanted to see me?"

"That's right, Klein. Cheating is a very serious offence. You obviously cheated on the midterm," Mr. Graham said sternly.

"What? No sir, I didn't cheat," Gabriel assured him.

The teacher perused Gabriel's exam, running his hand through his thinning white hair. In the silence of the otherwise empty classroom, Gabriel heard the loud stroke of the clock above the blackboard. It was one of those round white classroom clocks without a second hand, whose minute hand clicked sonorously to announce the passing of each minute.

"You got a perfect score. The only perfect score in the whole class. Now tell me how a stoner who got a 57% on the first test and a 42% on the second, who barely passed Grade 10 Math, suddenly turns into Carl Friedrich Gauss. Who'd you copy off?"

"I didn't, sir," Gabriel replied, deciding it was wiser not to point out that, if no-one else in the class had a perfect exam, his wouldn't have been perfect either if he had copied someone else's paper. "I've just.... I'm turning myself around. I've always been good at Math. I just stopped applying myself. This time... I studied. I did all my homework."

The teacher stared at him dubiously, narrowing his bushy white eyebrows. "Yeah.... I'm sorry, but I don't buy that, Klein. I'm going to have to report this to the principal," he said.

"Test me now," Gabriel suggested. "I can prove that I know the material."

"Alright," Mr. Graham said thoughtfully, glancing at his watch. He pulled two difficult problems out of his instructor's manual and told Gabriel to solve them on the board. Gabriel sucked in his lower lip and got to work immediately. Within fifteen minutes, he had found the correct answers, following the proper steps and using the correct formulae.

"Well I'll be damned...." Mr. Graham exclaimed, shaking his head. "Listen. If you're serious about turning over a new leaf, maybe I can help you. You realize that you're not in the advanced Math section right now, don't you? If you're really that good at Math, I can help you move up. Are you willing to do some extra work?"

"Really, sir? That'd be wonderful! Thank you!"

"Just don't disappoint me, okay Klein? You only get one second chance," Mr. Graham said as he handed Gabriel back his exam.

True to his word, Mr. Graham made rehabilitating Gabriel his pet project. For several weeks, he gave Gabriel extra homework and material. Every Monday, he gave of his own time to tutor the boy and administer tests. By April, halfway through the second semester, he determined that Gabriel was ready and took Gabriel to plead his case to Ms. Kang, the Mathematics Co-ordinator. While it was unusual to make a move so late in the term, Ms. Kang agreed to administer a placement test, which

Gabriel aced. As a result, the following morning he started the enriched Math class.

But Mr. Graham didn't stop there. He touted Gabriel's transformation to the principal and the other teachers at school. While one or two were skeptical – "Could a leopard really change its spots like that," Mrs. Leszychyn asked pointedly – most were positively elated to celebrate the prodigal son. By the start of Grade 12, Gabriel was placed in not only the enriched Math sections, but also enriched English, History, French, and Chemistry. In addition, he had earned a prominent spot on Mackenzie's *Reach for the Top* inter-collegiate quiz team.

His work ethic had transformed entirely during these few months. Without any friends to speak of or any social commitments, he went home every night to hit the books. His mission was to regain his status as a class leader after a year-and-a-half as shiftless laggard.

His parents marvelled at his new attitude, rejoiced at his metamorphosis. Even his relationship with them improved. The open hostility with which he had assaulted them for many years dissipated, to be replaced by civility and toleration. On weekends, they even occasionally enjoyed family activities together, playing *Risk*, taking walks, going skating. Of course, they were unable to recapture the joyous, loving relationship, the family harmony they had once enjoyed. For, once shorn of its precious petals, who can put the rose back together? But it was still progress.

Early on in Grade 12, Gabriel's academic rebirth led to a social breakthrough. The dominant student in several of his enriched classes was a girl named Jennifer Levenson. Fiercely intelligent, extremely competitive, she had earned a reputation throughout Grades 10 and 11 as the smartest student in class. Gabriel's emergence as an academic force put that title in question.

Acknowledging each other as kindred spirits, the pair became fast friends and fierce competitors. Both possessed powerful, flexible minds, allowing them to excel in all fields of study. If anything, Jennifer was the stronger of the two in the maths and sciences, whereas Gabriel's writing ability and skill in the social sciences and languages was unmatched. But they constantly jockeyed with each other for primacy, all the while studying together, introducing each other to their favourite music and television programmes, sharing their hopes and dreams. It didn't hurt that they partook of similar religious views. Both were traditionally Jewish. Jennifer attended a Conservative synagogue, although she was more observant than most of her fellow congregants, electing not to drive on the Sabbath or holidays. Although the Kleins attended an Orthodox synagogue, they were less observant than most, with laxer standards of Sabbath observance and kosher dietary laws. So Jennifer and Gabriel, meeting in the middle, had much in common. At long last, since he split with Jack in Grade 9, Gabriel had a close friend.

But Jennifer also had a large entourage that she welcomed Gabriel into: Aziz Shirazi, an Iranian-born student, whose passion was Physics; Selma Phillips, who adored the social sciences and dreamed of becoming Canada's first female prime minister; Lauren Resnick, who possessed an encyclopedic mind and could recite all the digits of pi up to the first seventy-five decimal points; and Steve Sheiner, who was not especially gifted academically, but who loved hanging around the brighter students, especially Jennifer. For the final two years of high school, these would be Gabriel's constant companions, the group of friends who shared his interests, his passions, his ambitions. What a distance he had travelled since slumming around with the Stoners!

"I'm going to *cr-r-r-ush* you, Jew-boy!"

Gabriel grinned. It was drizzling softly as he and Jennifer walked back from school to Jennifer's family bungalow in Bathurst Manor to do their homework together. Final exams were only a month away and the two friendly rivals, as they had all year, were jockeying for the best grades in their classes, challenging each other, jousting with one another, to bring out their best, each hoping to finish just far enough ahead to secure bragging rights. Jennifer reinforced her bold declaration with a hand gesture, showing her curved fingers slowly, powerfully crushing what could be imagined to be Gabriel's skull.

"Not a chance, Jew-witch. You're so-o-o going *down*!" Gabriel retorted.

Having each endured antisemitic slurs at various times in their public school careers, it was their private joke to taunt each other in this manner. To subvert their humiliation. To acknowledge their pain but avenge themselves by working harder and excelling where others fell short, a time-honoured Jewish strategy.

"You talk a great game, Gabriel, but you haven't beaten me yet," Jennifer said, as she turned into the driveway of her home. Gabriel admired her father's sleek, grey Lincoln Continental, which looked a damn sight better than the Klein's battered old Buick.

"What do you mean?" he asked, raising his shoulders. "I beat you on the History paper last term, on the Geography midterm, in English...."

"Oh, *those* don't matter. I mean where it really counts. In math or science," she said playfully, eliciting a groan from him.

They climbed the five stairs to her front porch. Jennifer pulled out her key, but the door was already unlocked. Several pairs of shoes clogged the entrance hall. A fabric softener jingle blared from the television down the hall. Jennifer conducted a brief scouting mission before returning to report.

"Hmmm.... Looks like a full house. My parents are both home today and watching TV in the den. My sister Karen's monopolizing the living room. I guess we can work in my room," she suggested. She led him through the kitchen, down a narrow corridor to a fair-sized room with a blonde wooden desk and chair to the right of the door, a large blonde dresser and armoire to the left and a twin bed with a white, daffodil-patterned duvet under the window on the far side. A poster of Bruce Springsteen in concert dominated the wall above her desk. A large cloth sunflower in a tall, psychedelic vase presided over her dresser. The aroma of lavender permeated the room. "Let me see.... I have Math to do, so I'm going to need to write on the desk. What are you doing?"

"Uh, I guess I'm going to study for my Geography test," Gabriel answered, a little overwhelmed by the undisguised femineity of her room.

"Well, then you can work on the bed."

"On your bed? Uh, okay," he consented, placing himself gingerly on the edge of the foot of the bed, tossing his school bag next to him. He had never been on a girl's bed before, at least not since he was a child, and it felt like a protocol violation to him, a trespass.

"Go ahead! Spread out! Make yourself comfortable," she instructed. "You're not gonna be able to work all bunched up on the corner like that."

As they worked, Jenny peered over at Gabriel on the bed from time to time. After a while, she kicked off her burgundy docksiders and propped her bare feet up on her desk as she leaned back, exposing the length of her creamy, fit legs from above the knee on down. She continued to gaze in his direction periodically, but he was too engrossed in his notes to notice.

"How's it going?" Jennifer asked casually, brushing her blonde hair away from her ear with her hand.

Gabriel looked up from his notebook. "Huh? Oh, okay I guess." Back went his nose into his studies.

She ran her finger slowly along her left leg and tried again. "So, do you know where you're going to apply for university yet?" she asked with exaggerated nonchalance.

"Well, yeah," he said, still bent over his work, his fingers slowly scratching his pantleg thoughtfully. "I want to go to U. of T. I guess I'll apply to York and McMaster, too. But if I get a full scholarship at U. of T., that's where I'm going."

"Not UBC?" she asked, making no effort to conceal her disappointment. "It would be so cool if we could be together for university, too."

He finally put his notebook down on the bed. "Why do you want to go there so badly?" he asked. Ever since he joined Jennifer's group, all she could talk about was enrolling in the University of British Columbia after graduation. Gabriel liked the idea of the group staying together in Toronto, but Jennifer's heart was set on Vancouver. It made him sad whenever he thought about it. He had finally found a group of friends to which he truly belonged. But that was over a year away, so he usually just pushed it out of his mind.

"Oh, lots of reasons," she explained. "We went to Vancouver on vacation once and I just fell in love with it. The mountains. The ocean. It's so green and beautiful! I'll be honest: I've never found Toronto very pretty." Again she patted her hair away from her ear and rubbed her right calf with the bottom of her left heel.

"Really? I've always liked Toronto. But I suppose I haven't been anywhere else. Maybe Montreal once or twice when I was young.... Cottage country." He shrugged his shoulders. "So you'd move to Vancouver just because it's a pretty city?"

"Well, yeah. I would.... But it's not my only reason. Not even the main reason. I really just need to get away from *here*." She pointed at the walls.

"You don't get along with your family?" he asked wide-eyed. Her family seemed the epitome of warmth and harmony.

"On the contrary. I love my family. But I find them stifling. My parents are bigwigs in this city. You know.... My mom is a well-known medical researcher, a Fellow of the Royal Society of Canada.... Everything she's set her mind to, she's achieved. And surpassed. My dad's a city councillor. His name's been on signs all over the city. He wants to run for provincial office one day. Everybody knows them. They're wonderful people, but it's kind of hard to be *me* around them."

"What do you mean?" he asked.

"You see, I've been pretty successful at school. I'm always the top of the class. I've won awards, science fairs. Next year I'm going to be class valedictorian...."

"Salutatorian," Gabriel corrected.

She wrinkled her nose, stuck her tongue out and repeated, "*Valedictorian*. But it's always expected. I'm Sam and Rhoda's daughter. Of course, I'd do well. It's never *my* success. It's theirs."

"So you need to get out from under their shadow," he suggested.

"In Vancouver, nobody's heard of Sam and Rhoda Levenson. Everything I achieve would be my own. My own.... I really want that.... And I *always* get what I want," she declared boldly, fixing him with her intense green eyes.

"That makes sense, I guess," he conceded, picking up his notebook again.

"No-one gives it to me. I *earn* it. Even if I have to wait for it...." she said wistfully.

"You'll only have to wait a year or so," he said, as he thrust his head back in his books. "But you *still* won't be valedictorian."

Jennifer sighed, pulled her legs off the desk and resumed working on her Math problems.

***

A few days later, on Friday night, the Klein's were sitting down to their Sabbath meal and catching up on the week's events. After reciting the blessings over the wine and the *challah*, the traditional braided egg bread, Isaac brought out a tureen of chicken soup from the kitchen to serve them.

"Ah," Gabriel grunted approvingly. "You can't beat Mom's chicken soup."

Esther sighed. No doubt she appreciated the compliment, but would rather have been respected for something other than her cooking. Isaac ladled some soup into her bowl first, then proceeded to serve Gabriel and himself.

"Did you hear about Manny Kalman?" she asked.

"What about him?" Isaac replied with a question.

"He's in the hospital again."

"Again?" Isaac repeated, shovelling a spoonful of soup into his mouth. "Didn't he just get out?"

"A few months ago, yes," Esther said. "But it sounds serious. They think it's...." She lowered her voice and whispered "Cancer," as if it were a contagious disease that one spread by speaking its name out loud.

"Oy vay!" Isaac exclaimed. "He's such a nice fellow."

They ate in silence for a few minutes, accompanied by the loud ticking of the octagonal dining room wall clock, framed in walnut. Esther drained her soup and lustily began sucking the marrow out of a large chicken bone.

Isaac turned to Gabriel with an eager grin. "So, Mr. Genius, how was your week? You got results to tell us about?" he inquired.

This question, which his father asked him in almost the same manner each week, grated on Gabriel's nerves, like rubbing his hand on sandpaper. But, over time, he had begun to understand that his father revelled in his academic success because he himself had never had the opportunity to develop academically. The son of poor immigrants, Isaac had been compelled to work throughout high school to assist the family. University was out of the question, as Isaac had required a steady stream of income to help support his parents and begin his own life. But he always held academics in high esteem and, now that he and Gabriel had largely reconciled, he derived a vicarious pleasure in Gabriel's successes. Of course, that meant that Gabriel's irresponsible behaviour at the start of high school had been like a dagger in Isaac's throat.

"Fine, Dad," Gabriel responded grudgingly. "No new grades. I'm getting ready for finals now and am plugging away on my Geography report."

"What's it about?" Esther asked.

"Urbanization."

"Urbanization?" Isaac repeated. "People moving into the cities from the country, right?" He was always eager to show that, although he was a manual labourer, he could hold his own weight intellectually.

"Yes," Gabriel nodded approvingly. "I'm focusing on the role of technology. How industrialization pushed people out of the farms and into the cities, where the factories were, while transportation technologies such as the automobile created a suburban residential ring around an industrial and commercial urban core."

"You see, Esty. Our son is gonna be a genius!" Isaac deadpanned. "The University of Toronto is going to come *begging* for him to go there."

Gabriel shuddered. "Actually, Dad, I wanted to ask you something. What do you think of me putting in an application to UBC, too, next year."

"UBC? You mean British Columbia? Why would you want to do that?" his father inquired skeptically.

"Well, I don't mean I necessarily want to go there," Gabriel said craftily. "But it's a really good school and some of my friends are going to apply there. So, I thought it wouldn't be a bad idea to apply there, as well as U. of T."

Isaac mulled this over while he cleared the bowls and brought in the main course. Esther, however, was quick to find fault. "Vancouver's so far away! We'd never see you," she complained. He was about to argue, but she continued, "And there aren't as many Jews as Toronto. You'd be so isolated."

Isaac, who had been eavesdropping from the kitchen, returned laden with a Corningware casserole of chicken paprikash. Placing it on a trivet near Esther's plate, he opined, "Mom's right. More importantly," Isaac said, looking down at his upended, calloused palms, "I don't have the money to send you there. If you get a full scholarship in Toronto, you can live with us. If you're in Vancouver, even with a full scholarship, I can't pay for an apartment or plane tickets. We wouldn't be able to manage. Why not just do Toronto?"

"Yeah, I guess that makes sense," Gabriel agreed. "It was just an idea anyway." In truth, the idea of committing himself to a faraway city that he had never been to seemed a bit daunting to him anyway. Still, it was too bad that he'd be separated from his best friend in a year. He tucked into the chicken leg that his father placed on his plate and listened to his mother's complaints about the poor manners of the customers in the cafeteria she worked in.

Over the summer, with Jenny's help, Gabriel secured employment through the school as a tutor for students taking remedial courses. It was an ideal summer job because it paid a high hourly wage, but he was only needed for about fifteen hours each week. This meant that he had sufficient free time and capital to enjoy the summer. This he took advantage of to get together with the group of friends that he developed during the year.

Popularity was a new experience for Gabriel. He had always been more of a loner, with few friends. Even when he was valued by the Stoners, he remained at the margins of the group, a hanger-on rather than a core member. Now, however, Jennifer placed him front and centre, included him, consulted him on everything. And, by virtue of her status as the sun around which the rest of the group orbited, her esteem made them defer to him as only a slightly lesser luminary, a Joseph to her Pharaoh.

Jennifer herself had become a permanent fixture of his summer. In addition to group activities – parties, watching videos at Steve's house, miniature golf, a Sunday at Centre Island – she was omnipresent on the telephone, meeting him for Slurpees at Seven Eleven, shopping with him at Yorkdale after work. She even had a knack for turning up, often unexpectedly, wherever he was: outside the classroom where he tutored, at the bus stop, at the video arcade. It was like the good old days with Jack, from whom he had been inseparable. They were together so often, like Siamese twins, that Esther inquired with the expectant grin that only a mother can sport, whether Jennifer was Gabriel's girlfriend. Gabriel laughed dismissively, explaining that she was his new Jack, his new best friend, nothing more.

One project Gabriel set for himself over the summer was to build a birthday present for Isaac. He had excelled at an after-school woodworking course he had enrolled in over the previous semester and decided to try his hand at making something practical. Isaac continued to tend his little garden lovingly, but was frustrated year after year by the attrition rate in his war against neighbourhood squirrels. Before he could enjoy his meagre harvest, the charcoal grey pests would carry off the best of the lot, leaving him with little to show for his labour but a few scrawny tomatoes and peppers.

Using his father's saw, hammer, screwdriver, and some lumber and wire he procured from a building store, Gabriel constructed a wood-framed wire cover for the garden. It was far from perfect, and the squirrels were eventually able to stretch the wire, gnaw away at the wood with their sharp incisors to gain entry. But Isaac was over the moon with his gift. Nothing Gabriel could have given him would have pleased him more, and the gift went a long way toward solidifying the new footing that their relationship found itself on.

For two weeks in mid-August, Gabriel's cousin Adina visited by Voyageur bus from Montreal and stayed with the Kleins. Since Esther and Isaac worked during the days, it fell to Gabriel to entertain her, a task that he complained about before her arrival, but thoroughly enjoyed once she appeared. He had remembered her from the last time he had seen her several years earlier, when the one-year age difference between them had proved a formidable barrier. As a result, he was initially reluctant to be saddled with his "baby" cousin. As it turned out, she was now rather good company and was herself eager to be shown around by her older, in her estimation "hunky," cousin.

Gabriel acted as tour-guide-in-chief for his cousin and accompanied her to such attractions as the Exhibition, the Science Centre, and a Blue Jay game, all of which he was able to splurge on courtesy of his tutoring wages. One afternoon, as they were emerging from the Yorkdale cinema, where they had just watched *A Fish Called Wanda*, they ran into Jennifer, with her uncanny knack for being in the right place at the right time. Gabriel and Adina were laughing heartly, recalling scenes from the film.

"I nearly lost it when that family walked in on Archie while he was dancing naked," Adina said, grabbing onto Gabriel's arm.

"Gabriel?" Jennifer called, surprised to see him.

"Jenny! What are you doing here?" he responded jovially. "Hey, there's someone I'd like you to meet. Adina, this is Jenny."

"Nice to meet you," Adina said pleasantly. "I've heard a lot about you."

"Likewise, I'm sure," Jenny harumphed, throwing a disapproving glance at Adina's gaudy, bright orange tee shirt.

"Hey, Jenny. We're gonna hang around the mall for a bit. Want to join us?" Gabriel asked.

"I'd love to, but I've got to go," Jenny replied quickly. "See you around," she said, before adjusting the Stiches bag over her shoulder and rushing off to the subway.

A few days later, after the completion of the Sabbath, Gabriel brought Adina to Maven's, a kosher fast food restaurant on Bathurst which served as a hangout for Jewish teens on Saturday nights. After gobbling down their burgers and fries, they were heading for the exit when Jennifer walked in.

"Jenny!" Gabriel exclaimed. "Good to see you!"

Jennifer's eyes brightened on seeing Gabriel, but when she noticed Adina nearby, she scowled, the left side of her lip encroaching upon her nose, her chin drooping. "Oh, hello," she muttered icily.

Gabriel wondered what had gotten into her. "Do you want us to wait for you?" he asked.

"No," Jennifer responded curtly. "I'll see you on Monday, I guess."

As they settled into the back of the number 7 bus for the ride home, Adina asked, "What's eating your friend, Jenny? She seems like a real bitch!"

"I really don't know. She's not normally like that. She must be mad at me for something, but I'll be damned if I know what I did," Gabriel replied, scratching his temple. He couldn't figure out what Jennifer's problem was. She wasn't the type of girl who was mean or blew hot and cold. It was completely out of character. He decided that he would call her on it the next time he saw her.

***

The following Monday, when Gabriel finished his tutoring hours, he waited outside the classroom where Jennifer was tutoring. As she emerged from her session, he pulled her aside. "Jenny, we need to talk," he announced.

"Where's your girlfriend?" she asked moodily, buckling the strap on her bag.

"Girlfriend? What girlfriend?" Gabriel was perplexed.

"You know. That Adina girl," she shot back. "The one you've been gallivanting around town with."

"You mean my cousin? She went back to Montreal. She was only here for two weeks," he told her, as they drifted down the hallway, past the lockers on both sides.

Her face lit up and she stopped just short of the main door. "Your *cousin*? Right! You mentioned that your cousin was coming to town. I just.... I thought your cousin was a he, not a she.... Oh, it's too bad I didn't have a chance to talk to her," Jennifer said.

Gabriel gaped at her wide-eyed, his shoulders easing backward. "Well, you *did*, but you practically bit her head off! What was that all about?"

Jennifer laughed giddily. "Oh, I'm sorry. I was...." She hesitated for a moment, then lowered her voice to just above a whisper. "Well... if you *must* know, I had my period, and was in a really bitchy mood. I'm *really* sorry. Please apologize to her for me."

Embarrassed, Gabriel scratched his head. Her *period*? I don't want to know about *that!* Boy, he thought, women are really complicated!

On a Sunday in mid-September, in Gabriel's Grade 13 year, he spent the afternoon at the Sheiner residence helping Steve with his Physics homework. Steve was having problems concentrating and appeared distracted by the glorious foliage swaying gracefully in the breeze outside the dining room window.

"Hey, Steve," Gabriel said, mildly irritated, "You need to focus. You're never going to understand inertia if you don't concentrate."

His classmate turned away from the window, his furrowed brow and narrowed eyes revealing the agony eating away at him. "So, what exactly *is* intertia?"

"Whoa! You mean you don't even understand the basic concept?" Gabriel asked with a distinct lack of tact.

"Not really," his friend admitted, his gaze returning to the window.

"Well," Gabriel began, "the idea is that objects will stay in the state they're in unless some outside force acts upon them."

"So a pizza in New York will stay in New York unless someone drives it to New Jersey?" Steve quipped, adjusting his spectacles.

"Basically...." Gabriel laughed politely. "But seriously, an object at rest is going to stay at rest unless some outside force — perhaps gravity, perhaps applied force, perhaps magnetism — acts upon it, making it move. An object in motion stays in motion, until a force like friction slows it down and stops it. You follow?"

"Yeah. Sort of.... I guess...."

"Now inertia is related to mass. So, in principle, the greater the mass of the object, the greater a force you'll need to change its state," Gabriel explained, twirling a dull yellow pencil between the forefinger and middle finger of his right hand.

"Yes, I guess it makes sense," Steve conceded. "But give me a practical example."

"Well...." said Gabriel, drawing out the word, "So it will take Superman to stop a train in motion, whereas I can manage to catch a baseball."

"Hey, that's *my* kind of Physics!" Steve declared with a grin. His smile evaporated quickly, though, and he returned to brooding out the window while Gabriel continued the lesson. Finally, having reached a difficult and noble decision, he blurted out, "You know that Jenny likes you, don't you?"

"Huh?" Gabriel muttered distractedly. "Yeah, I like her, too. She's my best friend."

"No, I mean *adores* you. Is completely *gaga* over you. Don't you see the way she looks at you?"

Gabriel looked at him quizzically. "I never really noticed. We're just good friends."

"Listen Gabriel, it's hard for me to say this to you. I wish she'd look at *me* that way. I've done everything I could over the last few years to get her to see *me* that way. But it's *you* she wants, not *me*," Steve said wistfully, almost choking up in the process. "You should go get her."

Gabriel saw the wound in his friend's dark eyes and realized what it had cost him to say what he did. He put his hand on Steve's shoulder. "You're a good guy, Steve. One of the best," he said. "I think Jenny's terrific. In every way. But I wouldn't want to ruin our friendship by trying to be something else. I'm sure you still have a chance with her." Steve looked at him dubiously through his thick aviator lenses and turned a page in his Physics notebook.

After that conversation, Gabriel began to pay attention to Jenny, to notice her – really notice her. He observed the sparkle in her eyes when she smiled, the way her ash-blond hair fell over her ears, how it rippled when she spoke. He noticed her slender body, her silky, supple neck, her graceful arms, how appealing her torso was in a tight, low-cut sweater, how cute and dainty her knees were when she wore a short skirt. *Why did I never notice her body before? She's quite pretty.*

He watched her intently in History class, when she gave a presentation on the plight of labourers during the Industrial Revolution. On the surface, she looked so confident, yet he observed with growing interest the subtle signposts of a more self-conscious, vulnerable girl that she tried to conceal. The way she nervously touched her hair periodically, as if she feared that someone might catch her in disarray. The reddish flush on the triangle of skin that her blouse revealed below her neck, just above the swell of her bosom. How she nibbled on her right pinky as she took questions from the teacher and the class. All of this made his heart flutter.

Most of all, he verified that Steve had been right, that she carried a torch for him that Niagara Falls couldn't extinguish. With his newfound attentiveness, he could hear her heart beat more rapidly whenever he entered the room, could see the colour rush to her face, could taste her palpable longing. Once, when they were walking to the bus stop with Aziz after school, her hand accidentally brushed against his. He could feel the electric tremor of embarrassed excitement in her skin, her nerves, as she quickly pulled away. He could sense her eyes on him, following him, boring into his back, whenever he looked away. All this awakened the germ of an idea in Gabriel, a possibility. *Why not?*

After all, Gabriel reasoned, *perhaps that's what love is, what separates it from lust. With other girls, like Lisa Ross, I was all hot and bothered by her. I was so excited, I didn't know how to act. But with Jenny, it's not like that. It's like we belong together. Like we were carved out of the same gnarled branch.*

On Chanukah, Jenny invited the gang to her house to kindle the candles and then study for their upcoming exams. She and her mother had prepared *latkes*, the traditional fried potato pancakes, and they made a party of it, together with Jenny's family. It was a pyromaniac's delight, as each member of the Levenson family had a dedicated *menorah*, each crowned with four candles to commemorate the fourth night of the holiday, together with a helper candle, the *shamash*. Each of the Levensons partnered with one of Jenny's friends: Mr. Levenson lit with Selma. Jenny's mother, Dr. Levenson, shared her *menorah* with Aziz. Jenny's two sisters partnered with Lauren and Steve. Jenny elected to light her *menorah* with Gabriel. As they sang together in the dark, by the glow of the tiny flecks of flame, Gabriel was overcome by a sense of peace and belonging, a sense of togetherness, that he had not experienced since he was a young child.

"I don't think my parents would ever have imagined that I would be celebrating Honika," Aziz said.

"Well, we're glad to have you with us, Aziz," Dr. Levenson said. "You're the best candle-lighting partner I've ever had."

"Hey, I heard that!" her husband complained, feigning injury.

"Oh, you're pretty good too, Sam. Now bring out the *latkes*, will you!"

"Yes, dear," he responded, bringing his fingers to his forehead in a mock military salute. He disappeared into the kitchen, returning shortly thereafter with a steaming plate of the golden pancakes and a frosted jug of lemonade.

"Great, Dad," Jenny said, her voice dripping with sarcasm, "but how are we going to eat these without forks?"

"Oh, come on! We've all got fingers. Dig in, everybody!" her father commanded.

And they did. Within minutes they polished off the stack of *latkes* sponging off their greasy hands on the napkins that Jenny's sister, Rachel, fetched from the kitchen.

"Wow!" Selma, observed, "Honika has a different vibe than Christmas. It feels... I dunno... less formal."

"It really depends," Dr. Levenson explained. "Some people are much more formal, more rigid. We just like to go with the flow here. I'm sure people celebrate Christmas in different ways, too."

While watching the proceedings as both participant and observer, Gabriel marvelled at how far he had travelled in a few short years. He had begun his high school career in a dystopian spiral, a freefall to oblivion, a social outcast drowning in a sea of alienation. And here he was, at the pinnacle, surrounded by a wonderful group of friends, celebrating the most beautiful, most harmonious Chanukah he had ever experienced. It made him feel tender, almost brought tears to his eyes. And it was Jenny who made it all possible.

Later that evening, while they were reviewing their Chemistry notes, he found himself alone with Jenny in her room when the others raided the kitchen for a snack. Still high on the afterglow of the Chanukah celebration, he decided to seize the moment.

"Jenny," he said to distract her from her floral covered spiral notebook.

"Mmmm?" she said absently.

"Do you want to go to a movie on Saturday night?"

"I don't know. Maybe," she said perfunctorily. "Let's ask everyone else when they get back."

"That's not what I mean, Jenny.... I mean just you and me."

She wrenched her head up from her notebook quickly, unable to conceal her rapid intake of breath. "You mean... like a date?"

"Why not?" he asked. "Why not...."

Looking back at that night years later, he realized it was the only time he was ever at ease asking a girl out on a first date. The only time without that nervous, feverish seasickness in his stomach. The only time he was certain of her response.

Jenny borrowed her father's car and picked him up. The movie they chose, *Mississippi Burning*, was playing at Yorkdale.

Their conversation in the car was stilted, as neither of them was certain quite how to act. Were they the close friends they had always been, or was this something else? When they reached the cinema, the awkwardness continued. At the cash, Jenny reached for her wallet uncertainly, but Gabriel insisted on paying. Reluctantly, she consented.

Once inside the screening room, Gabriel naturally gravitated toward the front, where he usually sat. It hadn't occurred to him that she might like to sit elsewhere. As he approached the second row, the hesitation in her eyes, visible even in the dim lighting, stopped him in his tracks.

"Where do you want to sit?" he whispered.

"Anywhere's fine," she replied non-commitally.

"No, seriously," he insisted. "Where do you usually sit?"

Once again, she hesitated. Before she reined it in, her head briefly inclined toward the back of the room. But then she said with an uncharacteristically weak, almost squeaky voice, a feeble smile, "Up front is fine."

"Hey, Jenny! Please be honest with me. Always. Don't worry about me. I want you to be happy. Do you want to sit in the middle, in the back? I'm just happy to be here with *you*," Gabriel said earnestly. A woman at the end of the first row grinned and needled her husband, "Now *that's* how you talk to a lady." Gabriel blushed. The husband threw Gabriel a look of exaggerated offence, as if to say, "You see what I have to put up with? Now look what you've done!"

Jenny smiled and relaxed visibly. "Well, if you don't mind, I prefer to watch movies from the back of the theatre," she declared. "I get dizzy if I sit too close."

"The back it is," Gabriel conceded graciously with a slight nod of the head, as they began the climb to the top of the cinema, where they installed themselves in the centre of the back row. They removed their heavy winter coats and placed them on the seat next to Jenny, hoping that no-one would want to sit there.

With the coming attractions advertised on-screen, Gabriel confronted his next dilemma. Should he drape his arm around her shoulders, or would that be too forward, too awkward? *Gosh*, he thought, *why can't there be a handbook for dating your best friend?* He opted not to, but then feared that would appear too stand-offish, too uncaring. So, he lifted his arm to slide it around her just as she was leaning in to whisper something to him, resulting in a brisk elbow to her cheek.

"Oh, I'm so sorry! Are you alright?" he blurted out too loudly, garnering angry glares from the spectators in the next row.

Jenny laughed nervously, pulling her hand from the offended cheek. "Oh, it's nothing. I'm fine."

Chastened by his clumsiness, he refrained from another attempt and settled in to enjoy the movie, hoping he wasn't causing any offence. The film, about two white FBI agents investigating the disappearance of three civil rights volunteers in 1960s Mississippi, was not typically first-date fare. The racism and violence it depicted disturbed them, and they emerged from the theater in sullen frames of mind.

Rather than going out for coffee after the movie, Jenny suggested that they finish the night at Marky's kosher delicatessen for a late dinner. The restaurant, which tended to be busy on Saturday nights, was packed on this night with teenagers, university students and middle-aged couples all seeking a post-Sabbath deli-fix. Gabriel and Jenny had to wait in the drafty entranceway for over forty-five minutes for a table. Once seated, they chewed over the movie.

"I think the most powerful scene for me," Jennifer commented while twirling her fork in her hand, "was the rally. You know, where the townspeople brought their children to hear the Klan leader speak that horrible rot about black people and Jews. It really brought home Pell's wife's observation that hatred isn't something you're born with, but is taught to you."

"Yeah," Gabriel nodded. "That sent chills down my spine. But I can't help wondering what the movie was trying to say about laws and procedures. Was it right for Ward to give up on proper procedures and let Anderson act like a thug to get the convictions?"

"What choice did he have? They weren't getting anywhere going by the book, except causing more violence against the black community, so his only choice was to.... You know, use other methods."

"So, you're saying the end justifies the means?" he challenged, his lower lip between his teeth. "I have a hard time going that__"

As he was talking, Gabriel had the uneasy sensation that a woman in a floral print blouse at the table diagonally across from him, with her back to the mirror that extended all along the side wall, was watching him. Surreptitiously, while bending to pick up his napkin, which he had deliberately dropped, he took a closer look at her long, angular face, but didn't recognize her. Her gawking discomposed him.

Observing his disquietude, Jenny asked nervously, "Is everything alright, Gabriel?"

"Yeah. It's fine.... It's just that the lady over there has been staring at me this whole time."

"Do you know her?" Jenny probed.

"No. I've never seen her before in my life," he replied.

"That's so weird," Jenny judged.

"Yeah.... Anyway, the town was completely corrupt – the police, the mayor, the judge – and the murderers deserved to go to jail. But I'm uncomfortable allowing the FBI to break the law in order to get a conviction," Gabriel resumed, while keeping a wary eye on his mysterious observer.

Jennifer was still not satisfied. "I agree, but... I don't know.... It's more complicated. That's why I like Math. Math problems have clear solutions. No ambiguity."

The Oracle of Spring Garden Road

The woman in the floral blouse left her companion at her table, ostensibly to visit the restroom. Gabriel watched her departure with some relief. In the meantime, the waitress arrived with their food. As they tucked into their sandwiches, the intrusive woman bubbled up to their table with a triumphant smile of recognition.

"*Now* I remember you," she announced to Gabriel and, it seemed, half the restaurant. "I met you in my house once."

Jenny was bemused, but Gabriel was discomfited. "No, I'm sorry, but you must be mistaken," he replied uncomfortably.

"Oh no! No mistake about it. It took me a while to place your face, but now I've got it. It must have been Canada Day because you were wearing an apron with the Maple Leaf on it. Does that ring a bell, dear?" she asked with an insinuating edge to her voice.

All the colour drained from Gabriel's cheeks. He pleaded with her using his eyes not to divulge the details of that meeting. The woman smirked broadly, clearly enjoying watching him squirm. She turned to Jenny and asked, "Is he your boyfriend?"

Jenny reddened, liking the sound of that word. Boyfriend. "We're on our first date," she answered shily.

"I see," the woman said. "I see…. Well, I think you'll like him. From what I've seen, he's *very* impressive. Very impressive indeed!" Gabriel hung his head, his stomach a cement mixer, fearing the worst. But the woman simply said, "Well, enjoy your dinner," and retreated magnanimously to her table. Gabriel breathed audibly.

"What was *that* all about?" Jenny asked in wonder.

Gabriel glanced downward at his sweating, trembling hands. Instinctively, he reached for his glass and gulped down some water, almost choking on it, spilling some on the table. "Someday I'll tell you about it, but please don't ask now. Okay?"

"Gabriel?" she said, her face a portrait of bewilderment.

"Can we just leave now? I really need to get outta here."

Jenny's jaw dropped, her shoulders slumped. "We didn't.... We haven't even finished our food yet.... I mean, if you *really* want to go...."

Gabriel reached into his wallet and pulled out a twenty-dollar bill, which would more than cover their order, and tossed it on the table. Then he stood up and collected his coat. Jenny followed suit and they slunk out of the delicatessen.

The mood in the ice-cold car with its frosted windows was sullen as Jenny slowly inserted the key into the ignition.

"Wait," Gabriel pleaded. "Don't start it yet. We need to talk." She complied, waiting for him to begin, but he just sat there, nervously playing with his fingers. After what seemed like an eternity, he found his words. He said rapidly, almost tripping over his tongue, "Listen, this has been the date from Hell. I've been so nervous, I think I've done *everything* wrong. Please don't hold that against me, Jenny. It's just.... we've been friends for so long that I'm so afraid of messing up."

"Aw, Gabriel," she countered, "I don't need a date to decide whether I like you or not. I've known you for so long. I know your strengths and your weaknesses...."

"Weaknesses?" he asked, pretending to take offence.

"You don't have many, but you've got 'em.... I'll take you anyway, warts and all. You don't need to be nervous with me."

"I just.... I wanted everything to be *perfect*...." he mumbled.

"Hey, it's *me*, Gabriel.... I don't want perfect. I want *you*.... I've *always* wanted you...." Her voice faltered as she said this. Gabriel unfastened his seatbelt and embraced her. With a joyous sigh, she kissed him with abandon, exalting that, at long last, after all the sweet, agonizing pain of longing, he was hers.

After a few minutes, she pulled herself away from his mouth, rapturous tears in her eyes, still cradling his hand in hers. Trying to inject a note of haughtiness into her mellowed intonation, she spat out, "Hey, just because we're going out together now, don't think I'm gonna go easy on you or anything." A soft, sweet smile crossed her face, making her look more like an angelic little girl than a teenager on the cusp of womanhood. "I'm still going to cr-r-r-ush you, Jew-boy!" Then she sidled over to kiss him some more.

One Saturday a few weeks later, Jenny and Gabriel had lunch with his parents after they returned from the synagogue. Afterwards, the young couple took a walk. As he normally did, Gabriel set a course for Earl Bales, his destination of choice, the geographical constant in his life, to wander the snow-painted hills and ravines. The weather had been unseasonably warm over the previous week, and to his disappointment there were muddy patches showing through the thinning snow. He had wanted everything to be perfect for her.

As if reading his thoughts, Jennifer smiled modestly and declared dreamily, "These have been the best weeks of my life!"

"Mine too," he echoed.

"You're not so great at first dates – frankly, you get an F for that," she teased. "But aside from that, you're alright, Jew-boy!"

"Well, I'm not as tough a grader as you. I think you're awesome at everything," Gabriel gushed.

"Hah! So, I beat you again!" she taunted.

"I guess you do. But you'd better enjoy it, because you're going to have eat my dust when I become valedictorian this year."

"Valedictorian, my foot! I think you'll make a fine salutatorian."

"Yeah, dream on, Jew-witch. Hey, is something wrong?" Gabriel had observed a change in her expression.

"No. Quite the contrary. I, uh... I need to talk to you about something, though," Jennifer said uneasily.

"Sure," Gabriel said. "Is everything okay?" Privately, he marvelled at the real Jennifer that he was getting to know. As a friend, she wore a suit of armour, a mask of confidence, bravado, unflappability. Now that they were sweethearts, she peeled back the curtain to display her vulnerability, her volatility, her insecurity. She could be playful one moment, serious the next. She could run the gamut from tender and loving, dependent even, to diamond hard and competitive in the span of a moment. He could never have guessed what lay beneath her surface. *She's impulsive, unpredictable, exciting, he thought. And she shows it to me and nobody else!*

"Oh, no," she replied, shaking her head, the pom-pom on her lavender toque flopping foolishly from side to side. "It's not something bad.... well, I *hope* you won't think it is. I just.... Gosh, this is embarrassing...."

"Don't worry, Jenny. It's *me* you're talking to. I don't bite. At least not too often," he said mischievously, leaning over to nip her gently on the neck. She giggled like a schoolgirl.

"Listen, Gabriel," she persisted, regaining her composure. "I.... Well, I haven't ever... you know...." She gazed at him significantly. "I haven't done it before."

Gabriel understood and became serious. "Oh.... That's okay. We don't have to...." Sex is a touchy subject for observant Jews. Most avoid sexual relations until they marry, to elevate sex, imbue it with a sacred and beautiful purpose. Many refrain even from touching or kissing before marriage. Gabriel himself had planned to abstain from sex until after his wedding, but his actions while under the influence had left him rather confused in this regard. He had been uncertain how Jennifer, who was not Orthodox would behave, but thought it was likely that she too would eschew sexual relations. So, he was perfectly ready to accommodate her wishes as he understood them.

"Oh, Gabriel.... I'm not saying I don't want to," she said flirtatiously, her face flushed. "I'm just not ready yet. You don't mind waiting?"

"For you, Jenny, I'd wait until the glaciers melt," he replied gallantly, waving his left arm in front of him and bowing low, a courtier of old.

Jennifer laughed and performed a curtsy in response. Suddenly, however, her smile evaporated and her ordinarily confident demeanour dissolved. She seized his wrists and asked plaintively, "Oh, why did you take so long, Gabriel? We're going to graduate in only a few months!"

The honesty, the pain of her overture was more than he could bear. "I... I don't know. I just.... It took me time to see what was right in front of me, I guess. I wish I could do it all over. All of it. I wasted my first two years of high school," he admitted ruefully. He shuddered as he recalled waking up next to Joey, or what he presumed was Joey, in the basement.

"Had you gone straight from the beginning, I'm sure we would have gotten together sooner, maybe even in Grade 10. Oh Gabriel, high school would have been wonderful with you by my side."

"I don't know what to say. I messed up. I really messed up," he said sullenly.

They were silent for a while, each lost in their private thoughts of what might have been, the joys forsaken, the pain, the shame that could have been averted. It was like staring at a stillborn baby and mourning its lost childhood, the bedtime stories, the first day of school, family vacations. A few flurries floated upon the light wind.

Then, as abruptly as her mood had taken its mournful turn, her storm clouds cleared away again, her face brightened. "Oh, let's not dwell on what could have been. Let's just enjoy what we've got," she suggested.

Without warning, she pushed him into the patchy snow, reminiscent of the way he had done the same to Jack only a few short years earlier, laughing brazenly. "Hey!" he cried, but she fell on top of him and silenced him with a passionate kiss, trying desperately to make up for lost time.

The sights and sounds of those glorious weeks are carved indelibly on his brain, like the inscription on a tombstone. The way her jade green eyes glittered when she blushed. The silk of her hair tickling his neck as they kissed. The intoxicating jasmine and honey aroma of her shampoo. Walking hand-in-hand to the bus stop after school. Delicious sleepless nights when he couldn't stop thinking of her. The way others looked at him with more respect knowing that they were a couple. The musical Sabbath dinners with her family, as they sang traditional songs with complex, multipart harmonies. The velvety soft texture of her back, as he surreptitiously snuck his hand under her shirt while sitting next to her in the school cafeteria, hoping nobody would notice. The delicious impending sense of loss, knowing that it was all just a castle forged of sand, unable to withstand the impending tide.

One weekend in mid-May, when Jennifer's parents were away at the cottage with her younger sisters, Jennifer insisted on staying behind on account of an important Calculus test that upcoming Monday. She nervously invited Gabriel over for Friday night dinner... and, perhaps, Saturday lunch. Gabriel accepted with great excitement and more than a little trepidation. He left his parents a note saying that he'd be spending the Sabbath at a friend's house. Technically, he convinced himself, that wasn't a lie. Jenny *was* a friend. Just a special kind of friend.

He arrived at her house wearing his good blue twill suit and knit tie, carrying a single red rose and his overnight bag. Jennifer answered the door in a short, off-the-shoulder, black patterned dress, with black nylons. Gabriel had never seen her so beautiful. Like a thief in the night, she whisked him in quickly, self-consciously, fearing that her neighbours might detect something amiss. Once he was inside, she bolted and chained the door, denying him any avenue of escape. She threw her arms around him and kissed him before he could drop his bag. "Hi honey," she giggled, "How was work?"

"Oh, not bad," Gabriel played along. "My boss is an idiot and I'm underpaid, but at least I got my paycheque today. How was your day?"

"Great! I got the reactor I was working on online and found out I was shortlisted for the Nobel Prize. And I even found time to make dinner. Did you know you were married to Wonder Woman?"

He chuckled. "This is for you, Wonder Woman," he said, handing her the rose.

She kissed him again and led him inside to the dining room, where the table was set for two, with the China and silver cutlery her parents reserved for special occasions. The meal, however, did not come off quite as planned. To Jennifer's disappointment, she had overcooked the chicken and forgotten to add baking powder to the cake she baked for dessert. Gabriel didn't mind, though, and they both had a good laugh at the expense of her flat "pan"cake.

"Okay, so I'm not much of a housewife," Jennifer admitted haughtily. "I guess you're gonna have to quit your little job and take care of the house and the kids while I win my Nobel Prize."

"Oh really?" he said in mock indignation. "I'm not sure I'll have time once they appoint me Secretary-General of the UN."

"That's okay," she conceded with a mischievous grin, "We can always sell the children to the circus. I never liked them anyway."

In general, however, their conversation that night was forced and stilted, as it was on their first date. They were only too aware of the mountain they would imminently need to scale, awash in a mix of breathless anticipation and abject terror. Gabriel absently fidgeted with his cutlery for most of the meal, while Jennifer kept fussing about refilling his glass or whether the food needed more salt. It was as if they were awaiting the executioner.

After dinner, they both grew quiet and jittery. They started kissing on the sofa in the den. With one hand around his shoulders, Jennifer used her free hand to pry Gabriel's shirttail out of his pants and roam the length of his back. He kissed her neck, her shoulder, everywhere her low-cut dress provided access to. But at first neither of them dared to go further. Feeling the pressure, Gabriel excused himself to visit the washroom, mainly to take a few deep breaths and gather his nerves. Staring at himself in the mirror, he wondered, *why is this so hard?* When he emerged, Jennifer was no longer on the sofa where he had left her. He called her name, but she didn't respond. Fearing that he had upset her, he searched the kitchen and dining room before finding her in her bedroom. She was lying in bed with a fluffy white duvet cloaking her from the waist down, revealing only her naked torso. Inexplicably, the scene called to Gabriel's mind Mrs. Weiss on the floor of the synagogue office. He shuddered involuntarily.

"Is anything wrong?" Jennifer asked anxiously, fearing that she had done the wrong thing, that she had been too bold, that she had presumed too much.

"No, it's great! You're just too beautiful."

He was momentarily flustered, not knowing quite how to proceed. Although in principle he had done this before, it had been in a drug-induced stupor, and he had gleaned no practical intelligence from it. He was a born-again virgin. It was so important to him to get it right this time. To make it memorable. Conscious of her eyes on him, he unbuttoned his shirt and removed it, together with his tattered grey, ribbed undershirt, which he draped over her desk chair. He swore softly to himself. Why hadn't he remembered to wear a newer undershirt? He climbed onto the bed beside her and, without realizing it, began caressing her breasts in much the same way that Mr. Haberman had done to Mrs. Weiss. Then he gently lifted the duvet and joined Jennifer underneath.

Afterwards, they were simultaneously elated and relieved. The pressure off, they lolled around, luxuriating in their unprecedented freedom. Their mission accomplished, the box ticked, they were once again best friends, at ease with each other, able to talk about anything.

"Wouldn't it great if we could always be like this? Never having to go back to our separate homes?" Jennifer mused, running the sole of her foot down the back of Gabriel's leg.

"Mmmm...." he moaned, more an expression of pleasure than agreement with her sentiment.

"I wish you'd applied to UBC. It's going to be Hell to be so far away from you."

"Why didn't you apply to U of T.?" Gabriel asked.

"I did. But I won't go if UBC accepts me," she said firmly.

"Why won't you consider it?" he asked.

"*God*! I just have to get *out of here*! Sometimes I feel like I'm in a *cage*," she said.

Gabriel nodded. "I know what you mean."

"Then why did you only apply to U. of T. and York?"

He considered that for some time before responding sheepishly, "My parents wouldn't let."

"It's too bad we didn't get together earlier. Maybe we could have arranged things better," Jennifer reflected, before curling up against him and closing her eyes.

As Jennifer drifted off to sleep, the picture of contentment, ripples were bubbling up from below the surface of Gabriel's tranquil sea. Outwardly relaxed, relieved, at ease, he began to be shaken by a discordant inner note of hopelessness. What did it all mean? Sure, it had been a wonderful night, but what was the point? Already, while they shared a physical closeness unlike any other in his life, he felt them moving away from each other, into separate orbits, one more knot they would cut away on their paths to freedom. He knew how it would happen. She would move to Vancouver in a few months. He would remain in Toronto. They would probably call each other at first, more out of duty than desire. The calls would become less and less frequent, until eventually they'd stop, as their new lives retained no more space for an atavistic relationship. When she'd return to town on a visit, he'd be regrettably unable to see her. Surely, she could see this, too.

He lay in the strange, cramped bed brooding for a while before sleep finally overtook him.

The sunlight streaming through the gaps in her vertical blinds woke him. For a long second, he wondered where he was, until he felt Jennifer's arm around him, the soft fleshy cones of her breasts pressed against his back. His misgivings having vanished in the night, he greeted the day with his customary optimism and enthusiasm, this time savouring the unprecedented freedom of waking up without parental supervision, free of constraints, in the arms of his beloved. Beguiled by the dewy, lazy freshness of the morning, he gently turned around and woke her with the sweetest, most sensual kiss.

People usually talk reverentially about their first time, but Gabriel could never understand why. The first time was stressful. All the pressure of learning the mechanics, meeting expectations, the fear of the unknown. For Gabriel, it was the second, third and fourth times that Saturday morning, the tender, joyful, unrestrained lovemaking in the early morning light, and the fifth and sixth times after lunch, exploring each other's bodies, learning how to elicit pleasure, that he cherished above all. It was a more dizzying and satisfying high than ever he had achieved with drugs.

In between their bouts of intimacy, they enjoyed a companionship unlike their old friendship. They laughed without restraint, shared their most cherished dreams, their deepest-rooted insecurities. Lying together on the rumpled white duvet, emblazoned with a crimson smear to mark their communion, touching each other unreservedly, all airs slipped between them, all posing and artifice unnecessary. If this was the end of innocence, as he had read in books, heard about in songs, he couldn't comprehend why. There was nothing purer and more innocent than what they shared.

Aside from a short walk outside in the late afternoon, they remained indoors throughout the Sabbath. Although Jennifer would ordinarily have attended services in the nearby synagogue, she was truant this Saturday so that she could make the most of her time with Gabriel. As the end of the Sabbath approached, they clung to each other more tightly, aware that the fantasy had to end. At the appointed hour, Gabriel helped Jennifer tidy up, to remove any evidence of their crime. He then kissed her wistfully and departed for home, doubtful that he would ever know such happiness again.

Later that week, Gabriel retrieved the mail from the rectangular metallic mailbox just inside the entrance of his triplex. On top of the pile was a letter addressed to Mr. Gabriel Morris Klein from University of Toronto Admissions. Breathlessly, he ripped it open, his hands shaking. "Yes!" he shouted at the top of his lungs. They had offered him a full tuition scholarship, together with the opportunity to defray his living expenses with Work/Study opportunities on campus. He had done it!

Since it was still early and his parents wouldn't return from work for a while, he decided to take the bus to Jennifer's to share the good news with her. On the way, it occurred to him that, with the opportunity to work part time, both on campus and off, he wouldn't need to live at home, uptown. If he shared an apartment with others, he could live frugally near campus, which would be better for his studies, but also afford him more independence. Yes, he decided quickly, that's what he would do.

When he arrived at Jennifer's, she was surprised to see him. "Oh, Gabriel. What are you doing here?" she asked, with a marked absence of enthusiasm, with discomfort even. She kissed him perfunctorily, distractedly.

"I got my acceptance letter," he waved it at her to substantiate his claim, "and thought I'd share it with you...."

"Congratulations!" she said. "I got mine, too."

"From U. of T?"

"Huh? Oh, yeah. I got that yesterday. But my UBC letter came today," she said, a guilty look in her eyes.

Gabriel looked down at his hands. "Oh, you didn't say anything...." he muttered.

"Listen, Gabriel," she proposed, "I'm going out to dinner with my parents to celebrate. Do you want to come?"

He searched her face for signs of welcome, but saw nothing. He glanced furtively at her house. It was the same bungalow they had inhabited only days before, where they had been closer than he had ever been before to anyone, where they were, in the words of the Bible, like a single flesh. Yet now, with her parents back, her ticket away from him in hand, it was as if it had never happened. Like they were mere acquaintances. He felt like an interloper. Mr. Patel, his Biology teacher, had taught the class about the appendix being a vestigial organ. Useful in an earlier stage of human evolution, but now unnecessary, atavistic, an artifact of a bygone era. That's how he felt now. Vestigial. He declined Jennifer's offer, mumbling something about needing to share his good news with his parents. He said goodbye and trudged home, feeling discarded, like the dried-out husk of a maple seed pod lying uselessly on a driveway.

***

The Oracle of Spring Garden Road

Gabriel climbed the two flights of stairs to his parents' upper triplex apartment. Was it always as dreary as this, he wondered. The boots and shoes scattered haphazardly around the inevitable rubber mat outside the door on each landing. The stench of ammonia mingled with cooking odours from the night before, sometimes fried chicken, sometimes liver and onions. The narrow west-facing windows on the staircase, framed by dingy lace curtains, letting insufficient light in from Bathurst Street. The institutional cream and sable bubble pattern on the floor tiles and the stairs. Clearly, the only motive of the architect and landlord had been to keep costs down. Either that or to inflict psychological harm on the tenants. Was there a Mengele School of Architecture out there somewhere that taught students how to design these artless, charmless homes?

He turned his key in the lock and entered his home, the only home he had ever known. The hallway, the kitchen, the living room were all dark; his parents were still not home from work. Gabriel dropped his knapsack and explored his home, as if for the first time. How ugly and unpleasant it was! The loud humming of the refrigerator. The dismally lit hallway. The living room, with its chairs and sofas covered by pallid floral cloths to prevent fading, as if enough sunlight could enter these sombre rooms to do them harm. The white plastic ant and roach traps in the corners. The amateur watercolour of the Danube that his mother painted all those years ago. Why were people so fond of what they risked their lives to flee that they tried to reproduce it ever afterwards? Had he really admired it, obsessed over it when he was a child? The ever-present ticking of the timeclock that controlled the living room lamp. The unsightly stain on the ceiling from the time the roof leaked during a spring thaw, which had never been touched up. Had there ever been love in this apartment, real love? He couldn't remember. There certainly wasn't now.

Why hadn't he noticed before how desolate it all was? There were times, years ago, when he must have found it warm and safe. When this depressing, dark cage that he shared with his parents had seemed like home. What is it about childhood that makes you ignore the too obvious flaws and bask in a false comfort? Lion cubs in a zoo must find the bars of their cage comforting until they grow to apprehend the horror of their imprisonment.

He entered his bedroom. As a child, it had seemed cavernous to him. But there was barely enough room for a bed, a work desk – a small table, really – and a chest of drawers, with most of the metal handles either missing, tarnished or falling off. Still the same lime green paint that had made the room seem darker, more desolate than the original off-white, only now dirtier, covered in posters or yellow squares of tape where posters had once stood. He would not miss this apartment.

When his parents returned, he sat them down on the living room sofa, underneath the Danube. "I've got some news," he announced.

"Yes?" his mother asked, bursting with curiosity. "What is it?"

"About university?" his father pressed.

"Yes," Gabriel replied evenly. "U. of T. gave me a full scholarship." His parents cheered. "But they gave me even more than I hoped for. I'll have enough to live downtown, near the university."

"What?" Esther burst out.

"What's the point in living downtown? You'll live here," Isaac asserted.

"It would help me with my studies if I were near the library. And I could get together with lab partners more easily...."

Esther broke in, "Tova Halpern goes to U. of T. and she lives with her parents near us. So does the Wilmer boy – what's his name? David maybe? No, Daniel."

"Look," Gabriel asserted, "I'd be much happier living downtown and I can pay for it myself. I won't be that far, and I can visit often." Esther looked crestfallen and was about to argue, but Gabriel pre-empted her. "Besides, Dad, you promised that if I got a full scholarship, you wouldn't stand in my way."

The veins in Isaac's temples pulsed. "He's right, dear. I don't like him running off on his own. But he did earn the right. If he really wants to move out of the house, it's his decision," he acknowledged with a resigned sigh.

"Thanks, Dad. I think it's for the best."

Esther left the room in a huff. Isaac looked ruefully at his son. "Congratulations, Gabriel. Despite it all, I'm proud of you. I'm so glad you turned yourself around. Make the most of your opportunity," he advised.

Gabriel nodded and went to his room.

Later in the week, Jennifer was having second thoughts. She and Gabriel were lolling on his bed in the early afternoon. Their Calculus teacher had called in sick, which allowed them to leave school early and enjoy a few quiet hours before Gabriel's parents returned. The window was open and it felt almost like a lazy summer day. They had been silent for a while, listening to each other's heartbeats, the sound of the traffic on Bathurst Street.

"I've been thinking," she said, breaking the silence. "Should I just go to U. of T.? It's a great school... probably better than UBC. But isn't it stupid to tear us apart when we could both be happy here?"

Gabriel couldn't believe his ears. It was exactly what he wanted, what he had been hoping for. And it had been *her* who suggested it, not *him*. But his conscience refused to let him off the hook. "No," he replied sadly after mulling it over, averting her gaze. "You've got to follow your dream. You've wanted this for so long. You just can't turn your back on it now."

She grabbed his arm, turned him to face her. "But, what about *us*? I've wanted that, too!"

For a long moment he stared into her hypnotic eyes, a dull ache in his gut. "You'd hate me for it," he finally said.

"How could I hate you? You're all I've dreamed of for the last year!" she cried, kissing him gently on his lips.

"Even so," he said. "You can't ground a comet. You were meant to soar toward the heavens. You'd be miserable shackled here with mere mortals."

She knew he was right and loved him all the more for it. Just then, they heard a key turning in the lock. Someone else had come home early. Frantically, they rushed to straighten out the bed and make themselves presentable just in time to greet Esther when she opened the door to Gabriel's bedroom.

As the final semester wound down, on the cusp of the irrevocable changes that would re-order his life, Gabriel sat for his final exams. As he had done since his break with the Stoners, he had studied conscientiously and was supremely confident. For reasons, that he was hard-pressed to explain, however, he froze up on his biology final. In his mind, he blamed his disappointing performance on his parents interfering with his pre-exam sleep, on the teacher's unclear guidance about the exam's scope, on the weather, which made his head throb. If he were honest with himself, however, he would have acknowledged that he simply fell short, scoring a B- on the exam. The upshot was that, though Gabriel had sparkling grades, he didn't qualify for either valedictorian or salutatorian at the graduation exercises. Jennifer was awarded the former, while Selma was delighted with the latter honour.

Upon receiving the news, Jennifer was elated. But, after it sunk in, she began to feel pangs of sympathy for Gabriel, guilt even. How could she rejoice if her boyfriend was miserable? She found him in the schoolyard sitting near the trunk of a large red maple tree, twisting a helicopter-like seed pod in his hand. She squatted beside him and grasped his other hand. "I'm sorry, Gabriel. I wish you'd won instead of me."

He forced a smile. "Oh, it's okay. You deserved it. Congratulations! I'm really proud of you," he said with uncharacteristic graciousness. "You worked toward this from day one of high school, putting your all into it, while I was doping my life away. It wouldn't have been fair if I were to have managed to take it from you. I'm just glad to have been able to join you for the ride."

"You know, Gabriel," Jenny said, tears clouding her jade green orbs, "I'm prouder to be with you now than ever," as she buried her face into his chest.

After graduation, Jennifer and Gabriel were conscious of the ticking clock. In a few weeks, Jennifer would fly away to her new life. This led them to two different patterns of behaviour. At times, they would cling to each other, in a frenzied effort to bank as many good times together as they could before the axe fell. At others, they would hold themselves aloof, like stoics of old, wishing to cut the cord and minimize the inevitable pain of rupture. Nothing in either of their lives to this point had prepared them for the cataclysmic change that, for better and for worse, loomed on the horizon.

On the fateful day, Gabriel accompanied the Levensons to Pearson International Airport. Jenny's plane departed out of Terminal 1. In all his life, Gabriel had never before stepped inside an airport. He had travelled out of the city only by car, and only to places nearby, never farther than Montreal. Although he was in a state of nervous anxiety over Jenny's departure, he was amazed at the scale of the airport, the planes taking off and landing all around, the myriad of national and international destinations flipping noisily across the departure board, with a satisfying *tck-tck-tck-tck*. MONTREAL. FRANKFURT.

SYDNEY. BUENOS AIRES. VANCOUVER. It was a thrill unlike anything he had yet experienced.

On the surface Jenny was cool and collected, somewhat aloof, but Gabriel could see that she was concealing her inner anxiety. She kept to her father and her sisters – her mother was flying with her to help her set up in Vancouver – maintaining a respectable distance between him and her. His attempt to hold her hand was brusquely rebuffed. Her focus was on the practical: documents, luggage tags, the departure gate.

As she approached the security checkpoint, all too soon it was time to say their farewells after everything they had shared together. She leaned over and kissed him on his cheek, clearly searching for something fitting to say. But struggling as she was to maintain control, all that came out was "Good luck, Gabriel." Somewhat taken aback, Gabriel replied in kind, "You're going to do incredibly, like you always do." And then it was all over. He was standing behind, looking on as Jenny and her mother filed closer to the scanning equipment, on her way to her new life.

Suddenly, Jennifer broke out of the line and lunged at him, grabbing him and squeezing in desperation, with all her might. "I'm so scared, Gabriel!" she confessed. For a brief instant, she was his beloved Jenny, the Jenny he and no-one else knew. Brilliant but vulnerable; strong but uncertain, doubtful; at once a champion and a child. "I know. I am, too," he said. But the moment passed quickly, and she steeled herself, her armour once more intact. She took one long last look in his eyes before leaving him forever and whispered, "Knock 'em dead, Jew-boy," renouncing all future claim on him. They gave each other one last desperate kiss, a kiss on shifting grounds, caught between the past that they were consigning to their scrapbooks, and the enticing, mysterious, promising, terrifying future that beckoned them. And then she was gone.

Chapter 7

All rise! Court is in session! We will hear opening arguments in the matter of R. v. Haberman.

Crown Attorney: The Crown submits that the accused, Jonathan Haberman, a married man, violated God's sacred law and knowingly committed adultery with a married woman, Mrs. Naomi Weiss, wife of Cantor Meyer Weiss, in the synagogue office on the afternoon of February 25, 1985. The accused had opportunity, being the synagogue president, given that Mrs. Weiss was the synagogue secretary and worked directly for him. We call our first witness, Gabriel Klein, to the stand.

Witness, state your name for the record.
Gabriel: Gabriel Klein.
Do you swear to tell the truth, the whole truth and nothing but the truth, so help you God?
Gabriel: I affirm it.
Crown Attorney: Mr. Klein, please tell the Court what you were doing in the synagogue building on the afternoon in question.
Gabriel: I... I had forgotten my bag. So I went back to get it.
Crown Attorney: What bag is that? How did you leave it in the synagogue?
Gabriel: It was my knapsack for school. I took it with me for Rabbi Plotkin's shiur that morning, but accidentally left it under my chair.
Crown Attorney: For the record, Your Honour, a shiur is a Torah lesson, in this case led by the rabbi of the synagogue, Rabbi Jacob Plotkin. Mr. Klein, how often did you attend this shiur?
Gabriel: Every Sunday.

Crown Attorney: So, on this particular occasion, how did you discover that your bag was missing? What did you do at that point?

Gabriel: Well, I needed to do my homework and couldn't find it. So I went back to shul...I mean the synagogue...and got it from the library.

Crown Attorney: Was anyone else in the building at that time?

Gabriel: At first, I didn't think so. It was Sunday afternoon, and the building was dark. The morning services were over, as was the rabbi's shiur. I think there was also a daily service in the evening, but it was much too early for that. So I thought everyone had gone.

Crown Attorney: Is the synagogue office near the library?

Gabriel: Not really. It's upstairs....

Crown Attorney: "It" being the library or the office.

Gabriel: Sorry. The library's on the second floor. The office is downstairs, down a long corridor from the main staircase.

Crown Attorney: So what made you visit the office that afternoon if you thought nobody was in the building?

Gabriel: Well, when I came down the stairs with my bag, I heard a woman screaming.

Crown Attorney: Screaming? Like she was in pain?

Gabriel: Uh.... I thought so at the time.... I was just a boy....

Crown Attorney: What do you think now?

Gabriel: I... I think she was climaxing.

Crown Attorney: Sexually?

Defence Counsel: Objection, Your Honour! Counsel is leading the witness!

Overruled. The witness will answer the question.

Gabriel: Yes. I believe she was having an orgasm.

Defence Counsel: Objection! Assumes facts not in evidence!

Crown Attorney: Okay, Mr. Klein. So when you heard screaming, which you thought meant a woman was in pain, what did you do?

Gabriel: I... I was scared, but I crept closer to the office and heard that it was Mrs. Weiss' voice. So, I went inside the office to see what was wrong.

Crown Attorney: And what did you see?
Gabriel: I.... They were....
Crown Attorney: Please go on, Mr. Klein. This is very important.
Gabriel: They were naked on the floor.
Crown Attorney: Who was naked?
Gabriel: Mr. Haberman and Mrs. Weiss.
Crown Attorney: And what were they doing?
Gabriel: They.... He was touching her breasts.
Crown Attorney: And then what did you do?
Gabriel: I ran out as fast as I could.
Crown Attorney: Did they say anything to you?
Gabriel. He came out and ran after me. He tried to tell me that they weren't doing what it looked like they were. Then he offered me money not to say anything. But I just ran.
Crown Attorney: Where did you go?
Gabriel: I went to tell Rabbi Plotkin. I thought he would punish them.
Crown Attorney: And what did Rabbi Plotkin say?
Gabriel: He said it was a terrible thing they were doing, but he couldn't, or wouldn't, do anything about it.
Crown Attorney: Why not?
Gabriel: Because Mr. Haberman was rich. Because he was a big donor and could get Rabbi Plotkin fired.
Crown Attorney: I see. And was all this a surprise to Rabbi Plotkin?
Gabriel. No.... I don't think so. He seemed to already know about them.
Crown Attorney: Thank you, Mr. Klein. I have no further questions. Does counsel for the accused wish to cross-examine the witness?
Defence Counsel: Yes, Your Honour. Mr. Klein, what was the weather like that day?
Gabriel: The weather? I.... I really don't know. It was so long ago.
Defence Counsel: I see. It was February. Were you wearing boots?
Gabriel: I... I must have been.
Defence Counsel: So, did you take your boots off before going to the library?

Gabriel: I don't remember.

Defence Counsel: You don't remember.... Were you wearing a coat?

Gabriel: Yes, I must have been.

Defence Counsel: You must have been. This is all so vague. Now Mr. Klein, you say you saw the defendant and Mrs. Weiss lying naked on the floor. Is that right?

Gabriel: Yes.

Defence Counsel: So, you saw them both completely naked?

Gabriel: Well, not exactly.

Defence Counsel: Not exactly? What do you mean? Did you see them naked or not?

Gabriel: Well, I believe they were naked....

Defence Counsel: You believe?

Gabriel: They.... They were behind her desk. I could only see them from... from their waist up.

Defence Counsel: And did they ever move out from behind the desk or did you check behind the desk.

Gabriel: No! I.... I just wanted to get out of there as fast as I could.

Defence Counsel: So you don't even know for certain that they were naked.

Gabriel: They were! I saw.... I saw her breasts. He was stroking them.

Defence Counsel: And you say the defendant chased you out when you ran. Was he naked then?

Gabriel: No. He must have thrown his clothes on when he ducked behind the desk.

Defence Counsel: But you didn't see that either, did you?

Gabriel: No.

Defence Counsel: So you don't seem like a very good witness. You don't know about the weather. You don't know what you wearing. You claim they were naked and committed adultery, but according to your own testimony, you didn't see them naked. How can you be sure they had sexual relations together if you can't even be sure they were naked below the waist?

Gabriel: They were!

Defence Counsel: Mr. Klein, you were only fourteen years old at the time, correct?

Gabriel: Almost. It was a couple of weeks before my fourteenth birthday.

Defence Counsel: Did you like Mrs. Weiss?

Gabriel: Yes. She was nice.

Defence Counsel: What do you mean "was nice"?

Gabriel: She was kind and let us take candy from the jar on her desk.

Defence Counsel: Were you in love with her?

Gabriel: What?

Defence Counsel: As a young boy who had just reached puberty, did you have a crush on Mrs. Weiss.

Gabriel: That's... That's just ridiculous.

Defence Counsel: Please answer the question. Did you have a crush on Mrs. Weiss?

Gabriel: I... I guess.... Well, yes....

Defence Counsel: And did you ever fantasize about her?

Gabriel: Excuse me?

Crown Attorney: Objection!

I'll allow it. The witness will answer the question.

Defence Counsel: Look, it's normal. You were a young boy with a crush on a beautiful older woman. Did you ever fantasize about her?

Gabriel: Fantasize about her.... I suppose I did.

Defence Counsel: You suppose you did, or you did?

Gabriel: I did....

Defence Counsel: So, is it possible you just imagined that she had sex with Mr. Haberman, perhaps to punish her for being out of reach for you? Is that why your story doesn't add up, why there are so many gaps and inconsistencies?

Crown Attorney: Objection! Badgering the witness!

Sustained.

Defence Counsel: No further questions, Your Honour.

Crown Attorney: The Crown calls Rabbi Plotkin to the stand. Rabbi, please state your name for the record.

Rabbi Plotkin: I'm Rabbi Jacob Plotkin.

Do you swear to tell the truth, the whole truth and nothing but the truth, so help you God?

Rabbi Plotkin: I affirm it.

Crown Attorney: On the afternoon of February 25, 1985, Gabriel Klein visited your apartment. Is that correct?

Rabbi Plotkin: Yes. That's correct.

Crown Attorney: Was it normal for him to call on you in your apartment?

Rabbi Plotkin: No. He had been there with his family once or twice when I invited them for lunch on the Sabbath. But other than that, I saw him only in the synagogue.

Crown Attorney: What was his state of mind on this occasion?

Rabbi Plotkin: He was very upset.

Crown Attorney: Did he tell you why he was upset?

Rabbi Plotkin: Yes. He said he saw something upsetting.

Crown Attorney: And what was it he saw?

Rabbi Plotkin: He said he saw... people in my synagogue having an affair.

Crown Attorney: Did he say who these people were?

Rabbi Plotkin: Yes.

Crown Attorney: Please tell the Court who he said he saw having an affair.

Rabbi Plotkin: The synagogue president and the secretary.

Crown Attorney: Both married to other people, correct?

Rabbi Plotkin: That's correct.

Crown Attorney: And what did he ask you to do?

Rabbi Plotkin: He asked me to throw them out of the synagogue.

Crown Attorney: How did you respond to his request?

Rabbi Plotkin: I... I told him that these things are more complicated than that.

Crown Attorney: Complicated how?

Rabbi Plotkin: Well, people sin. We don't expel everyone who sins from synagogue. If we did, no-one would be allowed in, myself included. (Laughs are heard around the courtroom). Instead, we try to work with those who sin in the hope that they can mend their ways.

Crown Attorney: And did you speak to the defendant or Mrs. Weiss afterwards to try to mend their behaviour?

Silence.

Crown Attorney: Rabbi Plotkin? We're waiting for your answer.

Rabbi Plotkin: No, I didn't.

Crown Attorney: You didn't?

Rabbi Plotkin: I... I should have, but I didn't.

Crown Attorney: Why not?

Rabbi Plotkin: Because... Because I was afraid of losing my job.

Crown Attorney: I see. Now, Rabbi Plotkin.... And this is very important.... Rabbi Plotkin, did you know that the defendant and Mrs. Weiss had been having an affair even before Gabriel Klein visited you that day?

Rabbi Plotkin: Oh, that's silly. How would I have known?

Crown Attorney: Mr. Klein testified that he left your home convinced that you had known already.

Rabbi Plotkin: Well, you'll have to take that up with him, then.

Crown Attorney: You're evading the question. Please answer directly.

Rabbi Plotkin: I... I can't answer that question. As a member of the clergy, I can't answer questions about confidential information I may or may not possess about my congregants' personal activities.

Crown Attorney: Your honour, Rabbi Plotkin is a Jewish rabbi, not a Catholic priest. Jews do not go to Confession and rabbis do not take a sacred oath of confidentiality.

The witness will answer the question.

Rabbi Plotkin: (sighs) Well, I might have suspected.

Crown Attorney: You suspected, or you knew?

Rabbi Plotkin: I had reason to believe....

Crown Attorney: Let me clear about this. You were aware of this violation of the Seventh Commandment by your synagogue president, with the synagogue's secretary, and you chose to do nothing because you were afraid it would harm your personal interests to interfere. This makes you an accessory after the fact.

Defence Counsel: Objection, Your Honour! She's badgering the witness.

Objection sustained.

Crown Attorney: No further questions, your honour.

Defence, cross-examination?

Defence Counsel: Yes, Your Honour. Rabbi Plotkin, did you ever see the defendant and Mrs. Weiss engaged in improper conduct.

Rabbi Plotkin: No. Never.

Defence Counsel: Did they ever hold hands in your presence?

Rabbi Plotkin: No.

Defence Counsel: Kiss? Make lewd comments?

Rabbi Plotkin: No. Nothing like that.

Defence Counsel: So you never saw any incontrovertible evidence that they were having an affair.

Rabbi Plotkin: Not exactly. No.

Defence Counsel: No further questions.

Crown Attorney: The Crown has demonstrated that the accused was naked with Mrs. Weiss, a married woman, in the synagogue office on the afternoon of February 25, 1985, and stroking her private parts. A witness has testified to this. In addition, the witness testifies that the defendant tried to cover up his crime with bribery. A second witness, the rabbi of the synagogue no less, testifies that he was aware of the adulterous liaison even before that date. With this incontrovertible evidence, the Crown rests.

Defence Counsel: Your honour, we will demonstrate that this case is entirely without foundation. We call one witness and one witness only, Mr. Jonathan Haberman, the defendant.

Defence Counsel: Please state your name for the record, sir.

Mr. Haberman: Jonathan Haberman.

Defence Counsel: What do you do for a living, Mr. Haberman?

Mr. Haberman: I'm a businessman. I have a company that imports sporting equipment.

Defence Counsel: Were you also synagogue president during the time of the alleged events?

Mr. Haberman: Yes, I was. And chair of the board.

Defence Counsel: Would it be fair to say that you had made a considerable contribution to the synagogue, not only in terms of money donated, but also in terms of the time you devoted to its operations.

Mr. Haberman: Well, I don't want to toot my own horn, but you could say that.

Defence Counsel: On the afternoon in question, what were you doing in the synagogue?

Mr. Haberman: We were.... The synagogue's annual gala – one of our main fundraisers for the year-- was in the planning stage. I stopped by that afternoon to review the finances and prepare a statement to the board later in the week on what kind of budget we could afford for the event.

Defence Counsel: Was Mrs. Weiss, the synagogue secretary, also present?

Mr. Haberman: Yes, she was. I had asked her to help me prepare the report.

Defence Counsel: Mr. Haberman, according to Gabriel Klein's testimony, when he walked into the synagogue office that afternoon, you and Mrs. Weiss were on the floor behind her desk. Is that correct?

Mr. Haberman: No. Of course not.

Defence Counsel: And why would he have said such a thing if that weren't true?

Mr. Haberman: I have no idea.

Defence Counsel: What were you doing when Mr. Klein walked into the office?

Mr. Haberman: We were sitting at her desk going over the annual budget and expenditures.

Defence Counsel: So, just to be clear, were you having an affair with Mrs. Weiss?

Mr. Haberman: Absolutely not!

Defence Counsel: And you didn't have sexual relations with her that afternoon or any other?

Mr. Haberman: No! Of course not!

Defence Counsel: Thank you. I know this has been a difficult time for you and I appreciate your cooperation. No further questions, Your Honour.

Does the Crown wish to cross-examine the witness?

Crown Attorney: Yes, Your Honour. Mr. Haberman, do you respect Rabbi Plotkin?

Mr. Haberman: Yes. Immensely so! He's been my spiritual leader for decades. A wonderful man!

Crown Attorney: Would you say he's an honest man?

Mr. Haberman: To a fault!

Crown Attorney: Then how would you explain his testimony that he thought you and Mrs. Weiss were having an affair?

Mr. Haberman: I'm as puzzled as you are. You'd have to ask him.

Crown Attorney: But if you were to speculate....

Mr. Haberman: Maybe.... Maybe he jumped to a hasty conclusion based on the fact that she and I spent a lot of time together in order to conduct synagogue business. And maybe the lies Gabriel told him poisoned his mind about us. It's really hard to say.

Crown Attorney: But Rabbi Plotkin testified that he suspected your affair even before Mr. Klein mentioned it to him....

Mr. Haberman: I really couldn't say.

Crown Attorney: Now Mr. Klein testified that you offered him money as a bribe to keep him silent about what he saw. Is there any truth to that?

Mr. Haberman: No. Not at all.

Crown Attorney: So what did you do?

Mr. Haberman: When?

Crown Attorney: When you ran after him outside the synagogue?

Mr. Haberman: Oh.... I just told him that he had the wrong idea.

Crown Attorney: The wrong idea about what?

Mr. Haberman: About Mrs. Weiss and myself.

Crown Attorney: Mr. Haberman, that's puzzling to me. Perhaps you can clear things up for me. If you were sitting at the desk going over the budget and not hiding on the floor behind her desk naked, why would you have run outside to clear up any confusion? (Gasps are heard around the courtroom.)

Mr. Haberman: I.... I.... Oh! Now I remember! I made a mistake. We were on the ground behind Mrs. Weiss' desk when he came in, but we were fully dressed. Mrs. Weiss had lost her contact lens. We were searching the floor for it when Gabriel – Mr. Klein entered. I feared that he might misunderstand. Might__

Crown Attorney: Let the record show that Mr. Haberman has now changed his testimony. Mr. Haberman, I'm still puzzled. While it would be unusual to see you both searching on the floor for a contact lens, as you now say you were doing, it's hard to understand why, if you were both fully clothed, that would lead Mr. Klein to conclude that you were having an affair. Were you in fact naked, as Mr. Klein has said?

Mr. Haberman: I.... No. No, we weren't. I don't.... I don't know why....

Crown Attorney: So, you've changed your testimony on what you were doing but you can't explain why you ran after Mr. Klein. No further questions.

Defence Counsel: This case is nothing but a tempest in a teapot. There is no evidence of adultery. We have the report of a confused thirteen-year-old boy, who can't recall any relevant information about the day. He is an unreliable witness, especially since he was in love with Mrs. Weiss at the time and imagined the affair because he couldn't consummate his love. We also have testimony from Rabbi Plotkin that he did not see any evidence that the defendant and Mrs. Weiss did anything inappropriate. Therefore, no-one has provided a shred of evidence to corroborate Mr. Klein's far-fetched story. The defence rests, Your Honour.

The court has reached its verdict. Guilty as charged. The defendant is remanded into custody for sentencing.

***

A man who has no present and no future revels in the past. For over twenty years, Gabriel spent his endless days tramping the city and scouring his past, in search of meaning. Reliving old memories, litigating past wrongs in the courtroom of his mind. The trials always ended the same way, punishing those who had betrayed him, vindicating him for his uncompromising, unflinching integrity. Yet, they never went exactly as he had planned them. They were unable to banish the traces of doubt that lingered somewhere in the shadowy recesses of his mind.

The morning was surprisingly cold for early June. The third frigid day in a row, with a howling wind. There were even traces of frost in the park. In this unexpected revenge of winter, Gabriel remained in bed later than usual, his bedclothes gathered tightly around him, condemning the accused. Eventually, he took the leap and charged out of bed. It wouldn't do to miss a Tuesday at the office. He rushed to get ready, skipping his bath on account of the weather.

He arrived at his office only to find it in chaos, with people swarming about, a police car with cherry lights flashing, a heated argument underway. Apparently, at the intersection on which his office stood, a red Ford Mustang ploughed into a silver Toyota Corolla which had stopped at the light. The Mustang's hood had folded up like an origami bird on impact and the rear of the Corolla had crumpled. The driver of the Mustang, a young man of medium height in a black sweatshirt, stood at the bus stop shouting at the Corolla driver for stopping short before the light turned red. A police officer was standing in front of the bank's silver depository – right in Gabriel's private alcove! – with the other driver, a tall, cigarette-smoking, middle-aged man in a brown suede jacket, who argued that the light had already changed to red when the impact occurred. Other onlookers, including the boutique owner and the pharmacist's assistant, had flooded the area to partake in the excitement.

This unwonted encroachment on his private space unsettled Gabriel. He attempted to box the intruders out of his alcove, but the police officer waved him away. "Quite a lot of excitement, eh?" the boutique owner said to Gabriel. Gabriel merely grunted and wandered off to the Public Garden, waiting for normalcy to return. He was grateful not to have witnessed the collision. He wouldn't have appreciated the police asking him too many questions. Inevitably, for their reports, they would need to ask for his name, his identification papers. Needless to say, he'd refuse to answer, but it would be unpleasant. He was better off not being involved.

When he returned to his office shortly before noon, normalcy had been restored. Aside from errant cigarette stubs strewn carelessly in his alcove, no evidence of the morning's excitement remained. As Gabriel settled back into his corner, brushing away the unwelcome debris with his feet, the teller rushed out of the bank, her eyes bleary and red, a forlorn expression on her face, which showed the scars of too many heartaches. Perhaps her boss had castigated her publicly again for one of her many failings. Or maybe there was a problem at home, with her mother, her son. Perhaps her marriage, which always seemed to be a struggle, was in jeopardy. Regardless, Gabriel, in his unsettled state, was moved to pity.

"Are you okay?" he asked, sidling toward her.

"Pardon?" she asked defensively, surprised by the intrusion into her thoughts by one perpetually so aloof.

"You seem upset. Is there anything I can do? Do you want to talk about it."

"Oh, no Eddie. It's.... I'm alright. But thank you. Thank you for caring," she said, suppressing a sob. She grasped his hand in friendship to show her appreciation.

Gabriel reeled in shock. No-one had touched him in so many years. The mass of humanity that passed by his office on Spring Garden Road had deemed him untouchable, subhuman, and he had accepted their verdict. Even those, like Jane, who saw him as a human being, as someone of genuine value, would never deign to have any physical contact with someone as dirty, as unhygienic, as he. The unexpected, unimaginable, touch of her skin, which, though chapped and raw in the surprisingly cold early June weather, was still soft and womanly, brought tears to Gabriel's eyes, as he recalled the many others, so long ago, that touched him, caressed him, even loved him. An overwhelming sense of loss engulfed him.

"Are *you* okay, Eddie?" the teller asked, witnessing his tears, perhaps fearing that she had upset him.

"Of course," he growled, struggling to regain his composure. "The wind is biting today. Getting in my eyes." He wrenched his hand away and turned brusquely away from her. "I'm going to go to the library to warm up for a bit."

"Sorry, Eddie. I didn't mean to...." she called after him, but he was already on his way and didn't turn back.

Later in the afternoon, after he returned from the library, Jane stopped into his office with a cup of hot chocolate for him.

"I thought you might need this on a windy day like today," she said cheerfully, holding the steaming beverage for him to grasp with the same hand that the teller squeezed earlier.

Still under the spell of his encounter with the teller, Gabriel was uncharacteristically unguarded. "I thank God for people like you, Jane. You're one of the few people that restores my hope in humanity," he said.

"That's sweet, but I have a lot more faith in people than I do in God," she responded.

"What's *that* supposed to mean?" Gabriel snapped, almost personally affronted by her callous dismissal of God.

"Well, I'll be honest with you, Gabriel. When I was young, I was brought up in a religious household. My parents were... well, let's say they were devoutly Christian. I used to go to church every Sunday, used to say Grace, pray before bed. But as I got older...." she let her voice trail off.

He waited for her to continue, but she seemed willing to leave it at that. Annoyed, he pressed, "As you got older, *what*?"

"Well, you know.... In school, at university, I learned to approach life more scientifically. I realized that I believed in God only because my parents taught me to. But when I thought about it, it really made no sense___"

"Nonsense! You're too *kind* not to believe in God!" he declared.

"What's kindness got to do with it? Religion is anything but kind. Look at all the brutality that's been committed in the name of God!" Jane argued.

Gabriel sighed. "Sure," he agreed, "but don't throw the baby out with the bathwater. If you want to condemn religion for the sins committed in its name, do the same with nationalism and even *love*. The three forces that have inspired human beings to write the greatest music, paint the most sublime works of art, design and construct the most magnificent structures, in short, uplift the human race, are love, nationalism and religion. Look at the most magnificent temples, the spectacular parliaments and national theatres, the Taj Mahal. Consider Shakespeare's sonnets or the stirring national anthems. Or the beautiful liturgy developed by any of the world's leading religions. Could we imagine a world without them? Would we want to? Yet, these same three forces have also inspired great barbarity. If you eliminate them, though, you remove this powerful impetus, this divine inspiration for great good. The key is to educate people and prevent them from using them destructively."

"Hmmm...." Jane considered. "That's an interesting argument."

Gabriel sucked in his lower lip. "Listen," he said thoughtfully, "I want to show you something. Can you come with me for a few minutes?"

"I... I don't know. I've got to be somewhere soon," Jane responded uncomfortably. She pulled at the top of the zipper on her coat in an effort to seal the widening crack through which the wind was afflicting her.

"It's up to you. You don't need to be afraid of me. I just want to show you something in the Public Garden. It's not far," he said.

"Well, that should be okay. But I really don't have long. I should get back to the hospital."

They started walking west on Spring Garden Road, toward the Lord Nelson Hotel and the Halifax Public Garden, passing a couple of tourists huddled in their windbreakers outside the craft store. Jane asked, "Are you okay leaving your things on the sidewalk like that," referring to the blanket and rolled up sweatshirt he used as a cushion. He had taken his hat with the few coins inside with him.

"Oh, that's not a big deal. No-one's likely to grab that," he said with an impish grin. "The smell is my special security system."

Jane blanched. She changed the subject to spare his dignity. "So, what does kindness have to do with believing in God?"

"Everything. Why should we be kind to one another if God doesn't exist? The only possible reason out there is the Hobbesian social contract. But that doesn't really work. In an anarchic state of nature, insecurity might compel us to renounce violence so that others do the same, but it can't mandate kindness. The social contract can't explain why *you* are so concerned about *my* well-being," he lectured.

She looked at him with puzzled admiration. "Kindness is human. Not divine. No-one needs to be taught kindness. It's built into our DNA," she countered.

They stopped at a red light on the corner of South Park Street, just next to the Lord Nelson Hotel. He gazed up at the building and commented with irony but not bitterness, "That's a far cry from where I sleep." Jane shuddered. "Two problems with what you just said," he continued, sucking on his chapped lower lip. "Number one, if its innate, where does it come from? God created humans and created kindness. But number two, most humans aren't kind, or at least don't act kindly much of the time. That's why God had to mandate kindness. If not, Western, liberal man – who liberal philosophers themselves tell us is selfish and acquisitive, putting his needs above others – would abuse others for his profit. You're not like that."

"I appreciate the compliment, Gabriel. I really do," Jane said as they crossed the street. "But I just don't believe in the idea of a perfect, supernatural being that created the universe and cares about our destiny."

They entered the park and travelled a short distance on the path before Gabriel veered off to the right, crossing a narrow bridge over a serpentine pond, stopping suddenly under a magnificent oak tree next to the caretaker's shed. He pointed up to it and said, "*That's* what I wanted to show you. Isn't it beautiful?"

"Yes," she agreed, her head tilted back to admire the oak. "But why did you want to show *that* to me?"

"It's staggeringly beautiful. But could you reproduce it?"

She stared at him, uncertain how to respond.

"There are too many elements of its beauty. You'd have to start with the size and shape, not described by any regular geometric term. The most irregular shape of its leaves. The dimensions. But that wouldn't be enough, would it? That's not what makes it beautiful. So next you'd have to reproduce its colours, the various hues and contrasts. The different greens and golds of the leaves, the brown of the trunk and branches, the little reddish-green buds. But that still wouldn't capture it. You'd be missing the depth. The leaves and branches in the foreground, those in the background, the bits of blue sky, of sunlight gleaming through. And yet that still isn't the whole beauty of the tree. You'd be missing the texture. See how grizzled and uneven the bark is, the deep veins on the leaves, the cotton ball appearance of the blooms?" Gabriel was growing more animated as he spoke.

"And if you could reproduce all that, you still wouldn't capture it, because you'd be missing the movement," he continued, as she followed him with growing admiration. "Notice how the tree sways irregularly in a gentle breeze," his gnarled hands danced back and forth to illustrate the point, "how it shakes wildly in all directions, each branch going its own separate way, in today's wind? Could you reproduce that? What about the delicate fragrance of the blooms? The gentle sound of the leaves rustling in the breeze? All of this makes up the startling beauty that we experience in a tree. I don't think a human being could capture all that. But even if one could, which I highly doubt, it would merely be a copy, a facsimile, rather than an original. Such a magnificent work of art could only have been produced by God."

Jane gazed up at the tree, trying to see it through his eyes. Then, stooping to pick up a fallen obovate leaf from the ground, she asked, "Were you an art teacher, Gabriel?"

He looked at her contemptuously. "No," he said. "Then you don't hear it?"

"Hear what?" She gently twisted the stem of the leaf between the thumb and index finger of her left hand. As she did so, the sun briefly broke through its cumulus cage and glinted off her diamond engagement ring, catching Gabriel's eye.

"The music...." he said grumpily. The clouds caught up to the sun, imprisoning it again after its fleeting escape. "Never mind. Another time I'll take you somewhere else." He retraced his steps to the main path with Jane in tow.

"You know, it's kind of funny. You make me think of the main character in *The Life of Pi*," Jane said as they exited the park.

"What's that?" Gabriel asked. They stood on the corner, where their paths diverged.

"You didn't read it? It's one of the most famous novels in recent decades. The main character tries to persuade his companion to believe in God."

"Never heard of it," Gabriel growled.

"Oh," Jane said quietly. It occurred to her, to her great embarrassment, that Gabriel might already have been on the street when the novel was published. "Well," she brightened, "maybe I'll bring you a copy to read. I think you'd like it."

"There's not much point," he said. "I wouldn't be able to keep it from getting wet where I live."

His frank admission opened up a window into his life that Jane had never imagined, that chilled her to the bone. How could he withstand the elements, with no shelter, no place to preserve what he cherished most? He was clearly an intellectual. Had he read *no* books in many years? That must have been unendurable for him, more painful than his physical discomfort. What could make a man torture himself in this manner, she wondered.

"I'll find a way," Jane vowed, more to herself than to Gabriel. It seemed like an important step toward improving his life.

"I could read it in the library, if you think it's worth it," he offered. "I go there now and again, mainly for shelter. But I also try to read a bit when I go."

"No," she insisted. "I'll figure out how to lend it to you. So you can read it when *you* want. Anyway, I've really got to go. I'll catch up with you soon, though." With that, she waved goodbye, crossed Spring Garden Road and made her way along South Park Street to the hospital, while he departed in the other direction, returning to his office.

***

The temperature dipped in the afternoon and the wind picked up, which was good for business. People felt sorry for Gabriel as he huddled in his corner seeking shelter. The boutique owner spied him from his shop window and made a special trip across the street to deposit a toonie into his cap. "You disappeared pretty quickly this morning, eh?" he said with a good-natured grin. "I guess you don't like all that bustle." Gabriel nodded. "I don't blame you. Hey, chin up, Eddie. It's supposed to warm up later this week."

As the boutique owner was crossing the street back to his store, a young woman walked toward Gabriel carrying a large Shoppers Drug Mart bag. Something in the way she moved, the way she carried herself, reminded him of Jennifer Levenson. It had been years since he thought about her. He wondered what had happened to her. Had she revolutionized space flight, as she had always said she would? Was she still living in British Columbia? Had she married?

He studied the young woman. She was slightly shorter than Jenny, her hair red and curly. There was no way anyone would ever confuse the two women. But she had that same determination as she walked, the same 'I'm going to conquer the world' attitude in her gaze. When Jenny put her mind to something.... Like when she decided that I, that oblivious young simpleton, was going to be her boyfriend. Boy, she got what she wanted!

Gabriel's thoughts drifted to what he considered his first time. His first sexual encounter. That weekend when Jenny's parents were away. How young they had both been! What did they know about life and love? Still, it had been a beautiful Sabbath, one of the finest moments of his life. Something he could hold onto, even on a bitterly cold day like today.

That inevitably brought to mind his last time. Suddenly, he was engulfed by a powerful wave of regret, of loss, of doubt. It must have been over two decades ago, perhaps longer. Was it all worth it? He began to lose heart. It wasn't the first time he had succumbed to bouts of uncertainty, to self-doubt. But they were coming more frequently now.

He recalled his last night with Jenny, on the eve of her departure to Vancouver. It was late August and the days were still long, the weather warm, although a chill breeze crept in after sunset. They had spent the afternoon walking around the Scarborough Bluffs, reminiscing about the past, dreaming about the future. For the first time, Jenny's intrepid eyes were assailed by fear. As if, on the precipice of the freedom she had always yearned for, it had finally occurred to her that there might be something of value in the past she was discarding, a precious pearl buried amongst all those regrets and recriminations.

She held onto his hand tightly as they wished each other goodnight for the last time before he accompanied her to the airport the following afternoon. "You'll be fine, Jenny," Gabriel said. "You're going to set British Columbia on fire!"

"Great," she quipped, "so now I'm an arsonist. I'm sure my parents will be proud when they bail me out of jail."

"Aw, you know what I mean."

"Yes, I do. And I appreciate it. I'm going to miss you," she said, smiling warmly, nostalgically, through her tears.

"Me too," he said, wondering whether that was really true.

She leaned over, parted his lips with her tongue and kissed him languorously on the mouth, taking her time, wishing to remember their last kiss. "The world is going to celebrate the name Gabriel Klein. Of that I'm one hundred percent certain," she declared as she pulled away. "*Nothing* is going to stop someone as brilliant and determined as you."

How wrong she had been, Gabriel reflected more than twenty-five years later. No-one had ever heard of him. He had accomplished nothing of significance to anyone but himself. Had his been a wasted life? What would Jenny say if she could see him today?

It was the same with Mr. Graham, he thought suddenly, liberating another long-suppressed memory. On the afternoon of his high school graduation, he found Mr. Graham on a metal stepladder in a deserted hallway, struggling to affix a banner over the lockers. *Congratulations Class of 1989*, it read in sparkling metallic red letters. "Mr. Graham," he said, "I've been meaning to talk to you. I... I really wanted to thank you for all you did for me."

"Oh, I really don't think I did much," the teacher said modestly, his thinning white steel-wool hair in disarray.

Gabriel grabbed a corner of the banner and climbed up on a locker shelf to assist him. "Yes, you did! If you hadn't believed in me when.... Let's face it, there really wasn't much to believe in.... If you hadn't helped me catch up to the rest of the class, I never would have gotten myself straightened out. Never would have gotten a free ride to U. of T. I owe you a lot. Thank you, sir!"

With Gabriel's help, Mr. Graham hung the banner and descended from the ladder. He looked intently into Gabriel's steel blue eyes and explained with astounding candidness, "Gabriel, I'm an old man. When I was young, I had dreams of doing something truly great with my life. I don't know what, inventing something, maybe getting a Nobel Peace Prize, or writing a great book, a masterpiece. Something that would make a lasting impact on the world. Well, I'll be retiring after next year and that ship has most certainly sailed. There's not much chance that I'll do *anything* that people will remember me for. But if I've helped you get back on track, if I *truly* made a difference with you, then you can help *me*, too. You've got so much talent, so much promise. Go on to do great things, Gabriel. For both of us. Okay? When you do something great with your life, I'll feel like I contributed somehow.... like I did something truly worthwhile.... Now go join your classmates for dinner in the gym, young man!"

Gabriel supposed he must have let Mr. Graham down too, somehow, but his guilt was only fleeting. It all seemed so far away from him now, beyond his grasp, like the faint light of a star obscured by clouds on a windy night.

His reverie was interrupted by the clatter of the bank manager locking up, wearing her permanent press, ever-ready scowl. "Goodnight, your worship!" Gabriel called to her sarcastically. She glared at him without responding, no doubt perplexed, maddened even, by the economic irrationality of his existence. Then, lifting her nose, she pivoted and marched away, secure in her superiority, the prosperity of her life. Across the street, the pharmacist's assistant was also leaving, his cellphone to his ear as usual, no doubt getting an earful from his wife. It was time for Gabriel, too, to call it quits for the day.

Another workday over, Gabriel picked up his cap and counted the day's haul. Eleven dollars and sixty cents. Not bad. That would allow him to splurge on dinner at the supermarket and still save five dollars. He reflected on the eventful day. Although it had not started auspiciously, was miserably cold, it was a productive one overall. He had earned a good sum of money. More importantly, he had made some progress with Jane. He would need her help to set his plan in motion, but he could never approach her as a supplicant, begging for charity. Today, however, he had lain the groundwork to do her a great service. If he could carry that off, he could ask for her help with a clear conscience, based on the principles of respect and reciprocity. Yes, he thought while making his way to the supermarket on Queen Street, it had been a good day after all.

Chapter 8

Gabriel's tenure as an undergraduate at the University of Toronto was in many ways the happiest period of his life. No longer trapped in his Bathurst Heights suburban prison, he felt free to partake of the best of the world. He had exchanged the claustrophobic confines of his parents' triplex, with its drab interior, the overpowering odour of stale food, the dreary smallness of it all, for the glory and magic of the St. George Campus. His nominal academic home on campus was the enchanting Romanesque Revival maze that was the University college building, with its individually painted tiles, third floor rooms that were accessible only by specific staircases, chambers that could be entered only through other rooms, and rumours of a ghost haunting the premises. But his classes took place in buildings all across the vast expanse of the downtown campus: in Larkin Hall on Devonshire; in Convocation Hall; at New College, a more modern, quirky, labyrinthine delight; at Lash Miller Labs; across Queens Park at Northrup Frye. The sweep of geography he travelled simply to attend classes was testimony to the broader horizons of his mind and spirit.

And how wonderful were the people he encountered! Rather than the same stultifying neighbourhood children he had suffered his entire life, the intellectually lazy, the bullies and thugs like Victor Runyon, the good-natured but simple, the Stoners, at U. of T. he mingled with the best and brightest that Canada and the world had to offer. In his first week alone, he had meaningful conversations with students from Calgary, Kapuskasing, Los Angeles, Moncton, Mauritania, Mexico, Thailand and Vancouver. How his frontiers had expanded!

Witnessing these students, hundreds of them, rushing to classes, milling about in front of Robarts Library or Sid Smith, jaywalking across St. George Street, mobbing the food trucks, congregating on King's College Circle, made the blood pulse faster in Gabriel's veins, gave him a thrill of existence that he had never before experienced.

To him, the university was a world of its own for its more than sixty-thousand students, faculty and staff. It was an independent country within the city of Toronto. With its own sports teams, a student government, theater and music ensembles, student-run newspapers, a police force. It *was* freedom. He lived without adult supervision. He selected the courses that interested *him*, rather than a slate of required subjects imposed on him by nameless, faceless administrators. He was not beholden to his parents for his income, which came from his scholarship and the part-time jobs he held during the term and throughout the summer.

But university life was richer than simply classes and work. It was endless hours in cafés or bars debating the essential mysteries of life: whether freedom was preferable to equality; whether free trade with the US would enrich Canada or hollow it out, make it dependent on Washington; the meaning of justice; the future of the Confederation after Meech Lake; whether Gorbachev would actually relinquish control over his Eastern European empire or whether it was all posturing; the Tragically Hip versus Blue Rodeo. It was all so exciting and adult. No, it was better than adult. Adults spent their time punching clocks, making mortgage payments. Their discourse was confined to childcare, root canals, back pain. They lived the unexamined life that Socrates derided, embraced all the chains that Gabriel dreaded. No spontaneity. No inspiration. It was a wonder they had the courage to emerge from the cocoon of their blankets in the morning to face the inevitable dreariness of their lives.

University students experienced life as it was meant to be lived. Fully. Exploring. Probing. Thinking. Free.

    To manage expenses, he shared a small, three-bedroom apartment on the second floor of a three-storey building near Spadina and Dupont with Aziz and a student he had not met previously, whose contact information he had obtained from U. of T.'s off-campus housing office. Hamiltonian Vail Sheppard, whom his mother, an avid skier and one-time member of the Canadian Olympic alpine team, had named after a ski resort, was the stereotypical engineering student, who never met a beer he didn't like. Unlike Gabriel, he personified the night owl, the extrovert, the life of every party. Although they roomed together all four years of their undergraduate careers, they frequently clashed over the commotion Vail inevitably made when he surfaced in the wee hours of the morning after going on a bender, his allergy to housework, his habit of leaving empty milk containers in the refrigerator without replacing them. Their relationship was surface-level, practical. Could you please pass the butter? And will you be out tonight or should I put the chain on when I get in? But when Gabriel needed advice on women, Vail was the first person he would turn to.

    When Aziz moved out after the second year, Vail and Gabriel brought in a replacement, Pablo Ramirez from Mexico City. Pablo was quieter, more cerebral, more compatible with Gabriel's lifestyle than Vail. Pablo's father was a diplomat, so he had grown up all around the world, in Chad, Yugoslavia, Argentina, South Africa, and now Canada. To one such as Gabriel, who had never travelled further than Montreal, Pablo was an exotic figure, a romantic one, with lots of precious life experience. Yet the Mexican's bookish ways, his innate shyness which people often mistook for haughtiness, for arrogance, made it difficult for Gabriel to break through to him, to forge other than the politest of bonds.

***

And friends? In a manner of speaking, yes, although they were more acquaintances than true friends. In fact, Gabriel never really had a close male friend again after his rupture with Jack Silverman in junior high. The men in Jennifer's circle had been *her* friends, not really *his*, and, though he blended right in with them, he truly hadn't connected to them on an individual basis like he had with Jennifer. And of that group, only Aziz and Lauren joined Gabriel at U. of T. Jennifer, of course, was in Vancouver. Selma had jumped at the opportunity to study at McGill. Steve, whose grades had not been good enough for U. of T. or to follow Jennifer to UBC, had stayed uptown at York. Gabriel, Aziz and Lauren initially tried to recreate the camaraderie they had enjoyed at McKenzie. They quickly discovered, however, that without Jennifer as the glue that held the group together, they had too little in common to remain good friends. Instead, he had his flatmates – superficial friends that they were – members of the Hart House Debating Society, his colleagues at The Newspaper where he worked on the editorial page, his classmates.

And, of course, there were women. Mature women. Intelligent women. Sophisticated women. In his classes. In the clubs. In truth, Gabriel was both awestruck and intimidated by the women he encountered on campus. As a rule, while he had always found himself comfortable in scholastic settings and with adults, he had always been ill-at-ease with his peers, especially with the fairer sex – except for Jenny, but she was now over four thousand kilometres away. He didn't quite know how to act around women, was always worried that he was saying or doing the wrong thing. And, thriving on clear oral communication, he was terrible at reading the many arcane signals that women used to communicate, which constantly got him in trouble. All the more so since the women he befriended were all paramours, women he had designs on or those who fancied him, rather than platonic friends.

A prime example was Angela Pietrangelo, his first new friend in the university. He had sat next to Angela in his first Introductory Psychology class, PSYCH 100, a class of sixteen hundred students in the circular Convocation Hall. She had smiled at Gabriel indulgently when he clumsily dropped his bag before class, spilling its contents on floor. Rather than help him clean up the mess, she giggled at him as he crawled around her feet to pick up the pencils and paperclips that had fallen, in the process, to his embarrassment, brushing up against her shapely legs, bare from the hem of her miniskirt down to her sandals. She teased him about that ever afterwards, saying that if he wanted to peek up her skirt, he could have been conventional and asked her out. Since Angela and her roommate Penelope were also in his Economics class, they quickly all became study partners and often hung around together at the Hart House café or the University College Refectory between classes.

Although Angela was stunningly beautiful, with her wavy auburn hair, piercing blue eyes and well-toned, model's body, Gabriel found himself comfortable with her because she was off-limits. As a Catholic, she would have no interest in dating him, he presumed, just as he had resolved to date only Jewish girls. He simply hadn't realized that, as a handsome and intelligent young man, he might attract unwanted interest.

Matters came to a head in February, when he arrived at Angela and Penelope's apartment to study for the third Economics midterm with them. Angela welcomed him in dressed seductively, wearing a short black skirt with a slit running almost to the top of her thigh, a low-cut, almost translucent white silk blouse. Her hair, which she normally kept clipped up, was hanging long over her bare shoulders. *God, she's gorgeous!* Gabriel observed.

"Would you like some wine?" she asked sweetly, her slight, sexy lisp accentuating the word "some".

"Um, no thanks. That won't help me study," he replied. "Uh, where's Penny?"

"Oh, she couldn't make it. She has this thing with her family. She's sleeping over there tonight...." The trenches were dug deeply, the escape paths barred. It was a full-out ambush.

"Really? Maybe we should do this tomorrow night instead, then," he said twitching awkwardly.

"No. She said we should go ahead without her," Angela said quickly.

By this point, Gabriel was aware that he was in trouble, but couldn't think of a way to extricate himself gracefully without insulting Angela. So, he tossed his bag on the kitchen table and reached for his books. But she took his arm and directed him to the futon instead. "Let's sit here. It's more comfortable."

Angela retreated to the kitchen briefly and returned with two glasses of red wine. She took an ample swig of hers and handed the other to Gabriel, who placed it warily on the coffee table without drinking. Angela switched on her stereo and slipped an Air Supply record onto the turntable.

"Hey, Angie! It'll be easier to work without music," Gabriel pleaded.

She seated herself right next to him on the futon, leaving barely enough room to wedge a strip of tin foil between them. He could smell the pleasant fragrance of her shampoo, could witness the heaving of her breasts in the red, lacy brassiere that showed clearly through her blouse. "It's just background music. Besides, let's talk for a bit first. We can work later," she suggested, taking his notebook from him and placing it out of reach on the coffee table. She sipped some more wine.

Gabriel consulted his watch uneasily. "I don't really have that much time. I want to get to sleep early because I have an early morning tutorial."

She threw him a coquettish look with her angelic eyes. "Relax, Gabriel. I've wanted to be alone with you for a long time." She gently reached for his hand — hers was softer than silk — and placed it on her thigh, under the open slit of her skirt. He quickly jerked it away and stood up.

"Hey! What *is* this, Angie? I just came here to study."

Angela smiled patiently, seductively. "What do you think? I was hoping we could get to know each other a bit better," she said invitingly.

He bit his upper lip. "This isn't what I signed up for," he said with growing determination. "I think I should go. We should try this again when Penny's back."

"Oh, come on! I *see* the way you look at me, my legs, my eyes. I *know* you like me, too," she asserted, her adorable lisp almost sealing the deal.

"Angie, you are the *hottest* woman I have ever known. By far. Probably the hottest I will *ever* know. I can't help but stare at you. I wouldn't be *alive* if I didn't. But let's just be friends," he pleaded.

"Why?" she challenged him, still speaking softly in almost a sing-song voice. "Since we like each other, why can't we just go with it and see where it takes us?" She moved a step toward him, seducing him with her eyes, the subtle movements of her head, her hair, as she spoke.

This was going to be difficult, he realized. He was hoping he wouldn't have to explain it to her. "Hey, Angie," he said softly, "Why ruin a good friendship?"

Angela guffawed. "Come on, Gabriel! We're not getting married. It's just sex!" she exclaimed, as she closed the distance between them and blew gently into his ear.

It was at that moment, as goosebumps emerged upon the skin of his neck and his legs dissolved into jelly, that he realized it wasn't really his friend Angela in front of him after all. It was

Satan in a black slit skirt. As irresistible as she was, he needed to leave immediately, before it was too late.

"Angie, really!" he said ineffectually, his voice wavering. "We need to stop this."

"Why?" She continued her assault on his ear with her moist lips, her tongue.

"You see...." he said uncomfortably, squirming out of both euphoria and guilt, feeling his resolve melt, "It wouldn't.... It wouldn't be fair to you. It couldn't go anywhere."

"What do you mean?" she asked coquettishly, as she began nibbling on the side of his neck, "I think we can go *pretty* far. As far as you *like*, Tiger...."

"Well," he tried to explain feebly, "I'm Jewish. I can't marry someone who's not Jewish. If we dated, it would put you in a terrible position where, at some point, either we'd break up or you'd have to convert__"

That got her attention. She quickly withdrew from his neck and glowered at him. "You want me to *convert*?" she blurted out. "I'm Catholic!"

"No. No. Not at all. I'm just saying that if we dated, there'd be no future since you wouldn't want to convert and I wouldn't marry a Catholic," he continued absurdly.

"So, let me get this straight. You're saying that you won't date me because I'm Catholic?" she asked angrily. Her whole body tensed. Her eyes, which had implored him only seconds before, now assaulted him with their merciless, withering glare.

"It's not just you. I wouldn't date *anyone* who isn't Jewish for that reason," Gabriel clarified, trying to appease her.

She turned away from him and stomped toward the kitchen. "You're such a bigot! Just forget about it," she snapped.

"Listen, Angie. I...."

"No, just get out," she screamed. "Take your books and get out. *Get out!*"

As he slunk out of her apartment, he heard Suzy Q's voice echoing in his mind: *you fucking yid!*

He dissected the situation immediately afterwards with Vail, who, as usual, viewed matters differently.

"What a dickweed!" Vail scoffed, while flossing his teeth in the kitchen. Gabriel would ordinarily have admonished him that the apartment had a bathroom for all his personal hygiene needs. But he was eager for Vail's advice, so he tried to ignore the etiquette breach. "Why didn't you just screw her?"

"Aw, Vail, you wouldn't understand. Not everyone thinks with their dicks," Gabriel replied sharply, employing language to which Vail could relate. "Angie's a friend. We don't have any future together beyond that. So why ruin a good friendship by screwing around?"

Vail stared at him dumbfounded. "You're hopeless! That babe is *hot*! I'm mean *smoking* hot! And she was practically *throwing* herself at you." He feigned a falsetto voice, "'Oh *please*, Gabriel. Defile me! *Ravage* me!' And you just walked away.... Think about it. You ruined your friendship anyway. So, what's the point?" In a twisted way, Gabriel reflected, he actually had a point.

"Why is it," Gabriel asked, "that I miss all the signals? I had no idea she was into me like that. It was the same with my girlfriend in high school. Jenny. She practically had to hit me over the head to make me realize that she was interested in me."

"Angie *should've* hit you over the head.... Listen, Gabriel. For reasons I can't fathom, women find you sexy. That's your superpower. And like Spiderman, with it comes great responsibility. You've got to be responsible and give them what they want."

"That's just it," Gabriel lamented. "I have no *idea* what they want. I'm not even sure what *I* want. I've been chasing Naomi Steinman all year, but she definitely seems immune to my superpower. She's positively repelled by it.... That's disgusting, Vail! Throw it out!" he snapped, as his roommate discarded his dental floss on the kitchen table.

Vail grimaced and removed the floss with an exaggerated, mocking gesture of obeisance. "Which one is *she*?" he asked.

"She's the one I was telling you and Aziz about. The girl I met at the JSU booth in Sid Smith...."

"The one with no tits?" Vail made a gesture with his hand across his chest.

"No, that's what you say about Julie Pomerantz. And that's not fair!" Gabriel protested. Julie was a girl Gabriel had taken out twice, mainly because she was available. They had no chemistry together and both moved on quickly.

"Well," Vail advised sagely, "here's the wisdom the great Vail imparts to you my friend: stay away from the titless wonders and say yes to girls like Angie. Even you shouldn't be able to screw that up."

Gabriel sighed and went to bed. Talking to Vail didn't help at all.

Overall, his first two years at U. of T. were tremendous in every respect, except socially. Yet it was that particular deficiency that he dwelled upon, that ate away at him late at night. He found himself feeling forlorn and hopeless, fearing that, after Jenny, he was fated never again to find love.

Without having a clear direction for his studies, Gabriel registered for a disparate handful of year-long introductory courses in his first year: psychology, philosophy, political science, classics, and economics. He was quickly captivated by philosophy and declared his major before the first semester was finished. In his philosophy classes, he encountered so many ideas that shaped his outlook on the world. He learned about Aristotle's assertion that what separated human beings from animals was their use of language, which empowered them to communicate abstract ideas, learn from the past, plan for the future. This powerful observation was tempered, however, by Wittgenstein's caveat that human beings were limited by language, constrained by it as much as they were liberated by it. The words they possessed limited their horizons, their ability to express ideas. If their vocabulary lacked a word to express a particular idea, concept or shade of meaning, people would be unable to conceive of it. Gabriel found that idea comforting. It explained why people could not truly comprehend God. They simply lacked the words to do so.

He was exercised by the Western liberal tradition, beginning with the Hobbesian state of nature. How could they imagine a world without God? To assume a mythical state of nature, a state of war of all against all, and assert that in order to escape that chaos all would need voluntarily to consent to the dominion of a powerful man, a Leviathan, who would provide peace and security. How hollow it all was! Or John Locke's claim that people are inherently free and equal irrespective of God. While Gabriel agreed with Locke's assertion that governments that fail to act in the public interest could and should be replaced, and while Gabriel was by nature and conviction a democrat, he believed that any edifice that justified itself solely in terms of man and reason, leaving God out of the equation, must inevitably fail.

What shook Gabriel to the core, however, was Rousseau's revelation that man is born free, but everywhere he is shackled by chains of his own making. Yes, Gabriel reflected, that's the essence of the human condition. Chains of convenience. Chains of duty. Chains of wealth. Chains of love. He refused to include chains of religion and would not travel with Marx to lament religion as the opiate of the deluded masses. He decided that man's greatest duty to himself was to shed the chains that shackled him. To free himself to unleash his full potential as a human being and thereby sanctify the glory of God.

Although he took issue with much of what he encountered, he absorbed it all and, strangely, incorporated core elements of it into his world view, despite the inherent contradictions. In the midst of this open-minded exploration of the canon of Western philosophy, therefore, Gabriel's views of God underwent a puzzling metamorphosis. In the absence of any formal Jewish education, which he stopped at age fourteen, and without ever attending a synagogue, Gabriel became his own religious advisor, his own rabbi and teacher. Consequently, his understanding of Judaism became much more personal and idiosyncratic, less directly tied to scripture and more a product of his own interests, the ideas he encountered in his secular studies, the particular quirks and foibles of his personality. As a consequence, although he still was a practicing Jew, he no longer took the commandments quite as literally, but began to view God in a more humanistic way.

This led him to religious and social views that were very difficult to square with any official conception of Orthodox Judaism. His views on sex, for example, were illustrative. During his college years, he began to oppose marriage as an institution, decreeing it an artificial construct that interfered with the natural course of love, which was God's greatest gift to mankind. Therefore, he no longer had any compunctions against pre-marital sex, and would be willing to move in with a girlfriend. It might be said, therefore, that his views on Orthodox Judaism became rather unorthodox during his college years.

It was an adjustment for Gabriel to live in a shared apartment with flatmates. On one level, it was a great relief to be free of his parents. Unlike his parents, his flatmates respected his closed door, never objected on those rare occasions on which he slept late, didn't lecture him incessantly on the merits of fibre or the importance of hard work, in general didn't mind his business. Yet he was surprised to discover that he missed his parents' regularity, their predictability. His parents were absent all day during the work week, allowing him the run of the house. They retired for the night routinely at eleven thirty. They never blasted technopop in the early hours of the morning while Gabriel was sleeping or vomited on the sofa after going on a bender.

The triumvirate, as Gabriel dubbed them, quickly established some basic rules, although they did not resolve all conflict between them and, paradoxically, sometimes inspired discord. Gabriel posted them in the form of ten commandments affixed to the fridge with a cheap souvenir magnet from Niagara Falls.

If thou makest a mess, thou cleanst it up.

If thou finishest the roll of toilet paper, thou replacest it before leaving the bathroom.

Thou shalt respect thine flatmates' privacy and property, including their clothing and non-communal food/utensils.

Each time thou servest thineself with communal milk, cereal or other staples, thou shalt deposit $0.25 in the communal grocery jar.

Every three months, when it is thine turn, thou shalt pay the entire apartment rent to the landlord on or before the first of the month.

Each week, thou shalt deposit an additional $10 in the communal grocery jar for communal supplies.

If thou finishest the last of one of the communal supplies (milk, cereal, bread, rice, toilet paper, facial tissues, etc.,) thou shalt replace it in a timely manner so that your flatmates suffer not.

Thou shalt not make noise after midnight without the express consent of thine flatmates.

Thou mayest have guests of the female variety sleep over on weekends. At other times, only with your flatmates' express consent.

Thou mayest host a party in the apartment only with the express consent of thine flatmates.

Aziz and Gabriel followed these rules fairly scrupulously. Vail, however, was too free a spirit to be bound by tedious regulations. Too frequently, Gabriel or Aziz would be in a hurry to get to class in the morning, only to discover that there was no milk for their cereal or no toilet paper on the roller. Invariably, Vail was the culprit, always with some inadequate excuse – "I *meant* to, but I was running late for my Electromagnetics lab" or "Oh, I didn't realize it was empty." At other times, they would stumble to the locked bathroom in their underwear late at night and wait patiently, to be greeted, when the door finally opened, by one of Vail's harem – as they referred to the women he brought home – who was sleeping over unannounced. When they called him on it, he'd always play the aggrieved party. "Chillax!! Don't have an aneurism!! It was a last-minute thing. It just *happened*. I couldn't just turn Brandy away. I mean, did you *look* at her?" And, of course, there were his trademark thunderous entrances in the wee hours of the morning after a night of heavy drinking.

There was also the matter of the Guns N Roses poster, a cross with five long-haired skulls against a black background, which Vail had affixed prominently in the living room. That was communal territory and they had agreed that nothing would be displayed there unless all three residents approved. Neither Aziz nor Gabriel were fans of the band, and they were both uncomfortable displaying a cross in communal areas. Yet, without their consent, one afternoon they arrived home to find it permanently ensconced above the futon. They both protested, but Vail waved their objections away. "Oh, come on!" he harangued them. "It's not a religious symbol.' It's rock and roll. And it's way cool!"

Annoying as it was, they tolerated his transgressions, often forgave him for them, because he brought life to the apartment, a dynamism they would never have achieved on their own.

Their apartment was a landmark on the social scene because of Vail. People were always stopping by. They hosted many parties. In essence, Vail made them cool. So, while it was often too lively for Aziz and Gabriel, who were quieter and more studious in nature, they were reluctant to mess with their special sauce by coming down too hard on him.

Tensions occasionally flared, however, as a result of shortfalls in the grocery jar. The idea had been to balance between communal need and disproportionate usage. From the outset, they had concluded that, while they could each have a separate section in the fridge, the freezer, the bathroom for their own sundries and food items – which was especially important given Gabriel's kosher and Aziz's halal dietary restrictions – it would also be practical to share certain communal resources. It made little sense for them each to purchase their own milk, facial tissues or toilet paper. Yet, to divide the costs of these goods equally would be unfair to whomever used them the least. So, after much discussion, the triumvirate agreed to a formula that required a fixed contribution each week from each party together with a nominal additional contribution into the grocery jar each time one of tenants or their guests used one of the enumerated goods.

The concept was simple enough, yet by midway through their first year there were too many surprising deficits. Because of his laxness toward the rules in general, the finger of suspicion naturally fell upon Vail, but he bristled uncharacteristically under his flatmates' suspicion and pointed his finger at them.

On one such occasion, Gabriel and Aziz were eating a late Sunday morning breakfast at the kitchen table, while Vail coiffed his hair in the bathroom, the door propped half-open. Vail obsessed over his hair, using only specialized shampoos and conditioners, spending hours in front of the mirror just to achieve the perfect 'natural-looking' wave. His flatmates teased him about that liberally.

"It's your turn to go shopping, Aziz," Gabriel said between spoonfuls of Corn Flakes. I need to give you fifty cents for breakfast and my ten dollars for the week." His fingers played absently with a fingernail-sized chip in the grey laminate that covered the table.

"Yeah, sure," Aziz responded. "I'll wait until Casanova in there has finished with his hair. I'll need his money, too. Hey, don't do that! You're making the crack bigger."

"What? Oh.... This table's a piece of garbage anyway. It wobbles so much that I can't eat cereal without getting my clothes splashed," Gabriel complained.

"Well, it's all we've got for now. So, treat it well. Hey, Pretty Boy! Are you finished in there?" Aziz called to the bathroom. Receiving no reply, he turned to Gabriel and said with a smirk, "He must be very absorbed by the mirror."

Vail emerged, still preening and patting his strawberry blonde mane with his hands in leonine fashion. "I heard you," he said. "Where's the fire?"

"Oh my God!" Gabriel feigned shock. "Is that Tom Cruise? His hair is *unbelievable!*"

"Very funny, wise guy. I haven't been able to find my regular conditioner, so it's not holding like it usually does," Vail explained.

"If you spend half the time on your work that you spend on your hair, you'd make the dean's list," Gabriel commented snidely. With a loud droning whoosh, the heat suddenly blew forth from the vent in the floor beneath the table. No matter what temperature they set the thermostat for, the apartment effectively had only two heat settings: infernally hot or Arctic cold. When the furnace was on, it blew warm dry air, until everyone and everything was febrile and chapped. Once it passed some unknown threshold, however, it switched off and eventually plunged them into hypothermia. It made dressing for around the house difficult, although they quickly learned to wear layers that they could peel off and throw back on as necessary.

Aziz brought them back on topic. "I need your weekly grocery contribution. I'm going to go shopping now." As Vail went to his room to retrieve his wallet, Aziz ambled over to the cupboard above the sink where they kept the grocery jar. He stared at the jar wide-eyed, his palms turned skyward. "Hey!" he cried. "What's going on? There's only two dollars in here!"

"What?" Gabriel asked stupidly. "That can't be!"

Vail returned with a crumpled ten-dollar bill in hand and anger in his green eyes. "There must've been over twenty dollars in there yesterday. Which one of you numb nuts has been pilfering from the kitty?"

Aziz and Gabriel glanced at each other meaningfully. "If you're accusing us of stealing, Vail, I find that offensive," Gabriel snapped. "*I* certainly didn't take any money from there. And I know Aziz didn't either...."

"How do you know that? *He* was the one who discovered the money missing. Isn't *that* convenient?" Vail thundered.

Gabriel was astonished, Aziz furious. "Are you accusing *me* of stealing?" Aziz exploded in response.

"I've known Aziz for years. He would *never* do something like that. On the other hand, *you* always have a problem following the rules and meeting your communal responsibilities," Gabriel insinuated.

"Oh, so it's like *that*, is it?" Vail said.

"Or maybe it was one of the tarts you brought into the apartment last night," Aziz suggested.

"Watch yourself, Ayatollah," Vail shouted, his fists clenched. Enraged, Aziz prepared to lunge at him. Instinctively, Gabriel positioned himself between his two flatmates to prevent it from escalating into a fistfight. But the damage was already done. The mutual suspicion and ill will that was engendered continued to fester, eating away at the benign, surface-level camaraderie that had thus far prevailed amongst the triumvirate, though it would be several months before it broke them apart.

As Gabriel prepared for his end-of-year exams, he managed stress by playing his violin. Although the imperfection of his sound still haunted him, the complexity of a piece of classical music helped take his mind off his worries. While he was playing away his cares one morning, however, the tension on his strings was too great and the bridge developed a large crack. He feared that if he ignored it, the bridge might snap entirely, causing the tailpiece to slam into the body of the instrument and render it useless. Despite the other demands on his time, therefore, he set off immediately to get it repaired, which led to one of the most important developments of his undergraduate years.

His first stop was to the U. of T. Faculty of Music. There he was directed by a kindly administrative assistant to a Music store not far from Roy Thompson Hall. She had told him that there were closer shops, but that the one she recommended was meticulous and reasonably priced.

Upon his arrival, Gabriel spotted a help wanted sign on the door, which started the wheels turning in his head. He entered and told the clerk he was there on two missions: to repair his violin and apply for the job. She grinned and said that, in both cases, he needed to speak to Mr. Balogh through the rear door.

He passed through wooden displays of sheet music and a wall of wind instruments — trumpets, saxophones, tubas — to a surprisingly out-of-place green baize door, which was slightly ajar. He pushed it gently, revealing an unexpectedly large, chaotic workroom with wind and stringed instruments of all kinds in various states of disrepair. It was like an automotive shop for musical instruments. The whole room was covered with paper — mainly yellow invoices — scattered haphazardly on tables and stools, pasted to the walls, on the floor. Gabriel marvelled at the array of tools, brushes, rags, pastes, wires and other materials affixed to the walls. In the middle of the room, either controlling the chaos or being mastered by it, was a short, slender man of about sixty with fine ribbons of white hair, pomaded and carefully arranged to cover as much scalp as possible, and narrow, rectangular steel-rimmed glasses, tinkering with the keys on a clarinet.

"Yes?" the man asked curtly. "Can I help you?" He had a heavy Hungarian accent, even more pronounced than Esther's. Gabriel instantly felt at ease, despite the man's aloof demeanour.

"Um, I'm here to fix my violin," Gabriel replied. "And...."

"And?" Mr. Balogh repeated tersely. "And what?"

"I'd like to apply for the job."

Mr. Balogh extended his hand impatiently. "Give it to me." Gabriel removed his violin from its case and handed it to Mr. Balogh, who began his examination. "I see. Too much tension on the strings. You need to be careful. I can fix. It be ready Monday. Fill this out." He handed Gabriel a blank invoice form.

"Great! How much will it cost?" It amused Gabriel that Mr. Balogh reached for the instrument and proffered the form with his right hand. Balogh, in Hungarian, was a name that loosely translated as "lefty."

"Don't know. Won't know til I fix." The repairman continued to examine Gabriel's cracked bridge.

Gabriel was so enthralled with the shop, the panoply of instruments and tools, the Hungarian proprietor, that he decided uncharacteristically to make conversation. "Ön magyar," he asked, using some of the elementary Hungarian he had learned at home to ask if his interlocutor was Hungarian.

Mr. Balogh's face lit up. "Igen. És te?"

"My parents are," Gabriel responded, reverting to English. "I was born here."

"But you speak the language?" Balogh continued in Hungarian.

"Yes.... Well, no. I understand it fairly well, but speak it only a little. I guess all those years of my parents trying to talk behind my back...."

The man smiled benignly and continued tweaking the strings of Gabriel's violin. After some time, he asked in English, "Which job you want?"

"The one you advertised on the front door," Gabriel replied.

"There's two jobs. One in the store and one helping me," Mr. Balogh explained. "Which one you want?"

Gabriel's eyes roamed the workshop dreamily. "Gosh, I'd love to help you fix instruments! But I know nothing about that. I guess the shop would be more appropriate."

"You good with your hands?"

"Well," Gabriel said reflectively, "I was good at woodworking in school."

"You play well?" Mr. Balogh queried.

"I'm okay, I guess," Gabriel replied uncomfortably.

"Play for me," Mr. Balogh demanded.

"How? My violin__"

"There," the proprietor insisted, waving his finger at a table. "Play that."

Gabriel plucked the violin off the table, marvelling at its workmanship. He had never held such an exquisite instrument. Using his own bow, he played the first piece that came to his mind. Monti's Czardas, which he had learned with Lyudmilla years before. Only on this quality instrument, it sounded better than he had ever played it before. The violin had a crisper, clearer sound that almost brought tears to his eyes, despite his small mistakes.

The man's face softened. "You learn quickly? Follow instructions?" Gabriel nodded. "And maybe learn to speak more Hungarian?" Gabriel nodded again. "Okay. You start Saturday."

"Seriously? No resume or references?" Gabriel asked incredulously.

"No need. I see you make good repair worker. I know. I do this many, many years."

"Oh, thank you. But... how much will I be paid? Also, I can only start after my exams, in late April. And, unfortunately, I can't work Saturdays. I hope that's not a problem," Gabriel declared with trepidation.

Mr. Balogh eyed him warily before answering. "Fine," he said. "You start at end of April, Monday to Friday. Eight dollars an hour. Now let me work." He put Gabriel's violin down and returned his attention to the nickel-plated clarinet.

In the summer between Gabriel's first and second year, his on-again, off-again relationship with his parents took a decided turn for the worse. All throughout his freshman year, to allay his mother's fear that she would never see him once he moved out, he had endeavoured to visit them with surprising frequency. As it was difficult to celebrate the Sabbath properly in his ecumenical apartment, especially with Vail's penchant for wild parties on the weekends, once or twice a month Gabriel would return home for Sabbath meals with his parents. In some respects, his relationship with them had improved markedly now that he was no longer living under their roof and subject to their directives. Rather than their chattel, he had become almost their equal, which relieved much of the tension on his end. And, while his parents wouldn't have readily admitted it, they found life considerably less stressful without Gabriel scrutinizing their every action, judging them from behind his merciless, disapproving eyes.

All that changed on a sultry July evening, when Gabriel stopped by unannounced to surprise Esther on her birthday. He mounted the stairs armed with a bouquet of colourful flowers and was about to knock on the door, when he decided that using his key surreptitiously would have a greater effect. So, he unlocked the door as quietly as possible and tiptoed, his steps muffled by the loud rumbling of the prehistoric, second-hand air conditioner they had bought for their bedroom, to the kitchen, where he heard them talking. "Surprise!" he exclaimed jovially. "Happy birthday!" But his mirth instantly soured, when he descried their embarrassment, their forbidden pleasures laid out on the table.

"Gabriel!" his mother blurted out guiltily. "We... we didn't know you were coming...."

"Apparently *not*," he snapped, his voice laced with bitter irony.

"Ah, Gabriel," Isaac moaned, "why do you have to make everything so difficult?"

"Is that all you have to say?" he asked, while his parents quickly cleared the pepperoni pizza off the table and back into the box. Gabriel clucked at them contemptuously for violating both the injunction against eating pig products and the parallel injunction against mixing meat and milk. Were there no limits to the depths to which they would stoop?

"Now that you don't live here anymore, do we still have to live up to your standards?" Isaac asked contentiously.

Gabriel was incredulous. "*My* standards?" he exploded. "Doesn't Judaism mean *anything* to you? Besides, you used the regular plates and cutlery. *I* eat with them, too! Now they're not kosher, and I can't eat here anymore!" he said. In truth, he was being somewhat disingenuous, since he ate off tableware in restaurants that had also been used for non-kosher food. But it was the principle of the matter.

"Well," his mother tried to appease him, "then we'll use disposables when you come to eat with us."

"That's not the point!" Gabriel shouted.

"What exactly *is* the point?" Isaac challenged him.

"This is supposed to be a kosher home," Gabriel said icily.

Isaac didn't want to have to justify his actions to his son. That wasn't the way it was supposed to work. A father set the rules of the house and the son complied. Not the other way round. But he was eager to defuse the situation. "Look," Isaac explained impatiently. "When you were young, we wanted to raise you with Jewish values and practices. To ground you. To make sure you knew who you were, where you came from. But your mother and I were never as religious as our parents were. Keeping kosher was something *they* did. It didn't matter to us. Then we did it stricter because it was important to you. But now that you're out of the house...."

"You're just going to throw God under the bus. Throw out His commandments." The rancour in Gabriel's voice was palpable.

"It's always God with you, Gabriel," his father complained. "You aren't God! You *also* make your choices. You do what *you* want. Not necessarily what God wants. Rabbi Plotkin, for instance, wouldn't eat at the restaurants you eat at, wouldn't find your kitchen kosher enough."

"Leave Rabbi Plotkin out of this. He's such a fraud!"

"Oh, so now the rabbi is a fraud? I guess everyone in the whole world is a fraud but you!" Isaac taunted, the artery in his forehead pulsating.

"I'm starting to think so...." Gabriel sputtered. "Do you even believe in God?"

"It's always 'do you believe in God' with you.... Yes, I do. No, I don't. What does it matter?" his father equivocated.

Esther tried to intervene. "Can't we just take it easy? You're right. We shouldn't have done this___" she began.

Isaac cut her off. "Oy, stop trying to appease him, like Hitler," he commanded. "Listen, Gabriel. God is just something we tell children to get them to behave, to treat other people properly. But no. I don't believe in God any more than I believe in the Easter Bunny or Santa Claus. Or even that Bogeyman you were so afraid of as a kid."

Gabriel's jaw dropped. His shoulders tensed. His whole body began to tremble. He had always suspected that his father lacked faith, but would never have anticipated this level of disrespect. Of chutzpah. It was too much for him to bear. "I don't even know why I came," he sputtered, shaking his head in disgust. He hurled the flowers contemptuously on the floor and stormed out, muttering "happy birthday" under his breath.

His head was pounding, his heart racing as he bounded down the stairs. How many times will they have to disappoint you before you learn, he berated himself. They're just no good! He clenched and unclenched his fists repeatedly. Once outside, he caught sight of his father's little vegetable garden. Seeing the few meager plants that his father had fussed over, put his soul, his entire being into, that mattered to his father far more than God, his anger rushed to his head. He was overwhelmed with the desire to hurt his father, to cause him intolerable pain. Lifting his right foot spitefully, he kicked the fragile plants repeatedly, digging at their roots with the toe of his sneaker, severing them, destroying the garden, like a dark, avenging angel.

Isaac, who had rushed out onto the balcony to call him back, screamed plaintively, like a wounded animal, "Oy! My garden! Why would you do that? You monster! You monster! Don't come back here! You're not my son!" Gabriel was immediately seized by guilt, wondering how he could have done something so terrible, so hateful. He staggered away furious at his parents, but even more disappointed in himself.

Gabriel's summer job at the Music store was a revelation for him, almost as challenging and enjoyable as his studies. Mr. Balogh was a tough taskmaster, demanding and unforgiving, but he treated Gabriel as a trusted apprentice, shared freely of his knowledge. Gabriel would arrive at ten o'clock each morning and do whatever Mr. Balogh required of him, organizing the chaos of the workspace, cleaning the tools, sometimes taking apart a soprano saxophone, screw-by-screw, key by key, other times restringing a viola. Of course, dismantling an instrument was the easy part. Learning to put it back together was the challenge, and Mr. Balogh showed little sympathy.

At first, the proprietor would ride him hard and impatiently, expecting his apprentice to know all that he had learned over a lifetime of work, not tolerating confusion. After Gabriel had toiled in the workshop for a month, his boss wanted him to stop watching and start doing. Believing in trial by fire, one morning he pressed the issue while examining a tenor saxophone that a customer had brought in for repairs. "There are air leaks, Gabriel," he snapped tersely in Hungarian. "Plug them!"

"But I don't know how," Gabriel protested.

"Haven't you seen me do it?"

"Yes," he replied, "but I don't think I can do it myself."

"Ach!" the white-haired man spat. "Dim the lights." Gabriel complied as his boss inserted a leak light into the neck. "You see? It leaks here and here." Gabriel nodded, seeing the light that escaped from cracks in the B and G keys. "Now fix it!"

Gabriel was flustered. "Is it a screw issue, or do I need to replace the pads?"

"Take a look!" Mr. Balogh commanded. "How does the pad on the B key look?"

"Okay, I guess...." Gabriel replied, not noticing any bends, tears or distortions in the leather.

"Right," his boss affirmed. "What about the cork?"

Gabriel hesitated. "It looks worn."

"Right. So, replace it." Using a sharp box knife, Gabriel cut a small piece from a sheet of cork that Mr. Balogh kept on a shelf. Then, after carefully removing the worn cork, he glued the fresh piece under the key.

Mr. Balogh inserted the leak light back into the instrument's neck, gently pressed the B key and grunted his approval. "Now the G key. What's wrong with it?"

Picking up the instrument again, Gabriel inspected the pad and the cork. "I don't see any problems with the pad or the cork," he declared tentatively.

"So, why is it leaking? Think!" his boss chided him.

"Do I just need to tighten the screw?" Gabriel asked cautiously.

Mr. Balogh nodded. "It's worth trying." Gabriel reached for a small instrument screwdriver and tightened the screw on the G pad. Inserting the leak light into the neck once more, Gabriel depressed the G key and noted with satisfaction that no light escaped.

"Next time, when a saxophone comes in with a leak, you do it yourself, without wasting my time," Mr. Balogh sputtered, splashing ice-cold water on Gabriel's triumph.

By the end of the summer, as Gabriel prepared to start his second year at the university, he had learned how to perform many routine repairs on most stringed and wind instruments. Mr. Balogh had trained him to diagnose instruments by himself when they were brought into the shop. If he could repair them himself, he was told to do so without bothering his boss, who would focus on the more complicated cases. Although he remained aloof and critical, Mr. Balogh exhibited a great deal of trust in his apprentice. They would talk little during the workday, but his overall attitude toward Gabriel had changed during the summer. Gabriel could sense that, despite his snarls, his tsks, his boss approved of his work. Indeed, the proprietor had increased Gabriel's wages several times without being asked to, so that Gabriel was now earning eleven dollars an hour, a great wage for a summer job.

In late August, Mr. Balogh approached him as he was restringing a cello and stood over him awkwardly. Having learned to let his taciturn boss initiate conversations, Gabriel continued his work, averting the white-haired man's gaze, and waited for Mr. Balogh to speak his mind. Eventually, his boss snapped in English, in an unsuccessful attempt to sound friendly, "You go back to school soon?"

Gabriel nodded. "I can work here for another ten days, but then school starts."

"And...." Mr. Balogh began, but seemed unable to continue. Eventually he said, "And you wouldn't want to work here full time? Forget school?"

Gabriel was flustered. "Leave school? No. No, I couldn't. No. Thank you, though. But no."

Mr. Balogh's plump, downturned cheeks registered his disappointment. "No. Of course. You're right," he admitted. "But you can work here during the year? Part time?"

Gabriel considered this for a moment. "Yes.... In principle, I could. I don't know exactly when or for how many hours. It'll depend on my schedule. But I'd love to continue working with you."

Mr. Balogh nodded curtly. "Good. You let me know when. I pay you twelve dollars an hour whenever you can work." He placed his hand stiffly on Gabriel's shoulder, letting it rest there awkwardly for a few seconds before withdrawing and leaving Gabriel to his work.

"Jesus Christ! Not again," Vail exclaimed. He stood with his elbow on the kitchen counter holding the grocery jar, which was completely empty. "I'm so fed up with this!"

Hearing no reply, he called angrily, "Gabriel! Aziz!"

With irritation in his voice, Aziz, who was studying in his room at his white, pressed board Ikea desk, yelled back, "What's your problem pretty boy? I'm studying for a midterm."

"There's no money in the kitty anymore. I put a quarter in yesterday and there was a bunch of money there. Now there's nothing."

With a guttural harumph, Aziz abandoned his desk to join his roommate in the kitchen. "I too tire of this. Maybe we should stop hosting parties and letting women run loose in the apartment so freely," he said reproachfully, glaring at his flatmate with his round, almost black eyes.

"That's just the *point*, man. We haven't had anybody here since *before* yesterday. It has to be one of the three of us!" Vail let that sink in before continuing, "I know *I* didn't take it. So, it's either you or Gabriel."

"If that's an accusation, I can assure you that *I* didn't take any money," Aziz replied with indignation.

"So *you* say," Vail snapped, as Aziz coloured. "But if you're telling the truth, then that only leaves Gabriel."

"Unless, of course, *you're* not telling the truth," Aziz countered.

"Aw, shut up! Seriously, how do you know you can trust Gabriel? They say those people have a soft spot for money. Why do you assume he couldn't have done it. If it wasn't you then it has to be him."

Aziz was silent for a moment while he considered the possibility. "No. I can't believe that. I've known Gabriel for a long time. I'm certain it wasn't him."

"Didn't you say that he went off the rails in high school, hanging around with a gang?" Vail pressed. "Maybe he's a bad apple at core."

Again Aziz was quiet. *It's true that Gabriel behaved immorally before I got to know him*, he thought. *But....* "No," he said finally. "Gabriel is a decent person. An honest one. A God-fearing person. He didn't steal our money. I'm certain of it. I will not listen to any more of this. I know nothing about you, however."

Vail snarled, "Fine! Stick together. I know it's one of you and I'm going to catch you red-handed one of these days." With that, he ran off to his room in a huff, slamming the door.

***

During the school year, Gabriel worked at the music workshop all day Sundays and Thursday evenings. His knowledge of instruments continued to snowball and his relationship with his boss, though still formal and awkward, continued to evolve. They talked more, even if the conversation was stilted. Mr. Balogh would ask Gabriel about his studies, about his parents' lives in Hungary and other such topics. On a particularly slow day in the shop in December, as Christmas approached, Gabriel took the initiative while tidying up the invoices and straightening out the tools. "Do you have a family, Mr. Balogh," he asked idly, just to make conversation, rather than out of genuine interest.

The old man shook his head sadly. "Nem," he said slowly. "No family." He sighed and stared at his shoes. After a long silence, he continued in English, "My wife, she die when we leave Hungary. It's too hard to leave her mother, her sisters. She die of broken heart. We never have no children."

Gabriel squirmed uncomfortably, chewing on his lower lip. He wondered how it was possible for a young woman to die of a broken heart, but he just nodded somberly. It saddened him to think of the man's lonely life, without family or friends, in a country far from home, whose language he still wasn't fully proficient in. Suddenly, his boss broke into a doleful grin and declared with moist eyes, "They are my children," pointing all around him to the instruments that he had repaired. At that moment, Gabriel felt closer to that awkward, crusty man from the old country that he had never even laid eyes upon than he had ever felt to anyone in his life, save his grandfather. Something caught in his throat, so he just nodded and continued arranging the workspace.

***

A few weeks later, Gabriel's longest running friendship came to an abrupt end. That blustery Sunday morning in early February, Gabriel and Vail made their fortnightly pilgrimage to the university's Athletics Centre to play squash. Gabriel wondered why he continued to do this, as Vail, who was much more athletic than he, always cleaned the court with him. On the way out, Gabriel reminded Vail to contribute the prescribed tithe to the grocery jar, since his roommate had partaken of the common goods during breakfast. Grumbling, Vail complied and observed that all was well that week, since the jar was stuffed with almost fifteen dollars already. They bid good day to Aziz, who opted to study in the quiet of the empty apartment before meeting friends later in the day.

The squash contest went as predicted. Vail ran circles around Gabriel, beating him in three straight games. After a short break, they played a second time with the same result. The closest game of the six was eleven to six, and Gabriel had the disturbing notion that his opponent had not been putting in his best effort. As his penance for defeat, Gabriel had to endure his roommate bragging about his superior play. After a quick shower, and sufficient time for Vail to style his mane exactly right, they finished off their exercise ritual with lunch at the Sid Smith cafeteria. In principle, it should have been a good bonding opportunity, but the games weren't competitive, and they had little to talk to each other about over lunch, making it awkward and uncomfortable at times. On this occasion, Gabriel opted to let Vail do most of the talking, which meant he got a steady diet about Vail's prowess with women, why Gabriel didn't have a girlfriend, and why Vail was convinced that Aziz was behind the thefts in their apartment.

They returned to their apartment in the early afternoon, chilled to the bone by the frigid winter winds blowing off the lake. After peeling off the layers of outdoor clothing, Vail stretched out on the futon with the remote control and switched on a basketball game. Gabriel was about to hide out in his bedroom to "fool around with his violin," but stopped into the kitchen first for a glass of milk. As he was about to deposit his coins in into the grocery jar, he stopped dead in his tracks. Instead of the fifteen dollars that were there in the morning, the jar now contained about seventy-five dollars. They quickly concluded that, as they had been out together, only Aziz could have added that money. Moreover, the only reason he would have done so is if he had taken the money initially – perhaps intending only to borrow it, Gabriel suggested – and was now repaying some of it.

For the next forty-five minutes, they sat staring at the door – Vail on the futon directly under the prophetic Guns N Roses doomsday cross, Gabriel perched on a kitchen chair, his stomach in his mouth, slightly nauseous – awaiting Aziz's return. As his friend's key turned in the lock, Gabriel felt faint and rose to escape to the bathroom. "Stay where you are, Gabriel! You can't wuss out on me!" Vail commanded.

Aziz crossed the threshold and immediately felt the weight of their stares. "What's up, guys?" he inquired uneasily.

"Where were you?" Vail pounced.

"I was out," he responded. "I met Zehra for lunch." Zehra was his ex-girlfriend. Ironically, they had become closer since they broke up and she had started dating someone else. It was a matter that Vail teased him about constantly, but today Vail let it pass without comment.

"Was anyone else here?" Vail pressed.

"What is this?" Aziz pleaded, turning to Gabriel.

"Just answer the question," Vail barked.

"I don't like your tone. Was anyone supposed to be here?" Aziz challenged, his dark eyes registering defiance.

"Listen," Vail explained. "We left together this morning while you were still home. Did anyone else come in here today?"

Evidently flustered, Aziz sputtered, "I... I don't know what to say...."

Vail pounced on his evasion. "What does that even *mean*? Did anyone come in here? Did you *see* anybody?"

Aziz's expression grew furtive. "I mean, I wasn't even here now. How should I know who came in while I was gone?"

"Well, we're the only ones with the key. So, if *we* were out together, *you* were the only one who *could* be here, unless you let someone in," Vail connected the dots, as Gabriel looked on with growing discomfort.

"What's this all about," Aziz asked, a trapped rabbit facing the wolves.

Suddenly, not wishing to prolong the interrogation, Gabriel challenged his friend, "Aziz, did you put sixty dollars in the grocery jar today?"

"No! I certainly did not!" Aziz protested. As his friends both observed, however, he did not seem surprised by the question.

"Well, then who did?" Gabriel followed up like a prosecuting attorney cornering an evasive defendant.

Aziz glanced around the apartment, as if seeking in vain for some support, an ally to come to his defence. "Why ask me?" he asked evasively.

"We've already gone through this," Gabriel pressed, losing patience. "You were the only one here. If it wasn't you, then who was it?"

"It's not fair of you to ask me this__"

"Why won't you just answer the question?" Gabriel asked in growing frustration.

"Don't you trust me, Gabriel? After all this time, don't you know that I'm not a thief?" A sour note of disgust permeated Aziz's voice.

Vail jumped in, "Listen, we *know* you took it. So, where's the rest of our money, Ayatollah?"

Bitterly hurt, Aziz appealed to Gabriel for support, but Gabriel just looked away. Humiliated, Aziz spat out. "I didn't take your money. But I won't stay here any longer. The semester ends in April. I'll move my things out right after exams." He glanced over to Gabriel again, hoping for a protest, a gesture of sympathy, but received none. He turned in a huff and left the apartment.

In the meantime, there was life. Books, exams, term papers. Days when the most critical decision to be made was what to wear to the debate club meeting. Girls in tight sweaters and short boots urging him to sign a petition against German reunification. Grappling with the paralyzing implications of Hume's problem of induction. The SAC elections. More handwringing over the imperiled Meech Lake Accord. The wind tunnel through the Robarts Library steps that would push passersby onto St. George Street on a blustery day. The buxom blonde in his Astronomy elective wearing the Star of David around her neck who kept giving him the eye, but also quite obviously had a boyfriend who picked her up after each class. Recruiting students for the campus Liberals in the hope of ousting Mulroney in the next election. The unctuous sweetness of the cinnamon buns at the bakery around the corner from his apartment. Endless hours of research and writing in Sig Sam Library before stumbling home in the early morning snow and collapsing into bed.

In March of his second year, Gabriel was persuaded by Peter Grossman, an acquaintance from high school, to attend a Jewish Student Union dance. Although Gabriel had frequented the JSU's brownstone house on Spadina Avenue, near The Newspaper's offices, as a source of kosher food on campus, he only rarely attended the organization's events. On this occasion, in the wake of his encounter with Angela Pietrangelo, he consented, hoping to meet Jewish women.

The venue was a social hall at a Harbourfront hotel. Peter offered him a lift, which he gratefully accepted so he wouldn't make his entrance ignominiously alone. As soon as they arrived, however, Peter peeled off to dance with someone, advising Gabriel as he abandoned him, "If you meet me here in a couple of hours, I'll give you a ride back." Gabriel glanced around the room and immediately regretted coming. The gaudy silver and mauve balloons – were they trying to signal sophisticated dance or tawdry brothel? – the hollow AM radio dance music, with its electric metronome beat; the in-group that knew each other well, flashing their superiority on their designer jeans, their Sperry Topsiders with the leather laces arranged as perfect tassels; the awkward and uncomfortable out-group, of which Gabriel was the poster child. Worse, although he recognized very few faces at the dance, those he did know were from his elementary school, his neighbourhood, whom he would have preferred to avoid.

After bringing a drink ticket to the bar, Gabriel stood around awkwardly, nursing a bad beer. What he would have given for a Red Baron by local Waterloo microbrewery Brick! It occurred to him that this had been a terrible idea, that he was completely out of place, that this was exactly the wrong venue for him to meet women. If he were honest with himself, he had never been smooth or easy with women. In the past, he tended to moon over girls, like Lisa Ross, for ages before getting the courage up to date them. Or, like with Jenny Levenson, the relationship would grow of its own accord through friendship or classwork. He wasn't made for dances, where you had to lay it on the line and introduce yourself on the spur of the moment.

Eventually, a young woman he knew from high school approached him with alcohol-induced enthusiasm and invited him to dance, practically pulled him onto the dance floor. Crushed in between tens of other hopping, gyrating partygoers, Gabriel felt sorely out of his element, like a rabbi at a prostitute convention. The DJ played the Time Warp from the Rocky Horror Picture Show, a film that Gabriel had never seen. To *his* horror, the song had an accompanying dance, with hand gestures, jumps to the left and right, and other frills that it seemed Gabriel alone was unaware of and couldn't coordinate. His dance partner eyed him contemptuously and broke off to dance on her own, leaving Gabriel to slink away from the dance floor in shame.

Humiliated, he retreated to an empty side room with tables and chairs, where he couldn't hear the music but still felt its mechanical, pulsating beat, and sat brooding by himself at a round table, nursing his disappointing beer. Every few minutes someone would wander through the room and look at him askance, making him feel even more self-conscious. He debated with himself whether he should simply leave now and return home by subway or whether he should stick it out a bit longer. After a while, his reverie was disturbed by a voice from behind.

"Is this the misfit section?"

He turned and found himself face-to-face with a young brunette woman of medium height and build in an ivory sweater and brown corduroy pants. He hesitated before answering. Was she mocking him? Or just being friendly? He couldn't decide. He elected to assume goodwill and respond with humour. "It's actually the leper colony," he joked.

"Oh, then I won't shake your hand. I wouldn't want it to fall off in mine," she responded without missing a beat. "I'm Cathy."

"Cathy...." he repeated, thinking *that's not typically a Jewish name*.

"Yeah. Short for Catherine. You're wondering what I'm doing at a JSU dance. Well, I'm actually Jewish. Cathy Blum. B-L-U-M. Rhymes with plum. Everyone thinks it should rhyme with gloom, and they're right. My parents were both rebels when they were younger and decided to break with Judaism. They changed the pronunciation of their last name and called me Catherine and my brother Christopher, mainly to stick it to my grandparents. In the end, though, the joke's on them. They gravitated back to the fold and my dad's even the president of our synagogue. I think our names are a source of embarrassment for them now," she explained, speaking rapidly in an enchanting vanilla cream voice. "Mind if I sit down?"

"Of course!" he said, as he stood up quickly and held out a chair for her. He was unsure of himself. Was that the right thing to do, the chivalrous and noble thing, like his mother had always drilled into him? Or was it insulting to a modern woman? In his confusion, he scraped his hand on the square metal chair frame. He hoped she didn't notice. "I'm Gabriel.... Gabriel Klein."

"Nice to meet you, Gabriel. Do you skulk around outside of dances often?" Her voice was soft and melodious. Her eyes glistened as she spoke.

"Well, I...." Once again, he couldn't be sure she wasn't ridiculing him, and it took him a few seconds to prepare his reply. "I was actually dancing earlier, but I was banned for committing choreographic crimes against humanity."

"I see.... So, *you're* the one. I've never talked to an international dance criminal before. This is so exciting!"

"You say that now," he deadpanned, "but just wait 'til you get charged as an accessory after the fact."

"Good thing my father's a lawyer," she said with mock relief. "I just hope he doesn't drop me as a client because of the heinous nature of the crime."

"Well, you can always get another lawyer. It may be a bit harder to find another father, though...."

"I suppose," she said with exaggerated deliberation, "I could always put in an ad in the Star: 'Sexy young woman seeks father figure.' Hmmm... I'm afraid I see too many ways that could go wrong."

He laughed unreservedly. As he grew more at ease, he studied her face more carefully, this delightful stranger that had rescued what had hitherto seemed an irretrievable failure of an evening. Her eyes were large, oval and enigmatic. At first glance they appeared green, like small round emeralds. At other times, he was convinced they were small blue topazes. But they had streaks of yellow and hazel inside, as well. And in some light, they looked grey. It made him think of the Rolling Stones song, *The Girl with Kaleidoscope Eyes*. They must have been singing about Cathy Blum and her bewitching eyes.

Her face was beautiful, a perfect rectangle, dimpled, with a small blemish on the left side of her chin – a small childhood scar that never healed completely – the slight imperfection that made her face all the more perfect. Was that a contradiction, he wondered, a paradox? He remembered his violin instructor's injunction about perfection being impossible with people. Was this God's way of driving the point home?

They talked at length about their studies, their goals, their backgrounds. Cathy was a History major in her first year, and intended to apply to law school after completing a three-year bachelor of arts. She had lived in Toronto her entire life and wouldn't mind settling down here eventually, but was eager to explore some of the wide world out there beforehand. Gabriel admitted that, beyond an interest in Philosophy, he didn't have any long-term plans. And from his perspective, living away from his parents was a big enough thrill, so he hadn't given much thought to travelling. But it certainly was something to consider.

"Okay, Gabriel," she said eagerly, having covered the expected ground, "Tell me something about yourself that you've never told anyone else before."

He was taken aback. "That I've never told anyone? Gee, I don't know...."

"You're thinking: 'I don't really know this girl. Should I really tell her my deep dark secrets?' And you know, you've got a point. But do it anyway." She had a way of putting him at ease while simultaneously keeping him off balance. He had never met anyone like her. What a fresh breeze she was in his too stagnant life!

"Alright...." he agreed, searching for something appropriate. "Well, I learned to repair violins for my part time job...."

"*That's* not the kind of thing I'm asking for. That's not personal," she chastised.

"Hey! Give me a minute! I'm not finished.... I also *play* violin – I'm told I'm not bad. But I'm never happy when I play because, at least to my ears, it doesn't sound perfect. I can hear each tiny flaw and it discourages me. When I play, I want to hear perfection. To play music the way God intended music to be when He created the universe. I can never achieve it, though. But when I repair a violin... well, it gives me a great sense of satisfaction. Because I imagine that, one day, I'll repair the instrument of a great virtuoso and that because of me, he'll be able to play divinely perfect music." He looked at her uncomfortably, afraid that he might have opened up too much.

Cathy just stared at him, admiration in her kaleidoscope eyes. Eventually, she said, "That's absolutely *beautiful!*"

Relieved, he turned the tables on her. "Now you tell me something!"

"Me?" she asked coyly. "Hmmm... I don't know.... What haven't I told anyone before...? Well, I could tell you.... No. I've shared that before...."

He waited impatiently, afraid that she would wriggle out of the obligation.

"Okay," she said decisively, "but it's very embarrassing...." By this point, Gabriel was listening to her so intently that he would not have noticed if a bomb were to have exploded in the room. "When I was in elementary school, the boys used to make fun of me, taunting me by shouting, 'Cathy Blum, show us your bum!' It used to make me so angry. I wanted to hit them. To run away and hide. As I got older, it didn't matter as much. And, to be honest, when I was Grade 11, there was this jock in Grade 12, Derek Newland, who was absolutely *gorgeous*. It was like his chest was chiseled by Michelangelo. I used to fantasize about him cornering me near my locker after school and saying 'Cathy Blum, show us your bum,' and me pulling down my pants for him. I guess I was a horny teenager." Her cheeks were burning, her eyes positively glowing as she said this, her voice a beguiling admixture of innocence and seduction.

Gabriel didn't know how to respond. *Did she really just say that?* he wondered. She was so completely disarming. She dazzled him.

"Wow," Gabriel said slowly. "Just wow!"

"Cat's got your tongue?"

"After that, there's not much I *can* say, is there?"

"Well, I'd tell you to ask me to dance, but I don't want to run afoul of the Geneva Convention. So," she suggested, "you could offer to take me home...."

Gabriel flushed from his forehead down to his neck. "Ahhh..." he stammered, "I, uh... I don't have a car."

"Who needs a car? Let's ride the rocket."

"My pleasure, Cathy Blum," he said, as they stood and fetched their jackets.

As it turned out, Cathy lived in the Annex, not that far from Gabriel's apartment. They laughed and teased each other during the subway ride from Union Station to Spadina. Gabriel had never felt as comfortable with any woman before. Not even Jenny. They walked slowly from the station to her apartment, savouring every moment. *It's funny,* Gabriel thought. *I've strolled these streets so often over the past two years, but have never found anything remarkable in them. Yet tonight, with her, they're magical. Is this what love is? Can I be in love with someone I met only hours ago?*

They stood outside the front entrance talking, laughing awkwardly for about fifteen minutes, each uncertain about what to do next. Then, Cathy took the initiative, saying, "Well, I'd better head upstairs. It was so great to meet you." She shook his hand and joked about it not falling off in hers. What kind of leper was he? Then, still holding onto his hand, she said slyly, "You didn't think I'd invite you up, did you?" Gabriel quickly mumbled "Of course not. I...." She said, "*Certainly* not. I've only just met you. Maybe another time, though...." she said naughtily, running her index finger lightly across his palm as she released it from her grasp and turned to enter the building.

The next morning, after a deliciously sleepless night in which he lay in bed reliving the evening, imagining the possibilities, he was eager to call her. His flatmate and relationship coach, Vail, doused him with cold water. "You don't want to seem too desperate," he advised. "Play it cool." So he waited two more days until he could stand it no longer. Ah, the agony of those restless nights staring out the window, making silent entreaties to the moon and the stars, as he so desperately wanted to cave in and dial her number, imagining her sweet voice at the other end, her frank, engaging candour. When he eventually did pick up the phone, he aborted three times because he lost his nerve, before finally reaching her roommate and leaving a message. When Cathy failed to return his call, he left a second message two days later, also in vain. He considered calling a third time – perhaps her roommate forgot to give her the message? – but decided, with Vail's guidance, that it would be prudent to concede defeat.

He agonized over Cathy for many weeks. *What did I do wrong,* he tormented himself. *Did I wait too long to call? Or was she just teasing me?* He found it hard to concentrate on his work, and even missed a deadline for a political science paper, incurring a small penalty. In time, however, to his great dismay, he reconciled himself to the fact that Cathy, who seemed so real, so fresh, so perfect for him, would not be a part of his life. The impassioned lyrics of the new Pearl Jam song hit him hard. Was Cathy destined to be a star in another man's sky after that perfect evening? How could that be? He recorded the song off the radio and played it over and over on his tape recorder for days, but eventually decided he needed to move on.

So, to distract himself, he threw himself into his studies and finished the semester with a straight-A record, including a rare A+ in his symbolic logic course, for a sessional grade point average of over 4.0. Instead of the girl of his dreams, he earned a spot on the Dean's List and cheque for $1,000 from the Principal of University College, presented at the annual scholarship dinner. While Gabriel appreciated the money and the honour, he believed he got the raw end of that exchange.

Aziz's departure that month left Gabriel in turmoil. From one perspective, it was a relief. Since their confrontation that February, no more money disappeared, for which he was grateful. He was glad they had found the culprit and closed the case. But, at the same time, life around the flat had become tense, like living in a minefield. Aziz had stopped talking to them if he could avoid it, and it was a relief when he wasn't around. Yet, after all the years they had been friends, Gabriel harboured private doubts about whether they had handled the situation properly. Sure, it was clear that Aziz was guilty. But still.... And his abrupt departure meant that Vail and Gabriel needed to cover his third of the rent until they could find a new roommate, which probably wouldn't happen until September, when the new academic year began. This presented no real problem for Vail, whose parents covered his expenses. But for Gabriel, that meant that – even with the Dean's List cheque – he would have to earn more money over the summer.

A few weeks after Aziz finally moved out, without uttering a word to Gabriel, leaving no forwarding address or phone number, Gabriel was sleeping in with a bad cold. Suddenly, he was disturbed by a thunderous crash above him. It sounded like something had fallen to the floor of the apartment above. He immediately thought of the widow, Mrs. Gupta, who lived above him. A kindly old woman, with no family in town, she often shared delicious, freshly-fried vegetarian samosas with the boys. Had she fallen? He'd better check, he decided.

Quickly throwing on his bathrobe, he bounded up the filthy, poorly-tended stairs to her apartment. As he emerged from the stairwell, however, he witnessed an unexpected and unusual sight. The landlord's fifteen-year-old daughter was locking Mrs. Gupta's door with her father's master key. The short, red-headed girl seemed startled and tried to hide the key.

"What's going on Melanie?" Gabriel asked suspiciously. "Is Mrs. Gupta okay?"

"Huh?" Melanie grunted in confusion. "Oh, yeah. Yeah, she's fine."

It was then that Gabriel noticed the money in her hand, which she had tried unsuccessfully to conceal by balling it up in her fist. On an impulse, he snarled, "You never put back the rest of the money you took from us!"

Melanie gasped, terror flashing in her grey-green eyes. "He... He *told* you?" she asked in disbelief.

Finally, it became clear to Gabriel. Oh, how wrong they had been! How they had mistreated Aziz! "No, he didn't! And we threw him out because of you. Are you proud of yourself?" The girl stared mournfully at her sneakers, with their Velcro straps instead of laces. "Now go back inside and put Mrs. Gupta's money back. Then you and I will have a talk and you'll tell me everything. And I mean *everything*, or I'll go straight to the police." Trembling, she complied, then accompanied Gabriel back to his apartment, where she offered up a full confession.

Twenty minutes later, Gabriel had the whole story. Melanie had fallen in with a bad crowd at school, much like Gabriel himself had at the same age. Alcohol. Drugs. Sex. Only to run with that crowd, she needed to pay her share, which was more than the pocket money her parents furnished her. She needed to lay her hands on serious money. One day, while she was accompanying her father on a maintenance call in the building, she saw him using his master key to gain entry to a unit and the idea struck her. If she were to use his key during the workday, when most of the tenants were out of the building, she could get access to loose cash without anyone ever suspecting her. She waited for opportunities when her father went out, leaving his keys behind, as he often did when he took her mother to the cinema some afternoons. This strategy had worked well for her for many months, and she had often looted the boys' grocery jar.

It all came apart, though, in February when she needed cash immediately and couldn't wait for the workweek. Her parents went for a drive on a Sunday morning, leaving the keys behind and she decided to risk it. She had listened at the door of their unit and heard not a sound, so she entered the apartment, heading directly to the kitchen and the money jar. That's when Aziz, who had been showering, emerged from the bathroom completely naked, expecting an empty apartment. When he startled Melanie in the kitchen, with her mitts on the grocery money, he rushed back to the bathroom to wrap himself in a towel and returned to confront her. Moved by her tears and his sense of honour, he agreed not to report her, provided she returned the money on her own. She consented gratefully, and provided the first installment early that afternoon, after Aziz stepped out of the apartment, although she financed that compensation by stealing from other tenants. When she heard that Gabriel and Vail had suspected Aziz and evicted him, she had felt terrible. But, with him out of the way, her secret was safe, and she never returned the rest of the money she had pilfered.

Gabriel could guess the rest. When he and Vail had confronted Aziz, based on the circumstantial evidence of the money's reappearance while they were absent, Aziz had felt dutybound not to betray Melanie. Therefore, he denied that he was the culprit, but refused to lie by saying that he didn't know who the thief was. When even Gabriel refused to believe him, he was crestfallen, and judged that his only honourable course of action would be to leave. Oh, how unfairly they had treated him!

Gabriel agreed not to call the police, provided that Melanie confessed her crimes to her father in Gabriel's presence. Left no other option, she broke down and agreed. Her father was aghast and promised to repay all her victims. Moreover, he compensated Vail and Gabriel by forgiving one month of rent, which alleviated the burden they faced now that Aziz had departed. But it couldn't assuage their guilty consciences.

That night, Gabriel tried in vain to locate Aziz, who had moved out without leaving them even a phone number. It took a while, but by contacting several of his old high school classmates he found the number of the friend Aziz was staying with temporarily. It was to no avail, however. Gabriel left several messages on that friend's answering machine, but Aziz didn't return his call. Eventually, Aziz's friend picked up the phone and told him never to call back. Aziz wanted nothing to do with him. It was a painful blow, but life moved on and, by the time the next academic year started, they had replaced Aziz with Pablo and put this unfortunate episode behind them.

Perhaps the intellectual summit of his university career was a course he enrolled in that summer. Concerned that he had accumulated too many electives during his first two years, as he explained "to sample extensively from the intellectual smorgasbord in all its breadth," and that he might not have the pre-requisites to graduate after four years, he signed up for two required philosophy courses in the summer term, during the evening. The Tuesday and Thursday advanced political philosophy class with an adjunct lecturer captured his imagination, positively enthralled him. The instructor, a doctoral student in the department, opened his mind to a range of ideas and arguments that revolutionized his understanding of the world.

Significantly, unlike the famous Straussian professor who taught the introductory political philosophy course as a performance, without entertaining questions or discussion from the students, the summer instructor encouraged student participation, actually revelled in it. Many of the classes, therefore, evolved into probing discussions between Gabriel and the instructor. During these exchanges, Gabriel challenged Bentham's utilitarianism as morally bankrupt because it had no place for God. As he saw it, not all happiness is equally worthwhile. In some ways, he preferred Burke's conservatism, his "dead hand of history," which privileged social goods over individual caprices. He admired the religious core of Hegel, but violently rejected Marx, not for his stinging critique of capitalism, which Gabriel thought brilliant, but for his rejection of God and traditional values.

The only drawback of the class was that Lawrence Linton from his old neighbourhood was also enrolled. No longer Leibl Lubov, Linton had now cultivated a heavy faux-Oxford accent and resided in a posh Yorkville penthouse apartment. Having severed all ties to his former life, he took great pleasure in sparring with Gabriel, putting him down whenever the opportunity presented itself. As if by besting Gabriel, the Hungarian Jew, the son of a garbage collector, he could erase the stain of his own humble origins.

After class each night, the instructor, who encouraged students to call him by his first name, Arthur, invited the students to join him at a pub on Madison Avenue north of Bloor to continue the conversation. Fortunately, from Gabriel's point of view, Linton was always too busy to participate in these extracurricular meetings. Over the course of the hours they whiled away there, they consumed sometimes as many as five beers each while they probed the contradictions inherent in political and social cooperation, the tensions between individual liberty and communal needs, the dialectic between rights and responsibilities, the interdependence of politics and the market. These "Madison Avenue tutorials," as the students called them, had a profound impact on the development of Gabriel's worldview.

Once again, Gabriel worked full-time in the music store over the summer. By this point, Mr. Balogh had complete confidence in him and tended not to interfere with his work, only standing nearby at times to observe and admire Gabriel's handicraft. On days when Mr. Balogh had errands to run in town, or when he left Toronto for a short vacation, he was completely comfortable leaving Gabriel in charge of the workshop, something he never would have considered the year before.

Once, during a lull at the shop, Mr. Balogh touched Gabriel lightly on the shoulder. "I want to show you something." Curious, Gabriel waited on his stool in the workshop, while his boss went to his car. Five minutes later, Mr. Balogh returned with a well-worn violin case. He opened it reverentially, with a rapturous expression, and produced the most beautiful violin that Gabriel had ever laid his eyes upon. The wood was magnificently striped, with a finely-carved scroll. The purfling was carefully inlaid, the chin rest, fingerboard and tailpiece crafted out of ebony, the strings close to the fingerboard. "My father made this for me in Hungary, for my twelfth birthday," Mr. Balogh explained, beaming, as he proceeded to play a piece by Dvorak that sounded simply heavenly. Even after working alongside him for over a year, Gabriel hadn't known that his boss played violin, and superbly at that. He clapped enthusiastically at the end of the piece to show his approval.

"You try it," Mr. Balogh ordered.

As soon as he grasped the instrument in his hands, Gabriel was charmed by it. He was surprised how light it was, how easily it fell into his hands, how it almost seemed to play itself, even in the upper registers. And the sound. Such a rich, deep, clear tone that he had never been able to achieve on his own violin. He had only heard such instruments on records, played by professionals. It gave him a thrill just to touch it. His boss could read the admiration on his face and beamed as he retrieved the violin and restored it to its case. "My father was a great luthier, no?" he asked.

"Yes," Gabriel responded almost breathlessly. "Thank you for letting me play it. It's the finest violin I have ever seen!" Mr. Balogh nodded emotionally, and Gabriel felt a pang of jealously. To have had a father like that, he thought.

On another occasion, Mr. Balogh pounced on him as soon as he arrived, had been waiting for him. "Are you doing anything next Wednesday evening, Gabriel?" he inquired eagerly.

"Uh, no.... Not really. I was going to work on my paper for class...." Gabriel responded.

"I see. But you could make yourself available. Correct?"

"Yes. Of course. But why?" Gabriel couldn't hide his puzzlement.

"Well, you have been doing a fine job, so I'm giving you a bonus," Mr. Balogh announced, with an uncharacteristic smile. "I've bought us tickets to Roy Thompson Hall. The most wonderful violinist, Maxim Vengerov, will be playing Beethoven's violin concerto in D major. It's an opportunity we can't miss."

"I... I don't know what to say," Gabriel gushed.

"Then just say 'thank you,' and get to work," Mr. Balogh snapped.

On the night of the concert, Gabriel wore a beige suit with a salmon-coloured knit tie, both of which he bought especially for the occasion. It was his first time inside Roy Thompson Hall, which simultaneously impressed and disappointed him. On the latter side of the ledger, the venue was much more modern-looking than he expected. In his view, classical music should be played in a more traditional-looking venue, with dark wooden panelling, red velvet carpets and gas lamps. But, oh the acoustics! He had read that performers had complained about them, but from his perspective the sound in the auditorium was superb. And Vengerov's skill! How effortlessly he played, how smooth and velvety the sound. Music as God intended it, on a violin that descended directly from the heavens – a Stradivarius no less, Mr. Balogh pointed out. Though the concert ended with a magnificent symphonic composition, Dvorak's Eighth Symphony, Gabriel had been carried away by the Beethoven concerto and positively idolized Vengerov. On the way out, he thanked his boss from the bottom of his heart for what remained one of the highlights of his life.

One Tuesday evening, just before class on the ground floor of Sidney Smith Hall – Sid Smith to the initiated – Gabriel visited the cafeteria in the basement, which doubled at night as the Student Administrative Council's (SAC) Hangar Pub, to purchase a bottle of iced tea to drink during class. On his way downstairs, he was contemplating the week's reading from John Stuart Mill's *On Liberty* and didn't watch where he was going as he pushed open the double burgundy doors leading into the cafeteria and ran straight into Lawrence Linton.

"Watch where you're going, Klein!" Linton chastised him. Instinctively, Gabriel mumbled "Sorry," with the characteristic Torontonian long-O, before glancing up to see his rival holding hands with the same young woman who had stolen his heart only weeks before.

Cathy turned beet red and inhaled sharply. "Gabriel...." she said, her vanilla cream voice wavering.

"Oh. You know each other," Linton said. "Do you want to join us for coffee before class?"

"Uh, no.... I've got to go do something," Gabriel sputtered. "See you in class," he said. Then, addressing Cathy, he simply said, "Bye," before spinning around and exiting the cafeteria without purchasing the beverage for which he had come.

That evening after class, at the Madison Avenue tutorial, Gabriel couldn't contain his anger, his contempt, his impotent rage at Lawrence Linton. The class was sparsely attended that night and only one other student – a quiet, but extremely intelligent Nigerian woman named Ifeoma – joined Arthur and Gabriel at the pub, so Gabriel felt free to let loose on his absent rival.

"What a phony! With his heavy British accent, as if he was a polo buddy of Prince Charles'! And that name, *Lawrence Linton!* His real name is Leibl Lubov. His parents came over with mine from Hungary in fifty-six. Why does he have to pretend he's the Goddamn Archbishop of Canterbury?" They were sitting outside on the upper deck, basking in the warm but breezy evening. Gabriel was so agitated that he practically screamed his accusations, causing patrons at nearby benches to turn around.

Arthur laughed, his long brown hair and bushy mustache rippling in rhythm. "The accent didn't sound genuine. I guess he thought he'd be treated better if he sounded like part of the elite."

"Yes," Ifeoma added. "In this society, if you look or sound like you're from the wrong part of the world, you do not get the same opportunities as others do."

"That's just bullshit!" Gabriel exploded, his inhibitions loosened by the four beers he had gulped down. "That's exactly what's wrong with society. It's all shadow over substance. Who cares if you're poor or have an accent? What really matters is what's inside you. Take my father, for example. He came over as an immigrant without a penny to his name. So he worked as a garbage man to feed his family, to put a roof over our heads. There's no shame in *that*...."

"Not at all," Arthur jumped in.

"Yet he always lied about it. He lied even to *me*, his own *son*! Like I would think any less of him because of what he did for a living. You know, this is all the fault of you Protestants and your stinkin' Protestant work ethic," Gabriel charged.

"Oh ho! So now it's *my* fault!" Arthur said, feigning injury.

"Yes. Yours and John Calvin's. The idea that wealth is evidence that you're worthy of being saved is fundamentally corrupt. It not only justifies theft and abuse, but it also equates poverty with sinfulness, making the poor morally culpable for their misery. As a result of its superficiality, good, decent, humble people feel ashamed. You know, when the Nazis were rounding up Jews in Hungary, my grandfather was penniless, living in bushes by the river. Yet he was the most noble, valuable person I ever met."

Arthur, ever the educator, pressed, "So, would you go as far as Marx in calling all private property theft?"

"Of course it is," Ifeoma responded. "Private property was acquired... that is, taken away from the common usage, through violence and coercion. The political and economic elites accumulate disproportionate amounts of wealth while others starve. This is indefensible on moral grounds. So the political leadership uses its authority to sanctify private property and justify their theft of public resources."

Gabriel took a draught of his beer, then sucked in his lower lip. The light breeze that had been caressing them all evening suddenly picked up momentarily, mussing his mane of chestnut hair. "No.... No, I wouldn't go that far. Marx's critique of the dysfunctionality of capitalism is brilliant. But from there to advocate a proletarian revolution – the tyranny of the proletariat – that's a bridge too far. To begin with, it would be dysfunctional in its own right. There would be no incentives to produce, no incentives to innovate. Civilization would grind to a halt. Instead, private property is essential, as liberal theorists argue, to encourage people to be as productive as possible for the society as a whole. The problem is that people deify wealth, make it more than simply a means to an end." In one part of his brain, Gabriel marveled at how articulate he could be under the influence of alcohol. Yet he was also somewhat queasy.

"Gabriel, your problem is that you're too *certain* about everything," Arthur observed, apparently no worse for wear from the alcohol that he had thus far consumed. "I don't inhabit a universe where there is certainty. I teach Marx, Hegel, Rousseau, Locke, Bentham and I understand them. I'm intimately aware of their arguments, their strengths and their limitations. There are elements of each that I find useful, that can explain contemporary problems, that can elucidate the fundamental tensions of social, political and economic interaction. But, unlike you, I can't definitively say one is right about this or wrong about that."

Ifeoma laughed. "Certainty is a Western disease. One can't live in Africa, where we are dependent on the rains, on security from the militias, from the government, and be certain of anything."

"Well," Gabriel conceded, "Maybe it's not possible to be certain, but to me that sounds like a whole different conversation about epistemology, which we don't want to get into now. You know, whether there's truth, whether we can know anything. Whether we can observe what is, as the positivists assert, or whether the postmodernist critique that we can only access perspectives on reality is closer to the mark. A worthwhile discussion, but let's focus on *political* philosophy tonight."

Arthur laughed. "I'm afraid you draw lines too clearly, my friend. I'm with Ifeoma. It's all connected."

When Ifeoma left at ten-thirty, Arthur and Gabriel brought their drinks inside to play darts. Gabriel started, hurling his three red darts wildly at the board. The first registered in the three zone. The second missed the board altogether, lodging in the surrounding cork panel. The final dart grazed the fifteen zone and miraculously managed to stick, for a meagre total of eighteen points. Arthur followed up with three lasers into the twenty, the triple band in the center of the fifteen zone, and the four zone just adjacent to the bullseye, for a yield of sixty-nine points. "Ho!" Arthur yelled in delight.

They played two more rounds, with spectators at a nearby table cheering them on. Arthur handily won them both. It was strange, Gabriel thought, as he swayed to the piped-in music. His own aim typically improved after his first beer, as it allowed him to filter out distractions, but declined precipitously after each one thereafter. With all the alcohol he had imbibed on this occasion, his hands were unsteady and his concentration poor. Yet Arthur seemed completely unaffected by alcohol. It made Gabriel admire his mentor even more.

After beating Gabriel soundly, his teacher pulled him to an indoor table near the dartboard. Arthur ordered two more beers and turned serious. "Listen, Gabriel," he said earnestly, squeezing his mustache between his thumb and forefinger, "I've been meaning to talk to you. What are you planning to do when you graduate?"

Gabriel was surprised by the question. "Honestly, I have no idea. I love being a student, but I can't imagine anything I'd truly like to do in the real world."

"I know what you mean," Arthur said with a rueful laugh, "I was there myself. But have you given any thought to grad school in philosophy?"

"No. Not really."

"I think you'd make a great teacher. A great *professor*. You're really passionate about philosophy – much more so than any of my other students. And you're really smart," Arthur declared.

"Thanks," Gabriel said, flattered by his teacher's praise, especially under the warming haze of the alcohol. "But are there jobs?"

Arthur guffawed. "I can't say yet. I *hope* so. Don't have any illusions. It's a long haul. I'm still in grad school myself. But you seem even better cut out for this than I am."

"Well, it's something to think about," Gabriel conceded.

"I'll tell you what. Let's wait until I see your final paper and exam for the course. If they're as good as I expect them to be, we'll talk again then. Okay?"

"Deal," Gabriel said, as he drained the rest of his bottle of Red Baron and settled his part of the cheque. He then stumbled down the stairs and walked home, still brooding about Cathy and Lawrence Linton.

The following Saturday night, Gabriel was up late working on his final paper for the course. He had chosen as his topic the centrality of God to Western liberalism, arguing that, while liberal philosophers bracketed out the role of religion in their analyses, their premises only held because of the Judeo-Christian values that defined Western society. Because of his admiration for Arthur, he was especially eager to make his paper memorable, so he had been obsessing over it for weeks and, now that the due date was approaching, he was editing the current draft, fixing the phrasing, correcting typos, strengthening the argument.

While he was thus engaged, the telephone rang. Annoyed to be distracted from the paper, he ignored it and let his roommate answer it. Before he could get back into his work, however, Vail shouted, "It's for you, Gabriel!"

"Who is it?" Gabriel yelled back, hoping Vail could take a message for him.

"I don't *know*! I'm not your fucking answering service!" came the curt reply.

Gabriel reluctantly abandoned his paper and picked up the phone in the living room. "Hello?" he said distractedly.

"Uh, Gabriel?" a woman's voice asked uneasily.

"Yes. Who is this?" he asked. Something about the vanilla cream voice sounded familiar, but he couldn't place it out of context.

"It's me.... Cathy. Cathy Blum."

The surprise hit him with the force of a freight train. The mere mention of her name unsettled him, excited him, confused him. "What...? I mean... what can I do for you?" He cursed himself for sounding so stupid.

"I... I'm sorry for not calling you back. It was just.... It's not what you think. Can you meet me for coffee somewhere now? I'd really like to explain," she pleaded.

He glanced at the clock on the microwave oven. Five past eleven. "I don't know. It's late.... You don't need to explain. I didn't know you were seeing Leibl. I mean *Lawrence*." His face puckered when he uttered the offensive name.

"That's just *it*," she said. "You don't *understand*. I need to talk to you. Let's meet at Toby's. I think it's open late."

"Well...." he hesitated.

"I promise I won't ask you to dance or commit any violations of the Geneva Convention," she said with a nervous giggle.

A little flustered, but mightily intrigued, Gabriel consented and abandoned his paper for the night. It took him a while to prepare, as he couldn't find the right clothing to wear, changing several times before settling on a pair of black jeans and his favorite grey sweater. Then he battled his hair, which resisted his comb and bunched up in an unsightly blob. By the time he was satisfied and arrived at the diner, Cathy had been waiting for fifteen minutes. She looked even more charming than she had at the JSU dance, sporting an emerald blouse and short grey pleated skirt over her shapely bare legs, with her dark hair falling below her shoulders, her kaleidoscope eyes a portrait of nervous apprehension.

"I was afraid you weren't going to come," she said shily, her voice quavering slightly.

"Oh, sorry. I wasn't.... I wasn't dressed, so it took me a bit of time."

She smiled, the sun rising over her slight scar. "It's better to be on time than to be dressed," she teased.

But Gabriel would have none of that. "Listen, you wanted me to come, so I'm here. But I'm not the kind of guy that's going to flirt with someone else's girlfriend."

"Gabriel, I'm so sorry about the way I treated you. I didn't mean to. But you've got to hear me out."

The waitress came to take their order, coffee for Gabriel, chocolate ice cream for Cathy. Gabriel absently surveyed the restaurant. Only a few scattered diners, who came to Toby's Good Eats no doubt, like they themselves had, because it was the only chain that stayed open late at night. A couple at a nearby table was arguing loudly about the man's drinking problem. Gabriel shuddered, hoping no-one was listening in to his conversation with Cathy.

"Well?" he asked impatiently when the waitress moved on to another table.

Cathy played absently with her napkin, obsessively folding and unfolding it. "You see, it's just.... Gee, why does this have to be so hard?"

Gabriel stared at her quizzically. "I'm not even sure what *this* is," he stated flatly, almost harshly. As he gazed at her dimpled face, her multicoloured orbs, his heart ached. She had hurt him once and, though he longed to be with her, he couldn't envision any scenario in which he could avoid another heartbreak. So he tried to steel himself against her charms.

"Come on, Gabriel. Give me a chance!" she pleaded.

"For what? Does your *boyfriend* know you're here?" he asked acidly.

"I'm not *with* Lawrence anymore," she blurted out.

All of a sudden, the storm clouds parted and blue skies appeared. There was reason to hope. Just then, however, the waitress brought their order, accidentally spilling some of his coffee on the table. She apologized and was about to fetch a rag to wipe it up when Gabriel impatiently waved her off, saying that it wasn't a big deal. He mopped it up himself with his napkin.

When the waitress departed, Cathy continued, "I dated Lawrence for a few months, but I broke up with him a couple of weeks before I met you. That night at the dance was *amazing*! I was so happy to get to know you. You and I had that spark that Lawrence and I never had. But then the next day, Lawrence called and said he needed to talk to me. He said his mother was sick. She has... Cancer." Cathy whispered the diagnosis, just like his mother always did. "I felt that he needed me. I couldn't just abandon him. So we got back together. I didn't know what to say to you when you called, so I just hid. Please don't hate me for it."

"Don't worry about it, Cathy. I don't hate you. I'm just sorry our timing was wrong," he said, taking the high ground. So she hadn't been as callous as it had seemed.

"But I'm not finished! After I ran into you at Sid Smith, I realized that I couldn't do it. I just *couldn't*!" she declared, before shovelling in a spoonful of ice cream, shivering as it froze her palate.

"Couldn't do what?" he asked. The alcoholic man pounded his table with his fist, mortifying the woman he was with. Was she his wife? His girlfriend? Everyone in the restaurant conspicuously averted their eyes.

"Couldn't stay with him. It wouldn't be fair for me to sacrifice *my* happiness just to make *him* feel better. I'm sorry his mother is ill.... Really, I am.... But that's not my fault. I don't love him, so why should I stay with him just because she's sick?" Cathy explained.

Gabriel wasn't certain how to respond. The waitress returned to ask if they needed anything else. Gabriel thanked her, but said they were fine. In the back of his mind, he wondered whether her real motive had been to eavesdrop on their conversation.

"So...." Gabriel began excitedly. "So, you broke up with him again? You're not dating him anymore?"

"That's right! I went over to his place this evening and told him that I wished him and his mother well, but that I didn't love him and needed to stop the charade," she announced with equal excitement. "I was sorry to hurt him again, but I had to follow my heart. The first thing I did after I returned home was call you. Hoping that I didn't screw it all up...."

"No. You didn't. You didn't at all. I wanted to do this so badly on the night we met...." he said, as he leaned forward to give her a kiss. But she recoiled sharply.

"Oh no! Please don't do that!" she snapped to his great surprise. "I'm not gonna break up with *one* boy just to run straight into the arms of another only *hours* later, am I? I'm not *that* type of girl!"

"So you called me here now, at this time of night, just to tell me that and go back home? Separately?" Cathy nodded. "You're a *strange* girl," he said, an amused smile on his face, despite the rebuff.

"That I am. Strange and wonderful...." She grinned. "Now go ahead and ask me out for next Saturday night."

Gabriel shook his head in amusement. "Miss Cathy Blum," he mimicked a southern accent and began in a tone of mock formality, "would you do me the honour of accompanying me to the thee-ater on Saturday night?"

"Well, Ashley," she played along, "Ah do believe ah.... Oh wait, I can't. I promised Lawrence that I'd__"

"What!?!" he asked in shock.

"Just kidding," Cathy declared with a winning smile. "Ah'd be honoured to."

To celebrate their "monthiversary," the first month of their courtship, which they dated to their clumsy encounter at Toby's, they took in a movie at the Carlton Cinemas and followed that up with a visit to a posh Yorkville bar, where patrons relaxed in plush leather sofas and armchairs. Gabriel and Cathy opted for a loveseat, where they could touch each other and kiss, rather than talking at each other across the distance of the table. It was an auspicious night for them. To this point in their relationship, they had not enjoyed the privacy to consummate their love, beyond holding hands or kissing. Both shared their apartments with others and, although it was the summer, their roommates were all working in town and frustratingly ever-present. Being private people by nature, neither Gabriel nor Cathy warmed to the idea of having sex for the first time in a crowded apartment. That week, however, Vail had travelled to Montreal with friends to watch a tennis tournament and Pablo, who had recently moved in, was touring the Eastern United States with his parents. This left the young couple the run of Gabriel's apartment for several glorious days.

Unlike Gabriel's first time with Jenny, neither he nor Cathy was particularly fearful or nervous. Although neither of them had had extensive sexual experience, it was not the first time for either of them. More importantly, their relationship just felt so right, they were as comfortable with each other as if they had grown up together, that it eliminated the anxiety, the fretfulness that he had suffered at Jenny's house.

As they sat together in the loveseat, their legs touching beneath their shorts, enjoying the live jazz pianist, Gabriel waxed nostalgic. "Life's finally gotten good," he lamented. "It's too bad we only have two years left."

"I don't know," she said. "U. of T.'s great, but I look forward to getting out and starting my life."

"Not me," Gabriel demurred. "This is probably as good as it gets. Here we're all philosopher kings and queens. Our best selves. Out there, we're just fodder for the next generation of adults, the next salesmen, the next corporate executives. Who needs *that*?"

"*We're* not going to sell out," she insisted.

"*Everybody* sells out!"

"Wow! That's cynical," Cathy observed with a bemused smile. "I'd like to think that there was at least *some* hope for us...."

"Oh, I don't mean *that*. You and I are different. We've got integrity. But it's easy to lose your integrity out there. That's why I want to avoid the 'real world' as long as I can. Why I'm thinking of going to grad school. The longer we can study – maybe travel a little, see the world – the longer we can avoid the trap that everyone falls into."

She took a sip of her Pina Colada, adjusted the silver bracelet on her wrist. "Don't you want to get married?" she asked, a little too casually. The pianist began a Scott Joplin ragtime.

"*Married?* Why would we want to do *that*? To become our parents? We're better than that. Our *relationship* is better than that. Purer. Holier."

"You're funny, Gabriel," she commented wryly, still twisting her bracelet. "You're a religious guy, yet you don't believe in marriage. Doesn't God want you to get married and, like the *Torah* says, 'Be fruitful and multiply?'"

Gabriel downed the last of his beer, placing the glass on the table a little too clumsily and loudly, and signalled to the waiter that he wanted another. "Yeah, you've got a point. But we can do that later, right? No need to rush into it. For now, we can live Socrates examined life."

"I see...." she said with exaggerated thoughtfulness, as if she wanted him to know that she was humouring him. "But please do tell, Mr. Socrates. If you want to avoid the real world and selling out at all costs, why on earth would you want to date someone who plans to be a lawyer?"

Gabriel reddened, recognizing that she had left him no graceful way out. He broke into an impish grin and declared, "Because she's strange and wonderful. That's why."

"That's right. That's the first sensible thing you've said all night, Mr. Dean's List. Now, unless you'd prefer to stay here putting your foot further down your throat, let's get back to your place and put your empty apartment to good use...." The blazing, triumphant look in the multi-hued orbs that were her eyes indicated that she enjoyed coming out on top.

"Yes, Ma'am!" he said sharply, bringing his right hand up to his forehead in a military salute.

As they settled into Gabriel's apartment that night – what would be their apartment and theirs alone for almost a full week – they embraced and each said "I love you." For both of them, it was genuine, heartfelt. But the words meant different things to each of them, had different emphases. For Cathy, it was I love *you*. *You* are the one I love. I want to devote my life to *you*, for whom my heart beats, without whom there is no sunlight, without whom my life has no meaning. For Gabriel, however, the emphasis was different. *I* love you. *I* who am Gabriel love you because of what you bring to *me*. At this stage of his life, love, for Gabriel, was an act of self-aggrandisement, like a state conquering a territory to make it richer, stronger, more secure. It was a demand for loyalty, for comfort, for fealty, rather than anything calling for extraordinary sacrifice or commitment on his part.

Despite these internal differences, or perhaps because of them, their week by themselves was blissful, brought them even closer together. Those were their days and nights of pure ecstacy. They were young and lithe and smooth, unstained by time, and joys abounded. Everything was new and their spheres were blissfully free of their parents' tedious orbits, pleasure and imagination their only frontiers. Free to experiment with love, a drug with no pernicious side effects, whose high is more intoxicating, more mind-altering than the most powerful hallucinogenic. It made them long for each other all the more when Gabriel's roommates returned, and they retreated to their separate living quarters.

While Gabriel was shopping at the Eaton's Centre in the autumn for a gift for Cathy, he had a chance encounter with an old high school friend. He was rummaging dispiritedly through a display of scarves in the entrance of a women's clothing shop when a voice from behind startled him, proclaiming in an assumed British accent, "Well, as I live and breathe. It's Gabriel Klein! Jolly good! Jolly good!"

Gabriel wheeled around to see Steve Sheiner – "call me Steven now, please" –grinning at him. Although Gabriel had by now moved on from high school and rarely thought about his old friends, he was surprised at how pleased he was to see Steve. "Steve!" he practically shouted. "I don't believe it! What are you doing here?"

Steven grinned and snapped, "Just because I go to York doesn't mean that I'm not allowed to go downtown, you know!"

"How's life at Camp York?" Gabriel teased.

"Oh, you know. I'm taking macramé and basket weaving this year," his friend deadpanned. "And what's it like at U. of T. with all the blue-blood elites? Have you become an intolerable snob yet?"

"Oh, absolutely," Gabriel replied without missing a beat. "I'd love to chat, but I'm late for a meeting with the finance minister. We're going on a foxhunt this afternoon."

"So, uh, why are you elbow-deep in ladies' lingerie?" his friend gibed.

Gabriel grimaced. "Scarfs are hardly lingerie! Do you have time for a coffee?" Steven nodded. "Great! Let's head to a café and I'll fill you in."

They installed themselves at a table at a café on the lower floor. "So you see, my girlfriend's birthday is coming up and I need to get her something," Gabriel explained.

"Cool!" Steven said brightly, but his smile masked some underlying sadness. "How long've you been dating?"

"Oh, almost five months now."

"What's her name?" Steven asked.

"Cathy. I met her at a JSU dance, of all places," Gabriel said.

Steven muffled a sigh by taking a sip of his cappuccino. "It's hard to believe that you're no longer with Jenny," he said wistfully.

"That's ancient history at this point. Do you still keep in touch with her?" Gabriel asked.

"I did. But I haven't heard from her in a while. I guess she's moved on," said his friend sadly. "What about you?"

Gabriel shook his head. "Not a word from her in over a year."

"The last I heard, she was seeing this medical student out in Vancouver. I guess she was always too good for someone like me," Steven lamented.

"Aw, I wouldn't say that. We just don't always get our first choice in life."

Steven glanced around at the nearby tables, glumly noting all the young couples. "I suppose," he said.

To change the subject, Gabriel discussed his mission. "Actually, maybe you can help me out. I'm trying to find the perfect gift for Cathy, but I'm way out of my league. I just can't think of anything," he confided. "What do women like?"

"Well," Steven considered. "To be honest, I think she'd like *anything*, just because it's from you. They're not like us.... They aren't looking for something cool just because they want it. They won't be disappointed if they don't get that power tool or Star Trek memento they were hoping for. They want something from the heart, something that'll have sentimental value for them."

Gabriel was impressed. He hadn't expected that depth of understanding and felt downright silly not to have figured out what Steven appeared to understand instinctively.

"Maybe go with a simple piece of jewellery that she can wear that'll remind her daily of how much you love her. Like a necklace or a bracelet. That can't go wrong," Steven concluded.

"You know, Steve... er, I mean Steven, you're pretty sharp. You're a very sensitive and perceptive guy."

"Yeah. Surprising that I can't find any women who think so...." Steven bemoaned. "Hey! What happened to you and Aziz? I heard he moved out and isn't talking to you anymore."

Gabriel filled Steven in on the misunderstanding. "I feel just awful about it. I'd love to apologize, but he won't take my calls. If you could let him know how awful I feel and ask him to let me make it up to him, I'd be eternally grateful."

"I can try," Steven replied. "But I don't think he's likely to budge. I've never seen him so mad. He says he's finished with you." He consulted his watch. "Look, I've got to get going, but it's been great to see you."

"Yeah. Awesome!" Gabriel agreed. "Hey! Gimme your number. I'd really love it if you could get together with Cathy and me at some point. I'm sorry we've lost touch. We should remedy that."

Steven ripped off part of the bill and scribbled his number on it. He passed it to Gabriel, saying "That'd be cool! See ya, Gabriel!" Gabriel watched as he mounted the stairs and passed through the revolving glass doors onto the street. *How is it that I never realized how much smarter he is than I am, how much more intuitive and practical?*

Although they were both by nature private people, over time Cathy and Gabriel conceded the necessity of sleeping over in each other's rooms even when their roommates were present. It made little sense, they concluded to wait for the far too rare occasions when they had the apartments to themselves. Their burning love, their urgent need to be alone with each other, simply couldn't wait. In compliance with the ten commandments that Gabriel himself had drafted for his home, Cathy slept over at Gabriel's apartment only on weekends, whereas Gabriel would occasionally lodge at Cathy's, where no such regulations existed, during the week.

After a particularly intense bout of lovemaking one Saturday night, Gabriel was lying naked on his back, staring up at the ceiling in the darkness, registering Cathy's warmth, the regular rising and falling of her chest with each breath, beside him. On an impulse, he propped himself up on his side, reached into the drawer of his bedside table and pulled out a flashlight. He shined it on her lissome body, slowly examining every inch of her, like an appraiser of fine gems. Gently, he slid the light along her body, shining directly onto her skin, illuminating the flesh around its blue plastic casing in an eerie ruby glow, revealing the twisted, knotted blue veins beneath the surface. He manipulated her onto her side and beamed the light behind her, into the skin of her back, along her arms and legs, as otherworldly shadows danced on the ceiling above them.

"Hey, that's cold! What are you doing?" she giggled.

"I need to know," he whispered with an air of great solemnity. "Are you really what you appear to be, or is there a monster lurking inside you? You won't disappoint me… won't betray me, like everyone else has, will you?"

She kissed him. "No, Love, I'll *never* do that. We were made for each other."

"Mmmm...." he murmured, accidentally dropping the flashlight on the floor.

As he scrambled around the bed to pick it and switch it off, Cathy said, "You know, as soon as I met you, I just *knew* we would be together. Even when I didn't return your calls because I was back with Lawrence, I was sure that nothing would stop us from getting together."

Gabriel reacted harshly. "Don't *ever* talk about Lawrence again! It never happened," he ordered her.

"Are you jealous? Hey! I'm with *you*, not him. And what about you and Jennifer?"

"That never happened either. *Forget* about it. There's only you and me," he snapped.

Cathy was disturbed. "You can't just *forget* about people. They *existed*. They made us into what we are now. Lawrence wasn't right for me; *you* are. But I'm glad I went out with him."

"Well, *I* don't want to hear about him anymore," he groused.

"Gee," she said playfully, pulling him close to her and nibbling on his earlobes, "I guess you'll have to *make* me forget about him. If you can...." He eagerly accepted the challenge.

Steven Sheiner accepted Gabriel's invitation to join him for a Chanukah dinner at Cathy's. It was just the three of them, as Cathy's flatmate, Carol, had a night class to attend. They began with a candle-lighting ceremony in the living room, then sat in the dark basking in the flickering light, enjoying the serenity. After a while, they repaired to the dining room to the Chicken Cacciatore with Whole Wheat Rotelle that Gabriel prepared for the occasion, which they washed down with a chilled bottle of Sauvignon Blanc.

"You know, Gabriel," Steven reflected as he swirled the wine in his goblet, "the last time we spent Chanukah together was at Jenny's."

"Oh, so you're talking about the competition," Cathy said, with mock jealousy, studying her guest.

"Don't worry," Steven said earnestly. "There's no competition. With Jenny, I practically had to whack Gabriel over the head with a two-by-four to make him aware of the fact that that awesome creature was into him. With you, it's *totally* different. He's obviously smitten with you. He hasn't been able to take his eyes off of you all night!" Cathy beamed, as Gabriel flushed bright red. "And," he continued, admiring her in her brown corduroy pants, the snugly-fitting sweater that set off the amber flecks in her eyes, the pearl necklace that Gabriel had given her for her birthday, "if I'm not overstepping my bounds, I can see why."

"Ooooh! I *like* him!" Cathy cooed. "Why haven't you brought him here before?"

"I want to keep you to myself," Gabriel retorted. "It's not a great strategy to bring in men that you like, especially not men with velvety tongues."

"So, Steven, you've got to tell me. What was Gabriel *like* in high school?" Cathy inquired. Aside from Lawrence Linton, she hadn't yet met anyone who knew him before he started university.

"I only knew him for the last two years. He was off the rails before then...."

"Yes," Cathy interrupted. "I heard about that. But what about afterwards?"

Steven helped himself to a sip of wine and reflected. "Well, insanely intelligent, like now. But, sort of... angry, hard-edged. Like he had a chip on his shoulder. I always felt he was a man on a mission, but I was never sure what that mission was. Like...

well, like a brilliant comet blazing a trail to the empty reaches of the universe."

"Hey, guys!" Gabriel remonstrated. "I'm sitting right here!"

"You're on the hot seat, eh Mr. Dean's List?" Cathy cackled. "Here. The wine's empty. Go get some beer from the fridge and let me hear more, will you?"

Gabriel complied, as he eavesdropped on their conversation. "He was always talking about God and truth and righteousness, like he just dropped out the Bible or something."

Cathy smiled. "That hasn't changed much, I'm afraid," she said with a giggle.

"But he was a loyal and good friend. Ruthlessly honest. And as far as I can tell, he never betrayed me or humiliated me with Jenny, who I was hopelessly in love with.... Probably still am now, after all this time." Moved, Cathy touched his elbow in sympathy. "He never showed us he could cook like this, though. You've got him well-trained."

"Gabriel's not the sort of guy you can train," she ruminated. "But you're a good judge of character, Steven. And, you may not believe it now, but I'm certain that someone as sensitive as you will find a woman that's far better suited to you than Jenny ever was."

As he accompanied Steven to his car afterwards, Gabriel asked, "So? What do you think of her?"

His friend paused for a moment and thought. "I think she's *perfect* for you! Somehow, she makes you softer, more human. I don't mean to be rude. You're my friend, but sometimes you seem, well, harsh, cold, indifferent. With Cathy, you're just a better person. You'd better hang on to her."

Gabriel was taken aback by his friend's reply, but just said "Oh, I intend to," as Steven climbed behind the wheel.

***

As his third year at U. of T. drew to a close, Gabriel's life began to fall into place. He continued to excel scholastically, earning the attention and admiration of his professors. For the third straight year, he made the dean's list, with a grade point average above 4.0 because he earned A plusses in two of his courses. And his love for his studies, for Philosophy, only grew. It was only natural, therefore, for him to let Arthur, whom he met with at their Madison Avenue pub periodically throughout the year, persuade him to apply to graduate school. Gabriel now had dreams of becoming a professor, a modern-day philosopher, himself. As a professor, he decided, he would never have to leave the comforting confines of the university, would never have to sell out. He could live life on his own terms, free of the corruption of the 'real world'.

It was also clear to Gabriel that he had found his soulmate. Cathy was not, he decided, a temporary infatuation, a passing fancy that would fade with familiarity. As a child in Hebrew night school, he had been taught that Heaven chooses a single partner for every person at the moment of birth. It was incumbent on people, therefore, not to settle for an inferior match, but to search far and wide for their divine match – in Yiddish, their *bashert*. Cathy, he knew now, was his *bashert*, and Heaven had saved its finest work for him.

This knowledge, however, did not inspire thoughts of marriage in Gabriel. Far from it. They were young, with many joys, challenges, adventures ahead of them that marriage and convention would spoil. No need to rush into anything that might alter their bliss, to institutionalize their love. The eagle was free and glorious. Why cage it? Why burden it with practical considerations?

The only fly in the ointment was that their destiny beyond his fourth year was in the hands of university admissions committees. Gabriel was confident that he would have a strong record for graduate school. But Cathy was in a more precarious position. Unlike Gabriel, she struggled at U. of T., with only average grades. While her Law School Admissions Test results were fairly good, therefore, it was nonetheless unlikely that she would be admitted to law school in the universities that would best advance Gabriel's ambitions – Arthur recommended U.of T., McGill, UBC, Queen's – or even other universities nearby. She would most likely have to apply widely to weaker programs in less desirable locations and would need to go wherever she was accepted. This reality began to introduce an element of uncertainty, of fear, into their lives, as they grappled with the possibility that they might be compelled to travel separate paths for a few years and carry on a long-distance relationship. For the time being, however, in the Spring of his third year, Gabriel was as happy as he had ever been in his life.

By the autumn of their final year at U. of T., Cathy felt that their relationship had reached a critical juncture. With them both graduating the following summer and potentially moving on to different universities, they needed to commit to each other, or risk being pulled apart. For Cathy, the solution was as clear as a bottle of emerald Riesling: marriage bells. What better way to consummate their love and prevent fate from driving them apart?

Her plan had another practical advantage. If they were engaged immediately to be married by the summer, they could plan their next steps in unison. Specifically, since someone would need to support them, they could not both enrol in academic programs simultaneously. She believed that since law was the more lucrative profession and had a fixed three-to-four-year timeframe, it would make sense for her to complete her studies first, with Gabriel working full time to pay the bills. Once she passed the bar, she would return the favour and support his graduate work, however long that might take.

Over the previous summer, she had dropped hints, but Gabriel seemed obtuse and failed to pick up on them. By the start of school after Labour Day, she began to press the issue, but he shut her down each time. It occurred to her for the first time that his tirades against marriage and conformity might not simply be bravado, young adult posing, as she had assumed, but might actually constitute bedrock principles of his. But what was she to do? She was strung out on a tightrope wire, unable to retreat to security – she loved him too much to leave him – yet he would not allow her to reach the promised land of marriage, stability, a family, happiness. For the first time, this conflict introduced a note of tension, of rancour, into a hitherto harmonious, carefree relationship. It had even become a tug of war in bed, as Cathy tried unsuccessfully to use sex as a coercive weapon. Besides, as she put it, she felt less frisky now that she realized he didn't love her as much as she had thought.

Meanwhile, Gabriel, who believed that their relationship was just fine as it was, thank you, couldn't understand why she would want to interfere with the natural order of the universe by institutionalizing it. From his perspective, love was truest when it was free from coercion, from chains. Why mess with the perfection of their love by putting names on it, by involving others, by routinizing it? Besides, why add pressure by making him *responsible* for her before he had the reliable means to do so? He had to follow his dream of graduate school and only then could he entertain the confines of marriage. The more he protested, however, the more the fear that he might eventually abandon her crept into her brain, which made her press even harder.

The impasse had simmered for the first weeks of the semester and reached a boiling point by the end of the High Holidays in early October. Cathy had joined her parents uptown in their synagogue for Rosh Hashana and Yom Kippur and had been hoping that Gabriel would come, as well. But Gabriel, in compliance with his vow never to enter a synagogue again, prayed on his own. Cathy was miffed. She understood and respected his rejection of organized religion – or at least she humoured him about it – but believed that there were times when gathering together as a family should take precedence. She took him to task for it the evening after Yom Kippur, when she stopped by his apartment after breaking her ritual fast so that they could go out for a quick coffee together.

"Would it have killed you to join us for the *chag*?" she sputtered, using the Hebrew word for 'holiday'. She stood in his room with her arms crossed, her nostrils flaring, her back leaning on his closed door.

"Aw, come on, Cathy! I'm glad to see you. Don't be like that!" he pleaded. He sat on his hastily made bed opposite her, holding out his arm, beckoning her to join him. Instead, she held her position resolutely.

"I know you've got your principles, and I'm fine with them. I *admire* you for them. I *do*," she began. "But life isn't only about principles. There's people, too! It would have been nice for me if you had joined me. My parents also would have been happy to have us both with them for the holidays. Sometimes you need to give a little."

"Well.... Maybe I could stay at your folks' next time. But there's no way I'm going to *shul*," he proposed.

"Ach! You're so inflexible!"

"Hey! I thought that's what you loved about me!" he teased. He gave her one of his patented 'adorable' looks, hoping to cut the tension. Instead, she remained standing rigidly by the door, elbows out, rubbing her sandalled foot testily against the worn beige carpet.

"And why is it that I've never met *your* parents? We've been together for over a year, yet you seem embarrassed to show me to them," she complained.

"You *know* I don't get along with them! Why are you making a big deal about that now?" he shot back.

"It seems to me that if you were serious about us, you'd introduce me to your parents, regardless how you felt about them. I want to know that our relationship has a future. That we're going to commit to each other." As soon as the words left her mouth, she could see him stiffen.

"Give me a break, will you? I fasted all day," he shouted. Then trying to keep his voice down, he continued, "Do we really need to get into this *now*?"

"It's *never* the right time to discuss this. Either you have work, or your tired, or you've just fasted.... There's always *something*," she charged, a trial attorney badgering the witness.

"Geez! I don't know what's gotten *into* you, Cathy...."

"What's gotten *into* me? Really?" She squeezed her fists in frustration. Then, taking a deep breath to try to compose herself, she got to the heart of her appeal. "Look, Gabriel. I like you. No, I *love* you. I don't know *why* – you're *maddening* at times, sometimes I just want to *strangle* you – but I really *do* love you. We've been dating for a year-and-a-half now and we need to decide what comes next. You need to grow *up* already! We're going to graduate this summer and I need to know I'm not... well, wasting my time with you. Let's get engaged already." She had rehearsed on the way over, but it didn't come off exactly as she had planned.

"We've been over this before, Cathy," Gabriel replied cagily. "We're not ready to get married now. Neither of us are in a position to earn money yet. I want to go to grad school. You want to go to law school. We should wait until we can start off on the right footing."

"Who needs *money*? We can live as students until we get through school. You always say that people are happier without lots of money," she said. He grimaced, as he always did when she used his words against him.

They were interrupted briefly by a loud, metallic vibrating sound in the walls. Mrs. Gupta upstairs must have been using her built-in kitchen sink garburator. "You *know* that wouldn't work, Cath. After a while, we'd end up fighting over money. Let's just wait a bit," Gabriel pleaded when the vibrating ceased. Then a smile came over him and he sang a lyric from a Leonard Cohen song about love and chains.

It was exactly the wrong thing to say. Instead of lightening the mood, he poured gasoline on her open flame. "That's what it is, *isn't it*? I'm just a *chain* to you. I'm great for sex, but you wouldn't want to tie yourself down to me, *would* you?" she raged.

"Aw, that's not true. You *know* I love you," he protested. "But please try to keep it down. The guys can hear through these thin walls."

"I don't care *who* hears me," she shouted, stamping her foot for emphasis.

An idea came over him. "Why can't we just move in together and leave marriage till later?" he suggested.

"Move in together?" Cathy repeated, mulling the idea over. It wasn't what she was hoping for, but it was a step in the right direction, wasn't it? But no, she decided. Not good enough. She continued her offensive. "What would that accomplish? If you're worried about us fighting without enough money, what difference would it make if we were married or not? We'd still have very little until we start working. You just want to avoid a real commitment."

"That's not true," he responded defensively. "It's just that marriage is a big step. I'm not sure I even like the institution of marriage. Why can't we commit to each other by living together?"

"You're a strange fellow," Cathy charged, more annoyed than amused. "You're always talking about God and how we need to follow His teachings if we want to live a good life. Yet you'd rather move in with me and live in sin than marry me. How do you square that with your logic?"

Gabriel shifted uncomfortably in his chair. Of course he recognized that she was right, but that only made him dig in and argue more vehemently, like a cornered animal. "What difference does it make?" he challenged her. "We *already* sleep together. If that's a sin, getting married won't erase it." He vaguely recognized the absurdity of what he had just said, but was under assault and needed to defend the citadel at all costs.

"I don't want to be left high and dry if you decide to run off," she said, humiliated that she needed to state her case so directly, to name her fear.

"If you're afraid of me running off, I can do so even if we're married. We could get divorced, or I can simply run off and disappear. So there's no advantage to getting married from that point of view," he reasoned.

Cathy stared at him in horror. "You've actually given that so much thought? What kind of person *are* you? Is *that* what love is all about?"

"Not that I'm ever planning to do that. And no, I haven't given it *any* thought, but the arguments you're making don't hold any water," he said defensively.

"Look, Gabriel, I don't feel like going out tonight. I'm going back home. And I think we're at a crossroads here.... I've made up my mind. I'm not going to hang around anymore at your beck and call. If you don't want to marry me, that's your right. But I need to move on...."

"Aw, don't be like that!" he whined. But she had grabbed her jacket and made for the door.

"I'm serious!" she warned him, as she fought to master her tears, the frustrated tears of a woman who has waited too long for too little, who has been rebuffed when she wanted to be embraced. "I need more than you're willing to give me. If you aren't able to do this for me, then we need to go our separate ways. I'm *done* with this!"

"So..." Gabriel erupted, shell-shocked, rising from the bed to join her near the door, "so this is goodbye?"

"I... I think so," she said, as the tears began to flow. "Goodbye, Gabriel." She leaned over and kissed him sadly on his cheek before wrenching open the door and bursting out, leaving him sitting stunned in her wake.

Gabriel's initial reaction was indignant defiance. *If that's the way she's gonna be, good riddance to her! She seems to care more about marriage than she does about me! I'm better off without her. There're plenty of other fish in the sea; I don't need to chain myself to her.* As the shock dissipated, however, he saw matters in a strikingly different light. *How could I just let her walk out like that? I'm never going to find someone like her again. She's one in a million. Maybe I should run after her.* But then the reality of the conflict reasserted itself. Since he was unwilling to get married so young, what good would running after her do? Their differences were irreconcilable.

After turning the matter over and over again in his mind, he decided he needed a stiff drink. He trudged into the kitchen for some of the whiskey they kept in a cabinet under the sink. There he found Vail and Pablo, who had listened to the fight through his paper-thin door, waiting for him.

"Wow! Tough break, dude!" Vail ventured.

"I'm sorry, Gabriel," Pablo offered more diplomatically.

"You heard the whole thing?" Gabriel asked sullenly, as he retrieved the bottle of Canadian Club.

"Most of it," Vail said callously. "She really went to town on you! You have a problem keeping the hot ones, don't you? First that Angela girl and now Cathy."

"Gee, Vail, you're a big help!" Gabriel griped. He poured himself half an eight-ounce tumbler full of whiskey, that time-honoured elixir for hard times. Pablo grew concerned.

"Hey, Gabriel! Go easy on that," his new flatmate admonished him.

"Oh, don't worry. I can handle it," Gabriel said, as he took a large draught, swished it around his mouth and swallowed. It tingled his tongue and cheeks gently at first, but burned, not altogether unpleasantly, as it travelled down his throat.

Vail offered his sage wisdom. "You're better off without her, dude," he opined. "You're only twenty-one. That's *way* too soon to think of tying yourself down to one babe." Vail helped himself to some whiskey, as well. He showed the bottle to Pablo, who shook his head.

"I know," Gabriel agreed, breathing out fumes of rye and alcohol. "But how can I just let her walk away like that? She's the girl of my dreams!"

"Hey! I know you were really into her – frankly, your lovey-dovey act with her kinda made me sick at times – but *trust* me. You dodged a bullet today. If she truly loves you, she'll wait for you. If not, she's not worth it. Better to wait for someone who cares enough about *your* needs, too," Vail pronounced. Then he turned to Pablo and said with a wink, "You see? Better advice than Dr. Ruth and he doesn't even need to bare his deep dark secrets on the radio!"

But Gabriel wasn't so sure. He drained the rest of his whiskey. Having fasted all day, however, the drink unsettled his stomach, made him queasy. He returned to his room and crawled morosely into bed without changing or switching off the light and remained there in fetal position without sleeping for many hours.

At work the following afternoon, Gabriel could hardly concentrate. He made several basic mistakes that he might have made in the early days, but that were surprising at this stage. Noticing his agitation, the redness in his eyes, Mr. Balogh called him on it. "What's wrong, Gabriel? You're not yourself today. Is everything okay?"

"Yeah, I'm fine," Gabriel lied.

"Sit down, okay?" his boss commanded. Gabriel complied, shifting his weight onto his wooden work stool. "You don't want to tell me. Fine. But you're not okay, and I'd like to help if I can."

"Aw, it's nothing," Gabriel said evasively. But, feeling the weight of Mr. Balogh's stare, he caved in quickly. "It's just that I think my girlfriend and I broke up last night."

"Oh, I'm sorry. What happened?"

Gabriel was uncomfortable sharing details with his boss, especially since Mr. Balogh had always been rather stiff and formal, had never been particularly talkative with him. Nonetheless, he wanted to unburden himself with someone, and his traditional advisor, Vail, had not been of any help. So, he reluctantly related Cathy's ultimatum to him.

For quite a while, Mr. Balogh was silent, lost in his own thoughts. Gabriel assumed that he was embarrassed by personal details of that sort in the workplace and immediately regretted telling him. In time, however, Mr. Balogh said slowly in Hungarian, "I want to tell you a story." Gabriel sat on his stool with his hands clasped together awkwardly, as his employer continued. "My wife... my Róza... was two years my junior. She was one of three fraternal triplets, all girls, all pretty." Gabriel interrupted him briefly to inquire what 'testvéri hármasikrek,' meant, having never heard the term for fraternal triplets before. Mr. Balogh translated that as 'three twins that didn't look like each other,' from the word, 'három,' meaning three. "But my Róza was the prettiest by far," he continued. "So beautiful... she completed the heavens. Long, flowing hair, the colour of clover honey, the biggest, warmest, brownest eyes you've ever seen. Such pale skin, but when she smiled, or blushed, her cheeks were as red as Macintosh apples. I'd love to show you a picture of her, but we were too poor when we came here and didn't own a camera. But I have picture right in here." He pointed his thin, arthritic index finger to his forehead, smiling sadly, sheepishly. "Unlike me, she never gets any older...."

"When I was in my first year as a student at Szeged University – just as you are a university student now – Róza was still finishing high school. I saw her for the first time one glorious afternoon at the university, near the fountain outside. I found out afterwards that her mother worked there as a receptionist in the History department and Róza used to wait at the fountain for her every Tuesday afternoon after the art class she took nearby. She was a talented painter. I know it sounds impetuous and foolish, childish even, but I fell in love with her right then and there. But what could I do? I couldn't *talk* to her. My heart sank into my stomach just looking at her. You know, Gabriel, that I'm not a man of words. I never have been... especially with women. So, I said nothing, and that was that."

"I returned to the fountain every afternoon that week in the hope of encountering her again, but to no avail. I had almost given up hope the following Tuesday, when I found my sweetheart sitting on the top bench around the fountain, her back to the main building of the university and its ivory façade, her beautiful legs draped over the two benches below. Oh, how I rejoiced!" The workshop telephone rang and Gabriel hopped off his stool to answer it, but Mr. Balogh waved him away, wordlessly bidding him to ignore it and return to his stool. Gabriel had long tried to convince his boss to purchase an answering machine for the store, but Mr. Balogh was skeptical about technology and refused to trust a newfangled gadget like that with his calls. He simply let the phone ring on while he continued his story.

"I was still too shy to talk to her, though. So, I sat on the bench opposite her, on the other side of the fountain, and pretended to read, all the while drinking in her beauty, imagining what it would be like to talk to her, to stroke her hair. I did this every Tuesday for the next few weeks, never getting enough courage

The Oracle of Spring Garden Road

to initiate a conversation." After several rings, the telephone fell silent. "Of course, I knew that she saw me looking at her. I could feel in my bones, I don't know how, that she was flattered by my attention and was eager to talk to me, too. I *knew* that she liked me too, you understand. A man can *sense* these things. But I was just too nervous, too frightened to open my mouth and talk to her. It was agony! I was so ashamed, so afraid that I had blown my opportunity."

"But one day I had my violin with me – the one my father made, the one I showed you – and, instead of talking, I pulled it out and played for her. A little bit of Beethoven, a bit of Dvorak, whatever came to mind. I swear to you that I've never played so sweetly, before or afterwards. It was like God was playing for me, using my fingers, helping poor tongue-tied Balogh so that he could get his Róza. As I played, she inched closer, sat down right next to me listening not just with her ears – what beautiful ears! – but with her whole body, her eyes as wide as the sun, her cheeks fiery red. When I finished, she started to talk to me, and it was too late to be nervous. From that day onward, we met every day after school, Tuesdays at the university, on other days near her high school, and I played my violin, we talked. Eventually, I worked up the courage to ask her to marry me and she agreed, making me the happiest man in all of Hungary."

"But, as so often happens in life, it wasn't a happily ever after story. We knew it wasn't going to be so easy. Her father was a communist, high up in the government before the 1956 revolution. *My* father was a fervent Catholic. He hated the communists and had been a political prisoner after the Communist government took power in 1949. They jailed him for over a year. He was never the same afterwards. What unspeakable things they must have done to him, my poor father! Well, when I approached Róza's father to ask him for his blessing, he cruelly and coldheartedly refused. There was no way, he screamed, that he would let his daughter marry the son of, in his words, a traitor. It was terrible! Oh, how we cried! We continued to see each other secretly, in defiance of his edict, but we had no real hope that we could ever marry."

"I pleaded in vain with Róza to run away with me and marry without her father's blessing. That was out of the question for her. If her father were to cut her off, she would be unable to speak to her sisters, which for her would be a punishment too terrible to bear. So, we just carried on as we had, without hope." At this point, Mr. Balogh stared at Gabriel pleadingly, as if asking him for absolution. "You understand," he explained, "that I'm not someone who defies authority. I think it's right that a father should decide whether or not to give his blessing. But how could he condemn us both to such misery?"

"Anyway, this was around the time of the 1956 revolution, and I became involved in protests against the regime at the university. I had never liked the communists and now identified communism as a system that kept me away from my Róza. When the Red Army came in to crush the revolution and the Nagy government, I knew I couldn't stay anymore. One of my comrades told me he believed we were all going to be arrested for our part in the protests and that he was going to escape to Austria that very night. Would I join him? It didn't take me a minute's thought to say 'yes'. There was no future for me in Communist Hungary. In a frenzy, I ran to Róza, who was by this time a university student too – we had known each other for over a year by then – and pulled her out of class. I told Róza that I was going to get out that very night and begged her to come with me. She couldn't believe it. 'You're not going to leave me, leave Hungary!' she cried. But I told her I had no choice and that this was our only chance at happiness. She was horrified at the thought of leaving her sisters – they were so close, they thought the same thoughts, breathed as one – never seeing her parents again. But when she understood I was serious and that I couldn't wait, she kissed me and said she couldn't live without me. If she had to cut out one organ, she said, better her eyes or her ears than to cut out her heart. Being proper and respectable, that was the first time we had ever kissed. Oh, how sweet and wonderful it was, despite the fear, the danger. While I went to bid farewell to my parents, who supported my decision tearfully, she ran home and gathered a few essentials. We left Szeged that night and never saw either of our families again."

The door swung open and Suzanne from the front of the store entered the workshop. "Mr. Balogh, Mr. Singh from the TSO has been calling! He wants to talk to you about his cello," she announced. "Didn't you hear the phone?"

"Can't you see we're busy here?" he scolded. "I'll call him back when I'm ready. Now, please let us work in peace!"

Suzanne grumbled and shot Gabriel a disapproving glance that seemed to say, 'what an ill-tempered, unreasonable man!' Gabriel grinned uncomfortably.

"We snuck out in the dead of night, in a farm tractor, loosely covered with hay. It brought us to a small farmhouse on a canal, where we were put into a rowboat and smuggled across the canal into Austria. It was still early enough that the Russians hadn't yet set up extensive patrols to control emigration. It was scary, but also very romantic, and Róza, in her fear, held me tightly during the trip. Our first order of business when we crossed into Austria, was to get married quickly in a local church. It wasn't a Catholic church, but we couldn't afford to be picky."

"When we arrived in Canada, it was very difficult. Neither of us spoke much English or French, and we had no-one here. *I* was okay starting anew and building a better life with my Róza, but I wasn't a triplet who had spent my entire life sharing everything with my sisters. For Róza, it was unbearable. I found work in a factory with the help of the local Hungarian community. But she stayed home alone all day pining for her sisters. She tried to write to them, but never received a reply.

Perhaps they never received it; perhaps her father refused to let them respond. In any event, she was heartbroken. While we delighted in each other's company, it wasn't enough to keep her steady through the interminable workdays, her long sleepless nights."

"After almost two years, we were ecstatic to learn that she was pregnant. I had hoped that the baby would occupy her during the days, give her a sense of purpose and fulfillment. But, as so often happens, fate had other plans. When she went into labour, something seemed wrong. She said she didn't feel the baby kicking at all." Mr. Balogh paused to suppress a sob. "She delivered a stillborn baby and any hope she still had drained out of her, like air from a leaky balloon. From then on, she cried bitterly all day and all night, never sleeping, never smiling. Nothing I did could comfort her. It was heart-wrenching. Two weeks afterwards, she...." Mr. Balogh's face convulsed, and a few tears escaped his chalky, cavernous eyes before he quickly regained control. "She... well, she died... while I was at work. I found her in the bathtub when I returned, still holding a sprig of dandelions that I had picked for her on my way home."

Mr. Balogh fell silent, perched on his stool, peering off into some unseen distance. Gabriel was unsure of whether he was finished or not and didn't want to disturb him, so he simply sat and waited, feeling infinitely sorry for Mr. Balogh, for Róza, for all who suffer. After an eternity, Mr. Balogh stirred, tried to compose himself, and addressed Gabriel solemnly.

"Although I have known such misery and have missed her terribly every day, every minute, since she passed, I never once regretted marrying her. The two years we had together as man and wife were worth more to me than any suffering I have endured, or will endure, even if I live another hundred years, you understand?" Then Mr. Balogh glared fiercely at Gabriel, as if he was staring directly into his soul. "Listen, Gabriel," he charged. "I don't go around parading my sorrows in public. If I do so, there's a reason. What I want to tell you is this. If this girl is just another girl, then let her go and forget her. But if your Cathy is so important to you, like my Róza was.... As important as the water you drink or the air you breathe, or even as your violin.... And if you'll regret forever that you lost her just because you weren't ready to get married.... Then put aside your pride and your fear. Go! Run and beg her forgiveness and don't ever let her go. You understand? Marry her, do whatever you need to, but don't give up the chance of happiness just because the timing isn't ideal. You hear me?"

Gabriel was overwhelmed and unable to respond. He looked away, trying desperately to fight back his own tears. Mr. Balogh didn't wait for a reply, instead admonishing him dourly, "Now go home and decide! Don't come back here until you've resolved this and can concentrate on your work. I can't afford to have you waste my time and money with your foolish mistakes. This is a business, not a gossip society!" With that, he turned his back to Gabriel, hoisted the telephone receiver curtly and returned Mr. Singh's call.

Gabriel wandered the streets of downtown Toronto, lost in thought. Eventually, he returned to his apartment long after dark in utter turmoil, mulling over Mr. Balogh's tragic story, his passionate advice, wondering how he could live without Cathy. Yet he was torn. He was too young, he was certain, to marry. Too young to tie himself down to one woman for the rest of his life, to a life of mortgages and children, orthodontist appointments and carpools, to punching timeclocks. But it was more than that. He had only recently escaped the stultifying confines of his parents' house, its mind-numbing conformity. For a few very short years, his life had been wide open, with infinite possibilities, without constraints, without humdrum averageness. Could he really give it all up at so young an age and lock himself into the same drab, meaningless, charmless existence as his parents had? Yet, how could he ever be happy knowing that he gave up Cathy, the most wonderful woman he had ever been privileged to encounter?

When he entered the apartment, the radio was blaring in the living room, yet no-one was around. Rock music filled the apartment. As he often did, Vail must have been listening and forgotten to switch it off when he left. Like Gabriel, Pablo preferred classical music. Annoyed, Gabriel was about to switch it off, when he found himself riveted in place by the lyrics of the Melancholy Grapes song that was playing, the heartfelt pain the lead singer conveyed with his raspy voice.

> *Love is the only law, you always say*
> *I never listened, so you went away*
> *Now I'm under the rain*
> *And you're gone without a trace*
> *Ah, my soul is in flames*
> *'Cause he's taken my place*

Oh no, he recoiled in terror. I couldn't *bear* that. To think of Cathy with someone else. No! A thousand times no! The music was a sign from God, he decided, telling him what he needed to do, just like God playing Mr. Balogh's violin for him by the fountain. He couldn't let this go on any further. He needed to take decisive action. Immediately, he donned his jacket and rushed out the door.

Fifteen minutes later, he buzzed Cathy's apartment from the antechamber between the glass doors at the entrance to her building, hoping that she and not her roommate would answer. After receiving no reply, he buzzed again and then a third time impatiently. Finally, Cathy's distorted voice came over the intercom. "Yes?"

"Cathy! It's me. Gabriel. I've got to see you," he announced.

Silence.

"Cathy?"

"It's late, Gabriel. I was in bed," came the garbled reply.

"I've got to see you now. Please let me in," he pleaded. A young man with white plastic grocery bags on each arm entered the antechamber and pushed past Gabriel to unlock the door. As he entered, Gabriel momentarily considered following him into the building, but then thought better of it.

He could hear her hesitation on the other end. "I'm not sure I want to see you," she said. "I told you. I can't do this anymore."

"*Please*! Let me just come up to talk to you. I know.... I know I messed everything up and I'm sorry. Please give me a chance to set it right again. I don't want to live without you, Cathy."

"I don't know...." she said, before the intercom disconnected. He pressed the button once more and waited for her to answer again. She took her time, but eventually a metallic distortion of her voice challenged him over the speaker. "What do you *want*, Gabriel?"

"Listen, Cathy. Remember how you called me late at night and talked me into meeting you at Toby's to give you a chance to explain why you never returned my calls? Remember our first 'date'?" He waited for her to reply, but she remained silent. "Well, we've come full circle. Now it's your turn to let me talk. Please let me up."

She still said nothing, but his heart leapt as he heard a loud buzz over the intercom and the door lock clicked. He pulled the door open and bounded up the stairs to her apartment where she awaited him through the chained door, clad in her bathrobe and slippers.

"That's as far as you get!" she announced sternly. "Now what do you want?"

"You won't let me in? I'm in the hallway where the whole floor can hear me. What I have to say is better said in private," he reasoned.

"I told you, Gabriel. We're done. I won't stay in a relationship that goes nowhere. You're not welcome here anymore. Now, I'll ask you again, what do you *want*?"

"I want *you*!" he almost shouted. To his embarrassment, a door opened down the hall and one of Cathy's neighbours, from the looks of her also a university student, emerged to watch the unfolding spectacle. Nonetheless, he soldiered on. "I've *always* wanted you. I've wanted you from the first time I laid eyes on you, when you rescued me from my lonely dance hall purgatory."

"I'm listening...." she said.

"I love your confidence, your quirkiness, your twisted sense of humour. I love how you're never flustered or frustrated by crises, but instead are amused. I love you because you're strange and wonderful. And..." By this point there was a small crowd of spectators in the hallway, two from apartments to his right, three from apartments to his left. Yet, with Cathy still unflinching, still peering out at him from the narrow slit of her door, he continued. "I wouldn't want to face the world without you by my side.... So, what I'm trying to say is, Cathy, would you do the honour of marrying me?"

The first spectator, with tears in her eyes, let out an "awwww!" The others waited anxiously for Cathy's reply. Cathy herself was breathing heavily, saying nothing, until the first spectator interfered, asking, "Hey, shouldn't he be on his knees?" Gabriel flashed her an irritated glance, imploring her to butt out, but Cathy said, more to Gabriel than to the woman, "Yes, that's right. I think he should be."

Gabriel glanced around self-consciously, red in the face, but, remembering Mr. Balogh's advice, complied. With six pairs of eyes on him, he kneeled in front of her door and repeated, "Cathy, love of my life, please marry me."

With a bemused, slightly sadistic smile, she looked at him prostrated before her and said "Hmmm...." Then, twisting in the knife, in a breaking voice she said, "I don't know. I need to think about it."

"Are you *serious*?" he burst out in despair.

"No, not really, silly," Cathy said with a big grin as she disengaged the door chain. "I just wanted to make you squirm. Now, come inside and squirm some more, and maybe I'll forgive you." Cathy's neighbours cheered as she threw the door open and Gabriel clambered off his knees, into her arms.

True to his word, Gabriel's surrender was complete. He agreed to a summer wedding, after which he would look for a job to support Cathy while she went to law school. He would postpone his own graduate education until Cathy was able to work as a lawyer. She applied widely, but was accepted only to two programs, of which the University of New Brunswick in Fredericton had the better reputation. Fredericton, therefore, was for better or worse their next destination.

In the meantime, Gabriel concentrated on his final semester as an undergraduate. He made a special effort to update his professors, and especially Arthur – whom he felt he was somehow betraying by delaying his grad school applications – about his plans and his firm intention to continue his studies in four years' time, to ensure that he could rely on them for support and letters of recommendation when the time came. Overall, he was dejected that his U. of T. years were coming to a close in this manner, but he did his best not to let it show, not to spoil Cathy's unbridled joy. He hoped, without much conviction, that he could pick up right where he was leaving off when he returned to a university once Cathy was a practicing lawyer, but he doubted that anything could ever parallel the magic of undergraduate life.

As he was working on an editorial on jaywalking at the *Newspaper's* office during his final semester as a student, Gabriel was disturbed by a telephone call. Of late, growing criticism had been levelled at the U. of T. community for ignoring traffic lights and interfering with local traffic. This was especially prevalent on routes such as the intersection of Wilcocks and St. George, which students crossed multiple times a day to travel between Sid Smith and the buildings on King's College Circle. The municipality and the Toronto Police had begun a campaign to issue warnings and draw people's attention to the dangers of crossing illegally.

Rather than reinforcing the 'responsible' position, Gabriel's editorial argued that jaywalking was part of the cultural fabric of the university community that would be wrong to stamp out. Universities, he argued, are venues for iconoclastic and counterhegemonic thinking, which enables them to innovate and improve on outmoded conventional wisdom and practices. Jaywalking, he maintained, was both a by-product and an expression of this independent spirit, which was essential for universities to foster. It was impossible to imagine a Galileo, an Einstein, a Socrates emerging from a culture of conformity. Therefore, it behooved the municipality to make allowances for university students and faculty, especially since their behaviour had not been especially disruptive or costly.

As he was putting the finishing touches on his editorial, one of the editorial assistants yelled from down the corridor that he had a phone call. He grumpily pulled himself away from his typewriter, picked up the phone, and pressed the flashing button indicating the line on which a caller was on hold. "Hello?" he barked.

"Hey, Gabriel," a cultured Hispanic voice greeted him, "It's Pablo. You got a call from the music store. They need you to go there right away. It's urgent."

Gabriel was surprised. "Today's Wednesday," he said. "I'm not supposed to go in until tomorrow afternoon. Did they say why?"

"No," Pablo replied. "Just that it was urgent."

"Was it Mr. Balogh?"

"No. It was a woman," Pablo clarified.

"Okay. Thanks, Pablo. See you later," Gabriel said before disengaging the line. He immediately dialled the shop, but there was no answer. *I wish Mr. Balogh would either answer the phone or finally get an answering machine.* He hastily finished the editorial and rushed down to the music shop by subway.

When he arrived, he was perplexed to see that the front door was locked, with a sign informing the public that the store was closed. That made no sense. It wasn't a holiday. He knocked on the door, but no-one replied. *Strange*, he thought, *they called me in, but no-one's here!* Frustrated, he circled around to the back of the store, which opened onto an alleyway and tried the worn, green wooden door there. It too was locked. This was all so puzzling. *Why was the store closed*, he wondered. *And why did they call me in if they're closed?* He banged on the back door and was about to give up when it creaked open to reveal Suzanne from the front of the store.

"Oh, it's you, Gabriel. It's so awful, isn't it?" she sobbed.

"*What* is?" he queried. "What happened? Why are we closed?"

"Oh, you mean no-one told you?" she asked in amazement. "I.... You see. Oh, it's just *terrible*!"

With growing apprehension, he grabbed her hand to steady her and waited for her to continue. "It's Mr. Balogh," she breathed between sobs. "He had a heart attack this morning and died right in the store!"

Her announcement knocked all the air out of him. He sat down on the icy pavement outside the store staring blankly. Mr. Balogh? Dead?

Now it was Suzanne's turn to comfort Gabriel. She bent down and draped her hand over his shoulder. She wasn't wearing a coat and had begun to shiver. "You poor dear. You must have been very close to him, working together in the repair shop for so long."

"I...." Gabriel stammered. "Was he ill? I didn't know he was ill...."

"I don't know that he *was*. None of us knew very much about him," she responded.

"I see...." Gabriel said, without really comprehending. Suddenly a thought struck him. "What, uh... what's gonna happen to the shop?"

"I don't know. We'll have to see. I guess it'll remain closed until someone figures out what happens to it. In the meantime, did you speak to Karen? She said she was going to call you."

"No. She must be the one who left a message for me."

"She wanted you to go through the inventory in the workshop and see what you could fix and what needed to be returned to the owners unrepaired. Do you think you could do that?" Suzanne inquired.

"I.... I guess so," Gabriel said hollowly. "I just.... It's so hard to believe...."

"I know," Suzanne agreed. She threw her arms around him and squeezed him tightly, as her tears moistened his shoulder. She had never really liked her boss, had found him too aloof, too curt. But now that he was dead, she thought of him reverentially, strangely missed him.

As he entered the workshop that he had shared with Mr. Balogh for much of the previous three years, Gabriel was numb. He thought of all the lessons his boss had given him, all the disapproving grunts, the forbearing sighs. Gabriel absently picked up a guitar string winder and twirled it in his hand. But oh, what he had learned from him! And not just how to repair instruments and speak Hungarian. Mr. Balogh had, in his own terse, formal way, shared so much with Gabriel about life and love. Sitting on his stool for what would turn out to be the last time, he gazed around at the instruments on the tables, on the walls. *These are my children.* They were all Mr. Balogh had to show for his excruciating life. Was this truly that remarkable man's only legacy? At least now, Gabriel consoled himself, he would finally be reunited with his Róza... assuming, of course, that Róza was allowed into Heaven.

He wanted to cry for his friend, for in the end that's what Mr. Balogh really had been to him, but found himself unable to. His soul was encrusted in ice. Why was he numb, he berated himself. After growing so close to the man, why couldn't he cry for him? He merely felt empty, hollow. Even at the funeral, for which he served as a pallbearer, he felt more like a spectator, a moth on the window looking in, rather than a mourner.

A few weeks later, Gabriel's heart missed a beat when he received a letter from a solicitor requesting a meeting at her office. Why would he be summoned to lawyer's office? What could he possibly have done? He was convinced this couldn't be good news. Apprehensively, he dialled the number on the letterhead and arranged an appointment for the following Monday morning. When he tried to probe the receptionist for the purpose of the meeting, he was told that she "wasn't at liberty to discuss that," which only heightened his anxiety.

He arrived early at the storefront law office in a strip mall in the Pape and Danforth area. The office was locked. Everything about the place, its shabby appearance, the missing letters on the sign, the cheap, worn vinyl furniture he could spy through the glass door, made Gabriel shudder. This was no Bay Street law firm! Eventually, the receptionist arrived, wearing sneakers underneath her drab, olive skirt, and showed him into the waiting room. Forty-five minutes later, he was ushered into a small office with musty wooden panelling to see the lawyer.

"What's this about?" he asked her anxiously. He wondered whether it pertained in any way to his upcoming marriage.

"It's just a routine matter, Mr. Klein," she replied, "arising out of the last will and testament of Zoltan Balogh." Zoltan. Until the funeral, Gabriel had not even known his boss', his *friend's*, first name. "I represent Mr. Balogh's estate."

"But.... But what's that got to do with me?" Gabriel inquired, more than a little puzzled.

"You were named as one of Mr. Balogh's beneficiaries." Gabriel was astounded. *How could that be? I just worked with him.* "Yes, here it is. He bequeathed his violin to you. He wrote, 'I leave my violin to someone who will understand its value and treat it well, Gabriel Klein. Tell him to give my father's greatest work the legacy it deserves.'"

His father's violin! That most exquisite instrument! How could he leave it to me? Then and there, sitting across from the lawyer, Gabriel burst into tears, sobbed uncontrollably, filled with an immense sense of loss. Curiously, he wondered whether he would feel as empty had his own father passed away instead of Mr. Balogh. Gabriel received the precious instrument and returned home, unable to attend any of his classes that day. He merely lay on his bed fully dressed, staring at Mr. Balogh's violin case, which he had propped up on his desk, but could not bring himself to open.

Gabriel and Cathy were married that summer and, surprisingly, Gabriel swallowed it all graciously. He had initially lobbied for a small wedding, with little fanfare. But, in the end he consented to the grand affair that Cathy had always dreamed of, the engagement parties, Jack-and-Jill showers, the tuxedo, no expense spared. He had hoped, at a minimum, to limit his parents' involvement, but that objective too he conceded to Cathy and her parents' sensibilities. It wouldn't look right if the groom's family were conspicuously absent, they felt. So, he patched it up with them, at least temporarily. For their part, Isaac and Esther were pleased that Gabriel had found someone sensible, who they hoped would straighten him out, make a *mensch* out of him at long last.

The Blums, recognizing the disparity in their financial circumstances, agreed to pay for the wedding, provided it was held at their synagogue. The Kleins gratefully consented, offering to pay for the flowers and the photographer. Pablo and a morally indignant Vail, who believed that getting married at twenty-two was antithetical to the natural flow of the universe, acted as Gabriel's ushers. Steven, who had been dating a friend of his sister's for six weeks and seemed positively elated, was the natural choice for best man. He joked that it was an appropriate designation; Gabriel heartily agreed. When Cathy caught the best man hiding in the cloakroom with his new girlfriend, necking while the hors d'oeuvres were being served, she was delighted. "You see? I told you!" she said, reaching over to straighten her friend's lily-white wax flower corsage, which had been ruffled by his passionate embrace. "It was only a matter of time until you found someone who realized what a gem you really are!" He pulled Cathy by the hand and gave her a great bearhug.

Afterwards, courtesy of the Blums, the newlyweds travelled to Hawaii for a short honeymoon. What an adventure it was for Gabriel, who had never before flown on an airplane! And the time alone, far from everything and everyone, scantily clad in a luxurious villa on the island of Kauai, was enough to make Gabriel forget all his objections to marriage. Alas that it ended far too soon!

When they returned, they had only two weeks to close up shop in Toronto and prepare for their move. Then it was off to Fredericton to begin the next phase of their lives.

Chapter 9

On a hot, lazy Sunday, Gabriel meandered through the residential neighbourhoods around St. Mary's University. After several days of eating poorly, he was fatigued, listless, lightheaded. With only months to go before winter's onset, he was intent on saving enough money and subordinated almost all else to that overarching goal. The plan.

Outside a pretty red frame house, he espied a sign advertising duct cleaning services. It brought a heartfelt smile to his pale, drawn countenance, as he recalled his mother's perplexity at the need to clean her ducks. Yet the recollection also inflicted him with a stab of melancholy. He immediately changed his course and plotted a trajectory for the Halifax Central Library.

Many a time over the past few years, he had stared longingly at the payphone in the library, recessed into the wall opposite the men's room. A relic of times gone by. Payphones had been vanishing from the city like they were abducted by aliens, no doubt a tribute to the ubiquity of those hateful cellphones. Yet the one in the library still remained, beckoning to him, a last rickety bridge to the world he had forsaken.

On this day, overcome by nostalgia, by self-pity, he ambled up to the phone and cradled its cracked ebony receiver in his sweaty hand. It had been years, oh so many years, since he had measured its satisfying weight, the solidity of its casing. He listened to the low-pitched growl of the dial tone, like the roar of a prehistoric beast. How important this device used to be.

Hello. This is Cathy... Cathy Blum. I need to talk to you. Let's meet at Toby's.

Not a day passed without his using it.

Hello. This is Arthur Jameson from Atlantic Siding....

Now it was no more than a historical artifact to him, an ancient medallion unearthed at an archeological dig.

After much hesitation, he replaced the receiver and slowly trudged toward the door. This was a mistake. He couldn't simply pick up the phone and call. Not after all this time. Once out on the pavement, in the hazy sunshine, however, he berated himself. Why *shouldn't* he call? It had been so long now that there was no reason *not* to. And he could always terminate the call if there was any unpleasantness. Yes, he decided. He could do this on his own terms, as he did everything. His resolution, however, did little to soothe the queasiness in his stomach.

Once again, he entered the library and marched to the telephone, like a prisoner on his way to the gallows. This time, he grabbed the receiver and pressed it quickly to his ear, his heart beating furiously, his head spinning. Before he could lose his nerve, he punched o with his index finger. The ring tone had barely just begun when a woman's voice crackled over the speaker, "Operator!" This threw Gabriel into such a state of confusion, bordering on panic. He hadn't used a telephone in over twenty years! With his free hand, he grabbed onto the white, laminated shelf beneath the payphone in an effort to steady himself, as he laboured to catch his breath, check his anxiety. Hearing no response, the operator queried, "Hello?"

Gabriel gulped and said, "I'd... I'd like to place a call...."

"What type of call, sir?" asked the operator.

"What type? Oh... yes.... Collect. A collect call," he replied.

"Can I have the number please?"

"The number.... Yes," he said, searching the crevices of his mind. "It's... 416-636-42...". His voice faltered before he could finish.

"Sir?"

"416-636-42... 47."

"And who should I say is calling?" the distant voice asked. He wasn't sure if he could detect a note of annoyance in the operator's tone.

He hesitated. "Say.... Say it's Gabriel," he said, his stomach in knots, his voice weakening almost to a whisper.

"I'm sorry, sir, but I didn't get that," the operator said.

"Gabriel," he said louder, his voice wavering. He waited on the line, breathing heavily as the operator connected the call. Seconds later, a strange woman's voice reverberated in his ear. "Hello?" Was that his mother? No. It couldn't be. She sounded younger, her accent was different.

"This is Bell Canada with a collect call from Gabriel. Do you accept the charges?"

"From who?" the woman asked.

"Gabriel," the operator repeated.

"I think you have the wrong number," the woman said.

"Is this 416-636-4247?" the operator asked.

"Yes, it is. But I don't know any Gabriel."

Trembling in fear, Gabriel shouted over the phone, prompting a surprised scowl from the library's security guard, who was making his rounds nearby, "How long have you had this number?"

"Oh, about five years," the woman replied.

"Five years...." Gabriel muttered absently. He replaced the receiver without thanking the operator. "Five years...."

He was about to beat a hasty retreat from the library when another idea struck him. He lifted the receiver again and dialled 0. "Operator!" said a different voice.

"Yes... uh, how can I get directory assistance for Ontario?" Gabriel inquired.

"Which area code?" the operator asked.

"416."

"I'll connect you," the operator said. A few seconds later, he heard a new metallic-edged voice squawk, "Directory Assistance! For what city please?"

"Toronto.... No, North York," he stated.

"What name?"

"Klein, K-L-E-I-N. First name Isaac," he replied.

"Let me see.... I have no Isaac Klein, but I have twelve I. Kleins. Do you have the street address?"

"Is there one on Bathurst Street?" he asked hopefully, trying desperately to resist the bitter fog engulfing him.

"I'll check.... No, I don't see one. Do you have another address for him?" the distorted voice inquired helpfully.

Once again, he disconnected without saying goodbye or thank you, more isolated, more alone than he had ever been during all his years on the street.

What had happened to them? Did they move? Or, he shuddered as he made his way distractedly back to his office, *had something happened?* He calculated quickly. They would both be in their seventies by now. Is it possible that one or both had passed on? *How miserably ironic, he thought. Now, after all this time, when I'm ready to reconnect, they might no longer be here for me.* Then, suffering great pangs of guilt, he admonished himself. Had they died alone, all the while wondering about him? And, a chill descended his spine, who had said *Kaddish*, the mourner's prayer, for them? It should have been him, their only child. That was his duty, regardless of their shortcomings.

Without thinking, he ambled to his office and slumped down on the pavement, his back against the brown bricks of his alcove. Was there really no way to reach them? Was there no-one he could call who could tell him where they were? Maybe his cousin Adina, he thought. But no, she's probably married. Who knows what her name is now, where she lives? Too much time has passed, he lamented. They're lost forever.

Was he to blame, he wondered. Sure, they had behaved badly. They were dishonest. But had he betrayed them too somehow? Had they deserved their fate? In his melancholy mood, his mind strayed, opening other unhealed scars on his psyche. He remembered Angela Pietrangelo, how he had hurt her without meaning to. She had called him a bigot, but that wasn't fair, was it? It would have been wrong to lead her on and it wasn't bigoted to want to date someone who shared one's beliefs, one's core values. You can't live up to everyone else's expectations, their values, he mused. You just need to live up to your own. And he had always done that, hadn't he? But then there was Aziz. Had he treated Aziz fairly? A gnawing pang of doubt made ripples in his stomach, like the shadow of fear that crept up on him as a child, in the middle of the night, when the lights from the cars outside played on his wall and tree branches scrabbled against his window in the wind. He tried to dismiss it, assuring himself that he had always been above reproach, yet the shadow remained.

As he was agonizing thus, Jane stopped by for a brief visit. Her face was drawn and haggard nowadays, worry lines digging deep grooves into her forehead. "Hi, Gabriel," she said dispiritedly. "I'm just taking a bit of a walk. I needed a break from the hospital. I've been there all weekend. Hey! What are you doing here on a Sunday?"

"Oh, I don't know," Gabriel groused. "I just felt like it."

"Did you get a chance to finish the book?" she asked.

In his agitated state, he reached into the plastic bag he was carrying and tossed the book pouch Jane had given him contemptuously back to her, saying nothing.

"What? Didn't you like it?" she asked, disappointed.

"It's *horrible*! Who wrote that *garbage*?" he raged.

"It's a wonderful book! Whatever could be wrong with it?"

"You told me it was an argument for God. It most certainly is *not*! God is just a better story than the miserable truth? That's a bunch of self-satisfied Western liberal claptrap! I'm sorry I wasted my time, my braincells, on that *garbage*," he replied acidly.

Jane was taken aback. "I'm sorry. I didn't mean to offend you. Next time I'll bring you something you might like better," she said.

Her tone, her expression of disappointment, the sorrow in her bloodshot eyes rebuked him. "I don't mean to sound ungrateful," he said. "It was nice to have a real book in my hands that I could read outside the library, to turn its pages. Thank you. But the book itself upset me."

"I'm surprised. I really liked it. It's become a modern classic," she said defensively.

"That doesn't surprise me," Gabriel declared. "It's a perfect statement of the nihilism of our times."

"I suppose I can see why you say that. But you have to admit: there really is no way to prove God's existence. Either you believe it, as you do, or, like me, you don't."

He groaned in annoyance. "You do yourself a discredit," he said severely. Then he lifted himself off the pavement. "I'll show you the argument for God. Right now. You must come with me."

"I... can't," she said. "I have to get back to my husband. He's very.... I'm afraid for him. Some other time, okay Gabriel?"

"Don't wait forever. Your problem is that you've been clouded by Yann Martel and his ilk. I need to show you a real argument for God. A positive one. If you let me do that, one day I'll ask you to help me, too," he said, looking at her significantly.

His openness surprised her. He had always rebuffed any offers of assistance, resented any suggestion that he needed any help. "I promise," she said. "I just need to go back to the hospital now."

She turned to go, but then hesitated. There seemed to be something she wanted to say, to ask. Fixing him with a penetrating gaze straight into his cold steel eyes, she tried to peel away all the layers of hair, of grime, of pain and get directly to the heart of the matter, communicate straight to his soul. "Gabriel, why are you here?" she asked suddenly, earnestly.

"Huh?" Gabriel responded sluggishly. "I already told you. I just felt like coming in today. Sunday doesn't mean much to me."

"That's not what I meant," Jane clarified, speaking with an intensity that surprised him. "Listen. You don't drink. I can see that. You're never drunk. You're not a druggie. You're better educated than most. You seem to have everything going for you. So, what exactly are you doing here?"

Gabriel stared out into the street, gathering his thoughts before answering. "Let me tell you a story," he said cryptically. "When I was a kid, my community was trying to do its part to help free the Jews of the Soviet Union, who were being persecuted for trying to practice their religion or for wanting to emigrate to Israel. The youth group of my synagogue had a fundraiser, whereby we sold red buttons that you pinned onto your clothing, saying "Let My People Go!" The money raised was donated to the cause. As an incentive, community businesses and benefactors donated prizes that would go to the children who raised the most money."

A group of students walked by, singing loudly. Annoyed, Gabriel waited for them to pass before continuing. "There was a teenager in my synagogue, a serious girl, we all looked up to her. She was active in the youth group, in the community, what you Christians might call an altar girl. She worked tirelessly to sell the buttons and brought in more than twice as much as anyone else. Oh, how I admired her! One Saturday during services, I ran into her and told her how cool I thought she was, raising all that money to help people in need. You have to understand, Jane, that I was only about nine or ten at the time and she must have been about sixteen or seventeen. I can still remember the sneer she gave me, as if I just fell off the turnip truck. 'Don't be a dork,' she said. 'It was the only way to get the Walkman!' She was only doing it for the prize. It didn't mean anything to her.... The lives, the suffering of all those people didn't mean *anything* to her, except the Walkman...."

"Oh, come on, Gabriel. She was just a teenager. Don't give too much importance to it...." Jane began, but then stopped. "So, what are you saying? That people are sometimes selfish and dishonest? Of course they are! Is that a reason to run away? To spend your winters freezing in the streets? To let a brilliant mind go to waste?"

Gabriel glared at her icily. "I think you should go back to your husband now. Don't you?"

Jane nodded sadly, realizing that she had pushed too hard. "I'm sorry," she said as she left, her gaze dropping to the sidewalk. "I didn't mean to intrude."

When Jane departed, Gabriel too abandoned his office to stroll through the city in the hope of clearing his head, finding comfort. He hadn't been to the harbour in a while, he decided, so he cast off in that general direction. On the way, he took a detour via Bishop Street to stand in the shade of the twin elms bordering Government House and enjoy the vista downhill toward the water. Those trees had always been a source of joy for Gabriel, but on this day, they were unable to soothe his troubled soul.

He passed a crowded café with outdoor table service, in sight of the water and the visiting tall ships, and watched the patrons lounging under the umbrella-shaded tables sipping iced-coffees in their shorts and polo shirts. But overpowering everything else for Gabriel was the sweet, unctuous aroma of hot cinnamon buns. They smelled heavenly, and Gabriel had not eaten much that day. Just a few scraps of bagel he had scrounged in the dumpsters and a half-litre carton of milk he had purchased at the supermarket. His mouth watered. At that moment, he wanted one of those buns more than he wanted anything else on earth. Consulting the chalk-scrawled menu board in front, he discerned that they cost three dollars and twenty-five cents. Plus HST, no doubt. Oh, how he yearned for one! Surely, he could spare four dollars for such a prize. Couldn't he?

As he was deliberating, a flock of geese, no more than twelve in all, lazily crossed the sky in their characteristic V pattern, honking loudly. Gabriel monitored them warily. "That's true," he said aloud to no-one in particular, earning cautious stares from some of the café's patrons. The birds will be flying south for the winter soon, he reasoned, and he would need all his money by then. The price was too steep. Discouraged, he backed away from the café slowly and leaned against a lamppost, still hungrily eying the patrons.

Just then, a man emerged from the café with cinnamon buns in a small, grease-stained brown paper bag, passing directly in front of Gabriel. Ah, the agony of it all! He caught himself thinking, at least partially in jest, how easy it would be to trip him and grab his bag. No, he thought with a giddy laugh. That would not do. The *Torah* was clear on that. He ought not to covet. *Thou shall not covet thy neighbour's wife. Thou shall not covet thy neighbour's house, nor his servant, nor his maid, nor his ox, nor his donkey, and above all, certainly not his cinnamon bun!* How would he atone for that on Yom Kippur? Well, he thought, one such as me shouldn't cave in so quickly to hunger and desire. I fast routinely on Yom Kippur each year, neither eating nor drinking for twenty five hours. Surely, after eating something – admittedly not much – today, I can withstand the lure of this diabolical pastry.

The thought of Yom Kippur sent his malnourished head, already unable to focus, flitting from idea to idea, down yet a different rabbit hole. *Ha!* he thought. *How long has it been since I last heard the sound of the shofar? It must be over thirty years! Can that really be? How can I consider myself an observant Jew without having heard it?* He resolved to stand outside the synagogue – he still refused to enter – at the end of Yom Kippur this coming September and listen to the single extended *shofar* blast that ends the fast. How could he start a new life in good conscience without fulfilling all of God's commandments?

As he stood unsteadily, propped up against the post, engaged in frenetic, haphazard thought, he was distracted by a young woman, no more than twenty years of age, wearing a white tank top and bright saffron shorts. Her appearance – her coarse, stringy blonde hair, her pimpled, freckly face – was rather plain. Homely even. But something in the way she stood was inexpressibly beautiful. Though she stood upright, her two legs were each angled slightly to the left, one slightly more than the other, her knees almost touching. Her torso, too, was arched slightly to the left, so that, although she appeared to be standing straight, there was nothing vertical about her. For reasons he would have been hard-pressed to explain, Gabriel began to weep. Who used to stand like that? Was it Cathy? Jenny? Oh, how it made him long... for what, exactly? *Perhaps, he told himself, perhaps, when I re-engage.... Perhaps.... But no.... It's too late! I'm too old. That part of my life ended decades ago.*

Seeing him in his dishevelled state, hearing him crying unreservedly, onlookers avoided him, concluding that he was drunk. One middle-aged woman in a wide-brimmed straw hat, however, took pity on him. She approached him and asked solicitously, "Are you okay, mister? Is there anything I can do for you?" He stared at her in confusion, in shame, for an eternity, and then responded, "If you must know, I'd really like one of those cinnamon buns...."

Later that evening, lying in his bed in the early twilight, before the park closed, with barking dogs still unleashed on the paths, eluding their owners for a few more minutes of liberty, another dive into the water, Gabriel reviewed the day's troubling events. No matter how important it was to save money, he could never allow himself to be so hungry again, to unravel as he had. What a difference that cinnamon bun made! A man can't function without adequate nutrition, it's a mistake even to try. Afterward, he had understood his folly and sought to rectify it with a visit to a takeout stand, where he spent over nine dollars on an egg sandwich and a cup of vegetable soup. Sure, it was an extravagance, but it was worth it.

It was essential for him to learn the lesson, he implored himself. To carry it with him. His plan amounted to a marathon, not a sprint. You can't bring a grand design like that to its fruition without adequate fuel. Every little bump in the road looms as an insuperable obstacle when you haven't eaten. You lose your will. You break down. If he was going to move to the next phase of his life on his own terms, he had to steel himself for the long haul.

Oh, he lamented, how money had changed him! He had never carried much money around with him before, usually spent it right away. Soon after devising the plan, however, he began to worry about the clinking of the coins, afraid it would attract thieves. To counter that threat, he made a point of exchanging his coins for bills whenever he had more than five dollars of loose change. It amused him at that stage to think of himself as a businessman.

But as the wad of bills grew, so did his fears. He grew concerned about the rain. How do you protect so much money alone in the elements? That problem exercised him for many a troubled night. *Look at me,* he thought. *For the first time in my life, I'm just like the rest of them. Obsessing over money. This is what I've always tried to avoid.* Initially, he wrapped the wad of cash in a ripped plastic bag. But that was too bulky and crinkled too much. He worried that it made him more of a target. Eventually, he scoured the shops and found a plastic money envelope in an office supply shop. It seemed ironic to have to spend precious dollars only to safeguard money, but what choice did he have?

And where to store it? At first, he had buried his savings in his bedroom, but when it grew to over a hundred dollars, he decided that the safest course of action was to keep it on his person at all times. But what about when he bathed? Or on the Sabbath, on Jewish holidays, when carrying money was forbidden? In the past, he would hide whatever loose change he had in his sleeping gear, which he hid in the bushes and brambles of his bedroom. In the improbable event that people were to stumble upon it, they were unlikely to take any interest in a homeless person's smelly, soiled bedclothes. But when his stash exceeded one hundred dollars, the risk seemed too high. Yet, he couldn't exactly open a bank account, could he? With no identification, no address? Maybe a corporate account, he chuckled acidly. The thought of a locker at the train station occurred to him, but he would still have the same problem with the key. Eventually, he resigned himself to hiding it in his bedroom, but this gave him a heavy heart every time he did so and made him reluctant to stray far from his bedroom on the Sabbath.

Money's no good, he bemoaned. It changes you. He found himself surreptitiously patting his pocket a thousand times a day to verify that his nest egg was still in place. And today he nearly starved himself just to squirrel away a little more money. What madness! Never in his life had he ever concerned himself with money. Even before – as a boy, in university, when he worked in Fredericton – his needs had always been small, he never lusted for wealth or opulence. His goals were always intellectual. In his new life, money had been largely irrelevant, as he spent his days in pursuit of truth, the beauty of the world, the glory of God. Money was at best a means to an end, more often just an afterthought. Now it was almost all he ever focused on. Would he accumulate enough money on time? Could he keep it safe? Would he earn it only to lose it carelessly? How trivial! How bourgeois!

Oh well. It wouldn't be long now. Once he got himself secure for the winter, he wouldn't have to worry about money again. With a full stomach, Gabriel slept like a prince for the first night in many days, full of hope that the next morning's sun would bring him the peace that eluded him today.

Chapter 10

In retrospect, it should have been obvious that their move to New Brunswick would end in disaster. Nothing went quite as planned. Everything was new, unsettling, ominous. Foreign. After living in metropolitan Toronto his entire life, Gabriel found Fredericton small, strange, provincial. His first impression of his new home, arriving late at night with the rented van that they drove from Toronto, was of oppressive darkness, so unlike the bright lights of Toronto. It was like the city was entombed in darkness, snuffing out any possibility of hope. He was by no means insensitive to the city's natural beauty, its historic architecture. But it struck him as a place to visit, rather than to live. Moreover, he found it hard to connect to the locals, who viewed him with suspicion. People in Atlantic Canada have a love-hate relationship with Toronto, which sucks up a disproportionate share of the country's oxygen. Gabriel perceived, whether justifiably so or not, that his neighbours, his colleagues at work, viewed him as an interloper. As a result, he was never able to achieve more than a polite, formal relationship with those around him. It was like he was wrapped in cellophane, able to see and hear others, but unable to touch them, to really connect to them. In many ways, he felt invisible, a biblical Joseph before his rise, lost in Egypt, a strange land with strange people and strange ways.

To support Cathy and himself while Cathy went to law school, Gabriel took a job as a regional sales manager for Atlantic Siding, a company that manufactured aluminum siding. His responsibilities included coordinating the efforts of the Atlantic provinces sales division of the company, which consisted of six full-time salespeople, and contacting contractors, construction materials suppliers and large project managers to push the company's product line. The job was completely demoralising. All those years of higher education, studying Kant, Hume, Aristotle, Rousseau, aspiring to a higher plane of thought and existence, merely to sell a product he didn't believe in? Was that what life was all about?

Although he had rejected the Marxism he had studied at U. of T., he suddenly identified with Marx's concept of alienation, capitalism's capacity to estrange the human being from nature and the self. Now, working from eight-thirty in the morning to five-thirty in the afternoon each day, Gabriel had become an automaton in the service of a surplus-squeezing bourgeois corporation, which concerned itself solely with sales and profits and cared not a whit about Gabriel's sensibilities. To add insult to injury, although he got along well enough with his boss, the hierarchical nature of the workplace galled him. Why did he have to take orders from someone obviously less intelligent than he was? Life had clearly taken a disappointing turn for Gabriel.

Even Cathy was not the same woman he had fallen in love with. In the first month, while they set up their home in Fredericton, married life started out swimmingly. It was like that Sabbath he had spent with Jennifer all those years ago, only it didn't end at sundown. With his salary, they rented an ample one-bedroom apartment in the downtown core, which, given the scale of the city, was walking distance from both the University of New Brunswick and Gabriel's office. They had enjoyed playing house, purchasing discounted furniture, taking walks when Gabriel wasn't at work.

But, in short order, Cathy started her program at UNB and was always busy. Not surprisingly, she was either in class or the library most days, while Gabriel was at Atlantic Siding. What disturbed him, however, were all the evenings and Sundays that she needed to spend studying at the university or preparing briefs with classmates. Even on Saturday mornings they would go their separate ways, as Cathy attended services at the city's only synagogue, whereas Gabriel recited his prayers and studied the weekly *Torah* portion at home. Given that Gabriel knew not a soul in Fredericton, had no friends, he was heavily dependent on Cathy for companionship. With her away so much, and exhausted when she was able to stay home, Gabriel found himself completely isolated in a strange small town, far from all that he knew. In time, he grew resentful. *How can she treat me this way,* he wondered. *I made a heroic sacrifice for her, putting my life, my career, on hold for her, and all she does is ignore me.*

It wasn't just her absence that disturbed him, though. More alarmingly, now that they were married, her personality seemed to undergo a disturbing metamorphosis. Their courtship in the rear-view mirror, Cathy became more assertive and demanding, more irritable with him, less patient. Whereas in the past he could always count on her sunny disposition, her quirky, naughty humour, her fresh, unpredictable candour, now he was more apt to meet a disapproving scowl, a sharp reproach, an impatient shrug. And the tenderness that had characterized her bearing toward him through the more than two years of their acquaintance had largely vanished, to be replaced at times with an indifference bordering on outright hostility. In fact, Gabriel reflected in his darker moments, he would have preferred hostility to the cold detachment with which she often received him. At least, it would inspire emotion, anger, rather than the hollowness that choked him now.

The toughest parts were the nights. Lying beside her in their double bed, only millimetres from her downy skin, yet unable to reach out to her for fear of rebuff. Too many times he had tried to roll over to her side, to cuddle her, to kiss her, only to be cut down with a surly, "I'm tired," "I have a headache," "I need to sleep because tomorrow is a busy day," or even, worst of all, "I'm not in the mood." So, he lay, rigid as a cold steel pipe, feeling the warmth that emanated from her body on a frosty night, inhaling the soft jasmine scent of her shampoo, listening to her heartbeat, her regular intakes of breath. Anticipating every tick of the clock, every crackle of the radiator, the settling of the pipes. More alone than he was during his solitary days in the endless purgatory of his job.

The first manifestation of these untoward alterations in her attitude had been in the second week of her program, when Gabriel decided to surprise his new bride at the library after he clocked out of work. He bought a colourful autumn bouquet and packed a Tupperware container of leftover lasagna together with a bottle of white wine into a picnic basket. He found her at a carrel in the stacks, snuck up behind her and covered her eyes with his hand. She jumped, wrenched his hand away and scowled. "Gabriel, what are you *doing* here?" she asked, as she quickly ushered him out of the reading area, toward the cafeteria. Her tone was frosty.

"Well, I knew you had to work late, so I thought we'd have dinner together here," he answered graciously. As he handed her the flowers, he shuddered, observing the harshness in her expression, her multicoloured eyes converging on ice grey.

"Don't *ever* do this again," she snapped. She couldn't have hurt him more had she stabbed him with a dagger.

On another occasion, when her parents were flying in for a visit, Cathy was preparing a mock trial for her Criminal Law class. Recognizing that she was overcommitted, Gabriel volunteered to meet her parents at the airport and take them back by taxi so that she could have more time to work. Cathy's outburst had been completely unexpected. "Absolutely not! You want to show me up with my own parents?" she raged.

Gabriel's jaw dropped. He simply couldn't comprehend her antagonism. "Come on, Cath!" he said soothingly. "I'm just trying to help you out."

"Well, no, thank you!" she snapped. "I don't need you to act like Superman, able to work and cook and make the dean's list and handle *everything*, while poor hapless Cathy can't even manage to pick up her parents!"

Much of this, no doubt, was a reaction to the intense pressure she was under in law school. The program was a challenge for her. Although she had been a strong student in high school, she had found university more of a struggle and her grades had been disappointing. It was for this reason that most of her law school applications had been rejected and she had been compelled to accept a spot further afield, in New Brunswick. Rather than finding it easier in a smaller school, she was dismayed to learn that her cohort was comprised of hyper-motivated, cutthroat aspiring lawyers for whom law was a passion rather than merely a vocation. Eager to succeed but fearing that she lacked the academic aptitude to compete, Cathy threw herself into her studies with a tenacity, a single-mindedness that excluded all else, including her husband. Her rationale, as she had explained to him, was that there was time for everything else later. If she failed out of law school or was unable to get an articling position or a job afterwards, then it would all have been in vain. But, once her career path was established, she could reward Gabriel for his sacrifices later, not only by allowing him to pursue a doctorate in Philosophy, but in other ways, as well.

Gabriel, however, remained unconvinced. From his perspective he had been neglected, abandoned, mistreated. Rather than thanking him for putting his own career on hold, for wasting his best years at a dead-end job in some God-forsaken provincial town, entirely for her benefit, she treated his sacrifice as a given, as a requirement, a necessity that needed no further comment or consideration. Furthermore, she continued to pile up the demands, heap on abuse. She seemed callously determined to squeeze as much out of his lemon as she possibly could, regardless of the effect it had on him. It was more than he could stomach.

Yet there were *times*. Times when the storm clouds parted and Cathy – the Cathy of old, the Cathy he had been smitten by at the JSU dance – shone through the drab, alienating, humdrum routine of their lives in Fredericton. Like the time in her second year when he had persuaded her not to return to Toronto to visit her family over the Christmas holidays, as she had done the previous winter, but to travel to Puerto Vallarta with him instead. From the moment they boarded the first aircraft, all the course obligations, the pressure to succeed, the knot of tension that had replaced the sunshine of her smile, evaporated, leaving the playful, unpredictable Cathy he couldn't resist. They spent much of the week walking along the beach hand-in-hand, skipping stones or exploring the neighbouring islands. When they weren't in bed, of course.

The highlight of the trip was an excursion to a nearby island that was accessible only by boat. They had hired a water taxi and thumped on each wave, drenched by the spray, for the twenty-minute ride, while, to their amazement, dolphins tumbled acrobatically into the water port and starboard, only metres away. After exploring the small island village, gloriously untouched by the twentieth century in its innocence, its holy simplicity, Gabriel and Cathy wandered off hands entangled to investigate the beaches. Clad only in their bathing suits, the sun drenching their hair, their skin, in a Garden of Eden lost in time and space, they were overcome by each other's beauty. Breathless, unable to resist each other, aching to touch each other, they embraced in a passionate kiss, hungrily pressing their mouths together. On a wild impulse, Cathy pulled away and led him to a secluded stretch of beach, sheltered from view by a small grove of trees, where they made love with wild abandon, their bathing gear discarded haphazardly in the sand beside them. It was the zenith of his love-life, a scene he would replay in his mind endlessly afterwards, even after all that happened in the ensuing years. When they became aware of a local woman observing them with a broad, knowing smile as she carried her wicker basket full of berries back to the village, Gabriel gasped. Cathy silenced him with a hand to his lips. "Don't worry," she reassured him. "They're not as... well, prudish here in Mexico as we are in Canada." They carried on only slightly inhibited, ignoring the intruding eyes.

The trip restored him. Reminded him why he had married her, why he had agreed to put his life on hold for her.

Or the time on his birthday, when she surprised him by cutting class. He woke at six-thirty, as usual, to dress for work. To his confusion, Cathy wasn't in bed next to him when the alarm sounded. As he stumbled out of their bedroom toward the bathroom, she stopped him, smothered from head to toe with whipped cream, wearing no clothing that he could discern, in her right hand bearing a flute of champagne with an orange slice affixed to the edge.

"What am I supposed to do with this?" he inquired, still wiping the sleep from his eyes.

"Drink it," she ordered.

"But It's too early. And I've got work."

"Call in sick, silly!" she said, as she pushed him back into the bedroom. "It looks to me like you've got a *terrible* fever." As they reached the bed, Gabriel sipping the champagne, Cathy suggested, with a mischievous lilt to her voice, "You know, if I jump into bed now, it'll make a terrible mess. You're gonna have to lick this off first...."

But those moments were too few, becoming rarer, four-leaf clovers that were ever harder to find. Most of the time, it was like he didn't exist. Worse, she treated him like he was in the way. An obstruction, a drain on her precious time, which would more profitably be spent on case summaries and hypotheticals, with the empty suits in her programme who would sell their souls to become successful lawyers. Was *this* what she had had in mind when she insisted on getting married?

He began to wonder whether he ever truly knew her. Love is a gamble, he reflected. What do we really know about the person we marry? How do we know that she won't change dramatically after marriage, that she wasn't merely putting on a show for us during courtship, a grand bait-and-switch once the deal is sealed? In the final analysis, it's just a monumental leap of faith.... No, he chastised himself. This is Cathy we're talking about. She'll come around. I just need to give her a bit of time to get acclimated to law school. But that didn't settle his growing doubts.

The one distinct pleasure that Gabriel indulged in was his lunchtime walks along the St. John River, across the old railway bridge to the other side. He had always adored nature, but the beauty of a small town, unmarred by the urban sprawl and concrete megaliths of Toronto, with fresher, unspoilt air, offered him easier access to it. The river, moreover, was to his mind of a more human scale, more approachable, than Lake Ontario. He could cross it by foot, explore its banks, the verdure that surrounded it.

Because of Atlantic Siding's peculiar hours and location, Gabriel could indulge in a lengthy lunch break. Although the company's manufacturing arm was located outside the city, its headquarters and sales office were housed in a small office building near the old barracks in the downtown core. To create a more relaxed work environment and accommodate their own preferences, the brothers who owned the business opted for an 8:30-5:30 workday, giving employees a two-hour lunch break, which they could take from 11:00-1:00 or 12:00-2:00. Gabriel opted for the latter.

Each day, except in inclement weather, when he was forced into the shelter of an indoor mall, he would change out of his suit in the washroom at the office, bring his bagged lunch to the river, cross to the far side with the wind lashing his face, and eat amidst the bushes and brambles on the bank near the site of historic Fort Nashwaak, allowing his mind to wander. Then he would explore the brush on both sides of the river, tramping through the clover and purple loosestrife underfoot as he peered across the St. John. Without tall skyscrapers, the city would virtually disappear behind the trees along its shore, only the spire of Christchurch Cathedral, the cupola of the New Brunswick legislature peeking through the foliage on the other side. He could imagine himself in a deserted wilderness, far from the banal pettiness of civilization. Staring into the river, which surprised him with its waves that lapped the shore — he had thought that only lakes, seas and oceans had waves — he was awed by its width, its mercurial might, its blustery, swirling waters, the blackness of its depths. There was something mystical about it. He wondered if the Danube had been as wide, whether it too pounded the shore with its all-seeing waves.

On days when Cathy expected to return home long after dark, he would again stroll its comforting banks in the evening, taking solace in the few shimmering lights reflecting off the obsidian of the water. Not only did these walks help alleviate the stress and misery of his workplace, but it also helped him feel connected to his Zaidie, a critical counterpoint to the isolation, the alienation he experienced in his strange new home. This was *Gabriel's* Danube River and, as the weeks and months trudged along, he felt an integral, organic part of it, identifying with its power, its struggles, its permanence. As it traced its path through the city, the river shaped Gabriel, altered his perceptions, his needs. By the time he left Fredericton, he had become dependent on water, would crave it, would seek out its calming influence on his soul

.

* * *

Time is relative. Not only in the sense that Einstein explicated, where speed and acceleration affect the passage of time. But time moves differently, is experienced differently, depending on the perceiver's state of mind. For Gabriel, who was enthralled from the outset, his four years at the University of Toronto had blown by with the force and velocity of a locomotive. Try though he may to hold on to it, to slacken its pace so that he could savour its succulent delights just an instant longer, it was over in the blink of an eye. All he could do was mourn its passing, like the death of his oldest and dearest friend. Conversely, the three years of Cathy's law degree and her additional year of articling, although numbering no more than the years he had spent on the St. George campus, dragged on endlessly, like the sand in a congested hourglass.

With Cathy largely AWOL, the main focus of Gabriel's life was, sadly, his job. Aside from the drudgery of it all, he experienced an alarming degree of culture shock, being a Torontonian, a traditional Jew, an intellectual. His employers were friendly, welcoming even, and open-minded, but Gabriel always felt awkward around them, with his colleagues. Worse, he felt that he just couldn't explain his requirements, the little things that made him uncomfortable. He feared they wouldn't understand.

His discomfort began early on, on his first day even. Gabriel had placed a call to a building contractor in Moncton. "Hello. This is Gabriel Klein, regional sales manager from Atlantic Siding," he recited from a prepared script. "I was hoping I could set up a meeting between you and one of my representatives to discuss what our company can do for your business.... I see. But we can supply you with a better product than the competition's and.... I see.... Still, I think you might find a meeting worth your while, at least to gain an understanding of what we bring to the table, even for the future.... Well, okay. I'll reach out to you again in a few months, then. Thank you for your time."

Mr. Willoughby, his kindly supervisor, who Gabriel had decided was a dead ringer for Josef Stalin – an older, plumper version, down to the Slavic smile and the thick, double bird-wing moustache – had been eavesdropping at the door. After Gabriel finished the call, he entered and rested a comforting hand on Gabriel's shoulder. "Listen, Gabriel," he said gently. "Your approach is good. So is your tone. But I have a suggestion. A lot of people around here – I'm not saying they're right – but a lot of people in these parts may not respond well to a sales call from... from someone named Gabriel Klein."

Gabriel was stunned. "What are you saying exactly?" he asked, more than a little offended.

"Look, I hired you. So, *I* don't have a problem with you. I'm glad to have you with us. But why don't you take a more... generic name. How about Arthur Jameson? When you make sales calls, just say 'Hi, this is Arthur Jameson from Atlantic Siding.' You may find that works better. But you're doing great!"

Gabriel felt too weak, too discouraged, to argue, and he adopted that *nom de guerre* for the three years he remained with the company. But he felt, well, eviscerated. He disliked the job, but it was all the more painful to have to hide behind a phony name in order to fit in.

Another time, the company arranged a working lunch for the entire sales force. Mr. Willoughby had asked his secretary to order sandwiches for everybody, so Gabriel didn't bother to pack his own lunch. Midway through the presentation on "Getting Your Foot In the Door," which Gabriel privately found both stultifying and morally offensive, Ms. Youngblood placed a tray with a packaged sandwich, a chocolate chip cookie and a can of soda in front of each of the participants. As he reached for it ravenously, he was dismayed to discover that it was a ham and cheese sandwich. He withdrew his hand and dined on the cookie and drink instead. He was mortified when another of the sales managers asked him, "Aren't you going to eat that, Klein?"

"No," he replied, averting her gaze. "I'm not really hungry." What was it about this place that made him so timid, he wondered to his own shame. In Toronto he would have had no trouble explaining his dietary restrictions.

Walking by the river over lunch one afternoon in late May, with the sun's blazing reflection off the water blinding him, Gabriel reflected on the emptiness of his new life. He had now endured his purgatory in Fredericton, at Atlantic Siding, for nine months. A full academic year! He could have been finished with the first year of his Master's. Instead, he was languishing in an antiseptic office in an unwelcoming town selling siding. Was this really what life was all about? Had God created such a magnificent universe just for him to sell building products?

Passing a white dogwood tree on the far bank, he sighed. Just the previous week that tree had been in full bloom, its cottony white flowers dazzling onlookers, contrasting majestically with the pink and yellow blooms on nearby trees. Yet now, only a heartbeat later, the blooms were gone, the green leaves no different from those of its neighbours. Only the discarded, trampled petals scattered around its trunk bore testimony to its former beauty. It struck Gabriel that he was just like that tree. Only a year before, he had been in the spring of his life, in full bloom during his undergraduate years, full of promise, at his intellectual peak, his physical peak, a handsome and vibrant young man with a bright future ahead of him. Now, in the span of months, he had begun to wither. Still good-looking, still intelligent, but no longer at his peak. His mind, which had been free to ponder questions of justice, truth, the sacred mysteries of life, was now harnessed for the sole dubious purpose of selling more units of aluminum siding. His hairline had started receding, shedding its precious blossoms into the shower drain. Like the dogwood, his spring had passed. Only the tree would get many more springs in the years ahead, many more opportunities to bloom. Not he. His one and only spring had passed, his fallen flowers now scattered to the wind.

It's unfair, Gabriel reflected acidly as he watched a seagull swoop down into the river, that we have so much potential when we're young, cruel even. We start out life full of promise, a *tabula rasa* with infinite possibilities. Over time, however, we shut one door after another with our choices. Others are slammed on us with every failure, each time we fall just short of the mark. So that eventually, when we graduate high school or university, we realize to our painful dismay that all our dreams, our ambitions, were nothing more than wind. Mere phantasms. Instead, our potential all spent, we settle into our mediocre existences, wondering in bewilderment what happened to all our promise, consoling ourselves that our children will be exceptional.

Life cannot help but disappoint, he decided. Despite all our youthful potential, very few of us ever achieve anything extraordinary. Out of a population of over thirty-five million Canadians, only two or three per decade become prime minister. A genius of Albert Einstein's or Isaac Newton's caliber emerges less frequently than Halley's Comet. Our economy, our society, not unlike colonies of bees or ants, require an ample supply of drones. For labour. For middle management. Yet parents of young children always marvel about how the sky is the limit. "She's so articulate. She could be Prime Minister one day." "With his scientific mind, he could discover a cure for Cancer." "He writes so beautifully. He'll become the next Mordecai Richler or Margaret Atwood. He'll win the Nobel Prize for literature." They never say, "What an intelligent child! He'll make a good hardware store manager." Or hospital orderly. Or regional sales manager for Atlantic Siding.

As he watched a white petal borne away by the river's current, he decided that he needed to shake himself up, prevent the atrophy, the rot that was starting to take hold. He couldn't let Atlantic Siding define him. Looking at the turbulent waters of the river, an idea came to him. Perhaps he could do something creative, engage his stagnating brain. Yes, that's it! He could write some poetry. Over the next week, he brought a pad and pen to the river on his walks, and he sat on its bank scribbling. At first, he wrote only a single word: *Alone*. Try as he might, he could think of nothing more. By the end of his break, to his discouragement, that was all he had. The word *Alone*, which he underscored and circled, and nothing else. In time, however, more came, and by the time the week was over, he was satisfied with his first short composition.

> *Alone. Abandoned. Alone. Unyielding. Alone.*
> *The river flows on, indifferent to the march of time,*
> *to the greenery on its banks, the fauna within.*
> *More of a piece with the sun and the moon than with anything so ephemeral.*
> *Untouched by pain or sorrow.*
> *Unperturbed by man's perfidy.*
> *It flowed long ere his birth,*
> *would remain unchanged long after his inevitable demise.*
> *The eternal secrets entombed in its basalt vault inscrutable to him.*
> *Its constancy a tribute to a higher truth.*

For the first time since they had moved to Fredericton, Gabriel felt alive. At work that afternoon, as he made cold calls to businesses using Dunn and Bradstreet leads to request meetings for his sales crew, all he could think about was unveiling his poem to Cathy in the evening. Perhaps she'd like it. Perhaps she'd think it has potential. On the way home, he was nervous, agitated, excited. Something akin to hope had crept back into his parched ego. For what, he was not sure. He had no fixed idea of what writing a poem would do for him, how it could rescue him, other than to give his repressed creativity, his frustrated intellect, an outlet, which it had lacked since he graduated. But it made his blood race.

After work, he busied himself with preparing dinner for them both, and listened to some music to pass the time. His heart leapt as he heard her key turn in the lock a little after seven o'clock, as the third movement of Dvorak's seventh symphony, Gabriel's favourite, blared over the stereo. Cathy stumbled inside, a weary expression on her face. "Hi, Babe. How was your day?" It was a scene that played itself out with few variations on a nightly basis. They were too young, Gabriel reflected, to dig such deep ruts.

"I wrote a poem," he said, beaming at her meaningfully.

"Really?" she said somewhat condescendingly. She removed her burgundy penny loafers and stepped into her slippers, unleashing a heavy, world-weary sigh. "Can you turn it down a little? I've got a bit of a headache."

Gabriel was desperate for more enthusiasm. "Do you want to read it?" he asked, his voice almost breaking with impatience, as he switched the stereo off.

"Well, I'm kind of busy tonight...."

"It's very short," he said with some acrimony, following her into the kitchen, where he had laid the table.

"Oh, very well," she conceded reluctantly. "Let's see it." He handed it to her and watched her scan it quickly, impatiently.

"Uh, it's nice," she said with a polite smirk. "But I wouldn't quit your day job...."

He was sullen all through dinner, barely touching the pasta primavera he had cooked. After the meal, he decided to try again, as she plopped down exhausted on the grey faux-leather sofa. "No, really, Cathy. What did you think?"

"Huh?" she grunted. "About what?"

"About my poem," he responded, gritting his teeth.

Cathy's eyes, always the most expressive part of her, broadcast her irritation. "I don't know what you want me to say.

It's fine. No, really. It's good. It's just.... *I* don't know. I'm not a poetry critic. But it's just sort of like a high school poem. You know...."

"Yeah," Gabriel muttered. That ended his career as a poet.

Gabriel constantly felt his position at work was untenable. He wasn't like the others. His behaviour, his hobbies, such as they were, his entire demeanour were different. No-one seemed to like him. And he had no love for the work. One afternoon, he popped in for an unscheduled visit to Mr. Willoughby's office to talk things through.

Mr. Willoughby was on the telephone, his white moustache flexing in and out, up and down, as he spoke, but graciously waved Gabriel in, motioning toward a chair. Gabriel perused the prized artifacts lining his supervisor's walls. An avid hockey fan, Mr. Willoughby was a collector of Montreal Canadiens' memorabilia. His office was a shrine to the team. On his desk sat a puck autographed by Guy Lapointe, perched on a metal stand and encased in a plastic bubble. His walls were adorned with a signed poster of Ken Dryden in his red, white and blue goalie mask, standing tall against his net, leaning on his stick in his signature pose; a poster of the Stanley-Cup-winning 1971 Montreal Canadiens team, the trophy sitting in front of team captain Jean Belliveau; a small, framed Parkhurst hockey card featuring Rocket Richard; an autographed home-white, number 17 Murray Wilson jersey; a framed black-and-white photograph of a younger Mr. Willoughby, sans Josef Stalin moustache, shaking hands with Guy Lafleur; and several other precious keepsakes.

Gabriel was puzzled. Sports had always been a mystery to him. Yet another fraternity from which he was barred. Perhaps it was because his parents were immigrants, who had little time and money to devote to sports, and less interest in inculcating what was in their estimation a low avocation in their son. Or perhaps it was just that the point of professional sports eluded him. Why would people care so much about, invest so much of their time, money and attention in, a trivial game? In the grand scheme of things, what could it possibly matter if someone did or didn't knock a round black disk into a rectangular net with a curved stick? Surely there were bigger problems in life, worthier pursuits.

"Quite a collection, eh?" Mr. Willoughby asked proudly after hanging up the telephone. Gabriel nodded politely as his boss became animated. "This puck was actually used in game two of the 1977 Stanley Cup finals. Boston was under pressure and Brad Park cleared the puck over the glass. I caught it in the stands. A few years later, I got Guy Lapointe to sign it at an oldtimers' game. You a hockey fan, Gabriel?"

Gabriel shook his head. "Not really," he admitted.

Mr. Willoughby's face fell. "Well, maybe I can take you to a Fredericton Canadiens game sometime. That may hook you," he offered.

"That would be nice," Gabriel replied doubtfully.

"So, what can I do for you, Gabriel?"

Pulling his eyes away from the sports memorabilia, Gabriel became momentarily flustered. His purpose had seemed so clear when he had walked in. But now, it was hard to figure out how to begin. "You see, Mr. Willoughby," he began, "I wanted to.... I mean, I'm not quite sure how it's all going...".

"What? You mean how you're doing here?" Mr. Willoughby asked. Gabriel nodded hesitantly. "Oh, you're doing fine, son."

"Thank you, sir. But it's just.... I get the feeling that people don't really like me here.... That whatever I do is no good. I seem to get the cold shoulder from everybody here."

"Listen, Gabriel. *I'm* your manager and *I'm* really happy with your work. So don't worry too much about the others, okay? Sure, you sometimes seem to lack enthusiasm, but your work is very good, very efficient, and you're always polite. As far as everyone else is concerned, you've got to realize that you're very different from most people 'round here. Try to loosen up a bit. Try to go the bar with your colleagues after work. Talk about the things they talk about. It's just a matter of breaking the ice."

"I can try...." Gabriel said dubiously.

Mr. Willoughby smiled broadly, reminding Gabriel of the photograph of Stalin at the Yalta conference that appeared in his high school History textbook. "Let me tell you about Rocket Richard," he said, pointing to the framed hockey card on his wall. "He was a nasty piece of work at times. He once broke his own teammate's nose deliberately. He punched a fan and knocked him unconscious. He even beat up a referee. But did anyone care? He was the greatest goal scorer ever! So, they loved him.... You follow me? As long as you keep doing good work, people will respect you for what you bring to the firm. All right?"

Gabriel thanked his supervisor and went back to work, taking time on the way out to inspect the small photograph of Rocket Richard.

Among the few bright spots in Gabriel's otherwise monotonous life in Fredericton, were his in-laws' periodic visits. While many men found their in-laws intolerable, Gabriel truly enjoyed their company. Seymour Blum, a partner at a large Toronto law firm specializing in tax law, was extremely intelligent and gregarious, a combination that made him the perfect companion for Gabriel, isolated as he was and in need of intellectual stimulation. They would spend hours during evenings or on weekends discussing politics, exploring philosophical controversies, or studying the Talmud and other Jewish scriptures. His wife, Deborah, who did not hold a job but was active in numerous community and philanthropic causes, was less interested in philosophical discussions. But she was an accomplished amateur painter, who loved discussing the arts and literature. She was also a gifted cook, who spoiled them with her culinary creations, which she proudly paired with the best wines. So, their visits transformed their one-bedroom flat into a vibrant Parisian salon, where the conversation never abated and the wine flowed freely.

As an added bonus, the Blums always brought a cooler filled to the brim with meat from a kosher Toronto butcher shop whenever they visited. Since Fredericton didn't have a large enough market to support its own kosher butcher, the Jewish community relied on occasional meat deliveries from Montreal or Toronto. The meat that arrived in this manner was typically frozen and was snapped up quickly by anxious consumers, fearing that they might miss out for another month or so. The Blums, however, always bequeathed them an ample supply, including the choicest steaks and lamb chops. That alone made their visits noteworthy events.

The Blums adored their son-in-law, although that had not been fore-ordained at their first meeting. Initially, they had been less than thrilled with the match. Could the son of a garbage man ever be good enough stock for their only daughter, the daughter of a professional, of urbane socialites, they complained. But Gabriel had quickly won them over with his intelligence, his good looks, his refined manners, the unreserved love that he had exhibited for Cathy, the way Cathy had beamed in his presence. Paradoxically, his strained relationship with his own parents, far from being an embarrassment or a warning sign, was actually an advantage to the Blums, even if they would have been reluctant to admit it, may not have even thought about it consciously. Not only did it mean that they didn't have to be seen around the uneducated, unsophisticated Kleins, but it also assured them that there would be no rivalry for holiday visits. During visits to Toronto, the young couple would, by their own choice, stay at the Blums, rather than the Kleins.

Perhaps more importantly, when children eventually entered into the mix, the Blums would not have serious competition for their grandchildren from the other grandparents. By this point, after two years of marriage, the Blums viewed Gabriel more as a second son, rather than a son-in-law. For Gabriel, who was not close with his own parents and had few friends aside from Cathy, the feeling was mutual.

Seymour's only disappointment with Gabriel was that he would not accompany him to the synagogue on Saturday mornings. This he found odd for a clearly traditional Jewish young man with a deep commitment to the religion. As a pillar of his community in Toronto, an officer in his synagogue, Seymour would dearly have liked to bring his son-in-law with him, have him by his side on the dais. But, he reasoned, he himself had rebelled against religion as a young man, had absented himself from synagogue for several years. So how could he hold Gabriel to a double standard? He was a decent young man; he'd come around in time.

On this particular visit, in March 1995, toward the end of the young couple's second year in Fredericton, the Blums were unsettled. The easy, relaxed loving relationship that they had become accustomed to between Gabriel and Cathy appeared strained. In retrospect, they would profess to each other sagely that they had discerned the signs of tensions building during previous visits, but that was, at best, an exaggeration, a reinterpretation of past events in light of new evidence. It alarmed them to see such disunity between Gabriel and Cathy, especially so early in the marriage, and they resolved to do something about it. Seymour and Deborah cornered Cathy in the kitchen on the Sunday morning of their visit, when Gabriel went to the grocery store.

"Cathy," her mother asked, "Is everything alright?"

"Sure, Ma. Why wouldn't it be?" Cathy responded wearily, dismissively. While she spoke, she scratched at the label of a salad dressing bottle with her fingernail.

"If you don't mind my saying so, you two don't look very happy," Deborah ventured. With her blond hair, now dyed, her narrow pale blue eyes, her thin, drawn, almost gaunt, cheeks, it was hard to see any connection to Cathy, who resembled her father in most respects, down to his rectangular face, his oval eyes.

"I'm *very* concerned," Seymour pitched in. "Gabriel looks dispirited. This is no life for him. A man like *him*.... He needs a challenge, needs to engage that first-class mind of his. This town's too small for him. His job is killing him, I can tell. But what worries me most is that you seem to have no patience for him. You can't leave him out in the cold like that!"

"Oh, come on!" Cathy bristled. In her agitation, she scratched through the label rather than peeling it off in one piece, as she had unconsciously been trying to do. Somehow, it added to her irritation. "He knows that it's just for a little while. I have to get *my* career on track and then he can focus on *his*. It's not like you guys, where it's only Dad's career that matters."

"Oh, don't be like *that*," Deborah countered. "Your father and I also believe in an equal marriage, but... maybe because we're from a different generation... our division of labour is different. You can't judge our marriage with a set of slogans or a pre-set formula."

"Isn't that what you're doing to mine?" Cathy asked snidely.

"Listen. Don't you care about Gabriel?" Seymour demanded.

"Did he put you up to this?" Cathy asked angrily, evading her father's question.

"No, of course not!" Seymour replied. "But we can *see* how unhappy he is. He's like a caged lion here. And, rather than helping him, you seem to be freezing him out!"

"You seem to care more about him than me," Cathy said caustically.

"Oh, that's ridiculous!" Seymour scoffed. "Has he done anything wrong to you? Is there anything that we don't know about that explains your behaviour toward him, which seems deplorable to us?" Cathy shook her head. "Then you've got to stop."

"You can't *treat* him like that. He's a good boy, a good husband. You can't just throw him aside!" Mrs. Blum insisted.

Cathy shrugged her shoulders brusquely. She hated it when her parents ganged up on her. Especially when they were right. "I've got a lot of work to do and don't have time to argue. If we *must* talk about this, let's wait 'til I'm under less pressure." With that, she retreated to the bedroom, leaving her parents eyeing each other with concern. For the rest of their visit, they were especially solicitous of Gabriel.

A few days after her parents' intervention, Cathy approached Gabriel after dinner, while he was reading. "I'm such a *bitch!*" she wailed. "You must *hate* me!"

Lifting his head out of his novel, Michael Ondaatje's *The English Patient*, Gabriel eyed her somewhat circumspectly. "Well, you certainly *have* been unpleasant since we moved here," he agreed.

Cathy winced. "You sure don't make it easy for anyone to apologize, Gabriel!"

He inserted the ripped envelope – covered in scribbled telephone numbers, appointment times and other arcane scrawls – that served as his bookmark into his book and closed it before answering, recognizing that this was going to be a lengthier conversation than he had initially assumed. Of late, he and Cathy interacted a lot less, except over meals, as she devoted an increasing amount of time to her studies. The farther she got through the programme, the further behind she felt she was, the harder she had to work. In consequence, he began to retreat inward himself, reading more, wandering off on long walks, even when she was home. "Is that what this is?" he asked somewhat testily. "An apology?"

Cathy threw a disdainful glance at his bookmark. How she hated the way he scribbled on used envelopes! Why couldn't he just use the notepad by the phone like a normal human being? Instead, the apartment was cluttered with various and sundry envelopes, credit card statements and advertisements, all marred by his illegible scratchings. She resisted the urge to snap at him, as she often did nowadays. Instead, she forced the frown that had started to form off her mouth, bit her lower lip and said earnestly, "It's just that I'm in over my head. I don't even know why I want to be a lawyer. I'm just not sure what else to do."

Gabriel's expression softened. "Ah, you'll do fine, Cathy. It's a tough programme, but you'll get through. You're gonna be a *great* lawyer," he assured her.

"Do you really think so?" she asked with more than a healthy dose of skepticism.

"Absolutely. You can do *anything* you put your mind to." She remained doubtful, but for the moment it was good to have him in her corner, to hear him say that. On an abstract level, it seemed silly to her that she could be comforted by mere words, by sentiments that were so patently improbable, but strangely it encouraged her, infused her momentarily with hope. She rushed toward him with tears winding their way down her cheeks like wayward mountain streams.

They hugged each other gingerly, each nursing their idiosyncratic wounds, their toxic insecurities, and said "I love you." Yet, though they had both changed, they still each meant something different. Gabriel was saying, I love you. I need you. I need you to be the woman with whom I fell in love in Toronto. You're the only thing that can make me tolerate the pain of this life in Fredericton, so please don't abandon me. Come back to me! Cathy, however, was saying, I love you, Gabriel, so please give me the space I need to finish my programme. Don't crowd me. Don't make demands on me. We'll take care of your needs later. Sadly, what they each required from love was irreconcilable, a portent of inevitable frustration.

As time grated on, a rift between Gabriel and Cathy opened and widened, fuelled by the accumulated resentments that were hard to put aside. After a steady diet of neglect, cutting comments, impatience, indifference, Gabriel grew increasingly isolated and angry, like he was being punished for sins he could not even fathom. As he began to react more angrily, to take her to task for her behaviour, Cathy became more resentful, wondering why he couldn't be more supportive of her studies. Consequently, they grew more aloof from each other, bickered often.

If Gabriel had had a friend to confide in, he would have said that their love was broken. But broken didn't mean finished or beyond repair to him.

When he was a young child, perhaps three or four years old, his grandfather had bought him a painted wooden rocking horse which, for reasons he would have been hard-pressed to explain, he named Window. It was his favorite toy. He loved the horse so much, he would bounce on it day and night with the full force of his growing boyish frame. After months of wear and tear, the wooden supports gave way and the horse collapsed. He ran to Isaac inconsolable, crying, "It's broken, Daddy! It's broken!" His father brought the wounded equine into the building's backyard, where he housed his tools in a rusted metal shed, and, to Gabriel's delight, within forty-five minutes he had restored Window to the land of the living, a little worse for wear, but still serviceable.

That was how he viewed his relationship with Cathy. It was damaged, no doubt, but not beyond repair. Indeed, his conviction was that the change in her personality, in her entire outlook on life, could be attributed to the difficulty she was having in law school. Once it was over, he reasoned, they could try to rebuild what they used to have.

Once, he got a brief window into the depths of her struggle. Waking up thirsty at three-thirty in the morning on a worknight, it surprised him to discover the light still burning in the dining room. He found Cathy slumped over her insurance law casebook, fast asleep, her lovely neck and back contorted. On the coiled, blue-lined spiral notebook which lay open beside her, in between sketches of some sort of spacecraft and a four-eyed monster – she had always been a doodler – beside the term *estoppel* with a large squiggly question mark next to it, was scrawled the desperate admission "I just don't understand!!" underlined twice in red ink. At that moment, despite all the pain she had inflicted upon him, despite her many sins, despite all the bitterness, he experienced an indescribable tenderness for her. *That's my Cathy,* he thought warmly. *My wonderful, quirky, free-spirited, monster-drawing Cathy.*

He marvelled at how one can both love and hate the same person simultaneously. They weren't mutually exclusive emotions. They could coexist uneasily like sun and snow in the universe of contradictions that was the human soul. Not daring to disturb her, he kissed her hair ever so softly, like an angel's breath, drank a glass of water and returned to bed.

By the following morning, however, the winds had changed again, the status quo ante restored, the closeness he had felt toward her the previous night far off, like an echo off some distant canyon. He stopped into the dining room to greet her before donning his *tallit* and *tefillin* to recite his morning prayers in the living room area. "*You're* up early!" he said cheerfully. "Did you sleep well?"

"Oh, just *peachy,*" she replied frostily, her voice oozing with sarcasm. "I've got an Insurance exam tomorrow and Tax on Friday, with not enough time to prepare. I was up almost all night! But I hope *you* had a nice beauty rest."

"I didn't.... Well, I...." He let his sentence trail off, realizing that anything he said would simply make it worse. He made no mention of what he saw the night before. Instead, he simply retreated to the living room area to nurse his wounds and pray.

Over breakfast, though, Gabriel sat with his eyes clouded, his shoulders hunched. He appeared to be chewing on something in his mind, sucking in his lower lip, as was his habit. At last, he blurted out, "Cathy, do you love me?"

"What kind of a question is that?" she responded with a bemused, slightly irritated, smile. Just like his father, he noted in frustration. Responding to a question with another, evasive question.

"It's a straightforward one, which deserves a straightforward answer," he stated flatly, more of a challenge than a clarification.

The hollow smile remained on her lips, but, despite herself, her eyes assumed a colder, harder aspect. "Would I have married you if I *didn't* love you?"

"Stop playing around," He commanded her. "Just tell me. I need to know."

Cathy stubbornly refused to answer immediately, on command. Instead, she glared at him harshly, angry that he was making such a fuss of it all. Eventually, she said bitterly, with hostility, "Of *course*, I love you. But why do you have to make a scene of everything? Why do you have to make *everything* so *hard*?"

That was too much for Gabriel. "Am *I* the one who makes things hard? Really? I get the feeling it's *you* who's making our lives miserable. I've tried everything to make you happy. I put my life on *hold* for you. I'm working at a job I can't *stand* just so you can go to school. Yet you treat me like dirt! I can't *take* it anymore!" he raged, as he stood and paced into the living room.

She wouldn't let herself be cornered, however. "Don't try to make me feel guilty," she snarled, following him, unwilling to let him escape her wrath. "I'm doing all that I can to keep up with my studies. It's not easy. I'm really not sure I'm cut out for this, but I have to try. It'd be easier if you were to support me... *really* support me." Gabriel's eyes widened, his jaw dropped in disbelief. "Oh, I know you've sacrificed for me, but you don't do it with a good heart. You always let me know in none too subtle ways how much you hate this. Can't you just be supportive? Without all the guilt?"

In frustration, he pounded his fist on the wooden end table, upending the photo frames that it housed. "I haven't given you guilt. I just want you to stop acting as if I don't even *exist*!"

"Oh, come on, Gabriel! Don't *you* play the wounded martyr now," she bellowed as she bent demonstratively to straighten out the pictures of her family that he had disturbed. "You didn't even *want* to marry me. I practically had to *beg* you! So don't make it sound like *I'm* the one who hurt *you*!"

What? he thought. *Where did that come from?* He didn't know how to respond, was tired of fighting anyway. He gathered his lunch and his briefcase and grunted at Cathy before shuffling off to work like a wounded animal.

By the middle of the third year, the tension between them had become so great that they fought constantly. The small mounds of resentment, which began as mere ripples on the otherwise placid landscape of their relationship, over the course of many squabbles, countless thoughtless remarks, gained mass, density, permanence. So that after a while they were mounds no more, but hills, immense, immutable cliffs of hostility looming ominously over their day-to-day existence.

Their fights would arise over the most trifling of casus belli: someone had used the last Q-tip without replacing it; Gabriel played his music too loudly; Cathy had mistakenly put one of

Gabriel's socks in her drawer; Gabriel's notepad envelopes were cluttering the floor. All the day-to-day friction that's routinely ignored in a healthy marriage, that's laughed off, suddenly rose to the status of a federal offense, would trigger all the hostility they harboured in their breasts.

On one such occasion, the trigger was the security chain on their apartment door, which Cathy neglected to engage after she arrived tired and hungry after a long day at the university. It had started innocently enough. Gabriel had been in the washroom when she arrived, so she called out, "Hi Gabriel! You home?" as she threw off her jacket, kicked off her shoes, dumped her bag on the floor.

He emerged from the washroom with some difficulty. The lock had been sticking of late, so he needed to fiddle with it in order to open the door. "Hi," he said. "We're gonna need to get the landlord the fix this door before somebody gets stuck inside."

"Oh, can *you* call him? I've got a lot on my plate right now," she responded, somewhat impatiently, but without rancour, as she flopped onto the couch, stretching herself out.

He nodded. "How was your presentation?"

"It wasn't great, but I don't think it was *terrible*," she responded, wincing slightly, as if reliving some of the more cringeworthy moments of her talk.

"Oh," Gabriel said simply, as he scratched a mosquito bite on his arm. "I... I hope it went better than you think."

"Thanks, but I don't think it did. I'm afraid that I'm not really cut out for law school. I don't live for the law like the machines I go to school with. I'm not even sure I really want to *be* a lawyer." She had returned to this theme a lot lately and it annoyed him every time. Why had she dragged him through three years of Hell if she wasn't even sure she wanted to be a lawyer?

"Then why are you killing yourself?" he asked moodily.

She shrugged defensively, as she squeezed the tweed sofa cushion between her hands. "I almost forgot. You got a letter from Revenue Canada. I picked it up on my way up but left it in my bag. Can you do me a favour and bring it to me?" she asked. "I left it at the door and don't feel like moving."

"Sure," he grumbled. "Maybe it's my refund cheque." As he bent to retrieve her bag in the entranceway, however, he noticed the chain dangling from its frame.

"Aw, Cathy," he sputtered. "You forgot to put the chain on again." The irritated, sanctimonious tone of his voice could not have been calculated to get her back up more.

"Sorry," she said tersely, "I forgot."

"You *always* forget!"

"Why can't you let things be? I *said* I was sorry," she snapped.

"It's not *safe*!" Gabriel shouted. He could smell the aggression rising in himself, could see her feeding off it and responding in kind. Yet he couldn't restrain himself. In spite of himself, he persisted, escalated, until there was no ladder upon which to climb down. Though he had waited all day through his isolation to be with her, though he longed to talk to her, to be loved, he couldn't surmount his pride, his need for justice. "Somebody could break in. Why do we even have a chain if you never use it?"

Like a spring that had been compressed with too much tension, she snapped bolt upright and yelled back, "Oh, come on! This is *Fredericton*, for God's sake! Not New York City! No-one's gonna break in__"

"It's there for a reason!" he exploded. "Why can't you just__"

"Aw, why can't you leave me *alone*? I've had a *miserable* day and I just don't have the *energy* for this."

"That's how you get out of *everything*! You're never responsible for *anything* because you've had a tough day. I've had *three years* of tough days, but that doesn't seem to bother *you* at all!"

They were interrupted by a loud bang on the wall. Their neighbour was annoyed about yet another nighttime shouting match.

"Why is it always about *you*?" Cathy screamed.

Gabriel couldn't believe his ears. "About *me*? About *me*? I've done nothing for *me* since we moved here! I put my career, my *life*, on hold for you, so you can go to law school, and you have the nerve to say it's always about *me*?"

"Look, I'm having a hard time right now. Law school is breaking my back. Cut me some slack, will you?" she shouted.

Gabriel inhaled deeply before replying, trying with little success to restrain his anger. "Then why *do* this if it's sucking the life out of you? Why do you *need* to be a lawyer? Do something you like, something you're good at, instead."

Cathy bristled at the suggestion. "So now *you* have no faith in me either, Gabriel? You don't think I'll be a good lawyer?"

"I didn't *say* that...." Gabriel protested.

"But you *thought* it!"

"I just mean, if it's such a challenge and you're not enjoying it.... If you're not even sure you want to do it, then why make yourself... make both of us, miserable?"

"AAAARRGGGHH!!" she screamed in frustration. "I don't have *time* for this shit! I've got *work* to do." Without another word, she stormed out of the living room and sought refuge in the bedroom, locking the door behind her. That night, he slept on the sofa in the living room, the first of many such nights.

In the midst of his growing estrangement from Cathy, from the world, a curious thing happened one April day on his noontime walk. As he sat in the bushes on the riverbank, hidden from view, with the city lost in the trees, without warning the sky darkened dramatically, the wind whipped up. It was as if day suddenly turned into night. Although he was shivering in his short-sleeve polo shirt and jeans, Gabriel found himself unable to move from his perch, transfixed by the river's black, swirling waters, which seemed to call to him.

What are you doing, Gabriel, it seemed to ask with its timeless wisdom. *You don't need them. Any of them. All you can expect from them is betrayal. I won't betray you. God won't betray you. You can trust us. We stood by your Zaidie and we'll be with you, too. It's not too late.*

As the rain started falling, Gabriel was awakened from his near-trance and slowly pulled himself back to the city, back to work. He would later come to understand this moment as his burning bush, where God gave him a sign. For now, however, it merely left him perplexed, confused, disturbed.

During their third summer in Fredericton, just before Cathy started her articling position at a local law firm specializing in employment law, Cathy proposed that they dine out and enjoy a night on the town. While the summers, when Cathy was not in school, were always better times, by now they had dug and fortified their trenches and it was often difficult to de-escalate their war of attrition, even when the pressures of school had abated. Gabriel consented warily, wondering at this point whether it was even possible to heal the growing rift between them. Whether he even wanted to.

She came girded for battle, with the short black dress that he found irresistible and black nylons, her hair down, pushed back on one side to expose her ear. A peace offering, he wondered, or something more sinister? Something in her comportment, her demeanour, reminded him of Angela Pietrangelo – *Satan in a black slit skirt*. He shuddered.

In the rather damp evening air, much cooler than it should have been in July, they moseyed down the sidewalks of the downtown core, no longer clinging to each other as they once had, but separately, aloof. Deliberately, Cathy reached across the gulf between them and pulled his hand into hers. He let it remain there limply, without conviction. But, at the next street corner, he withdrew it to press the pedestrian crossing button and kept it to himself. They spoke only sporadically during the walk, their conversation forced.

At the restaurant, a small Italian bistro, they sat facing one another sullenly through the dim lighting. He could see the machinations behind her oval eyes, still as lovely and multi-hued as ever. Clearly, she was working through something. She had an agenda for this dinner. He wondered almost dispassionately what it was. Did she intend to ask for a divorce? He had begun to consider that himself of late. Perhaps that would be for the best, he mused. But that seemed out of synch with her sexy attire, her attempt to hold his hand. Did she want to reconcile? He would have jumped at the opportunity only months ago. But now the scars were too deep, the acrimony too palpable.

The waiter brought them menus and they took their time studying them. Eventually, they ordered, *Pizza Margherita* for her and, appropriately enough, *Penne Arrabbiatta* – Angry Penne – for him. Gabriel surveyed the other diners. They were mostly couples. A couple in their late teens on what appeared to be their first date, eyeing each other awkwardly, uncertain whether this would lead to more dates, perhaps a romp in the back of his father's car, or whether it was a dead end. A couple about Gabriel and Cathy's age, sharing inside jokes, playing footsie under the table, eager to put the dinner behind them and move on to more exhilarating pursuits. An older couple, perhaps in their fifties, no longer in the throes of passion, but quite at ease with each other; soulmates that no longer needed to ride the rollercoaster of frantic sexual intercourse, but were perfectly content in the company of a loving and reliable partner, who could be trusted completely. Gabriel shivered momentarily, overcome with a sense of loss.

He stared coldly at Cathy. "So, what's on your mind?" he asked.

"What do you mean?" she responded cautiously.

"Well, you know.... The dinner, the dress. It's not like we've been on good terms for the last while." He felt a sudden weariness. Let's just get to the point and move on, he thought.

She considered this for a minute, apparently wondering whether to proceed or beat around the bush. It did not appear to be going as she had planned. She took a sip of water and ploughed ahead. "Gabriel, let's have a baby," she said simply.

"What?" he asked incredulously. It seemed a strange request to him, as, although they still shared a bed together, they had not made love in months.

"We've become so estranged from each other. It may be the only thing that can bring us back together." She glanced momentarily at the middle-aged couple. How many children did they have, she wondered. Were they always that comfortable with each other or had they experienced hard times, too?

"Now?" Gabriel said dismissively. "*Now*'s not the time for that. You've got one more year before you can get a full-time job as a lawyer. I'm going to be applying to graduate school in the Fall. If you have a baby now, how are we going to manage if you aren't able to work?" He stopped short of saying that, besides, he didn't even know if he *ever* wanted to have a baby with her, didn't really believe the marriage had a future.

"So you'll delay grad school for another year until I can get back to work," she responded. If she had been trying to anger him, she couldn't have come up with anything more incendiary to say.

"No way in *Hell*!" Gabriel sputtered. "I've worked here for *three miserable years*. This next one's my *last*. That's what we agreed on." He could finally see the dawn at the end of a desperately black night. Nothing could make him renounce it.

"Grow up, Gabriel!" she retorted. "Sometimes you need to make sacrifices. Look at your father...."

"Leave my father *out* of this!" he thundered. Nothing embarrassed him more than making a scene in public, but his rage got the better of him. The other diners turned their heads, as the waiter deliberately looked away, trying to appear discrete.

Paying no heed, Cathy continued. "Do you think your father *wanted* to be a garbage man? No! He did what he had to to take care of you, to give you the opportunities that you had. Well, I'm not asking you for the same *kind* of sacrifices, but so you'll work at Atlantic Siding for another year or so. *Big deal*!"

"*You lying bitch*!" he shouted at the top of his lungs. "You agreed that this was our last year in this...." He glanced around at the diners, who were pretending not to notice their fight. "In this... in New Brunswick. All I can say is I'm not staying another minute! Absolutely *not*! And we're not having a baby either!" He shoved his plate, making a great clatter, before standing and storming out, leaving her to pay for their dinner, which hadn't yet arrived, and walk home herself.

Nasty as it was, after that fight their relationship began to show signs of improvement. As Cathy began her articling position, Gabriel noticed that she wasn't as irritated as she had been. Though still pre-occupied with work, with a career she felt she lacked a handle on, she was nonetheless more attentive to him and his needs than she had been. Periodically, she'd suggest that they take a walk in the evenings, or go to a movie, a club. Or just sit watching television together from the safety of separate armchairs. Usually he would decline, citing fatigue or work that he had taken home with him that he needed to complete by the following morning. Or some other excuse that he could manufacture to preserve the aloofness, the stoicism he had resorted to of late. But occasionally, when he grew weary of the trenches he had dug to protect himself from her, he would relent and they would spend the evening as husband and wife, trying gingerly to recreate their prior easy intimacy, to mixed results.

One evening when he arrived late from work, he found Cathy in the kitchen putting the finishing touches on his favorite dish, Chicken Paprikash, which he hadn't enjoyed since his rupture with his parents. He didn't know how to react. Although he had longed for such an olive branch from her throughout their miserable sojourn in New Brunswick, by this time it was almost too late. Ensconced high upon his rampart, he could see no reason, no easy path, to descend. Besides, he had lost the essential trust that had defined their relationship in the early days. He muttered rather coldly, non-commitally, "This wasn't necessary."

Cathy observed his remoteness, the scars he was nursing, and started crying. "Oh, Babe," she sighed pitifully, her cheeks puffing up with sadness, accentuating her dimples. "I'm so sorry. I've been such a bitch! I've really botched this up, haven't I?"

Gabriel thought, *Yes, you have!* But he said nothing. He stood in the doorway of the kitchen, his hand resting on the white louvered door, watching her warily, as a springbok might eye a lion.

"You don't know how hard it's been for me...." she pleaded.

"That's no excuse!" he snapped. "We could have faced the challenges together. Like a couple. Instead, you shut me out. You hurt me more than you can ever imagine."

"You're right. I *know* you're right. I guess I cracked up under the pressure. And I resented you because everything always comes so easily for you. I know it's silly, but it's true. The more I struggled, the more I wanted to lash out at you because you *never* struggle. What is it that makes us hurt the ones we love most?" she asked pitifully.

Gabriel considered that for a moment. "Who else *can* we hurt? No-one else cares enough to suffer," he said wryly. He leaned his shoulder fully on the doorpost, feeling the oppressive weight of the universe to be too much for his legs. He was, after all, only human.

Cathy unleashed a long and pitiful sob. "It's not too late for us, is it Gabriel? It's still me. Cathy. Remember? Strange but wonderful?" It was a desperate plea and it moved him, made his heart ache.

"I don't know, Cathy. I really don't...." Gabriel stared out the kitchen window out into the distance. The sun was setting, but it was obscured from his vision by clouds. For some reason, that saddened him almost as much as his problems with Cathy. Without being able to articulate it, to define it clearly, he felt as if the sunset had everything to do with him, that he oughtn't to let it be marred by obstructions. But, of course, it was beyond his control. He gazed mournfully out the window for some time, before turning back to Cathy and pushing himself off the doorpost, unfurling himself to his full, imposing height. "We're clear that this is our last year here?" he inquired in a tone that, while not aggressive, brooked no disagreement. "That next year I can quit my job and go to grad school no matter what?"

"Yes, of course, Gabriel. I know that's what you want. That's what we agreed," Cathy confirmed.

He nodded. "I suppose we can try...". His eyes were glistening, his body trembling with emotion. She rushed to him, to hold him, but he rebuffed her with a wave of his hand. "Not yet. Not yet. Let's take this slowly and see where it goes," Gabriel advised. "Let's start with dinner."

He led her to the table, and they ate together, not as belligerents, not as husband and wife, but as two wounded combatants hoping for rescue, uncertain if the rustle in bushes ahead of them signified friend or foe.

The Oracle of Spring Garden Road

***

Gradually, they began the delicate work of dismantling fortifications and rebuilding shattered trust. It was more difficult than one would imagine to open oneself up again, to expose one's vulnerability, one's fragility, after being belittled, callously betrayed, profoundly wounded. The resentments were everywhere, like shrapnel littering the battlefield. But they both committed to making every effort to surmount them.

It took a great deal of time and patience, however, to overcome Gabriel's skittishness. From the outset, he stressed to Cathy that he wanted to take it slowly and steadily, not merely to dive in. Though they worked to rebuild their tattered intimacy, he refused to resume their physical intimacy as if nothing had happened between them. As he explained to her, sex for him was the highest expression of love, of oneness. If he performed the act without truly feeling, it might satisfy his physical lust, but it would be bereft of meaning, would cheapen their conjugal love, would build a flawed foundation for their rehabilitated marriage. Sadly, she assented, allowing him to take all the time he needed.

At first, they spent their time talking, about their pain, about their past, their dreams for the future. They took long walks together along the river, revelling in the healing natural beauty of the scenery. Once, early on, he reached for her hand, took it in his, as he had done so many times in the past. The touch of her all too familiar, silky soft skin, however, hit him like an electric shock, bringing back the bitterness, reminding him of the as yet unhealed wounds. To her dismay, he dropped it quickly, bruskly, like a cursed chalice.

In time, as the autumn colours blazed gloriously across the city, reflecting in the river's stippled sheen, they allowed themselves to heal. While the aestival majesty of the New Brunswick countryside had begun to wane, preparing the region for a long, dark winter, Cathy and Gabriel were just beginning to emerge from their own hibernation, their love starting to bloom anew. They would now gaze into each other's eyes, seeing only a little of the pain that had occupied those fragile orbs before. Again they touched each other, kissed each other, at first tentatively, remorsefully, but soon with all the passion and lustre of old. They stopped there, however, as Gabriel was still not ready to take the final step back to conjugal reconciliation. Life, however, was looking better for them than it had for quite some time.

Gabriel's healing was bolstered by the application process for graduate school. After soliciting information from various programmes and contacting Arthur, now an Assistant Professor at the University of Manitoba, for advice, he narrowed his options down to four schools: McGill, Queen's, UBC and, of course, his *alma mater*, U. of T. Having decided to pursue a Master's degree first, to retain his flexibility, rather than applying directly to a Ph.D. programme which usually provided funding to its students, he quickly dismissed the idea of applying to U.S. schools, whose price tags would be prohibitively high.

If it were up to Gabriel alone, his preference would have been to go to McGill. While U. of T. had the best reputation in the country, he had already spent four years there and was familiar with most of the Philosophy professors in his area at the institution. It made sense to him, as Arthur had suggested, to branch out and expose himself to new ideas and approaches. Queen's and UBC were also good programs, but after spending several years in Fredericton, he was eager to return to a big city, in the part of the world he was familiar with. Although he remembered Jenny singing its praises, UBC was far away, and Queen's was in a smaller city with fewer amenities for traditional Jews.

Cathy, however, had raised a red flag regarding McGill. Since the Quebec legal system, regulated as it was by civil law, was unique in Canada, she might not be able to practice there. Nor did she speak French very well, which could also interfere with her job prospects in Quebec. Unless she were to find a job in Ottawa, which would complicate their lives together immensely because of the commute, she would be unable to support him during his studies if they were move to Montreal. Moreover, her job prospects would be considerably better in a larger city, meaning that Toronto and Vancouver made the most sense to her. Her preference was, of course, Toronto, where her family lived, but she agreed that he should choose between the two on the basis of academic and professional criteria. In light of these practical considerations, Gabriel decided that UBC should be his first choice, followed by U. of T. They could decide later how to choose between Queen's and McGill if it were to come to that.

Having reached these momentous decisions, he began the process of filling out application forms, writing cheques to cover the application fees, requesting letters of recommendation from his professors at U. of T. Most importantly, he spent his evenings carefully crafting his statement of purpose, explaining which aspects of philosophy interested him most, which thinkers, and what he hoped to achieve during his studies. How wonderful it was to put his mind to something worthwhile, challenging, rather than to sales ledgers and cold calls! In his mind's eye, he could already see himself in the classrooms of his new academic home, wandering its pathways, sitting in its cafes debating the mysteries of the universe: justice, truth, divine law. Returning to the campus, the only place he had ever truly been happy, where he had ever fully belonged.

Cathy embraced the process enthusiastically and did her part to help him with his applications. In the evenings, on Sundays, she would proofread his written statements, which he tailored to the specific departments, to the professors with whom he hoped to study, and suggest edits. Then, after he made his corrections, she would take his clumsily hand-scrawled notes and type them out neatly on their old Smith Corona typewriter. She did everything she could to leave him no doubt that she wanted his success and his happiness, that she would grant him the same latitude to pursue his dreams as he had given her.

One brisk Monday afternoon in mid-October, when both Gabriel and Cathy were able to leave work a little early, they enjoyed a brief shopping excursion in the downtown core together. Gabriel bought a geometric tie, in hues of royal blue and cherry red on a slate grey background, that he could wear to work with his blue suit. Cathy bought a pair of versatile tan leather boots that would be equally appropriate in the synagogue or in the law firm at which she was articling. On their way back home, as the sky darkened ominously, they stopped to take out a cup of ice cream. While they were inside the ice cream shop ordering, the heavens exploded in a dazzling lightning display, with deafening, rumbling thunder peals that set off a spate of car alarms outside. Within a matter of minutes, the torrential deluge that followed soaked the downtown streets, before subsiding to a light, steady rain, which they needed to brave to get back home.

As they sloshed their way along Carleton Street's slick, wet sidewalk, with Gabriel trailing the shopping bags from his left arm, they each spooned out their ice cream as they walked and chatted happily about their days, their plans for the week, the trip to Toronto they intended to take over the holidays in December. As they were thus engrossed in conversation, a large U-Haul truck sped through the street, spraying them both with filthy water from the flooded gutter. Gabriel, who occupied the outside position, bore the brunt of it. His suit pants, protruding from underneath his trench coat, were completely drenched. Even his ice cream was inundated with the foul run-off. He grunted miserably, like a wounded animal. To add insult to his injury, Cathy burst out laughing. "You look like a sorry excuse for a human being," she howled with delight.

His anger kindled in him. *What a nasty, inconsiderate bitch!* He was about to chastise her, tear into her, when another thought struck him. *How do I know she's trying to be mean? Maybe she is, but perhaps she's just uncomfortable and doesn't know how to respond. Maybe her laughter is a nervous response because she fears my reaction. Or maybe she's just being strange and wonderful. Which is why I fell in love with her to begin with.*

It was then that another insight struck him, as he veered toward a nearby garbage can. *Maybe that's it. Maybe it's all an act of volition. We have the power to react to events, both good and bad, as we wish. If we get angry, then we cause more conflict, bitterness, estrangement. If I blow up because she laughed at me, we'll end a good day together in hostility and mutual recriminations. If she hadn't responded to her difficulties in law school with rancour at home, we would have avoided the unpleasantness of the past few years. Anger begets anger. Hostility begets hostility. But laughter should beget... what? Maybe it's all up to us!*

All this flashed through his brain instantly, in a manner of seconds, but the impact on him was profound. As he approached the bin and tossed out the remains of his soiled ice cream, he banished the scowl from his face. "Yeah, I do look a little silly," he acknowledged with a slightly forced giggle, proud of himself for restraining his anger. "A little?" she guffawed. They continued laughing on the way home, as Cathy continued to tease him playfully about his appearance.

That evening, as Cathy transcribed the final version of his essay for McGill on the dining room table, she caught him sitting diagonally behind her, staring at her, watching her fingers caress the keys, her hair bob and ripple each time she returned the carriage, her chest expand with every intake of breath. She turned and caught his eye. "What?" she asked shily.

"Nothing," he answered, as he stood up and approached her. With his hand almost trembling, he smoothed back her hair and kissed her on her exposed neck, bit her playfully.

"Hey, Babe!" she teased. "I'm not finished typing...."

He gazed into her kaleidoscope eyes and said, "Leave it 'til later." He lifted her out of the chair and whispered under his breath, "Cathy Blum, show us your bum," as he led her by her hand to the bedroom. An act of volition.

As they renewed the holiness of their marriage, Gabriel's position at work grew more precarious owing to two adverse developments. The first was his supervisor's departure. Having reached sixty-five, after fifteen years of loyal service to the company, Mr. Willoughby announced his imminent retirement in mid-September. He and his wife wanted the opportunity to travel, to spend time at their cottage in Pleasant Valley while they could still enjoy it, to visit Montreal to attend the occasional Canadiens' game. The company feted Mr. Willoughby at an elaborate dinner at a downtown restaurant, where the alcohol flowed freely. The Hobart brothers, the co-owners of the company, capped the evening by presenting him with a silver plaque and, more meaningfully for him, an autographed Guy Lafleur jersey to add to his collection of memorabilia.

Gabriel was sorry to see Mr. Willoughby go. Despite coming from very different worlds, they had grown to understand and respect each other. Mr. Willoughby had always treated Gabriel fairly and made accommodations for Gabriel's religious restrictions where possible. During the winter months, when the Sabbath begins early – often before the workday has ended – Mr. Willoughby allowed Gabriel to leave at two PM, provided that he made up the lost time on other days. He also allowed Gabriel to use his vacation time during Jewish holidays.

His replacement, a young, red-haired, ruddy-faced man named Abernathy, took a different view of these matters. From their first encounter, it was clear that Gabriel and his new boss were on a collision course. During his inaugural speech to the sales division, Mr. Abernathy announced a lunch meeting on Saturday afternoon at which he would introduce a fresh new approach to "getting to yes" that would constitute the core of their messaging to potential customers. Later that afternoon, Gabriel knocked on his new boss' door.

"Um, Mr. Abernathy? I'm Gabriel Klein, in charge of the Atlantic provinces," Gabriel stated diffidently. "I, uh... I just wanted to let you know that I can't make meetings on Saturdays. But if...."

His supervisor cut him off. "In general, I don't think we'll be meeting much on the weekend. But this Saturday is a mandatory meeting for the entire sales staff. No exceptions!"

"I'm very sorry, sir, but I won't be able to attend. Can we arrange a one-on-one meeting at a different time to__"

"Why not?" Anger flashed fiery red in Mr. Abernathy's eyes and his short, sinewy body knotted up as he said this.

"Well, sir," Gabriel said, swallowing hard, "I'm Jewish and I don't work on the Sabbath."

Abernathy stared at him icily, utter contempt in his expression. "I don't care if you're the Pope himself. This is a *mandatory* meeting."

It was clear that Mr. Abernathy had developed an instant antipathy toward him and, as far as Gabriel was concerned, the feeling was mutual. Unfortunately, he would need to develop a modus vivendi with this disagreeable man if he was going to remain gainfully employed for the rest of the year. He cleared his throat, repressed his anger and tried again. "I'm really sorry, Mr. Abernathy, but when I was hired, I made it clear to Mr. Willoughby and Mr. Hogan that I'm unable to work on Saturdays. If you'd like to check with Mr. Hogan...." Gabriel suggested.

"Well, we'll *see* about that, Klein...." Abernathy huffed.

In the end, Mr. Abernathy ordered Gabriel to get a synopsis of the meeting from another sales manager and then submit a plan to incorporate the new ideas in his region by the following Friday. His supervisor's contempt for him, however, was undisguised. Gabriel had won the first round, but at what cost?

The second storm cloud on the horizon concerned the company's dismal performance over the previous fiscal year. Facing increasing competition from larger American manufacturers that, taking advantage of the North American Free Trade Agreement, began to crowd the market, Atlantic Siding was losing market share. The Hogans were despondent and somewhat resentful. In their view, Canadian construction companies should remain loyal to local manufacturers, rather than embracing cheaper American products. But that was the way of the world. As profits began to slip, everyone at the company began to worry about their jobs and finger pointing was rampant. Under these inauspicious circumstances, having a supervisor with a grudge against him was a distinct liability.

At an October sales meeting, with the elder Mr. Hogan present, Mr. Abernathy put Gabriel directly in the hotseat. "Atlantic region. Klein," he said with relish. "Sales down eleven percent this quarter. How do you explain this?" He glared mercilessly at Gabriel.

Gabriel gulped. "It's been a tough quarter all around," he replied. "And my Charlottetown sales rep quit early in the quarter. We've only just replaced him."

His supervisor licked his already chapped lips and tore into Gabriel. "Well, Klein. It seems to me that if you weren't always missing work for your little holidays, your division would be doing better."

Gabriel was both mortified and incensed. Although he restrained himself from yelling, his voice rose to a plaintive whine. "Mr. Abernathy, I respectfully disagree. I haven't missed an hour of work since I've been here. Whatever time I miss on Fridays, I make up on other afternoons. My holidays are deducted from my vacation time. So, it has nothing to do with my sales numbers. Also," he continued, as his stomach churned, "the whole company has been suffering. Not just me... my section. So, it wouldn't be fair to blame *me* for that." He took the temperature of room through the corner of his eye, without turning his head. From the sneering expressions on their faces, his colleagues' sympathies clearly lay with Abernathy. Though Gabriel had worked there for three years, he had made no friends and his colleagues resented his special requirements. His differentness. They seemed overjoyed that a new boss was finally going to read him the riot act.

Abernathy sensed it too and was emboldened to twist the knife. "Is that so?" he asked, his voice rising with the thrill of the kill. "I'll thank you to let *me* do the managing and *you* stick to the sales, Klein. Maybe that way you we'll get better *results* around here."

Gabriel was about to protest but was overwhelmed by the futility of it all. "Yes, Mr. Abernathy," he responded through clenched teeth, as his new supervisor glared triumphantly, the top dog biting the neck of an upstart rival.

He returned to his desk after the meeting agitated and annoyed. Yes, sir! No, sir! It was like he was in the army. Why should he have to toady up to inferior minds? Just because he needed to earn a living, he had to prostrate himself before a know-nothing anti-Semite? Was it really worth it, he wondered. Or should he just throw over the whole damn lot of them? They could get by on Cathy's salary, small though it was, couldn't they? It would be a squeeze, but.... Well, I shouldn't be so rash. We're going to need as much as we can save to cover our upcoming move. I just need to hang on for another ten months or so....

As the trees began their annual symphony of autumn colours, therefore, Gabriel grew increasingly worried about whether he'd be able to keep his job.

After a particularly trying day of work in mid-November, in the midst of a heavy rain, Gabriel was sitting on the faux-leather recliner with his feet up, his shoes kicked off and discarded haphazardly on the carpet, reading the *Globe and Mail* when Cathy unlocked the front door and walked in dripping wet. She was home earlier than he had expected, as he thought she had said something about working late when he had walked her to her firm in the morning, which he had started to do of late. He thought little of it, though, grunting his greeting, his eyes still half focused on the front-page article about the horrible plane crash in India. All day, as his boss had taken him to task for his region's falling sales numbers, Gabriel had comforted himself with the knowledge that he would submit his graduate school applications soon, that this would be his final year of crushing his soul for Atlantic Siding's benefit. Now if only he could keep his job long enough to manage until then. With all that on his troubled mind, he failed to notice Cathy's agitation.

"How was your day?" she asked tentatively.

"Dreadful!" he grumbled. "I don't know if I'll be able to hang on to my job much longer."

"Oh!" she exclaimed in distress. "That's *terrible*! You *need* to keep it."

"For a few more months. I know...." He had hoped she might be less concerned.

"Maybe longer...." she said under her breath, as a loud peal of thunder rattled the windows.

He bristled. "No way! We're *out* of here as soon as you finish your year and pass the bar, as we *agreed*."

She gulped. "It might not be that simple...."

"What do you mean? What's going on, Cathy? Is something wrong?" He tossed the newspaper on the end table, sat up and scrutinized her, at last aware of her excitement, her nervousness.

"No.... I don't think so.... I hope *you* won't either," she said timidly, dropping her attaché case and kneeling beside him on the floor. She took his hand in both of hers, brought it to her lips and gazed up at him hopefully.

"Well? What's going on?" he asked, completely befuddled.

"It's just that I.... We.... We're going to have a baby...."

Wrenching his hand free, he lurched out of the chair and shouted down at her, not quite grasping the situation. "We *discussed* this! *Now's* not the time! Let's worry about grad school first and then talk about the right time."

"You don't understand! We're *going* to have one. In July. I'm pregnant, Gabriel."

He stared at her uncomprehending, incapable of speech. After a few seconds he sputtered, "But.... How...? How is that possible? We've been so careful...."

"I don't know, honey. These things happen...." she replied, looking away.

Gabriel slumped back down in the chair despondently, burying his face in his hands. "Oh my God! Oh my God!" he moaned as the rain raked the windows mercilessly. "What are we going to do?"

She kneeled beside him, draping her arm around his back. "We'll get by Gabriel. It can be a good thing for us," she suggested.

"I can't push off grad school for another year. I just can't!"

"I understand, Babe," she commiserated. "I just don't know what else we could do."

"I suppose we'll figure it out," he said, without conviction. "Maybe we could ask your folks for a loan that we can pay back once you start working...."

"Oh! I'd rather avoid that, if possible," Cathy declared. "I don't want us to be beholden to them...."

"We may have no choice," he said reflectively, as he rose from the chair once more and paced back and forth across the living room. He halted abruptly. "Are you sure? That you're pregnant, I mean. Maybe it's a mistake...." He was grasping for a lifeline, a reprieve.

"No mistake," she said. "I saw the doctor this morning."

Gabriel glanced at her quizzically. "You mean you suspected it? How come you didn't say anything to me?"

"I, uh.... I didn't want to worry you," she replied.

Something didn't feel quite right to Gabriel. Suddenly he remembered their fight that summer, the short black dress. *Satan in a black slit skirt*. "Did she say how this can happen while you're on the pill?"

Cathy hesitated. "I didn't ask her."

"You *have* been taking the pill, haven't you Cathy?" he asked with growing agitation.

Guiltily, she averted his probing gaze and confessed, "Well... no. I stopped taking it...."

"You *what*?" he sputtered, "You *what*? How...? How *could* you? We *discussed* this. You had no *right*!" In his rage, he flexed his stomach, the blood rushed to his head, blurring his vision. A sour, metallic taste filled his mouth as bile rose from his stomach to his throat. Like a wounded bear, he began circling the room wildly, swinging his forepaw at some unseen enemy.

"I... I should've talked to you about it. I know.... But... I just didn't want to wait forever. I didn't want to get stuck working for years before having a baby. I don't want to be one of those older moms that don't have the energy to juggle their jobs and their kids. We can make it work," she pleaded. "I *know* we can!"

"That wasn't *your* decision to make! How could you do this without even consulting me?" Gabriel was apoplectic. *Was this what she had in mind all along? Was she just pretending to reconcile to spring this on me?* He continued circling the room, kicking obstacles out of his way savagely as he encountered them: her briefcase, library books, a potted plant. "You're a monster!!" he shrieked.

As their neighbour banged on the wall to express his displeasure, Cathy began to weep. "I'm sorry, Babe. I really am. But I couldn't wait. And I really thought you'd be happy. That a baby is what we need to *really* get us back together. Be like we used to be. You've *got* to believe me. I did it for *us*." She stared up at him pitifully, like a supplicant, her large oval eyes brimming with tears, but she could no longer hope to reach him.

He glared at her, enraged by the monstrosity of her betrayal. The betrayal of all betrayals. Suddenly, the weight of all he had endured for her benefit over the previous three years, the loneliness, the bitterness, the hollowness inside, overwhelmed him like a tidal wave of tribulation. "You're a monster! I don't *know* you anymore. I don't *want* to know you."

His pronouncement had the finality of a divorce. Those were the last words he ever spoke to her. As she rushed to him to touch him, to plead with him, tears flowing down her guilty cheeks, Gabriel forcefully pushed her aside, knocking her to the ground, and stalked to the door, slamming it on his way out.

Chapter 11

Gabriel stumbled blindly through the rain-soaked streets of Fredericton, without coat or hat, turning this way and that, all the while muttering to himself, shaking his head. There were few pedestrians on account of the storm, but passing drivers assumed he was mad. Spiralling down a vortex of shock, indignation, rage, acid corroding his innards, he perceived little of the outside world. *How dare she*, he kept repeating, half-crazed in the fog that smothered his brain, clouded his eyes, over and over, like a mantra. *How dare she decide for me? Without consulting me. Without respecting my wishes, her promises. She used me these last four years. Used the best years of my life. Squeezed me dry. And now, the crowning insult, she wanted to lock me in with a baby. To who knows how many more years of meaningless, soul-killing work. Knowing that I had said 'No.' How dare she?*

A fiery crack of lightning briefly illuminated the rain-soaked city in a ghostly, ethereal light, exposing its treachery to Gabriel's febrile eyes. Oh, how he *hated* Cathy! Hated all of humanity! What a deceitful, despicable race! He had had his fill of them. The sky erupted in a mighty blast of thunder that left a several frightened cars howling in its wake. But Gabriel took no notice. All his life he'd been brutally betrayed by those he trusted, those he loved. His parents. Jack. Rabbi Plotkin. Now Cathy with the most callous betrayal of all. All except Jenny. But she would have betrayed him too if he had given her the chance he knew now. Oh, how easy it was for her to leave him and start a new life in Vancouver as if he never existed. Yes, the human race was rotten.

"She stopped taking them! She just stopped taking them!" he suddenly sputtered, choked by a spasm of rage. Under the heavy barrage of rain, his white button-up dress shirt had become almost translucent, adhering to his body like paint. His drenched charcoal suit pants, bunching up in places, had lost their shape, would be ruined. His shoes and socks were inundated. Yet, he took no notice, marching onward, sloshing through puddles, continuing his vitriolic diatribe against his shameless Jezebel, at times aloud, at times in his head. He was being sucked into a twisted tornado of anger, shame and revulsion, in which considerations of grooming and attire, of social convention, had no place.

Why had God ever created human beings in the first place? What a terrible experiment that had been. No wonder He brought the flood to destroy them. It was then that he noticed the downpour, thinking, *Yes. Bring down the rain to wash them all away, every pitiful one.* But wait! God saved Noah. Alone in a wicked world, Noah persevered. Just like Zaidie. Turning his back on everyone and everything, hiding out by the river. Knowing that the rest of the world didn't matter, as long as he was true to himself, to his principles, to God....

It would be incorrect to assert that Gabriel had at that moment decided on the direction he would take for the rest of his life. He was too incensed, too confused, too manic to develop any clear plans. But the germ of an idea began to sprout at the back of his mind.

He wandered blindly along the downtown streets glancing from time to time into the windows of the shops, now closed for the night. All these useless products that nobody needs, he groused. Is that what man was put on this earth to do? Produce unnecessary garbage and then push it on others in a never-ending quest for a buck? A flash of lightning lit up the hollow eyes of a store display mannequin. That's what people were, Gabriel shook his head angrily. Soulless mannequins. He'd be better off without them.

Without having planned it, when he caught sight of the intercity bus depot in front of him, he nodded. That was exactly what he needed. He had to get away. From her. From Atlantic Siding. From everything and everyone that had ever disappointed him. Once he had some distance, he could think about what to do next. He entered the terminal and studied the departure board. What time was it now? Was it nine-thirty already? How long had he been wandering the streets? It looked like the next bus was to Halifax, departing in twenty minutes. Gabriel nodded, to no-one in particular. Halifax. It was as good a destination as any, he supposed. He had travelled there once on behalf of the company to meet with the sales' representative there, but he remembered little of it.

He approached the ticket counter and asked how much a one-way ticket on the next bus to Halifax would cost. Twenty-two dollars, the clerk responded disdainfully, eyeing Gabriel's wet clothing, the small puddle he had left near the departure board, with disapproval. Retrieving his soggy billfold from his back pocket, Gabriel proffered two damp bills to the clerk, receiving a ticket and three loonies in return. "You might want to dry yourself off in the bathroom before you board," the clerk admonished him. But in his confusion and turmoil, he didn't quite understand. Instead, he headed straight to the bus, which was already accepting passengers at the designated stop.

He boarded the bus, still dripping, his shoes sloshing with each step, and presented his soggy ticket to the driver, a kindly grey-haired woman with a blue company cap. "Welcome aboard," she greeted him. "How far you going?"

"Halifax," he mumbled.

"No hand luggage?" she asked in surprise. Gabriel shook his head.

Reaching beside her she extracted a roll of brown paper towels and ripped off a large section, about half a metre long. "Here," she said with a friendly smile. "Why don't you towel off a bit? You don't want to wet the seat." He nodded absently and grabbed the towels, but then shuffled straight off in search of a seat, still clutching them angrily in his hand. The driver sighed knowingly. In her line of work, she had seen far too many souls in distress. Here was another one whom life had kicked around more than it ought to have.

As he made his way back, his shoes squeaking pitifully with every step, he continued muttering to himself, jerking his head violently, still reeling from the shock. Seeing him approach, several passengers nervously placed their travel bags on the vacant seats adjacent to them to bar him access. Near the middle of the bus, he found an aisle seat and sat down. The woman in the window seat next to him winced as she apprised his bedraggled appearance, his mildewy smell, his erratic behaviour. She glanced around fearfully and spotted a vacant aisle seat in the rear of the bus, to which she eagerly moved, leaving Gabriel by himself as the bus departed, sliding off into the wet, gloomy New Brunswick night.

Even once he was riding the bus, on his way to Halifax, he still had no clear idea that he would never return, never depart from his next destination, would make it the only home he would know for the rest of his life. In the dizziness of his troubled mind, he merely needed to get away, to put some distance between him and his tormentors. To find somewhere safe where he could think, plan his next move.

Eventually, the rumbling of the engine, the rotation of the wheels, the streetlights refracted through the prism of raindrops on the windows, all had a soporific effect on him and he dozed off. In his agitated state, his sleep was restless, his dreams menacing. Early on, he dreamt he was on a train, travelling into enemy territory at night, smuggling a very important package. He crept along the long, narrow corridor to the dining car stealthily in the darkness, in terror of being discovered. As he entered the dining car, the conductor called out that it was time to play Hide and Seek. So, Gabriel ran back into the corridor and ducked into the synagogue office to find an appropriate hiding spot. He crouched behind the secretary's desk, unsettled because his head protruded from one end. Just then, Rabbi Plotkin announced, "Ready or not, here I come!" and Gabriel heard Cathy's treacherous vanilla cream voice in the corridor announcing, "Look in there! I saw him go in there." Annoyed that she had given his location away, he bent his knees and concealed his head. But as the rabbi twisted the doorknob to enter, Gabriel recoiled in alarm, realizing that he had lost the package he needed to deliver. What would he do? What would they say when they saw him without it? He had to run. But before he could do so, the synagogue dissolved, as did the train he had been riding.

He now stood on the steep incline of an arid, rocky mountain. As his eyes grew accustomed to the blistering sunlight, a white-haired man in a white robe and primitive sandals approached him. Though he was very old, with a long white beard, he was strangely hale and agile, and his face glowed with an otherworldly radiance. Gabriel immediately recognized him as Moses. "It's not too late," the old prophet said in a sonorous voice that resonated throughout the mountain. "You can still join us." "Who else is here?" Gabriel inquired fearfully, but the old man had turned and bounded up the incline with the agility of a goat. Gabriel quickly clambered after him. As he passed through a thicket, he came upon a mountain stream both wide and deep. On the far bank, he saw his grandfather, sitting on a twisted log, tossing breadcrumbs into the water. "Zaidie!" he cried joyously. "Zaidie, it's me!" But his grandfather showed no sign of recognition. At that moment, the bus decelerated rapidly, and Gabriel's eyes jolted open momentarily. He shifted his body in his seat, and fell back asleep almost instantly, but the dream had been displaced.

Later that night, he had another, particularly unsettling dream. He was playing baseball, perhaps in the field next to Hart House at U. of T. He was the pitcher and was preparing to deliver a pitch, when he noticed that the batter was holding a violin instead of a bat. "You can't do that!" he shouted. But the umpire told him not to delay the game. With an uneasy feeling, he hurled the ball. The batter swung the violin quickly, blasting a sharp line drive directly back to the pitcher's mound, hitting Gabriel hard in the stomach. Moments later, he was in the hospital being examined by Dr. Levenson, Jenny's mother. Only it wasn't really Dr. Levenson. She looked more like Deborah Blum, who told him that she needed to amputate his arm. In a panic, he explained that he was hit in the stomach, not his arm, and that his arm was fine, but she paid no heed and called for the circular saw. He woke up screaming in abject terror, "No, it's okay! I can move it! I can move it!"

He looked around feverishly, wondering where he was. Then he felt his wet clothing, glanced at his waterlogged shoes and, with a sudden sinking feeling in the pit of his stomach, remembered what had happened, why he was on the bus surrounded by strangers pretending not to stare at him. It all had an unreal quality. Had she really betrayed him? Did he just imagine it all? In his weariness, part of him wanted to return home and pretend it had all been merely a bad dream. But then he remembered the pain of the past three years, her cruel neglect, the manipulations and machinations of Satan in the black slit skirt, and he understood that he had no choice but to escape her nefarious trap.

He was calmer now than he had been. The little sleep he had, turbulent as it was, had done him some good. He began to think dispassionately about the situation. Staring out the window into the blackness — the rain had already stopped — watching the occasional passing light distorted by the bus's speed, he decided he needed to plan out his next moves carefully, rather than thrashing about on instinct as he had done all night. For now, he concluded, the most productive use of his time would be to sleep. Tomorrow he could take his bearings, get organized and chart out his future. Wearily, he nodded his approval, as if the course of action had been proposed by someone else, shut his eyes and drifted off.

He awoke early the next morning as the bus pulled into the Halifax bus terminal. Other passengers were already jostling in the aisle, retrieving their bags from the overhead bin, queuing to disembark. As he prepared to follow suit, he perceived that his pants were still moist, adhering softly to the brown vinyl seat. One of his first orders of business would be to replace his dishevelled, musty smelling clothing.

After picking up a local map from the display outside the information booth, which at seven-thirty was still closed, Gabriel bounced out of the terminal and into the early morning cold. As he explored the streets near the bus station, he caught sight of a café that was just in the process of opening. Only then did he realize that he was ravenously hungry, that he hadn't eaten anything the night before. He had been waiting for Cathy to join him for dinner, which their fight had pre-empted. He pushed inside and ordered a cup of coffee and a bagel with cream cheese, which he devoured greedily while studying the map. When he finished, it was still before eight o'clock, more than two hours until the stores would open, so he ambled over to the waterfront and sat on a bench by the ocean thinking.

The morning was chilly, with a brisk breeze, but otherwise pleasant for November. Without a jacket, his clothes from the day before still damp, however, he began to shiver, his teeth to chatter. After only a few minutes, he beat a hasty retreat to the cafe and ordered another coffee, which he smothered with both his palms to steal its warmth. Clearly, he would need a jacket and a hat in addition to some warm clothing. Checking his wallet, he noted with satisfaction that he had an ample supply of cash to start with. Instinctively, he wanted to avoid using credit cards or his bank card; he wasn't ready to be tracked down just yet.

There was something delicious in his anonymity in this city. No-one knew him here. No-one *expected* anything from him. He had no work to do in Halifax, no siding to sell. No-one here required him to play the supportive husband to an ungrateful, unworthy wife. Or a loving son to deceitful parents. *Sometimes*, he thought, *I wish I could just disappear. Vanish off the face of the earth....*

Eventually, as the morning wore on, Gabriel abandoned the coffee shop and trekked toward the commercial district. Because he needed to conserve his cash, he selected a military surplus store as his first destination. There, he procured a warm khaki field jacket and a cheap tan canvas duffel bag. From there, he visited a discount clothing chain and purchased a sky-blue tee shirt, a pair of navy corduroy pants, and a white sweatshirt with a moose head motif. After paying for his purchase, he changed in the dressing room, storing his damp clothing in the duffel bag. He completed his outfit with a pair of grey crew socks and a black tuque from a nearby pharmacy. Already he felt more human. He would dearly have liked to replace his dress shoes, which had begun to warp after the previous night's ordeal, but he wanted to keep enough cash for food, a cheap hotel and whatever else he might need. Who knows how long he might have to stay here, he mused.

In his new, warmer attire, Gabriel began to appreciate the city more. It charmed him. It had a larger, more cosmopolitan feel than Fredericton, yet possessed a distinctly maritime charm. Despite the clouds, he was captivated by the staggering blueness of the sky, the omnipresence of water, in the air, the sky, framing the city on all sides. Even in his distress, it was hard not to smile at the cheerful pastel colours of the clapboard houses, the greenery throughout the city's parks and open spaces. A man could live here, Gabriel mused, without ever pining for Toronto.

He sauntered back to the waterfront and installed himself on a bench overlooking the inlet. Staring at the silvery black harbour, he was instantly beguiled by its hypnotic, swirling waters. Always glittering, shifting, rippling. It amazed him that all that turbulence, its ceaseless, restless motion, could soothe a troubled heart, could inspire a measure of tranquility. He watched a large gull with a white head, grey wings, a charcoal tail, and pale, rust-coloured, ducklike feet, hunt for food in the water.

Now to re-examine my predicament, he thought, as the houseboats bobbed gracefully on the gentle current. The idyllic peacefulness of the scene seemed out of place to him in his gut-wrenching turmoil. What a monstrous betrayal! How could he have been so wrong about her? Had there been any signs, any clues that he could have picked up on before he married her? But this wasn't helping, he told himself. He needed to make decisions, be practical, not wallow in his misery. There'd be time for that later, he concluded, as the gull pounced on some unseen prey, submerging its head while its hindquarters shot up in the air like an arrow. The gull re-emerged triumphant with a small crab in its mouth and flew off, leaving ripples and expanding rings in its wake.

Should he call her, he wondered. No. Let her worry about him. She doesn't deserve any consideration. In any event, he was through with her. She had committed an unpardonable sin. There could never be any question of reconciliation now. Nor would he call the office. He'd be damned if he had to kowtow to Mr. Abernathy or anyone of his ilk ever again. What a waste of over three years of his life! He was done with all that. Yes, at least some good would come of this. A brief, sad smile crossed his lips, but it was like the morning after a migraine; the sharp pain had departed, but the throbbing fog kept him in its dull grasp.

Catching sight of a massive, grey naval cruiser transiting through the harbour, his mind began to wander. What is it that makes one love somebody, with one's entire soul, and then suddenly stop? He had loved Jenny. He really did. Yet when she left, they both moved on. In a way, he still loved her, but not like that. No, not ever again. And Cathy, well he loved her more fiercely, more completely than he had ever loved Jenny. A forever love. Yet, by the end, they were just going through the motions, struggling to keep it together. Was it a weakness in him, a deficiency that made it impossible for him to love forever? Or perhaps biologically humans were never intended to mate for life. And the greatest source of unhappiness stemmed from the illusion that they could.

Okay, he told himself, focus. Now for next steps. He would apply for graduate school, as planned, only without Cathy's help. McGill, which had always been his personal preference but was problematic for Cathy, would now be his first choice, UBC his fallback. Of course, without Cathy supporting him, money would be tight, especially if he didn't have access to the money he had put away in their bank account in Fredericton. But he could live frugally. He didn't need a life of luxuries. He could sustain himself with part-time jobs, perhaps in the library, as a tutor, or even at a local music store. These were noble, worthwhile pursuits that he could enjoy with an unburdened soul, that would help him expiate his years shilling shamelessly for Atlantic Siding. Yes, that was the right approach. All he needed was some time and distance to see it all from the right perspective, to formulate a careful plan. Now everything would be all right, he assured himself.

And did he think at all at this point about the child Cathy was carrying, *his* child? In truth, he didn't. He was too focused on the wrong done to him to consider the rights of others, his theoretical obligations. *He* was the aggrieved party, the righteous victim. It was *his* life that had been upended. To the extent that the child existed in his mind at all, it was simply an abstraction, a machination through which she betrayed him. Not an actual person. Nothing to which he had any connection.

And throughout his deliberations, one phrase echoed in his mind: "It's not too late." He couldn't even place where he had heard it twice now, and didn't yet connect it to his dream on the bus, to his burning bush. Yet it held out hope. More than that, it was a beacon for him, promising to lead him out of the darkness that had engulfed his soul. *It's not too late.*

The broad outlines of his plan of attack largely complete, he stood and embarked upon a leisurely stroll along the waterfront as he worked out the details of his next steps. Issues like money, where he would live until his program started next autumn. Vexing logistical problems. He would have to get his clothes and other essentials – Mr. Balogh's violin – from the apartment. That should be done during the day, when Cathy is at work so as not to run into her. Then... back to Toronto? Or where? It was too much to decide all at once. Yet he needed a plan.

So intent was he on his calculations, so focused on the future, that he wasn't paying attention to where he was going. As a result, he walked right into a burly man in a jean jacket and a Montreal Expos hat. Mortified, Gabriel apologized profusely. The other man graciously accepted his apology, patting Gabriel gently to show that he bore no hard feelings. The incident made Gabriel realize that he was still shaken up by Cathy's betrayal and his unplanned flight from Fredericton, that he should probably find a hotel quickly, eat lunch and rest a while.

On an impulse, however, he moseyed into a bar along the waterfront instead. It had been so long since his evenings with Arthur in the pub on Madison Avenue. How carefree his life was then. Hanging his jacket on a wooden peg near the wood-framed door, he installed himself at a seat at the bar with a view of the window, through which he could watch the gentle bobbing of the boats, the gulls circling. The brass rail, surrounded by the richly-stained mahogany of the bar, had a welcoming, satisfying appearance, which appealed to him in his agitated state. The bartender, a young man of about twenty-five with a full head of dark hair, approached him, polished the counter in front of him with a white cloth rag, and said jovially, "Hello there! What can I do you for?"

"I, uh.... Do you have a Red Baron?" he asked diffidently.

"Sorry, mate!" the bartender replied. "We have some local microbrews, though, if you'd like."

"I guess.... You know what? Give me a gin and tonic instead, please," Gabriel requested.

"Sure, mate!" A few minutes later, the bartender returned with his drink. "Do you want to start a tab or pay for this now."

Gabriel glanced out the window and then at his watch. Three-fifteen. There was no harm in sitting here a bit and savouring his freedom from work, from Cathy. "I'll start a tab, please," he said.

"Where you from?" the bartender asked amiably.

Gabriel eyed him suspiciously. "Oh, here and there," he evaded.

"Will you be in town long?" the bartender continued undeterred.

"I don't really know."

The bartender, recognizing that some clients wanted conversation while others, such as this fellow, wanted seclusion, backed away graciously.

After a few drinks, Gabriel felt more relaxed. Everything became much clearer to him. He began to take a larger view of the matter, no longer trying to react to Cathy's provocation, but seeking to understand how he had gotten into this predicament in the first place. He reviewed his life to this point, his choices, his priorities. It occurred to him for the first time that it all had gone astray since he entered high school. Then, he had been so concerned with chasing women, chasing vanity, that he had fallen for every vice under the sun: drugs, sex, booze. His fall hadn't been just a short-term, eighteen-month detour on an otherwise righteous life. Instead, it was the beginning of a turn away from God. Ever afterwards, he continued in his errant ways, drinking and fornicating. He had corrupted Jenny, who would never have behaved loosely were it not for his importunate advances.

Feeling a little lightheaded from the alcohol, he nodded at the gin and tonic in his hand deprecatingly, as if to say, "Oh, this one drink won't hurt. I'll get back on track tomorrow." He beckoned to the bartender and ordered another drink.

They say in vino veritas, Gabriel reflected. And here am I, gaining piercing insight from the bottom of a gin and tonic. Surely, that was the cause of his troubles. What kind of man sleeps around outside the holy union of marriage? What could he have expected from a woman who dreamed of men asking her to show them her bum? He had brought it all on himself.

The bartender delivered his drink and asked if everything was alright. Gabriel peered out the window, noticing that night had fallen outside. The inlet was no longer visible outside the window at the left of the bar. He consulted his watch. Seven-thirty. How did that happen? Had he been here for over four hours? Yes, yes, he assured the bartender, slurring his speech. Everything was just peachy. Only it wasn't. His life had fallen apart, and it was his own doing. He had made a mess of everything.

More time passed. To Gabriel's amazement, it was already nine o'clock. At the other end of the bar, a middle-aged man was loudly regaling the bartender with a tale about a member of the local junior hockey team. "So, I gets a call from dispatch in the middle of the pouring rain last week to pick up a fare from the Lord Nelson. Turns out, it was my boy! Alex Tanguay himself, in the flesh, taking his dad to the airport. They was as nice as all get out! Just regular folks. I asks him if he's gonna break the scoring records and he shrugs, all shy and all. Says 'I'll sure try.' And then they gave me a twenty spot as a tip. Alex Tanguay himself, Bill!" Gabriel's attention was drawn to the commotion, briefly wondering what it signified, before returning to his devastating self-critique.

It was more than all that, Gabriel told himself, as the bar spun all around him. Much more. He expected too much from people, when they were nothing but a corrupt lot. Yes, that was his error. He had put his faith in man, rather than trusting God. Ever since junior high, he had been straying from God. First, he had put Rabbi Plotkin on a pedestal, practically worshipped him, like he was a deity in and of himself. How could he have failed to disappoint? Oh, now he understood! Like the moment of clarity after the rain, having escaped the horror of the previous night in Fredericton, he now finally realized what should have been obvious his whole life. Like Noah, he wasn't created for life with men. He had never been comfortable with people, never really had close friends, had been a terrible judge of character. Trying to interact with them, to accommodate the people he knew, had led him astray. He'd be better off without them. Instead, like Noah, he should have separated himself from a corrupt world and dedicated himself to God, to truth. "It's not too late," he said aloud with drunken conviction, to the amusement of two twenty-something women in jeans with shredded knees and low-cut blouses at a table near the bar.

He ordered another drink. Was it his sixth? His seventh? Ah, well.... It would be his last. The bartender brought it, together with the bill. It was nearing closing time and his head was swooning. The light above the bar now seemed extraordinarily bright to him. He stared at the bill for an eternity, trying to bring its dancing figures into focus. Eighty-seven dollars and forty-six cents? Was that possible? Gabriel instinctively reached into his back pocket, but something was wrong. Where was it? In his drunken daze, he couldn't quite grasp the nature of the problem. Unsteadily, he patted his other back pocket, which also lacked the familiar leather bulge. He stood up unsteadily and swooned onto the floor, where he fumbled around under the barstool in a vain search.

"Is there a problem?" the bartender asked warily.

As he scrabbled to stand up, his head collided against the edge of the bar, causing him to yelp pitifully. "I.... I donnn't unnndershtannnd," he stammered. "Itt was jussst heeere!"

"What are you looking for?" the bartender queried, already anticipating the inevitable answer.

"Mmmmy... mmmmy mmmmmonnnney! I jussst hadddd ittt!" All the jostling, squatting, crawling and standing had upset Gabriel's stomach in his inebriated state. His head began reeling and he started to retch. Grabbing hold of the bar with the claw of his right hand, his knuckles white, he steadied himself while he vomited on the floor with four violent heaves.

In a flash, the taxi driver sprinted down the bar. "Need any help, Bill?" he offered.

"The boy don't have any money and he can't hold his whiskey. What am I supposed to do, Hank?"

"I can take him home for ya," Hank volunteered. "You can send him a bill tomorrow." To Gabriel, he asked, "Where d'ya live, buddy? Can I drive ya?"

Gabriel processed the question through his stupor, through his pounding headache, but said nothing.

"He ain't from around here, I don't t'ink." Bill suggested.

"Well, can I take ya to your hotel, buddy?" Hank asked.

"Nnnnnoooo hottttelll!" Gabriel stuttered. "Nnnoooo!"

"So, what do I do?" the bartender asked in irritation.

The taxi driver scratched his balding, square head, sparsely covered with unkempt curls that were still reddish in places. "Ya can't leave him here and ya can't toss him out on the street like this. I guess you should call the cops. They'll know how ta deal wit' him." Hank concluded.

Forty-five minutes later, Gabriel was sitting across the desk from a duty officer of the Halifax Regional Police, handcuffed to his chair. He had been unable to answer any questions the responding officer had asked him at the bar and had vomited again in the squad car on the way over. He kept muttering incoherently. At one point, it sounded like he was saying "It's not too late." The officers in the front seat asked him what he meant, but to no avail.

"So what's the deal with this fellow, Kyle?" asked Sergeant Clark, the duty officer, a tall woman in her forties with her dyed dirty blonde hair in a tight bun.

"I'll be damned if I know. He got drunk at a bar and couldn't pay his tab. No ID on him, no wallet. Can't get a name or an address from him. Barkeep says he's not from here," Constable Mackle, a young, wiry officer with short, sandy brown hair and a baby face, responded. He looked more like the lead in a high school drama production than a police officer. His partner, a more seasoned veteran of the force stuck him with the dirty work of offloading this drunk, while he relaxed in the breakroom. Boy, he thought, it sucks to be the new guy.

"That what he was arrested for?" Sergeant Clark inquired.

"He's *not* under arrest," Constable Mackle corrected. "He didn't really do anything, except vomit all over the bar." The duty office grimaced. "And, of course, failure to pay his tab. But barkeep isn't pressing charges. Just wants to know who this guy is and where he lives so he can collect later."

The duty officer looked up sharply. "So why the cuffs if there're no charges?"

"Uh, Danny thought it would be best," Mackle explained. "For his own protection. He's been stumbling about. Already banged his head from the looks of it, as you can see from that gash near his temple."

Sergeant Clark sighed and raised her voice to address Gabriel. "Sir," she inquired with authority, "can you tell me your name?" Gabriel didn't respond. He just let his head float, lost in his drunken dizziness. "Do you know where you are, sir?" Again no response. "You're in the police station." That penetrated his consciousness. His face registered alarm and he shook his head slowly, unsteadily, from side to side. "Do you know why you're here, sir?"

"I... I ddddiddn'ttt dooo ittt!" he stammered frantically.

"Didn't do what, sir?" she pressed.

"Ddddiddnnnn'ttt shtttteal lllliqqqquorrr. I jjjjusssttt bbbbrrokkkke the ggglasss. Ddddiddnn'ttt Shttttealll."

"What's he talking about? Did he break his glass?" Sergeant Clark asked Mackle.

"I dunno. May have done," Mackle responded.

"Listen, sir. No-one is accusing you of stealing. You'll pay the bar later. But can you tell me your name?" she tried again.

"I ddddidnnnn'tt doooo itttt!" Gabriel rambled incoherently. "I bbbbbrokkkkke thhhhe winnnndddddow, bbbbuttt I ddddddiddddn'tttt sssshttttteallll annnny llllliqqqquor... I... sssshaw Ggggoddddd accccrosssss the sssshttttreetttt at Annnnnshei Ddddrilddddzzzz andddd He wwwwouldddn'ttt letttt mmmmeeee dddooo itttt!"

"Okay, Kyle. This isn't working. He's not making any sense. I guess take him down to holding and lock him up for the night. Check the missing persons reports and, if you can, take his fingerprints. Maybe we can find a match and learn who he is. If not, we'll figure this out in the morning when he's sober." Mackle nodded, unshackled Gabriel and led him away. He left Gabriel in the cell muttering, "It's not too late. It's not too late!"

***

In the morning, Gabriel awoke with a splitting headache, lying on the linoleum floor of an unfamiliar grey cell, next to a steel cot built into the wall. No gurgling sound this time. No Joey lying underneath him. Gradually, as he observed the bars separating the chamber from the institutional hallway, he began to piece together the events of the night before. *I got drunk*, he remembered. *And... I couldn't find my wallet*. Instinctively, he patted his back left pocket again, to no avail. *So they arrested me.... So, if I don't have my wallet, I don't have any identification.... Maybe they don't know who I am.* In a flash of insight, he remembered the man he bumped into on the waterfront. *He must have picked my pocket.* Gabriel smiled through the cobwebs clouding his brain. *God works in mysterious ways....*

It's not too late. That's what Moses said in my dream, he finally remembered. *I can still turn back to God. People never fail to disappoint me. What was it Lyudmilla said? Perfection is impossible when people are involved.* He touched the bruise above his temple. *Ow, I must've had a nasty bump. Okay, let's think this through. I won't go back to Cathy. I'm not going back to Atlantic Siding. But why go back at all? Why go to graduate school and meet more corrupt people who will inevitably disappoint me? Why not just... disappear? In Halifax, where they'd never find me. It's not too late.*

A police officer approached the cell and peered in. "How're you feeling this morning?" he asked.

"A little hazy," Gabriel replied.

"From what I hear, you were pretty far gone last night. You ready to come upstairs with me? D'ya want some coffee or something?"

"Yes, please. That'd be great. Do you have anything to eat?" Gabriel stood at the door of the cell, waiting for the officer to unlock it.

"Oh, it's not locked. You're not under arrest for anything. They just couldn't figure out what to do with you," the officer said apologetically. "There's some doughnuts upstairs. I'm Officer Larose, by the way. And you are...?"

Gabriel had to think quickly. "Uh, Eddie," he said. It was the first name that popped into his head.

"Nice to meet you. Eddie what?" Larose asked.

"Actually, can I use a bathroom, also? The toilet in here isn't all that private," Gabriel said sheepishly.

"Yeah, sure. Follow me," the policeman said. He led Gabriel through the maze of occupied cells in the secure area, out into an office area, up a set of drab steps which led to the large bullpen he had been in the previous night. In a side corridor was a restroom, which Gabriel used to wash his face and clear his head. He would have to be cagey now, not give away any identifying detail.

When he emerged, Larose led him to a desk with a box of Timbits on it. "Help yourself, Eddie. I'll get that coffee. What do you take in it?"

"Cream and a teaspoon of sugar," he replied, as he scooped out a couple of the doughnut holes. "Thanks!"

The officer returned with a steaming Styrofoam cup and a napkin. He handed them to Gabriel and motioned to him to sit down. It was good to get some food into his stomach, and the coffee made him more alert. He hadn't eaten much in the past forty-eight hours, which probably contributed to his breakdown at the bar.

"Okay, Eddie," Officer Larose said, a yellow ballpoint pen in his hand, "I just need to ask you a few questions to close out our report, if you don't mind."

"Sure. Go ahead," Gabriel said somewhat uneasily.

"Can you give me your full name, please?" the officer asked.

"Eddie," Gabriel said.

Larose stared at him in surprise. "Eddie *what*?" he pressed, trying to restrain his impatience.

"Just Eddie," Gabriel replied, staring uncomfortably at his hands.

"No last name?" Larose asked incredulously.

"Just Eddie," Gabriel repeated guiltily.

"And where do you live, Eddie? Can I have your address and telephone number?"

"No telephone. I live out there." He pointed toward a window at the end of the bullpen. "On the streets."

The police officer whistled in amazement. "You expect me to believe that you live on the streets? That you're homeless?" Gabriel nodded awkwardly. "I'll be honest with you, Eddie," Larose persisted. "You've got a fairly expensive watch. Your shoes are ruined, but they're Florsheim dress shoes, the suit pants in your duffle bag – sorry, we looked inside to see if we could find any identification – are fairly high end. I find it hard to believe you're a homeless man. So, what's the deal?"

"I wish I could help you, Officer Larose, but I can't," Gabriel stated flatly.

Larose tapped his pen thoughtfully against a metal Ikea desk lamp, generating a series of hollow metallic pings. "Can you tell me how to get in touch with your relatives?" Gabriel shook his head. "Alright, I get it. You don't want to be found. Are you in some kind of trouble, Eddie?"

"No. Of course not," Eddie replied.

"Say," Larose exclaimed, lighting upon an idea, "you've got a pretty big bruise on your forehead. You must have banged yourself pretty hard. Are you experiencing memory loss? You should probably get that checked out."

Gabriel had to think before replying. At first glance, amnesia would be a convenient explanation of his inability to furnish his name. On further reflection, however, he realized that it would require further monitoring, a hospital visit, more opportunities to be identified. "No," he said at length. "I'm fine. Really." Officer Larose looked doubtful. "Listen, officer. You say I'm not under arrest. Can I go now?"

"I don't have any cause to hold you. But I need to check with my supervisor first, if you don't mind." Gabriel nodded. Larose let his eyes linger on Gabriel's bruise for a few seconds, an expression between concern and disappointment on his face, before searching for the sergeant.

Larose waited for his supervisor to finish the call he was on. As soon as he put down the receiver, the junior officer asked, "What do I do about that drunk they picked up last night?"

"What d'ya mean?" Sergeant Singh snapped. "I told you to get his details and send him on his merry way."

"It's not so simple. He won't give me his name or his address. Or his next of kin. Just a first name. Eddie. If his name is really Eddie, I'm a monkey's uncle."

"That's odd. What d'ya think that's all about?" Singh asked distractedly. His wife was eight months pregnant, and he hoped to check in with her before the morning staff meeting to see how she was feeling.

"Well, he got hit pretty bad on the head. Has a horrible bruise. Maybe that messed him up? But my instinct tells me that's not it. I'm guessing he just doesn't want to be found...." Larose opined.

The sergeant scratched his chin thoughtfully. "Why don't we send him to the hospital for evaluation?" he asked.

"Already suggested that," Larose explained. "He refuses. Says if he's not charged with a crime, we have to let him go."

Sergeant Singh sighed. "They never make it easy, do they? Did you turn up anything with his fingerprints?"

"No."

"Nothing in the missing person reports?" Singh persisted.

"Nothing."

Sergeant Singh sighed again thoughtfully. "Then I guess we've got no choice. You can let him go. I wonder what he's hiding, though," he said, as he picked up the phone to place a quick call to his wife.

"Can I go?" Gabriel asked when Officer Larose returned to his desk.

"He says 'yes.'" The policeman responded dourly. As Gabriel stood and collected his duffle bag, Larose tried once more. "Are you sure you don't want to get yourself checked out? You got a pretty hard knock on your noggin."

"Thank you, Officer Larose. You've been very kind. And I'm sorry to have been so much trouble. But really, I'm alright. Truthfully, I've never been better." And in a weird way, Gabriel meant it. The only dark cloud for him was the fact that he had to leave Mr. Balogh's violin behind. She would probably sell it, he presumed. What a waste! But it was a price worth paying for his soul.

As he cruised past a portrait of the queen and stepped through a lightly-stained wooden door – one of four encased by glass that guarded the entrance to the brown-brick police headquarters – onto the pavement of Gottingen Street, with no possessions save the clothes on his back and the contents of his duffle bag, he felt lighter than he had in years, perhaps than he ever had. He hocked his watch at a nearby pawn shop to begin his new life with some cash. How free he felt! Freed from the shackles of convention, from a deceitful woman, from all of wretched humanity.

The rest of that day, Gabriel began exploring the charming city that he would call home, using the map from the bus depot, familiarizing himself with its parks, grocery stores, and other important landmarks. After a rough patch during his first two weeks on the street, he availed himself of the services of a local homeless shelter until winter passed. Unpleasant though it was, he viewed it as a necessary evil, a dose of cod liver oil until he could chart out on his own in the warmer weather. By late April, he had found the spot along the Northwest Arm he would call his bedroom, and with a full beard, bearing little resemblance to the man who arrived on the bus from Fredericton that autumn morning, his tenure at his office on Spring Garden had begun.

Chapter 12

"Do you hear it?" Gabriel asked expectantly.

He was walking with Jane in Point Pleasant Park. Her husband had taken a turn for the worse and she had come to him to seek solace from the only person who could comfort her. No-one else but Gabriel would speak the truth, regardless of how painful it was, would avoid hiding behind a veil of half-truths, evasions, lies. It was strange how she had come to depend on the words of a homeless man. But she knew by now that he was much more than just that. She had told him straight out that her husband had fallen into a coma and was dying. He had looked at her anguished eyes, her tear-stained cheeks and said gravely, "Then we shouldn't push this off any longer," and led her to the park.

He had veered off the path, into the woods. Jane peered around her anxiously, unsure of why he brought her here. "Hear what?" she queried.

"The music. God's music."

She strained her ears then shook her head. "No, I don't."

"Then you're not paying attention. Listen! Do you hear the wind blowing through the boughs, rustling the leaves? The waves just out of sight slapping against the rocks? The birds chiming in, different birds, different calls. Like the difference between a violin, a viola and a cello. Each with their own distinct tone." Gabriel lifted his hands to the sky as he said this, fluttering them delicately, as if he was conducting this serene, natural ensemble.

Despite herself, Jane smiled somewhat condescendingly. "Well, it *is* pleasant," she admitted.

"It's more than that," he corrected. "The rustle of a squirrel or a rabbit in the underbrush. The pitter-patter of rain as it falls into the channel. The metallic humming of the bullfrogs in the brook. All of this is part of God's magnificent symphony."

He cocked his ear to capture every note. "And the wind is never the same," he continued, completely wrapped up in his sermon. "It always sounds different. It never blows at the same intensity or from the same angle. It resonates differently off different trees, different branches. The ones with the small, round leaves shimmer and shake clumsily with a loud rustle. The evergreens just let it pass right through, with only a soft whistle. And the taller, thinner trees give off a mighty whoosh, as their branches, their very boughs bend."

Jane was impressed by his passionate eloquence, but still couldn't connect anything he said to her, to her husband lying unresponsive in the hospital bed on South Street.

"Most people go through life oblivious to this miraculous music. Then they laugh at God urbanely, deny his existence. But how can you *truly* hear this music, see the irreproducible beauty of a tree, smell the delicate fragrance of a rose, and doubt that God is the architect of it all?" He believed that he had delivered his clinching argument. Yet he felt the need to go further, to dare say what a civilized person could not. "I'm sorry your husband is dying, Jane. There's nothing you or I can do about that. But the only way you'll be able to find any peace is if you understand what I'm telling you. If you hear God's music."

They wandered in silence through the woods for some time, taking in the sights, sounds and smells. It gave him particular satisfaction to notice the intense concentration in Jane's intelligent eyes. She had clearly been affected by his appeal. Their reverie was interrupted suddenly by two teenagers on bicycles speeding along the nearby path, yelling at the top of their lungs. No sooner had they blown through, disrupting the park's peace, than a man ambled by arguing loudly with his stockbroker over his cellular phone.

Gabriel spat on the ground in disgust. "*That's* the problem," he declared angrily. "God created this beautiful music for us and all we do is spoil it. Human beings spoil the world, pollute it with their very being."

Jane continued meandering, a quizzical expression on her face. When she approached a clearing that led back to the path, she stopped. "Gabriel," she said softly, "I think you may be missing the point. People are part of the music. You and me and everybody else. We're all part of the beauty of the world."

It was Gabriel's turn to shake his head. "All they do is ruin it," he complained. "They pollute the rivers, pollute the air. And they drown out the tranquility with their incessant noise."

"Listen," Jane persisted. "You've reminded me of the beauty that I admit I've often overlooked in my life. But now I need to return the favour. You're just not looking at it the right way. You could easily say the barking of a dog or the cawing of a raven spoils the serenity of the world. Or even the sound of the wind howling through the trees. Yet you don't. Because you realize that they're part of the symphony. Humans don't bark and don't caw. We ride bicycles and talk on cellphones. That's our part in the orchestra. You just need to learn how to appreciate it as much you do the violins and the cellos."

"Oh, those are a bunch of fine words, Jane. But the fact is, all my life I've watched people spoil everything that was decent and true," he said with hostility. "They're mean and low and selfish. And their hallmark is betrayal."

Jane fixed Gabriel with a look of boundless tenderness and compassion, believing that she was finally reaching the cancerous root of his pain. "You've got to forgive people for being human, just like you forgive dogs for being canine," she said, almost pleading.

But he just became agitated and stared at her icily. "They all got what they deserved," he sputtered venomously. "Every single one of them." With that, he trotted off in a huff, abandoning his surprised companion in the middle of the park with her sorrow.

That night, he lay in his bed in an agitated state, disturbed by his conversation with Jane. As he closed his eyes, his mind replayed a long-forgotten sermon that Rabbi Plotkin delivered on Yom Kippur when he was a boy. "Why," the rabbi asked, his orator's voice reaching a feverish pitch, ringing around the synagogue like a clarion before battle, "did God give us a Day of Atonement every year? Why should it be necessary?" He paused to let the question sink in. "If we truly repent for our sins and fix our behaviour, it should be superfluous! We should need one Day of Atonement and then no more. Yet God gives it to us every single year in perpetuity! The point is: God *expects* us to sin, *knows* we will sin. Why? Because he made us imperfect. He made us creatures that will sin and sin and sin again."

"Now isn't that puzzling? God, who is the personification of perfection, created imperfect human beings. How do we explain that? Did He make a mistake?" The rabbi paused to wipe a bead of sweat from his brow. "Not at all! Our imperfection is part of His divine plan. God deliberately didn't make us angels. Angels are perfect in every way. They're incapable of sinning. But what glory is there in their good deeds? They merely do what they're programmed to do. But human beings, they're something even more wondrous than angels. They're imperfect. They can sin. And *boy*, can they sin. Only days after getting the *Torah* on Mount Sinai, they worshipped the Golden Calf! Yet it's our very capacity to fail, to succumb to temptation, to sin, that makes our good deeds more transcendent, holier, more wondrous."

"So God, in His mercy, in his kindness, gave us Yom Kippur, a day to atone for our sins," the rabbi continued, his eyes surveying the sea of congregants clad in white to emulate angels, as was the tradition on Yom Kippur. "And He gave it to us in perpetuity, knowing that we will fall short every year. But if we can work on ourselves, try with determined effort to choose good over evil, to follow His commandments, to treat each other with compassion, dignity and respect, *despite* our imperfection, then ladies and gentlemen we can realize the beauty and holiness of God's master plan that our flaws make possible."

Gabriel opened his eyes in annoyance. *Now why should I ruin one of my last few nights thinking about that fraud?* He lay still under his tattered blanket, his eyes fixed on the shimmering moon on the surface of the water, lost in thought. In two, maybe three days, he should have enough money to put his plan in motion. First, he would get a haircut at the barbershop on Dresden Row. Then he would spend the rest of his savings on a suit, shirt, tie, socks and shoes. When he presented himself to Jane at her Tower Road apartment, she would be overwhelmed. Perhaps she won't even recognize him.

Then the doubts resurfaced. Could he really go back? After living a life of complete freedom, could he give it all up? Could he return to a world of punch clocks, Social Insurance Numbers, reference checks, paying rent, neighbours? It all seemed so silly to him, so surreal. Crazy Eddie the responsible citizen, working from nine to five. Would he join the Conservative Party next, perhaps even run for office? It was laughable. And could he abandon his realm of isolation and independence for the petty world of people? Gabriel shuddered. The only thing people know how to do is disappoint.

But what choice was there, he asked himself, as dawn broke across the harbour. He was getting too old for this life. Better to find a compromise that he could live with than die miserably in a ditch. And he could re-engage with society on his own terms, couldn't he? If it all crashed to the ground, he could always retreat again, perhaps to a warmer clime where an older man could endure longer. Yes, it was better this way, he told himself without much conviction.

When he wasn't in the office working, earning the last few dollars he needed to put his plan into action, he spent the next two days on a farewell tour of the places he would miss most. He toured the Public Garden each afternoon, visiting every beloved tree, the pond, the fountain, the ducks, all the inhabitants of his kingdom. He ascended to the citadel, with its views of the water that charmed him so. And, of course, he trekked every square inch of his cherished Point Pleasant Park, which had served him well as his home, his fortress, his temple, for so many glorious years.

During these final days, Gabriel was a mass of contradictions: irritable, yet somehow resigned; nostalgic, even dispirited, like a man awaiting the gallows, about to lose all that was dear to him, yet strangely eager to secure the remaining money that would accelerate his departure; fiercely determined to remain aloof from humanity, to preserve as much of his precious isolation as possible, even after re-engagement, yet also impatient to try to reconnect to his parents, if that was still possible. He was high strung, agitated, and found it difficult to settle down at night. He ate very frugally, relying on dumpsters and the foodbank to satisfy his hunger, rather than wasting precious funds on more satisfying fare.

At long last, by the Wednesday evening, Gabriel had secured the last bit of money he needed, thanks to a generous toonie donated by the bank teller on her way home. It moved him that she was the one to put him over the top, rather than someone he despised. He was uncharacteristically gracious, almost on the verge of tears, when he thanked her. "God bless you always," he said. "I hope you find that happiness that always seems to elude you."

Taken aback by his demeanour, the finality of his intrusive pronouncement, she asked with genuine concern, "Is everything alright, Eddie?"

"Yes, of course," he muttered, his voice catching in his throat. "Of course...."

On his way back to the park that evening, the most curious incident transpired. While Gabriel concentrated on the Victorian homes on South Park Street, etching them onto the canvas of his mind, lest he forget them, out of the corner of his eye he was certain he had spotted his Zaidie across the street beckoning to him. He turned quickly, his heart in his mouth, to descry the back of a man of his grandfather's build, the same thin wisps of cottony hair, wearing a navy blue windbreaker just like Zaidie's, turn quickly into a side street, moving very quickly for an old man. With great trepidation and even greater longing, he lunged across the street to pursue the man, even crying out once, "Zaidie?" but the man did not acknowledge him or slacken his pace. Gabriel broke into a trot to make up the distance between them, but the man once again darted into an alleyway. When Gabriel reached the passageway, goosebumps down his neck, his pulse racing, there was no-one in sight. The man had simply melted away.

The apparition profoundly disturbed Gabriel. What could it mean? Was his grandfather trying to tell him something? Or had he just imagined it? His grandfather was dead, had been dead for decades. Dead people don't simply appear on South Park Street in Halifax, he reasoned sardonically, even to reclusive wannabe prophets such as he. Yes, it must be his agitation, this impending change, the momentous upheaval in his life that would begin tomorrow. Still shivering, goosebumps sprouting down his neck and arms, he trudged back to the park in turmoil, no longer attentive to his surroundings.

That night, his last on the banks of his Danube, Gabriel ate his evening meal, consisting of discarded pizza crusts and the remains of a portion of French fries that he had retrieved from behind a pizza parlour, and went straight to bed. His sleep was fitful, punctuated by terrifying dreams. Several times during the night, Gabriel cried out in fear, in anger, in despair. In one very poignant dream, Gabriel was skating alone on a rink not unlike the one at Forest Hill Arena that he used to frequent as a teenager. The arena was completely deserted, except for a woman in the distance playing a haunting melody on a violin. Perhaps it was Lyudmilla. He couldn't be sure. All he could be certain of is that the instrument, of exceptional tone and clarity, was his own. Mr. Balogh's legacy. Suddenly, the woman played a shrill note and the ice cracked open, sending him sprawling into the ocean, unable to move his legs because of the heavy skates on his feet. Panic-stricken, he tore at the laces to free himself, but they only lashed onto him more tightly, cutting into his ankle. He called out wildly for help. On a jetty in the distance, he noticed his middle school friend Jack, still a fourteen-year-old boy, standing dejectedly, watching Gabriel. Jack yelled with a broken voice "I'm sorry, Gabriel. I want to help you, but I can't. I never learned how to swim! No-one taught me. I'm so sorry. Please forgive me!" "It's alright, Jack. I forgive you," he said magnanimously, still struggling in vain to free himself of his skates. "Jack?" the boy asked in surprise. "Who's Jack? My name is Adam...."

Gabriel awoke with a start, in terror, screaming out loud, "No, you're not! You're Jack! You're Jack!" All around him was dark, the blackness of the tomb. The night was cloudy, blacking out the moon. He could see nothing, except a faint light on the other side of the channel. Nothing that could shake his surreal dread. He sat up in bed breathing heavily, huddled in his frayed blanket, rocking back and forth to steady his nerves. It was just a dream, he told himself. Just a dream. He remained in that position for the balance of the night, sometimes dozing, justifying to himself the last two decades of his life.

And how had he viewed himself all these lonely years? As an unanointed prophet crossing the Jordan River to redemption, despite the perilous journey, the heavy toll on his aging bones, the scorn of an ungrateful multitude; Noah, forsaking a corrupt world to pursue God's glory; Moses, hurling God's holy tablets to the ground in fury to punish the wicked for their idolatry; his grandfather, escaping his nefarious pursuers and their craven collaborators to live in safety and sanctity on the banks of the Danube. The rectitude of his choices had never been in doubt. He had divine justice, truth, on his side. And yet....

The morning was golden, putting to rest the trauma, the uncertainty of the night before. Gabriel greeted the day confident in his decision, rueful but no longer ambivalent. He tossed aside his bedclothes, such as they were, was about to conceal them as usual, but realized with a shudder that it wouldn't be necessary. He would not be returning to them. The Northwest Arm was uncharacteristically warm that morning as he bathed with deliberate care. He wanted to remember it that way. It was like saying goodbye to his best friend. Like accompanying Jenny to the airport.

His grooming completed, he embarked on his last walk out of the park, at one point absently running his hands along the trunk of a particularly fine cedar tree. He might leave the park, he decided, but it would always reside within him.

On his way downtown, he mentally bid farewell to the houses he loved best on Young Avenue – the gothic castle with the red turret, the sand-coloured geometric wonder supported by tens of ivory columns, the grey, green and blue Victorians standing side-by-side. Sure, he expected to see them again, but he would be irrevocably changed by then and might offend them. Finally, he made his way back to Spring Garden Street, only steps away from embarking upon his new life.

He took a last languorous look at his office before proceeding to the barbershop on Dresden Row. Instinctively, he felt for the wad of bills, the pile of coins in his pocket. All was safe. As he approached the tri-coloured rotating barber's pole, exiting the shop was a young boy of about ten years old, sporting a crisp new Toronto Blue Jays baseball cap and a well-worn jean jacket. Gabriel stopped in his tracks transfixed, staring at the boy in an admixture of horror and wonder, as a long-repressed memory resurfaced.

Many years ago, perhaps seven or eight, Gabriel had been sitting in his office in front of the bank, drinking indolently from his water bottle, pondering, of all things, the concept of justice in Plato's *Republic*, and whether it represented the advantage of the stronger, as Thrasymachus claimed, or whether Adeimantus was closer to the mark in deeming it the advantage of the weaker. Or whether they both erred in thinking that justice could be comprehended so abstractly, acontextually. It was a windy autumn afternoon, a harbinger of the wicked winter that would engulf the city in a matter of weeks.

Down the block, a well-dressed woman of average height was leaving a clothing boutique with a young boy in tow, about the same age as this boy, when a strong gust of wind ripped the baseball cap off the boy's head. The woman gave chase, as the wind pushed it toward Gabriel. Instinctively, he stopped it with his leg and stooped to pick it up. As he straightened himself to hand it to the grateful but skittish woman, he recognized her instantly. The same brown hair, although it was already greying in places. The prismatic eyes still lustrous, but framed by crow's feet. Slightly plumper. And to the left of her chin, almost below the dimple, the blemish of an old scar. *The slight imperfection that made her face all the more perfect.*

Gabriel stood spellbound, his right hand with the sullied cap extended, paralyzed by shock, by the flood of emotions that engulfed him. *Cathy*, he thought stupidly. *After all this time....* How can one describe what he felt at that moment? His pain. His longing. His guilt. His head exploded with memories. Of love. Of intimacy. Of betrayal. *Cathy Blum, show us your bum!*

"Thank you, sir," the vanilla cream voice said with forced brightness as she gingerly retrieved the hat from his hand. Rather than handing it to the boy, she held on to it by the azure plastic tab on the back, clearly unhappy that a homeless man had sullied her son's cap. As he stood there transfixed, unable to utter a sound, she reached into her purse and rummaged for a loonie that she dropped into his hat. Oh, the insult, the accusation with which that coin clicked against the others there! His own wife did not recognize him, had looked right through him as if he did not exist. Was it possible not to know one with whom you have shared everything? Had he changed so much? Had she?

"Mom, can I have my cap back?" the boy, who had just caught up to her, asked.

It was then that Gabriel's attention turned to the boy. Her son. The child resembled him, had his eyes, his hair colour, his mother's wide forehead. This was *his* son, *his* heir. Suddenly, he couldn't breathe, as if Tank had punched him in the stomach again in the Mackenzie schoolyard. *Had I truly given this boy up, this treasure, discarded him like so much unwanted packaging?*

"Come on, Adam," Cathy urged, grabbing her son by the arm. "Thank the nice man for catching it and let's go get some ice cream."

Adam. My son's name is Adam. Like Adam and Eve. Before the sin of the Tree of Knowledge. Oh, the great sin of knowledge. We know too much. Far too much. Oh, God! Please help me! This is too much to bear.

"Thank you, Mister," the boy said sweetly, clearly too young to share his mother's revulsion, her prejudices.

Gabriel tried in vain to catch his breath, to speak to his son, but was choked by his tears. He shook uncontrollably, staring dumbly as Cathy drew his son away from him, hastening down the block. "Let's go," she whispered just loudly enough for Gabriel to overhear. "I think that man's drunk." Upon reaching the corner, they veered right and out of his field of vision forever.

That was it. The first and last time he had ever met his son. It was over in a heartbeat, leaving him standing numbly outside the bank wondering whether he had imagined the whole event, the tarnished coin in his hat the only tangible proof of its occurrence. When he was again able to breathe many minutes later – an eternity later – he kept muttering, "What have I done? What I have I done...."

Standing outside the barbershop all these years later, Gabriel had the sensation of tumbling down a never-ending staircase. Once again, he was dizzy, unable to breathe, trapped in an agony of guilt and longing. His right leg throbbing, he grabbed the barbershop's door handle, not to enter, but to steady himself, to stop his head from spinning. Again he asked himself whether it had really happened, or whether he had merely imagined it? When you live on your own with only sparse and impersonal human contact, it's often hard to distinguish between one's visions, dreams, fantasies and cold hard reality. But what did it matter? If it hadn't happened, it was a prophecy. That's how God speaks to people. In visions. Not face-to-face. God had announced his resounding verdict. *Guilty on all counts! The accused is remanded for sentencing.*

A terrible realization came over him. *All this time I've resented everybody for betraying me. But I betrayed my own son! My own son! The most terrible betrayal of all! I've been so blind, so foolish!* He was overwhelmed by all the wasted time, all the people he hurt, all the pain he could never make right. He thought of

Aziz. *How could I ever have doubted him?* And his father. *Was I such a monster as to trample his cherished garden? Why did I not honour him as we were commanded?* But above all, there was Adam. Nothing could excuse his diabolical betrayal of his own son. *Why didn't I see it before? Why didn't I set it right!* His whole life he had been so certain of his own righteousness, his infallibility. How wrong he had been! *Perfection isn't possible when human beings are involved,* he berated himself with bitter irony, *and I am nothing but human.* In his torment, he let loose a bitter, anguished wail from the depths of his troubled soul, causing passersby to cross to the other side of the street in fear.

In utter confusion, he glanced down at his right hand and noticed that it was clutching the money he had saved, the money that was intended to help him start anew. But the recollection had stabbed him in the heart, and he lost his courage. Through the pane of glass in the door, he stared dazedly at the barber, who was blow drying a customer's hair. *How simple it was all going to be....* "No," he muttered. "No, I don't deserve it. I'm such a sinner. I don't deserve happiness. God can't forgive me for what I've done. Shouldn't forgive me." With a brusque movement of his shoulder, he pushed himself off the door and staggered down the block before stopping to steady himself once more, slow his erratic breathing. Perceiving that he was leaning on the window of a liquor store, he lunged toward the door, all the while mumbling, "What have I done? How can I ever atone?" Once inside, he bought two bottles of whiskey, like a common wino. On his way out of the store, he saw one of his comrades from the shelter over the winter, one of the roommates he had ignored, despised, in his own makeshift "office" across the street, with a bright red bucket for donations. Gabriel crossed the street and, without looking the man in the eye, took all the money he had – all the money he had painstakingly saved over several long hard months – and, with a bitter sigh, dropped it in the bucket.

He trudged back to Point Pleasant Park in defeat and lay down once more in his bed, in despair. Having judged himself, heard Heaven's resounding guilty verdict, Gabriel unscrewed the cap of a whiskey bottle and administered his liquid punishment. Even if you spend your entire life breaking the chains that shackle you, he thought sadly, there were some chains, some sins, you can never escape....

Epilogue

The young man fumbled nervously with his black bowtie. "Ma, can you help me out?" he called downstairs. "I can't get this tie on properly."

"Just a sec!" his mother yelled back. A few minutes later he heard her climbing the stairs slowly. "For a violinist, you really are all thumbs," she teased as she entered his large, tastefully furnished room.

He laughed. "Just give me a hand, please." He handed Cathy the bowtie, which she quickly affixed to his shirt collar and straightened. Now a heavyset, matronly woman, she was still a brunette, only now it came from a bottle and her roots were of fine silver. Her eyes were the same multicoloured gems, but they had lost their lustre, as if the bitterness of life had hardened them somehow.

"Are you nervous?" she asked, as she instinctively straightened the ivory bedspread, frowning at the wrinkles that had bunched up in the middle.

"Nah," Adam responded. "Well... I suppose so. But it's good to be a little nervous. I play better when I am. Fear is a good motivator."

Tonight's program would be demanding: Brahms' Hungarian Dances followed by Sibelius' second symphony. The music was technically challenging and exciting, with a prominent role for the string section. After serving as an understudy for the University of Toronto student symphony orchestra for most of his first year, Adam was eager to play his first concert as a regular. He was doing his best, though, to master the pre-concert jitters.

He reached for his black jacket, on the wooden chair next to his violin case, and slipped it on. "How do I look?" he asked.

She studied him carefully. "You look so much like your father.... He was in his second year when we met. Just about the same age you are now. I can't believe how much you take after him.... In looks, I mean."

"Mom...." he started, but seemed to think better of it.

"Go on," Cathy insisted.

"Well, I know I've asked before, but you never really gave me an answer.... Why did he leave?"

A fly buzzed around Adam's room, settling for the moment on the wall above his dresser. Cathy turned to look at it, unable to face her son directly. "You'd have to ask *him*, wherever he is. I really don't know. I've asked myself that many times. Honestly, I guess that he was just an irresponsible...." Her voice broke as the familiar anger overwhelmed her. It hadn't been easy raising Adam on her own. "At core, I guess he was just a really *bad* person."

Adam sucked softly on his lower lip. He felt sorry to upset her, but it was important for him to know. "Then why did you marry him in the first place? I mean... if he was so bad. There must have been *something* good in him."

Cathy responded thoughtfully, "When he was at his best, he was *wonderful*. Kind. Caring. Charming. Incredibly smart. Funny. But all these years later, I guess I realize that most of the time he was selfish and petty. I just didn't notice it then. Or I overlooked it... made excuses for it. Sometimes, when the heart's involved, you don't realize these things until it's too late."

"Grandpa says___"

"I know what Grandpa says," Cathy snapped, her multi-hued eyes hardening. "I don't want to hear about it. Grandpa always had a soft spot for him. Even after he ditched us.... Anyway," she said more softly, "it's all in the past now. It still hurts, but we've got to move on."

Moved by her pain, Adam enveloped his mother in his arms and hugged her. "Sorry for bringing it up, Mom."

Lost in her bitter reminiscences, she didn't respond. He released her and walked to his violin case. "At least he left me his violin," he mused. "It's one *awesome* instrument!"

"Well," his mother said acerbically, "he didn't exactly leave it to *you*. He just left it behind when he skipped out on us. Just one more thing he abandoned...."

"Where did he get it?"

"It belonged to his teacher or someone he worked for. After all this time, I don't really remember.... Oh my gosh!" Cathy exclaimed. "Look at the time! We've got to get moving! They can't have their first violinist late for the concert."

"I'm not the first violinist. If anything, I'm the last violinist, sitting in the back row. But that's fine with me for now." He picked up his instrument case, unlatched it and peeked inside. Seeing that all was in order – violin, bow, rosin, music – he snapped it shut and carried it by the handle. Ushering his mother through the door to his room, they hurried downstairs and out to the car.

Constable Owens brought a thick sheaf of files to his already cluttered desk and sat down on his rusty metal office chair. He took a sip of coffee from a Tim Horton's cup. Damn, he thought, cold again. He never seemed to have the time and space to enjoy it hot. Sighing, he flipped the pages of the break-and-entry report he had taken from a homeowner on Edward Street, although it was hard for him to concentrate. His mind kept meandering back to the new Shimano fly reel Barb had given him for his birthday. The weather was getting warmer. Perhaps he'd be able to go to his brother's cottage on the South Shore, near Mahone Bay. A spot of trout fishing would do him some good before the long winter.

"Busy morning, Gord?" his supervisor, Sergeant Mackle, asked, disturbing his reverie. The sergeant was trying with his tongue to dislodge a morsel of bacon that was wedged between his molars during breakfast.

"Just the usual shit," he replied. "B & E on Edward. Perp took some jewels and some cash. Owner was at work when a neighbour called her because of the alarm. A drunk and disorderly at a restaurant down the block last night. He's still cooling in the tank. Domestic assault at an apartment on Wellington. Husband found a pair of men's shoes in the closet that weren't his and started pounding his wife. Just an ordinary day in this Shang-ri-la of ours..."

"Is the husband in custody?"

"No. She refused to press charges. You know how it goes," Owens lamented.

"Yeah. That gets old quickly," Mackle agreed, grimacing. "Did the neighbour who called in the B & E see anything?"

"No. She just heard the alarm. And she didn't call it in. The owner did. The neighbour called her when the alarm kept ringing." Owens felt weary. Somehow he'd expected policework to be more glamorous than this. Yet this was what it was like most of the time. The only time he felt energized nowadays was when he was out at the shore with his rod in hand. But at forty-eight, he was too young to call it quits.

"I see. And did you ever get the coroner's report on that John Doe floater in the Northwest Arm?" the sergeant inquired.

"Let me check," Owens said, as he flipped through the files on his desk. "Yes. Here it is." He skimmed through the report. "Cause of death: drowning. Had a high blood alcohol level. 0.14%. Geez! He was pickled! Blunt force trauma to the head. Their conjecture: he was toasted out of his mind and slipped on the bank in the park. He must've hit his head on a rock, tumbled into the water unconscious and drowned. What a waste!"

"I guess you should head out to the park later to see if you can find anything to corroborate that theory. Also, we'll need to work on an ID." To his dismay, although Mackle finally freed part of the food caught in his teeth, a smaller, more elusive piece remained trapped.

"Aw, Kyle, what's the point?" Owens burst out. "He's just some homeless guy. I think he's the bum who hung around Spring Garden. You know, that Oracle? We'll never find out who he is. And why *should* we? He was just a waste of life anyway. Just a selfish drunk who never did anything for anyone else, never contributed to society. Probably has a family somewhere that he ran out on, people who were worried about him. But that was never *his* concern. As long as he got his whiskey...."

"Wow! That's harsh, Gord," his supervisor pronounced. "You never know why someone would check out of life like that. Maybe mental health problems. You really can't tell. And it's not for us to pass judgement. We've got to do our job and cross the T's, dot the I's on the file."

"Yeah, I know.... I'll follow up. But in my opinion, it's a waste of already scarce resources. I'm sure no-one'll miss him. What difference could a bum like him possibly make, alive or dead, to anyone? Mark my words. The world's better off without him."

Sergeant Mackle grunted and walked to the breakroom. Constable Owens took another sip of his room-temperature coffee, sighed, and returned his attention to the break and entry file.

A burly, older man with wispy grey tufts of hair peeking out of his black fisherman's cap struggled against the blustery wind to open the heavy wood-framed door and stumbled into the bar, rubbing his hands together to warm them up. He tossed his cap and his grey down-filled jacket onto a wooden peg near the door and pulled up a stool at the bar near the window facing the inlet. It wasn't his usual perch, at the right side of the bar near the dartboard, but some fancy party of well-coiffed men in suits had beaten him to it. What was this world coming to, he wondered, casting a disapproving glance their way.

"Hey Hank! What's shaking?" the bartender asked with a friendly smile.

"Aw, you can't even save a man's seat, Bill?" Hank groused.

"Wouldn't be good for business to chase away customers, would it?" Bill asked good naturedly.

Hank harrumphed. "Aw, just get me a beer, will you." He shifted on his stool with a disapproving grimace, as he surveyed the dimly-lit bar to see if any regulars were in attendance. Not seeing anybody he recognized aside from the serving staff, he buried himself sourly in the beer that Bill placed in front of him.

"So it seems your boy's gone AWOL, Hank," the waitress chirped with a broad smile, as she carried a plate of fried fish and onion rings past the bar to a table in the back.

Hank waited for her to return from her mission before querying, "Which boy we talking about now?"

"That bum. Crazy Eddie. Ain't been seen for a few weeks now. Got folks scratching their heads. Any theories why?" she asked.

"With those types, Charlene, ya never can tell. Maybe he moved on somewheres else. Maybe he got sick," Hank said thoughtfully as his big, hairy hands slid up and down the legs of his barstool, enjoying the satisfactory texture of the finished wood.

"You think maybe the police caught up with him?" the waitress asked. Her face was more animated than usual, no doubt enjoying the mystery, the intrigue, that brightened up her dreary life.

Hank considered this for a moment. "In the final analysis, I guess it don't really matter, does it? Whether he's here or there, in the joint or out on the streets. He never really did much for nobody, did he?" he concluded.

Turning his attention to the sports page of the *Chronicle Herald* lying open at the bar, Hank broke into a broad grin. "Hey! Zadina potted two more last night and the Mooseheads won again. Now *that's* my boy. He's on a pace to shoot past McKinnon when he was here."

"Aw, he's good," admitted the bartender, "but he ain't no McKinnon."

"Hey!" Hank interjected. "Did I ever tell ya about the time I drove Alex Tanguay and his dad to the airport?"

Bill laughed. "If I had a looney for every time you told me t'at ol' wive's tale, I'd be a wealt'y man. But seriously, Zadina couldn't hold McKinnon's jockstrap. They're in different leagues."

With that, the two friends began sparring over hockey while the waitress escaped to the kitchen to check on an order.

For the third time that day, Jane reconnoitred the stretch of Spring Garden Road that served as Gabriel's office in vain. He was still nowhere to be seen. She made inquiries in the nearby businesses, but no-one had lain eyes on him for several weeks. Not the bank manager, who expressed a malicious joy that the blight on the landscape had been cleaned up. Not the teller, who worried about him ever since his erratic behaviour the last time she saw him, who feared that he might have fallen ill, or worse. Not the local boutique owners or the pharmacist's assistant, who were puzzled by her concern for one such as Crazy Eddie.

Where are you, Gabriel? I need you! I really need you!

Her life was in complete turmoil. After a long battle, her husband had succumbed to his illness, and Jane found herself utterly adrift. Lost. Bereft of hope. Strangely, though she had many friends, it was Gabriel, the ragged, acid-tongued, antisocial homeless man she sought out. Only he could understand her, could comfort her.

But where was he? Had he moved on, to another part of the city or beyond? Had something untoward happened to him? Or had he finally escaped his self-imposed exile and found his way back to society at long last? It occurred to her to contact the local police, but she quickly dismissed the idea. The disappearance of a homeless would not be deemed worthy of investigation.

She sighed deeply and wandered aimlessly in her desperation, paying scant attention to her surroundings. The commercial facades of Spring Garden Road gave way to the colourful, stately Victorian homes of the South End, but neither setting held any interest for Jane in her grief.

Oh, Gabriel, what do I do now? My husband, my marriage, have been the core of my life for thirty-five years. How do I go on?

She stumbled on blindly, paying no heed to passersby, traffic signs, automobiles. Once, as she crossed Young Avenue from Southwood Drive without looking, a pick-up truck was forced to swerve wildly into the other lane, on the other side of the dividing island, to avoid her, the driver honking and cursing loudly. None of it registered on her.

With no clear purpose in her head, her feet carried her in accordance with their own plan, their own machinations, their own wisdom. Eventually, after passing the grain elevators, the shipyard on her left, she absently took the measure of her surroundings and suddenly understood where she was going, why she had trekked all the way here. She smiled a nostalgic, mournful smile and crossed the street to the entrance of Point Pleasant Park, remembering Gabriel's last conversation with her, his sermon at the park. It seemed so strange to her now that she had failed to grasp its importance at the time. As she traversed the park's pathways, Jane's senses came alive, awake to the nature, the trees, the birds, the breeze. Eyes glistening with both sadness and wonder, she revelled in the trill of the birdcalls, each with their unique timbre and pitch, the fluttering of the leaves as the breeze rocked the boughs, the squirrels rustling through the underbrush, the gentle lapping of the harbour's placid waves as they hit the shore. It was all so beautiful, so magical. So musical.

Almost in a trance, she made her way slowly, deliberately to the southern tip of the park, from which she spied the harbour, the ocean. To her surprise and wonder, she observed the large granite cross of the Halifax sailors' memorial. She had visited here dozens of times over the years, but had never truly registered its existence. Moved by the majesty of nature all around her, by the magnificence of this cathedral — for that's what the cross made it for her now — Jane fell to her knees in the gravelly sand near the water and crossed herself, tears flowing like a Halifax rain from her wrinkled eyelids. She peered up, addressing the turbulent sky above, "God, it's me, Jane. I haven't talked to you in a long, long time — far too long — but I need you. Oh, how I need you! Thank you for sending me your angel, Gabriel, to help me hear your music, to help me find my way back to you."

Acknowledgements

Writing a novel is a bewildering adventure. It requires one to get sucked into the vortex of the characters' minds, dream their tortured dreams, savour their joys, suffer their pain. Yet it is essentially a lonely endeavour, as one must lock oneself up in a quiet room for many months, communing with the imaginary, the hypothetical, at the expense of the real, hoping that one's poor words can approach the perfection in one's imagination. I would never have completed *The Oracle of Spring Garden Road* were it not for the support and forbearance of my wife, Nathalie, and my wonderful daughters. They gave me the space to retreat to my office, into my own mind, to think, to write, to edit, to obsess. Without Nathalie's unflagging encouragement, her willingness to read multiple drafts, her delight in the final product, I simply couldn't have gotten through the dark periods of doubt when nothing seemed to flow from my brain to the page as I had envisioned it. Her love appears on every page of this book.

I am grateful to Annette Freyberg-Inan, Monique and Stephen Wallace, and Ron Wener, who read and commented on earlier drafts of this novel. That was a huge time commitment and I know they must have agreed to do so with great trepidation. Yet their reactions are what gave me the confidence to go ahead with this project and not to leave it on the cutting room floor. I owe a debt of gratitude to T.V. Paul, for encouraging me to take the plunge and try my hand at fiction. I also wish to thank Edann Brady, Paul Fisher, Claire Friedman, Steven Lobell, Galia Press Barnathan and Jeff Taliaferro for their helpful advice and encouragement at various stages of this project. Finally, I'd be remiss if I didn't thank my parents, Toba and the late Michael

Ripsman, who taught me that I could achieve anything if I put my mind to it and don't give up when the seas are choppy.

>Norrin M. Ripsman
>Philadelphia, PA
>March 2024

Made in the USA
Middletown, DE
07 April 2024